If Ever in Love

by

Ann M. Trader

If Ever in Love

Cover Art by *Jennifer Greeff*

The Wild Rose Press, Inc.
PO Box 708
Adams Basin, NY 14410-0708
Visit us at www.thewildrosepress.com

Publishing History
First Edition, 2023
Trade Paperback ISBN 978-1-5092-4475-1
Digital ISBN 978-1-5092-4476-8

Published in the United States of America

Olivia swung around, shaking tiny water droplets from her feet before rising. Stuffing her stockings inside her shoes, she tossed them in her basket. She faced him, petticoat and bare toes peeking out from beneath her skirt.

"You, Captain Harry Fleming, are impulsive, hence you stand here with me rather than tending to your usual business. So...you must be after something." She lifted her hand and rested it on her cheek. "You like to give orders, not take them. And yet I've seen how deeply you care for those who depend on you—like Tom." They locked gazes. "I understand what it is to be sad, and I think something weighs heavy on your heart. Who or what caused the sadness, I don't know—but I recognize the signs just the same."

His heart filled to near bursting, and he pushed the air from his lungs. "God, I love your spirit. Marry me, Olivia Parr." He blurted out the words without forethought, without preparation. They were borne out of some inexplicable emotion he knew was not love, but something almost as potent.

"What did you—"

"You heard me." Harry inched closer.

"We—um, but—we hardly know each other, sir." Her face flushed a crimson hue.

The corners of his lips turned up. "You summarized me quite well a moment ago."

"You're ridiculous."

He scratched his chin, lips curving into a grin. "No...no, I believe the word you used was *impulsive*."

"Either way, I won't marry you." She ducked under his arm, but his hand found hers.

Praise for Ann M. Trader

"If Ever in Love is a lovely historical romance set just after the American Revolution. It's a story of second chances and forgiveness. Sometimes, the hardest to forgive is ourselves."

~*Sherri Lupton Hollister, author and member of Heart of Carolina Romance Writers*

~*~

"Crinkles All the Way has everything a reader could want in a holiday romance: a vibrant community, fun supporting characters, a swoony hero, a relatable heroine, and a touch of Christmas magic. "

~*Melissa McTernan, author The Wild Rose Press*

~*~

"The Gingerbread Cookie Code moves quickly, but it leaves nothing to the imagination and sends you on a steamy ride that is sure to capture your heart."

~*D. M. Grant, author The Wild Rose Press and blogger*

Dedication

To those who believe vulnerability is the highest calling
of the heart.

Acknowledgments

To see *If Ever in Love* published is nothing short of a dream come true! I want to thank my writing group and beta readers for helping me improve my stories. This is my third book with The Wild Rose Press, and I appreciate their commitment to author growth and development. I'm especially grateful for my editor, Judi Mobley, whose expertise, advice, and patience are priceless. And to my family, thank you for your unwavering love and support.

Part One

Nothing is as it Seems

Chapter One

April 1783

Fists balled by his sides, Harry Fleming lowered his gaze and blew out a breath. *One thousand, one hundred, eighty-seven.* That was the number of days he had been away from his South Carolina home, devising strategy, leading ambushes, and fighting for his life and that of their new nation. He flinched, the magnitude of that number exceeded only by the count of curses swarming in his brain. *I should have never left Redmond Hill in Uncle Zeb's hands.* He glared at the parade of scant fields, tangled primrose bushes, and rotten fence posts on his property. If nothing else, three years of fighting for liberty had revealed one stubborn, unfailing truth. *Should stood no chance against reality.*

"It's like I told you, Cap'n Fleming. The wood doesn't cut right. It's warped and ain't fit for mendin' no fence." Tom Harkett squared his shoulders, a stem of straw wedged between his teeth.

"It's not like the mercantile to deal in such poor quality." Harry kicked the timber with his boot, splintering it into shards.

"Aye, it ain't. But see—the owner passed away last year. Fancy new fella owns it now—some cousin of his."

He braced his hands on his hips. "Rest easy. I'll see to it you have the wood needed for repairs."

"Now I like the sound of that." The young man's cheeks rounded with his smile. "Thank the Lord you're finally home, sir. I still remember the rainy day when ye left, all set in your fine uniform."

"It was plain blue wool." Harry thought it a rather forgettable ensemble when compared to the decorated uniform worn by his elder cousin, Brandt Fleming, a graduate of William and Mary. Brandt's father, Zeb, had secured him a commission exercising military strategy against the Redcoats miles away from musket fire. He could not remember a time when Uncle Zeb had not held the best hand in the deck.

Harry blinked, sunlight filtering through the branches of the tall pines and casting a sunflower-yellow hue across the front porch. He turned his face into an oncoming breeze, the scent of sweet magnolia assailing him. *Thank God some things are still the same.* A smile inched up his face. His ancestral home was no longer a memory to call upon while hiding in the underbrush or keeping watch over camp in the pitch of night. Redmond Hill was real, and he was home. He gave the two-story rectangular house a cursory inspection, noting it bore marks from both weather and battle storms. While the roofline extending over the porch was sound, he ran his hand along one of the wood columns, discovering a jagged edge left by a musket ball.

Harry took a seat beside Tom on the front porch steps. "Where's everyone hiding?"

The lad removed his hat, dusted off the brim, and fixed it square on his head. "They're at church, sir. There's only Mum, Silas, and me around here nowadays. Everybody else mostly wandered off after time."

He swallowed an expletive about his uncle's

negligence and pasted on a dry smile. "And your sweet mother—how does Mary fare with your stepfather?"

"Forgive me, sir, but I only had one pa, and he's dead. Silas is Mum's husband. But she does well enough, sir. Canna complain."

Harry ran the back of his knuckles over his stubbled jaw. "Tell me, how old are you now?"

"Turned eighteen last month, sir."

He pushed himself up and strode toward the stable, Tom nipping at his heels. He kicked off the soil from his boot, propping it on the lowest fence rail and leaning against the weatherworn post. "Tell me what else is stirring in the back country?"

Tom beamed and let his gangly arms hang over the fence, regaling him with stories of the growing Catawba tribe and scores of newcomers arriving in the town of Camden.

"Lots of changes." He turned to Tom. "But my home's still standing, and I'm grateful to you for staying on—especially through the tough times."

The lad swiped the toe of his boot back and forth in the dirt. "Redmond Hill's my home, Cap'n. It's all I know."

Harry cocked his head. "You don't know how glad I am to hear that. You're loyal and responsible, and I don't want you helping anymore. I want you to work for me, and I'll pay you well."

He removed his flimsy hat, clutching it over his chest, squinting into the sunlight. "Wh-why thank ye, Cap'n. I'd be honored. Anything ye need, I'm your man."

Harry shook his hand, pleased his grip was steady and firm. "We'll get started at dawn. There's much work to be done to prepare Redmond Hill for my bride." He pulled a wrinkled envelope from his coat pocket and cast him a cautionary eye. "Take this to Paxton Cross straight away. It's important. Give it to Jon Hastings—no one else."

Tom threw his shoulders back and took the letter. "Aye, sir. Trust me—I'll put it in his hand myself."

"See that you do. Now," Harry said, relaxing into a smile, "I'm going to take a look around." He strode over to his horse, swung into the saddle, and spurred him to a gallop.

****

Olivia Parr landed on the log with a thud, her body slumped over at the middle and her hound by her side. The low-hanging branch of the sweet gum tree and the mossy ground cover were all the invitation she had needed to stop and rest. She smoothed her long dark tresses behind her ears, massaging her fingertips against the pounding in her temples, hearing Aunt Waneta's words.

"There is only one thing to do, my girl. It's time you say it out loud." Waneta drummed her fingers on the tabletop.

"I don't want to." Elbow on the table, Olivia dropped her chin on her palm. "Please, Aunt. I'm a good person and a good healer. Mr. Blake and his wife say I can stay with them."

"And how long until they tire of you? They cannot replace your parents. Elan and Betsey and me are your family now. And you can have—"

"Yes, yes. I can have James for my husband."

"He is a good Catawba man and has asked you to marry him. You should be grateful."

6

"I don't love him."

Waneta rose, and the chair skidded backward. "Your mother married for love, and look what it got her."

"But they were happy."

Her aunt stood erect, holding a graceful line between her neck, shoulder, and hips. "Best to be safe here with your Catawba family. You can learn to live with that."

Eyes downcast, she lowered her shoulders. "Yes, Aunt. I will do as you say."

Olivia sighed, shaking off the memory of the promise she had made hours earlier. A cool drop of rain landed on her forehead and trickled downward, mingling with the tears on her cheek. With a flip of her wrist, she coiled the length of her hair into a knot and tucked it underneath her wool cap. As more raindrops fell, tapping a soulful rhythm on the ground, she gazed at the hound dog beside her, his thick lips set in a pensive line. "Nay, Caddie—it's all right. I'll do what I must…but I don't have to be happy about it."

****

Raindrops pelted Harry's shoulders, trickling down his coat sleeves, and he slowed his chestnut stallion, steering them to shelter under a red maple tree. He dismounted, moving to cradle Gordie's neck, crooning gentle words in his ear. Rifling through his pockets, he produced a knife and apple. He cut into it, slipping a piece into his horse's mouth before popping another one into his own. As the shower continued, he flipped up the collar of his coat and relented to Mother Nature. As he fed Gordie the last slice, Harry spotted the twitch in his ears. He clamped his hand on his pistol, and his horse stomped his foot. Then he heard it, a light melody borne on a lifting breeze.

Harry wrapped the reins around a tree branch and walked toward the female singing with the rhythm of the rain. He squinted at the figure seated on a log, her back turned to him and hands rubbing the neck of a wet dog. As she stood and raised her arms in a graceful stretch, his gaze lighted on her small, lean frame. The words of her song—something about following His light and lifted burdens—left a hitch in his throat, and he stepped backward. A branch snapped under his boot, and he muttered an oath. Her hound turned, releasing a low menacing growl.

The woman pivoted in his direction, standing fast, and her eyes darkened like the storm clouds above them. "Who's there? Show yourself." A knife scraped against its scabbard. "I'm warning you. I'm armed."

A prickly silence enveloped them, then Harry emerged from behind a tree, hands raised. "Hold on. I mean you no harm, miss. Forgive my intrusion."

She balanced her weight evenly on both feet, wielding her knife as naturally as any adversary on the battlefield. The sight of her would have sent a lesser man running. *But not this soldier.*

"Stop! Don't come one step closer." She lifted her chin. "What're you doing here?"

"Taking refuge—from the rain, that is. I stopped to let the worst of it pass. My horse is over there." He gestured with his chin, and her gaze flicked to Gordie, then back to him. She held her defensive pose, her husky dog fixed a mere inch from her thigh. "I confess, I've ridden these trails my entire life and have never come upon such a sight."

"A sight? You find me amusing?"

"No," he said, only half-chuckling. "No. But I'm intrigued." He took two steps forward. "Please, forgive me. I'm Harry. Captain Harry Fleming, your servant." He removed his hat, a queue of tawny blond hair brushing his shoulder, then bowed and glanced up. "And you are, Miss…?"

"Parr. Olivia Parr, sir." She gave him a sideways glance, then slid her knife back in the sheath fastened to her waist, turning on her heel. Her canine kept a guarded eye on him.

"Pleased to meet you, Miss Parr," he said to the back of her head. From behind, he might have mistaken her for a lad, hide breeches and a cap, brown plaid shirt and vest swallowing her slight frame. The single feminine article of clothing she wore was an ivory gauze scarf tied around her neck.

"Fleming, was it?" she asked over her shoulder. "Are you kin to them? The ones who live at Glen Laurel?"

"I am. Are you acquainted?"

She turned to face him, patting the dog on his back. "Just a little."

He shrugged and crossed his arms, half-smiling. "Well, my Uncle Zeb's a bit of a brute. A controlling creature. Hopefully he's shown you his civilized side."

"You speak as though he's not in your good graces."

"Aye." His brow furrowed. "Nor I him."

She adjusted her cap over her ears. "Why? What's he done to you?"

Harry cocked his head. *Who is this young woman— this stray urchin staring up at me like a child waiting for her supper?* There was no inkling of understanding as to the impropriety of such a pointed question, and nothing cunning in her countenance. She was as transparent as the raindrops falling around them. "You are direct, Miss Parr."

She sucked in her breath. "Pray, please forgive me, Captain." With downcast eyes, her dark lashes fanned against her olive skin. "It-it's none of my business. Sometimes I speak without thinking."

Though his first thought ran to impudence, he judged her apology genuine. "It's all right. I'll answer you as best I can."

She lifted her head and gazed at him. With the clouds passing, the last traces of afternoon light filtered through the trees, highlighting her gently curved jaw and high cheekbones.

"It's not so much what my uncle's done to me. It is more what he hasn't done. He doesn't care whether I sink or swim—he's not pushing me into the water, mind you, but he's never going to toss out a rope to save me from drowning either."

A cricket's chirp lifted through the humid air between them, urgent and vibrant. In moments, an answer came from a different direction in several pulses. Their intertwined melody hinted of promise, of a connection defined by nature alone.

Olivia touched his arm, sending a tremor through his muscle despite the thickness of his jacket. Their gazes met. "Your uncle sounds rather harsh. In my experience nothing to do with family is ever easy. We must keep to His light."

"Oh, like your song?" He quirked a brow. "You've a lovely voice. I've heard the tune before—the one you were singing."

She dropped her hand and cleared her throat. "Um, it's a hymn actually."

"Of course. I knew that." He dragged his knuckles along his whiskers while she turned away, poking around inside her satchel. "Forgive me, Miss Parr, but might I ask why you're traveling alone along the trails of Pine Tree Creek?"

She turned around, one hand on her hip, the other fidgeting with her scarf. "I do it often enough. I was visiting someone. No need for concern."

"Would you allow me to escort you home? As a soldier and a gentleman, I must."

She removed her cap, shaking the droplets from it and releasing a mane of mahogany brown hair. With nimble fingers, she wove it into a thick braid down the front of her chest. "It's not necessary. As you can see, I'm in my traveling clothes. I set out on foot...and I can get home on foot."

"And is someone waiting for you there?"

She lifted her chin. "My father keeps his eye on me, sir."

A crease formed on his brow, and he crossed his arms. "With respect, Miss Parr, a gentleman always offers his protection to a young woman—even one who can clearly take care of herself. On my horse, I can have you home before dark, which would no doubt please your father."

The woody cedar aroma of juniper bushes wafted through the air, ruffling the scarf around her neck. Her tobacco-brown gaze met his for several long seconds. "Very well, Captain. I'll ride with you on one condition. You'll drop me off at the church."

That chin went up again, and he narrowed his eyes.

It wasn't every day he found a young woman and her dog traipsing through the woods—trails were taboo to most females. Though she had shown herself to be canny and capable, she was also kind. His muscle twitched from her earlier touch, and he uncrossed his arms. *Aw, hell.*

"Agreed." Harry offered her the crook of his elbow, and after throwing her bag over her shoulder, she accepted it. He led her to his horse and fitted her in the saddle, swinging in behind her.

"I'm taking up too much room, aren't I?" Olivia scooted her bottom back and forth, wedging it and her hips inside his thighs. She wiggled again.

Curse her breeches. He cleared his throat with a single cough and stilled her with one hand on her waist. *How in hell did I ever think she could be mistaken for a lad?*

"Better?" she asked, peering over her shoulder.

With his head down and chin tucked, he took in a deep breath, her scent of violet mixed with raindrops wafting up to his nose. In concealing a lopsided grin, he released a not-so-lopsided groan instead. "Aye. Something like that." Her guileless movements reminded him why women did not wear breeches. They alluded to certain feminine attributes better left hidden under skirts.

He pulled on the reins, dousing his randy thoughts with memories of Catherine's delicate tendrils and cornflower-blue eyes. His shoulders relaxed, calmed by the perfect harmony of her fair skin and primrose lips. It had taken his last ounce of patience not to descend upon Paxton Cross this afternoon and whisk her away. But he refused to risk any behavior that might lower him in Jon's eyes and jeopardize his plans. The path to securing

Catherine Hastings' hand in marriage went through her father. *Finally. Tomorrow. She'll be mine.*

Olivia shifted against him and fitted her cap on top of her head. He summoned a quiet smile, and with a click of his tongue, they set off, two strangers on horseback and one loyal hound meandering along the path toward Camden.

Chapter Two

By mid-morning, Harry was soaked with perspiration, his tunic sealed to his chest. He had labored for hours, ripping out an unruly maze of ivy laced across the southern face of the house, stopping only to drink water and mop his brow with a damp towel. Tom matched his pace and had the stalls cleaned, animals fed, and provisions secured in the barn in one morning.

Harry fixed his attention back to the house and took another step higher on the ladder. The ivy clung to the house with an invisible might, each stem strong on its own, but even more so when intertwined with one another. The unruly vines reminded him of his father, Joseph, and Uncle Zeb. Joseph was the younger by three years, a fierce and decisive man. He was a soldier in every sense of the word, forever steadfast in his beliefs. For what Zeb lacked in courage, he made up for with cunning and calculation. He had grit and possessed a keen ability to understand the workings of a man's mind. With a heaving groan, Harry ripped apart the last twist of vines and tossed them to the ground. He stepped off the ladder and dragged his rake across the debris, the tangled mess reminding him how jealousy had torn the two cousins apart.

Harry whipped out his pocket watch, then mopping sweat from his neck, barked out a few more orders to Tom and dashed toward the house. Inside his bedchamber, he shed his clothes and grabbed the soap and washcloth from the tray. The steaming water in the tub beckoned him, and he whispered a grateful thank you to Mary. *Right on time. She's a saint.*

After scrubbing and rinsing away the morning's grime, he draped a towel around his waist and stood in front of the mirror, shaving the shaggy stubble from his face. Afterward, he patted his cheeks with a fresh cloth and gazed at his reflection. *Whiskers certainly are more stubborn these days.* Blue eyes framed with fine creases at the corners stared back at him. *Where the devil did those come from?* He dragged his fingers through his hair, blaming hunger, fatigue, and countless skirmishes in the Carolina foothills for the slight. He leaned closer, counting close to a dozen scars on his shoulders and biceps. His gaze lowered to the burn mark stretching from his thumb up his forearm, and he ran his fingers over the slick skin. Doubt seeped into his thoughts, and he studied his reflection again. *Will Catherine still find me attractive...?* He scrubbed his hand along the back of his neck and closed his eyes. *Christ, how has she faired with her parents at Paxton Cross...?* He shook his head against the stampede of troubling thoughts, then combed his hair and dressed in his best clothes.

From across the room, he spied his small leather pouch on the dresser. *Just one more thing.* By the grace of God, he had kept the bag safe throughout the war. While its contents had no monetary value, the items were dear to him. *One is priceless.* He lifted the pale blue embroidered ribbon from the pouch, thoughts drifting back to their last evening together.

"Harry...stop. Please, we shouldn't." Catherine's *protest came amidst an airy breath.*

"No, you're wrong, Cee. We should. Now. While we can," he said, his lips skimming across her neck.

"Careful—you're crumpling my new skirt." She removed his wandering hands and placed them by her sides. *"There. Much better."*

"And you're crumpling my heart—amongst other things." Harry shifted his hips against the tightening in his breeches. *"We need to make memories tonight. You know what tomorrow brings."*

"Yes, you're leaving me."

"Nonsense. I'm taking you with me—in here." He took her hand and pressed it to his heart. *"Never doubt it."*

"But why must you go? Surely there are enough patriots in the fight. What if you're killed?" Her words caught deep in her throat.

"I won't be. I'll be careful. Father trained me for this since I was twelve. His skills, his tricks—aye, and his grit—they're mine now. I'm fit for the task."

"I don't understand why your uncle couldn't get you a post like Brandt's. He's not leaving." She folded her arms over her breasts.

With a clearing breath, he reached over to stroke her fingers. *"Brandt has a formal education—he's officer material. I'm not. Zeb knows this and simply negotiated to get his son the best commission possible."*

"Well, he ought to do the same for you. He's all the family you've got now. I don't understand why he keeps you at a distance."

"All the better to stay clear of his noose," he muttered to the wind. She frowned, confused. *"You know I prefer to make my own way, Cee. Besides, Brandt only has permission to stay here until he marries your sister."*

"Less than a fortnight away. Margaret swears a few headaches and dizzy spells won't keep her from marrying the man of her dreams."

Harry chuckled, rather envious of his elder cousin—wedding his sweetheart despite the tides of war. The couple was four years older than he and Catherine, and their betrothal was common knowledge. But the source of Margaret's recent maladies gave him a chill. In his experience, having lost his mother when he was eleven and his father last year, health and vigor were a gift, never a guarantee.

"And one day, will you make your wedding vows to me as eagerly as your sister does to Brandt?"

"Will you to me?"

Harry gazed at the pouty bow of her mouth and rubbed her chin with his thumb. "I've been in love with you my entire life, Cee. On my mother's grave, I promise I will marry you when I return. I fight for our freedom—and for our children's future. We need to be in control of our destiny—not some king who hurls threats across the ocean."

"What will happen to Redmond Hill while you're gone?"

"Zeb has promised to take care of it." He bristled at trusting the most important thing in his life—save Catherine—to his uncle.

"Things are changing all around us." She twirled her finger through a soft tendril, worrying her lower lip. "Papa shields me from as much as he can, and I love him for it. He's always had such a care for me."

"I'm grateful knowing your parents will protect you until I can make you my wife."

"Oh, Harry." She inched closer, hand on his thigh.

17

"I will miss you and pray for you every day."

He breathed her name. "Take your hair down for me. Please. I need you—need to burn every scent and touch of you into my mind." After a swift look left and right, she freed her mane, letting it spill over her creamy shoulders. "Sweet Jesus, you're the most beautiful woman I've ever seen."

He kissed the curve of her cheek, dipping lower to the slope of her neck. His hand slid higher, fingers running through the silken gold tresses. When she returned the gesture, drawing his head and mouth closer, his heart stirred.

"Harry..."

His name across her lips undid him. He groaned, his desire leaping like a flame to dry bracken. With each kiss, he was drawing the gardenia scent of her hair and skin into his senses. He wanted her...needed her. She softened against him, and the rest of the world faded away...

"Kitten...? Where are you?" Jon Hastings called out in the darkness.

No. It's not possible. It's unthinkable. *Harry crushed the thought.*

"You'll catch cold in the night air. Come inside, Kitten."

Catherine's breathing hitched. "Oh my, we...must stop."

"Your father knows you're with me, and he knows my intentions are honorable." He kissed her quivering lips. "Please, let me speak to him—"

"No. Why, I couldn't possibly let him see—or think. Oh, I must fix my hair and quickly. Please help me, Harry."

Catherine turned her back to him, and he bent downward, his forehead a lead weight on her shoulder. He could easier dam the Wateree River than his desire. He lifted his head and kissed the back of her hair. In the light of the stars, he studied it, an ethereal kaleidoscope of gold and silver-white. He held it in his palms and buried his face in it, engraving her scent on his mind.

"Wait." She turned around, meeting his gaze. "I do love you, Harry. Please take this with you—to remember me." She dropped her embroidered blue hair ribbon in his palm and closed his fingers over it.

"I love you, Cee, with all my heart."

Harry clutched the faded strip in his hand. It was more than a ribbon woven through Catherine's hair. It was his lifeline...*to her*...the kindest, sweetest, most beautiful woman he had ever known. Aside from Catherine herself, the ribbon was his dearest treasure. A smile lifted on his lips, and he tucked it inside his coat pocket and bounded out the door.

A short time later, Harry arrived at Paxton Cross. The scent of gardenia and lilac flanked the front door, and he breathed it in, hoping the sweetness might calm his nerves. He had played this scene over in his mind more times than he could count. He rolled his hand into a fist and expelling a gust of breath, rapped on the door. After being greeted and ushered to the study, he wiped his clammy palms on his coattails.

"By God, Harry Fleming—is it really you?" Jon Hastings crossed the length of the room, fit with several chairs and a cushioned sofa near a large window, and welcomed him.

"Aye, Jon." A smile overtook his face, and they shook hands. "You received my letter yesterday?"

He nodded, placing his arm around his shoulder and offering him a seat. "Glad you made it home safe, son."

Harry warmed at the endearment, rubbing his jaw. Jon filled a pair of glasses with a golden whiskey, and after placing one in his hand, they drank together.

"I must offer you my deepest condolences, sir. Catherine wrote to me about Margaret's passing. The last letter I received from her."

"I hope you never experience the loss of a child, Harry. The pain never goes away."

"I'm sure Catherine's been a great comfort."

Jon nodded before swallowing. "Yes, she's everything I could have asked for in an obedient daughter."

"She means everything to me, Jon. She's...she's my world." Hand trembling around his glass, he lowered it to the wooden table. He clasped his hat, digging his fingers into the folds. "Surely you ken my purpose. I've come home. I'm here to ask for Cath—"

"Harry. Please don't..."

He shook his head, undeterred. "Pray, sir, how is Catherine? I've not heard from her in so long, but the posts were unreliable. Tell me, did she receive my letters? Is she well? When may I see her?"

Jon rubbed a chubby finger around the rim of his glass. "She's well."

"Wonderful. I need to see her. Now please." He crossed his arms, and the silence between them grew.

"Not possible. Not today, Harry."

He watched Jon pull a handkerchief from his breast pocket and dab it around his neck. The house was eerily quiet for midday. His gaze traveled the room, finding no sign of Catherine's sketches or needlework. Had he not spied her mother through the window, basket in hand and cutting stems of purple gladiolus, he would have guessed no female was in residence.

"Why not? With all due respect, where is Catherine?"

Jon rose and crossed the room, pressing one hand against the mantel above the fireplace. "She doesn't live here anymore. My daughter married your cousin Brandt several years ago. They live at Glen Laurel. She gave birth to their first child in December—a little girl."

His heart hammered in his chest. "What the hell are you talking about?" He flattened his hat between his fists. "Catherine's my girl. *My* girl!"

Jon turned, shifting his weight between his feet. "Why, my daughter—she was hardly yours, Harry. There was no agreement between us. I wish I could spare you the shock of it. Truly, I do. But you've been away for years—"

"In service to God and country! You knew my intentions and those of Catherine. What's behind this?" He jumped to his feet, stomping back and forth across the room, then wheeled around. "Damn you, tell me who's behind this."

****

Some hours later, after sunset had faded into the pitch of night, Harry hunkered down in the saloon at the edge of town. The old place smelled of bayberry, stale smoke, and sour mash. A fetching young thing with lemon verbena hair strolled over to his corner table and poured him a shot of whiskey.

"Leave the bottle." He gazed up at her. "Please." He placed a few extra coins in her hand, and she cast him a titillating smile.

He drank liberally over the next few hours, the amber liquid in the glass slowly taking on the likeness of Catherine's golden hair. "Damnation, can I not drink in peace?"

Harry took a final gulp and placed the glass on the table with a thud, Jon's words rollicking around his liquor-soaked brain. With but a little coaxing, he had answered his question about what was behind the marriage. It was the usual motive—some drivel about the unity between their two families and security for his daughter. Jon regaled him with a simpering tale of a Brandt—so devastated by Margaret's death—that his only salvation was to wed Catherine. *Complete horseshit.* That Brandt was devastated, he could believe. That Brandt betrayed him, he could not—not of his own volition. Jon's final confession ripped through his heart like a rusty nail. Uncle Zeb had pressed for the marriage—insisted on it. *My own flesh and blood.*

Through heavy-lidded eyes, he glimpsed a candlelight shadow on the wall. When it took on Catherine's shape, he leaned forward and buried his face in his hands. His father's warning filled his head. *Zeb never forgave me, son. He despises me, and so will he you.*

"If you'd like, I could give you peace, sir."

The soft words snapped him out of his thoughts, the scent of lemon verbena tickling his nose. Skilled fingers walked up his bare forearm, and his muscle twitched.

"I could be your friend tonight."

Harry lifted his head, the tallow candles in the barroom rendering a glow over the pretty barmaid. She untied her hair bow, releasing a flaxen mane, and moved closer, encircling the silky tie around his neck, pulling it from side to side. His skin prickled from the friction, and he clasped her wrist. *I may be drunk, but I'm not a fortress.*

"Yes, I believe I'm in need of company." He pushed up from his chair, and the barmaid dropped her hair ribbon on the table. He grabbed her hand, leading her across the length of the room and upstairs to where he knew an empty room awaited.

Chapter Three

Harry preferred toiling in the dirt of his fields and not the empty cavern of his heart. He worked from dawn to dusk each day, sweat dripping from every sunbaked muscle in his shoulders, railing against the heartache with every swing of the ax and push of the plow. In the week since his life had turned upside down, he found solace knowing the beneficiary of his broken heart was Redmond Hill.

The crisp morning air glistened with streaks of sunlight piercing through the foliage of the elm trees. Save for the occasional song of the chickadee, he and Tom traveled the dusty road to town in silence. The team of horses pulling the wagon moved at a steady clip, stirring the arid soil into a bronze haze around their hooves.

The town of Camden greeted them with the clang of the blacksmith's hammer and the bleating of sheep corralled behind the butcher's market. Tom stopped the wagon in front of the mercantile store, a hub of activity in the cozy town, a place where a man could get a home-cooked meal and seed for planting, and a woman could stock her basket with flour, cornmeal, and muslin. It was a haven where men bartered and made deals, and women gossiped about stubborn men and undisciplined boys.

Harry swung down, landing on both feet, and gazed up at Tom. "You get the wagon loaded. I'll join you straight away." He watched the fellow speed into action, wishing he had five more men like him.

"Well, I'll be damned. Is it a ghost...or the man himself?"

The familiar tenor drawl stopped Harry in his tracks. He wheeled around to a strapping, robust man sporting a black waistcoat and polished boots. His queue of brown hair peeked out from beneath his tricorn hat. The fair-faced man flashed him a wide grin.

"Flesh and bone, my friend...flesh and bone." Harry removed his hat and took stock of Kitt Allington, his lifelong chum. "My God, it's good to see you."

Kitt threw an arm around his shoulder. "About time you've come home. Christ, but I've missed your ornery arse. C'mon, we need food and drink."

They drifted toward the alehouse—the noisy little eatery next to the mercantile—and took a table by a curtained window. The aroma of buttermilk biscuits and ham steaks filled the air, along with the nutty bouquet of coffee and sweet molasses. A portly woman wearing a kerchief to hold back her errant curls brought them an abundance of all four.

"Been wondering when you'd make your way home." Kitt sank his teeth into a warm biscuit. "How long you been back?"

"A week."

"You find much changed?" He dabbed a sticky drop of molasses from his chin with a finger and licked it clean.

"Changed? Aye, that's one word for it. Redmond's a wreck—my tenants have all but deserted me." He stabbed his fork into the ham and shoveled it in his mouth, half-chewing. "I find my funds are not how I left them—thanks to Zeb," he said derisively. "And there's the little matter of Catherine's marriage to Brandt—which I understand has already produced a child." He took a hefty bite out of a biscuit. "Yes, I'd say I find things much changed."

"You're stretched pretty thin...and rightly so." His friend shook out a square napkin, wiping his mouth before tossing it on the table.

"To the point of breaking, but I wouldn't dare give Zeb the satisfaction."

"I can't say I blame you. He's a surly bastard. But on the other point, be patient." Kitt waved to the serving woman who came over with her coffee pot. "You'll see your finances soon healthy again, and the men will return once word spreads you're back. There's plenty looking for honest work."

"Zeb was a tyrant—ran all but the weakest away. Silas, Mary, and her son, Tom, are all that remain." He scowled. "They're not the only ones he spirited away."

With arms folded on the table, Kitt leaned forward. "I'm sorry for your disappointment. I wrote to you about the marriage, but I guess it never reached you."

"Thanks, but it wouldn't have changed anything."

He chewed on his lower lip for a moment. "Have you seen your uncle yet?"

Harry replied with a terse shake of his head.

"Just as well. Besides, you've got your whole life in front of you. Put your energy into Redmond Hill. It will never forsake you."

"Aye, it's the only thing that gets me through the day." He sighed over his cup of coffee.

"Say, let me put the word out you're looking for hard-working field hands."

"I'd be obliged if you would."

"Done." Kitt smacked the table, then leaned back, rubbing his chin. "And I think you'd do well with some fresh company, my friend. Can't have you turning into some old codger held up on the farm." He snapped his fingers. "Have supper with us on Sunday—say two o'clock. Sarah's a fair good cook, and I'm sure she can find a suitable lady friend to join us."

Harry quirked an eyebrow. "And by suitable you mean...?"

"Unmarried, of course. One who's long on looks and short on temper. It's not good for a man to be alone too much."

He shrugged under his coat and averted his gaze. "I-I don't know, Kitt."

His friend leaned forward on both elbows. "Look, it'll be a pleasant meal and conversation amongst friends. If you two aren't rubbing along, just give me a sign—like a scratch of your nose—and I'll save you."

Harry disdained matchmaking mostly because he had never required it. He had given his heart to Catherine when he still had a squeaky voice and but a smattering of whiskers on his chin. She had pledged her love to him, and he had her hair bow to prove it. *But what is a ribbon compared to a wedding ring?*

He nursed his coffee. Though his heart still beat in his chest, it was cold like the bedrocks in the river. Every part of him rejected the notion he needed Kitt's intervention, but he was a man living alone and not so pleased about it. He looked up at his best friend's firm jawline and unwavering gaze.

Kitt cleared his throat loudly, purposefully. "Ahem."

He muttered a curse and lowered his mug to the table with a thud. "Fine. I'll do it."

"And another case closed." Kitt finished his coffee, smacking his lips in satisfaction.

Harry bit back a smile. Kitt was a master at persuasion. *No wonder he's so damn good with civics and the law.* Aside from the thicker waistline, a condition he attributed to his wife's fine cooking, the man had changed little over the years. Intelligent, honest, and amiable, Kitt Allington was the best kind of friend.

After he and Kitt parted ways, he rejoined Tom at their well-stocked wagon, checking the wheels and axels before joining him on the driver's bench. As they rambled down the road toward home, he wrestled with his thoughts. He longed to entrench himself at Redmond Hill, channel his energy into the earth, and salvage what he could of his life without Catherine. Maybe Kitt was right, and he needed some distraction. *Nothing better than a female for that.* He gave his head a shake when the image of a breech-clad young woman sprang into his mind. *Miss Parr. Now there's a female you don't see every day.* A smile tugged at his lips, and he wondered what it would be like to share Sunday dinner with her— and not some entirely "suitable lady friend."

Chapter Four

Long shooting rays from the late afternoon sun cast an amber glow on the streets of Camden, and that, along with the absence of workday routines, signaled a leisurely ride for Harry from the Allington home. No smells of wood, tar, and iron in the air on a Sunday. Regarding the afternoon's entertainment, Kitt had been correct in one respect—Sarah's cooking exceeded expectations. They dined on a brown-crusted chicken pie and a platter of steaming succotash. He had, however, been wrong in the other. Miss Emily Wakefield, visiting stepdaughter to the new owner of the mercantile, as congenial a package as she was, would not be one he intended to unwrap.

He turned the corner to King Street and sighed. Little more than the sound of light hooves and an ambling breeze brushing through the trees filled the air. He breathed in the sultry smell of dusk, closed his eyes, and willed his horse to lead the way. Moments later, a bark pulled him from his thoughts.

"Sit, boy. Stay put—right here."

Harry spun around in his saddle and spotted a canine curled up on a step. His gaze lighted on a slender figure—with dark hair swirled into a high knot— sweeping the front porch of the church. He recollected her voice and movements instantly, only this time she wielded a broom and not a knife. He pulled back, bringing his stallion to a stop under the cover of a mulberry tree. *Alone again?* In his experience, young women moved around like a gaggle of geese—and equally chatty. This female had only a fondness for a simple song and her faithful hound.

Olivia Parr wore a starched, peach cotton dress with an ivory kerchief tied around her neck. The few ruffles on the sleeves fell lazily around her forearms. As she swayed back and forth in rhythm with her broomstick and song, her small brown shoes peeked out from her skirt. She was not a beauty in the traditional sense of the word, but she had a natural allure. She reminded him of fresh summer corn, a golden treasure hidden behind a husk and a thousand soft silks.

He bolted to attention with Gordie's rousing snort, white knuckles gripping the reins. He gave his horse a soft click of his tongue and urged him into a walk. Once outside the shadows, he smiled, her dog still lying on the step, tail thumping.

"Good evening, Miss Parr."

She whirled about, hand over her heart. "Oh, my. Good evening, Captain Fleming." She fumbled a curtsey but managed a step forward, resting her free hand on the white railing encircling the entryway to the church.

"I'm surprised to find you here this time of day." He dismounted, slid his arm under his horse's neck, and led him toward the steps. His gaze drifted from her to her hound, his tail still wagging.

"Caddie remembers you."

He pushed the brim of his hat back for a better look. "I'm glad of it. He's quite devoted to you."

"He's my dearest friend and protector." The dog's ears pricked, and he licked his muzzle with one big sweep of his tongue.

Harry cocked his head. *Could she be more singular? Or lovely?* "Well, I'd say he lived up to his reputation when I came upon you in the woods." When she laughed, he fancied it a delightful sound. "What are you up to?"

"Just tidying up before folks arrive for service."

"This late?"

"*Evening* prayer service." She hid her smile behind her hand, her dark eyebrows slanting upward into a delicate arch.

"Well, thank you for enlightening me." He chuckled, rubbing his hand across the back of his neck. "I'm unfamiliar with such routines these days."

"God's house is open to all who wish to enter, sir." Olivia straightened her stance, broom handle propped under her fist and chin, eyes bright and beckoning. He nudged his horse closer, captivated by several wisps of hair that had fallen loose from their nest and were brushing across her neck. He liked the way she held herself—poised, yet uninhibited—as she smoothed another wayward strand from her cheek. The movement rekindled the memory of her seated in front of him on horseback, the same silky strands tickling his chin.

"You make it rather hard to say no." He averted his gaze, shrugging his shoulders under his coat. "Perhaps another time."

"As you wish, Captain." She turned aside, pulling the broom across the wooden planks once more.

Wait. No batting your eyelashes? No pouty frown? His horse whinnied and bobbed his head. *I agree—a most curious woman.* "Tell me, Miss Parr, do you live nearby?"

Her lips blanched into a fine line. "Not too far

away."

He took a step forward. "May I wait for you—right over there by the mulberry—and escort you home after the service? Forgive me, but I think it's unusual to find you alone again so late in the day. My father taught me to offer my protection to a young woman—"

"Even one who can clearly take care of herself." They chimed in unison.

"You remember?"

"I do." She leaned on the broomstick, using her free hand to smooth out some nonexistent wrinkle on her skirt. "You're very considerate, but I'll be meeting up with my father soon."

Her declaration rankled him. With a deep breath, he shook his head. "Well then—I suppose I should be on my way. It's been a pleasure talking with you again. Enjoy the service."

He brought his horse around and swung up into the saddle, his legs hugging the animal.

"Captain…?"

"Miss Parr?" He watched her dog lumber up the steps and take his place by her side. He stilled, holding the reins in one hand, gaze tracking the rise and fall of her chest.

"I-I trust I'll see you at the christening next Sunday?"

He ran his hands through his horse's mane, trolling his brain for some clue to her reference. "The christening? Of course, wouldn't miss it."

"We shall see you then, sir." With a bashful smile, Olivia curtsied and strolled around to the back of the church where she bid Caddie to stay before going inside. He stared, finding it hard to drag his gaze away from the figure lighting candles inside the chapel. She moved about the room, resuming her singing though it was barely audible from his post outside. Gordie roused him with a haughty flick of his tail, and he chuckled, clicking his cheek.

Back on the road, a deep lavender twilight peeking over the silhouette of dusty white pines, he rode at a steady trot and mulled over her words. *What christening?*

Chapter Five

May 1783

Blessed with glorious weather all week, Harry and Tom made steady progress in the fields at Redmond. An abundance of rain had fallen in April, rendering the soil prime for planting. Kitt was true to his word, having sent over a crew of men—some lean and robust, others hefty and brawny—all of whom were eager for work. He hired five of them for a reasonable wage and sweetened the deal by negotiating some compensation in the way of lodgings for three men with wives and children. His four tenant houses were pine log structures, plain and sturdy, but once filled with hard-working families, would shine again.

"It's a good thing ye done, Cap'n. Got some good men, I hear." Mary stirred the evening stew simmering over the fire, sipping from the spoon and smacking it between her lips before scooping it into four large bowls filled with white rice. She was the only housekeeper Harry had ever known, and he always enjoyed her roasted beef stew filled with as many vegetables as she could put her hands on.

They ate in silence for some minutes before Tom spoke up. "All three families are movin' in tomorrow. They're right happy about livin' here."

"Did you show them which houses to take?" Harry

looked at him over the steam rising above his bowl.

"Why, no, sir. I figured you—or Silas—would decide where to put them." He glanced at Silas, then his mother.

Harry took a long drink of ale and held on to the bottle. "It would be best if you took the first one, closest to the barn and the house. You can decide where to put the other three families."

"Me, sir?"

"Yes."

"A place of my own?"

Harry nodded, rather enjoying how the lad's face twitched.

"Glory, Jesus." Mary dropped her spoon and threw her hand over her chest. Silas leaned back, arching his brow.

"It's high time." Harry took two more bites, scraped his bowl clean, and wiped his chin with a cloth. "You're eighteen and still sleeping on a cot in the scullery. I won't have it any longer, and there's but one servant's room under this roof, and it's already taken." He waved a hand at the middle-aged couple, cocking his head. "What do you say, Mary?"

"Aye, you're right," she said, head bobbing. "Silas and me belong here. Ye do as the cap'n says and take the first house."

Tom's hazel eyes flickered, and he crossed his arms on the table, chewing his bottom lip. "I'll do whatever ye say. But I beg ye, may I please make a place in the barn instead? I canna afford to let go of my wages, not even for such a fine house. I've got to save for my future."

"I'm offering you the house in addition to your wages. It's yours for as long as you work for me—which

I hope is a very long time." He extended his hand to Tom, but he sat stone-still.

"Son?" Mary nudged his forearm.

He finally looked up, a smile curving his lips. "I don't know what to say except thank ye, Cap'n. Thank ye very much."

He shook Tom's hand, then stood, leaving their excited whispers in his wake. "See I'm not disturbed," he said over his shoulder, closing the door to his study behind him.

Harry welcomed the smells of leather and parchment from the furnishings that had belonged to his father and grandfather. A mahogany desk sat at the center of the room on top of a thick braided rug. The wooden chair behind it featured a tall, straight back, to which Harry had added two soft cushions for his comfort. A crimson glow from the fireplace snapped and crackled, filling the room with the scent of hickory. He crossed the room and poured himself a brandy. Easing back in his chair, he sipped his drink, releasing the tension in his shoulders and neck.

He thumbed through the stack of leather-bound books on his desk. Since his return, he had been studying the ledgers Zeb managed during his absence and determining the condition of his finances. He set his glass aside and began sifting through the few remaining pages. He populated each column with revenues and expenses, checking receipts and bills from one book against the other. Mindful to allow for the added expense of the new men, but whose output would generate additional income with the harvest, he was sure with time—and a bit of good luck—he could revive Redmond Hill.

With the late hour upon him, Harry stretched long arms above his head and turned his waning attention to several letters stashed in a nearby box. He opened and read each one, then stopped short, recognizing the seal on a note at the bottom of the pile. He tore it open and skimmed the script, tossing it aside, rubbing his temples. With a sigh, he drained the last bit of his brandy. Apparently, he would be attending a christening this Sunday—for one Catherine Margaret "Peggy" Fleming, granddaughter of Zeb, daughter of Brandt and Catherine.

****

The rising sun cast a stream of light on Olivia's face as she pulled a comb through her hair. Though she kept it in a braid at night, she was a heavy sleeper and always found it mussed in the morning. She gazed at her reflection in the looking glass, fanning her mane out across her shoulders, guessing it had been almost a year since her last cut, some months before her father's death. She swayed a little, the burden on her heart hampering her breathing. In two weeks, she would marry a stranger—live under his roof, share his bed, and benefit from his protection.

How will it feel to lie with a man? Her thoughts drifted—as they had in recent days—to Harry Fleming. She bit her bottom lip. *With him, I imagine quite nice.* From the moment she had met him on the trail, his every movement—every word—made her nerves tingle. He was the image of masculinity, from his broad shoulders down to the length of his riding coat barely concealing his nicely formed thighs. When she closed her eyes and inhaled, she could still recall his scent of earthy pine and sandalwood. The memory of riding with him on horseback, ensconced in his arms, was as vivid as if it were hours, and not weeks ago. *Don't be ridiculous. He was being a gentleman. Nothing more.*

Caddie brushed against her shift and sprawled out beside her. She pushed out a sigh and reached for her satchel, rummaging through the various pockets until she found her clippers. "Well, I suppose a husband is reason enough." She turned back to her reflection and stood straight, guiding them through the first strands of hair, letting the locks float to her bare feet.

****

Olivia arrived at her aunt's house before noon, dressed in camel-colored breeches and a gray cotton tunic. She sensed Waneta's probing gaze but plopped down on a stool at the small table, unaffected.

"You cut your hair." Waneta put a plate of warm hoe cakes on the table and tilted her head. "Still long, which is good."

"I feel like I must do—do something to get ready for…you know…"

"Your marriage."

Olivia bit into a cake and chewed, wiping her mouth between sips of water. "I'll gather my things this week and tell the Blakes I'm leaving. Oh, and I have nothing to wear."

"I never see you in anything but these rags."

"These," she said, motioning to her clothes, "make the most sense when I'm traveling—like coming to see you, Aunt. Skirts get in the way. But yes, I own two dresses—one peach and the other a pale yellow." She looked up and dropped her fork on the plate. "Wait. What do Catawba women wear when they get married?"

"Let your family take care of it."

Family. The word would take on new meaning once

she became James' wife and part of the tribe. She shivered, and not from the breeze sweeping through the room when Waneta opened the door.

"I will go back to town with you today. Elan is packing the wagon now." Waneta stood with her hands on her hips, sunlight washing over her face.

The Catawba traded with villages on the trail, and the town of Camden was one of the most active in the region. Olivia had visited the market a few times. The beautiful clay pots and vases made by Catawba women were growing in popularity with colonists. She had admired them from afar, having no means to either trade for or purchase one, nor a place to keep it even if she had. Being the daughter of a white pastor and a Catawba woman, she had little experience collecting material things.

"Come now, child. Your life will be good and happy with us, you will see." Waneta patted her cheek, then took a pitcher and refilled her glass of water.

Olivia wished she had some of her aunt's faith. Her lips in a tight line, she raised her cup in a silent toast, quite certain in this marriage she was bidding farewell to her heart.

Chapter Six

Harry did his best to blend in with the crowd at the christening. The pastor blessed the baby girl, and faces across the congregation beamed with a joy rivaling the sun shining down on the church lawn. Afterward, the celebratory mood shifted to outdoors where iced cakes, shortbread, and rose port were in plentiful supply.

"Well now, I'm surprised to see you here." Zeb slurped his drink.

Harry inched away, smiling through gritted teeth. "I received an invitation."

"It was nothing more than a formality."

"Likewise, is my presence."

"We sent Josie an invitation. Now there's a Fleming I'd like to see."

Hands clasped behind his back, Harry nodded to passersby. "My sister's place is at home with her husband and their wee sons."

"Pity. I shall call on her next time I'm in Charleston." He drummed his fingers on his glass. "But you've been back nigh on a month and haven't heard not one word from you. Not good to work too hard at Redmond Hill, my boy. What's happened to the young spitfire cloaked in our new flag who chased off after grit and glory?"

"He's still here." He tapped his hand on his heart.

"Some say you've come back changed through the

blood on the battlefield."

"A bloodbath is nothing compared to the wound inflicted upon me by my family." Harry finally turned an eye on his uncle. "How mistaken I was to think my only enemies wore red coats."

"Ah, now there's the cocky lad I know so well. Buck up, boy—life just moved on without you."

"Sorry bastard." He clenched his teeth.

"And you're a pathetic fledgling—no more than a smitten pup." Zeb leaned in and whispered, "Tell me, eh—did you hold Catherine's hand when you strolled through the garden? Steal a few sweet kisses on the porch swing, hm?" He smirked over his drink. "Took your eye off the prize, you did. You've only yourself to blame. You should have married her before you left."

He grimaced. *Should stood no chance against reality.* "Damn it, Zeb. Margaret was to wed Brandt."

"She died. Plans changed."

Harry shook his head. "It's maniacal how your mind works."

"You should damn well know how the world works by now."

"Indulge me. Help me understand how your world works." Several guests turned anxious gazes on them.

Zeb took his time lighting his pipe, puffing on it until the pot glowed red and a whirl of smoke circled his ears. "Possession."

"What? Land…? Property? Coin?"

"Yes. And people and legacy."

"You think we're all your personal bargaining chips?" Harry sneered.

"Precisely."

He choked back a laugh, head cocked. "Christ,

you're as arrogant and oblivious as old Lord Cornwallis himself."

"I'm a patriot, but I respect the man's military genius. I take that as a compliment." Zeb inhaled, letting the tobacco smoke fill his chest.

"It's an accusation."

As he exhaled, smoke kissed his cheek. "Bah! You're still nothing but a damned insolent pup." With a swift turn, he strode over and joined a cluster of old men in deep conversation.

Harry stood motionless, his arms taut by his sides, fists curled. He jerked his head when an arm fell across his shoulder.

"Just the man I'm looking for." Kitt spoke through tight lips, flashing a grin at several curious onlookers, nodding and leading him in the opposite direction. "Listen to me, Harry—forget about your uncle. Focus," he whispered. "Heads up on this one."

They took a couple of steps forward, stopping in front of a lanky man, late forties, sporting curly, wheat-blond hair.

Kitt waved an open palm in greeting. "Harry, may I introduce you to Mr. Reed Barlowe, local merchant and financier. Mr. Barlowe, meet Captain Harry Fleming."

"Pleased to meet you," Harry said, shaking his outstretched hand.

"Likewise." Reed sucked on the corner of his lip. "I've heard a good bit about you already."

Harry quirked a brow to both men.

Kitt stepped forward. "You see, Mr. Barlowe here is Emily Wakefield's stepfather. You made her acquaintance at dinner Sunday last. You'll recall Reed arrived in Camden last year after inheriting the mercantile and alehouse from his cousin."

"My condolences. He was an honest man. We surely miss him."

Reed rubbed his thin, blond mustache, touching a blemish on his cheek. "He was a distant cousin, so I hardly knew him."

"Glad to see you're keeping them both open for business." Harry crossed his arms, unflinching.

"Yes, they're profitable. I've made some additions—hope to increase their value." He folded his hands behind his back. "My Emily tells me you're an enterprising man—war hero, in fact."

"She's too kind."

Reed turned with a half-smile. "She's here if you'd like to see her. If you're lucky, she might make time for you."

He nodded, his jaw taut. "Thank you for the advice, sir."

"Well, good day to you, Captain Fleming. I hope to be seeing more of you soon." He scuttled off to join the line forming around the refreshment table.

"That one's a macaroni." Harry snorted. "And besides, I don't trust a man with short hair."

"Can you imagine it long?" Kitt nudged his elbow. "Even pulled back, why it would be like a big bush, all a-tangle with those whopping tight yellow curls."

Harry bit back a laugh, recovering just in time to meet Brandt's glare. He lifted his chin, assessing. *How do you measure up these days?* The stubborn Fleming eyes and square chin were unchanged, but his elder cousin could no longer claim height to his advantage. Brandt straightened, the cut of his coat and starched cravat accentuating his broad shoulders. Harry tugged at his lapels. *You're not the only one who fills out his coat.* His cousin wore his dark chestnut hair smoothed into a fashionable queue, the ends of his hair trim and blunt. Harry ran his hand over the strap holding back his wavy autumn-gold locks. *Still unruly, I know. Much like my disposition.*

As Brandt strode toward him, his coattails swinging, Harry's face darkened. They met head on, shoulders squared, and managed an embrace before stepping back.

Brandt clapped his upper arm. "You look well, Harry. We're all glad you made it home."

"And you're obviously fit, cousin. First a husband and now a father. How responsible of you to carry on the legacy." Harry plucked another glass of port from a server's tray to wash down the distaste rising in his gut. "Tell me, what other plans are hiding up your sleeve? Or more to the point, up Zeb's sleeve?"

Brandt rubbed his tongue on the inside of his cheek before answering. "The marriage was sudden, yes, but it was never any secret."

"May as well have been when I was off fighting hundreds of miles away."

"If I'd been in a better frame of mind, I would've written to tell you what was happening. But it wouldn't have made a difference. The old man had his mind set."

Since a childhood fever had made Brandt deaf in his left ear, Harry moved to his right side. "Tell me how is it Margaret dies, and then some months later you marry my girl? You think yourself so very different from Zeb. Seems to me you want whatever he wants, only you don't have the balls to wield the power as he does. The bastard's trained you well. You make a fine lackey."

Fury etched the hard line of Brandt's jaw. "I can see

you're not yourself, and I expected as much at our first meeting. But I refuse to say something I might regret later. I suggest you do the same."

"Keep your suggestions to yourself!" Nearby, several heads turned toward them. Harry raised a finger in his direction. "I don't take orders from you or Zeb." He bristled when Kitt grabbed hold of his shoulder.

Brandt's emerald eyes narrowed. "Don't mistake my tolerance for anything other than family loyalty. We share the same blood after all. You'll thank me later for my patience." He inched closer. "Now, come meet my daughter. It's high time you face Catherine too."

Harry glared as his cousin walked over to the steps of the church where a small gathering of people encircled the mother and child. He had spent the past few weeks sequestered at Redmond Hill, stewing in his juices. Gazing up at the heavens, he huffed, conceding to Brandt in one regard. *I need to face Catherine.* Tossing back the last bit of his drink, he turned to Kitt, gave him a flick of his head, and started walking.

As he got closer, Catherine's honeyed voice lifted through the air like a butterfly lighting on a daisy. Then her laugh came full, yet soft, and it stopped him cold. Kitt nudged him forward and was still strong at his back when they locked gazes.

Catherine's hand flew to her neck. Her berry-blue eyes were clear, yet moist with tears. He wondered if she shed them for him or their lost love…but alas, they were for her newly christened child. Brandt moved in beside her, placing his arm around her waist, gazing down at the bundle in her arms, and she regained her composure. *Well played, cousin.*

"Oh look, Brandt. It's Harry—dear Harry. We're so

45

happy you're home." He bent to kiss her outstretched hand, her warmth teasing his lips despite the kid glove. "We've missed you. I trust you're well?" she asked, ever the polite and delicate flower.

For once, Harry wished she was not so beautiful and decorous. He gave her a broken smile. "I'm faring well enough. And you are—I mean, you look..." He choked down what felt like a handful of nails before finding his words. His gaze softened. "Cee, you're lovely...as always. You look just like you did on our last evening together." He ignored the heat from Brandt's glare and the itch in his palms to take her in his arms. His gaze dropped to her breast where her daughter slept peacefully.

Catherine touched the ringlet of hair beside her cheek, biting her lower lip. "Some things about me are different though."

"Things, yes." He dragged his gaze to Brandt, then back to her. "But never you, Cee. Not ever."

Catherine glanced between them, and for a moment it seemed she had lost her breath. "It-it brings us so much joy to have you home. You and Brandt have always been close. I suppose you have a lot of catching up to do. You should visit soon."

A fresh rush of resentment ran up his spine. "I'm very busy. I've much to do at Redmond Hill—many things to set straight."

At his stabbing tone, Brandt stepped forward. "We know you'll come when you can. Things may be different, but we're still family, are we not?"

"Indeed. Now, if you will excuse me."

Harry gave a curt nod, then turned on his heel and crossed the yard, sidling up to Kitt. "You got anything harder than this damn fruity port?" His friend reached in his pocket and passed him a silver flask. He took a healthy swill, swiping the corner of his mouth with his thumb, and handed it back. "What the hell was that even...?"

"You, my friend, wising up to the fact the girl you left behind is gone. Catherine is no longer a lass. She's a wife and mother. The sooner you face it and move on, the better."

"Yeah—you know, I think you're right." Harry's head bobbed up and down, and he stepped backward. "I can't take any more of this. I-I, uh...I need to go."

"Harry, c'mon—get back here. Don't leave like this."

He whipped around, his friend's voice fading away as he darted past huddles of people milling about the lawn. He pressed on, the prattle of silly girls, meddling mothers, and pompous old men a blur around him. *I can't breathe.* He yanked at his neckcloth—once, twice, and once more—slinging it and his arm across his body and into a compact figure carrying flowers.

"Christ!" Harry pulled up short. "I mean, I'm sorry—beg your pardon, Miss. I—" He bent down to retrieve the vase, surprised the young woman was not flat on the ground with it and the scattered stems.

Olivia swayed and attempted a curtsey. "Please, Captain. Allow me." She took the vase and flowers from him and held them at her chest. "No harm done."

For the love of God. He groaned, pressing the heel of his hand to the ache spreading across his brow. "Miss Parr. Of course. I forgot you'd be here today. Seems I always find you fussing about the woods or this church."

She glowered at him. "I could say the same about

you, sir. Now, if you'll excuse me. Good day." With a flick of her head, she scooted past him and over to a nearby table where she began dropping the stems in the vase.

As he approached, his reckoning returned. *Same flattering peach dress.* Today, her healthy mane fell loose behind her shoulders, with only a few long strands secured with an ivory comb at the back. He stood a few feet behind her and waited. *But why should she acknowledge me? I'm a complete arse.*

"Miss Parr, please. I was very rude. I'm sorry." He bowed his head, then lifted his gaze. He took another step forward, close enough to catch her soft violet scent. "I'm not usually so boorish, but it's been one devil of a day. Will you accept my apology?"

She tilted her head, glancing over her shoulder, the corner of her mouth turning up softly. "I suppose I can forgive you." She resumed her handiwork, adjusting the greenery until it was in balance with the tulips, and turned around. "See there? All fixed." With the vase in both hands, she strolled toward the church. His gaze followed her, his heartbeat quickening before she gave him an about face, chin lifted. "Will there be anything else, Captain?"

"Actually, yes—"

From out of nowhere, a girl in pigtails ran into Olivia, pulling and tugging on her arm. "Miss Livie, Miss Livie—come quick!"

Olivia set the vase on the table and took off running.

Harry was close on her heels and reeled back when he saw the still body slumped over in his wagon. "Jesus! Tom! Can you hear me?"

"Aye, Cap'n. I-I hear you." Tom's eyes rolled back

in his head.

"What the hell happened?" He gripped the wagon railing.

"Old wood beam in the barn slid down on his arm, it did. Sliced right into it." Mary leaned over her son while Silas kept hold of the reins. "I wrapped it up best I could, but there was a good bit of blood."

Olivia motioned to Harry with a flick of her head. "C'mon. Help me get him to the barber-surgery."

"Tom—look at me. I've got to move you. Hold on to me." He slid in under his good shoulder, gathered him in his arms, and carried him down the street.

Once there, Olivia donned her apron and breezed through the room, grabbing clean towels and an assortment of bottles. He steadied the young man on the table and tossed his own coat to the floor. He jerked up his shirt sleeves while she tore the blood-stained tunic from Tom's shoulder.

"Get me the whiskey in the cupboard—top shelf on the right." Olivia barked out the order without so much as a sideways glance.

Harry gazed over her shoulder, watching her hands move with purpose, her mouth fixed in a firm line. As she leaned in for a closer look, appearing to know her way around a man's wounds, his eyes narrowed. *This one's full of surprises.* Before she had a chance to give another order, he grabbed the bottle and plunked it down on the work bench.

"You're going to be all right, Tom." She reached inside a nearby box and pulled out scissors, thread, and a needle. "But you need stitching up. I want you to drink the liquor to dull the pain. Captain Fleming here will help you."

He steadied the patient, and after he had downed about a third of the bottle, eased him back and placed his head on a pillow. He watched Olivia cleanse the wound with gentle strokes, getting underneath the torn skin and inside the raw tissue. She whispered words of encouragement to Tom while sewing neat stitches across the gash, sealing together folds of loose flesh. Then she smoothed a salve over the black threads and wrapped it with clean gauze. She sighed, stepped back, and rinsed her hands in a bin of water. Harry swiped a cloth from the cupboard and offered it to her.

"Thank you." She dried her hands, then dabbed it over her forehead and around her neck.

Tom blinked. "I'm beholden to ye, Miss Olivia. You're an angel." He inspected his arm with careful eyes. "I was scared, losin' blood and all. Think I passed out for a few minutes there."

"Sometimes nature knows what's best for us." Olivia moved aside, tidying up her instruments, folding a small stack of clean cloths, and reaching for a jar. "You must apply this salve and a fresh bandage every morning and night." She gave him a smile. "You won't forget?"

"No, miss. I won't."

Harry leaned back against the cupboard like it was an old friend, enjoying the tender display. *She is an angel, Tom.* As if hearing his thoughts, she turned around, capturing a loose strand of hair and smoothing it behind her ear. *My angel.*

"I believe the patient is all yours, Captain."

"His mother will take over, I assure you." He stepped over and peeked underneath the bandage to inspect her needlework. "Impressive. Good as any I saw in the field. And such able hands." *I bet they're soft.* He coughed to clear his throat…and thoughts. "Is that salve something Mr. Blake made?"

"No. It's one of my mother's remedies, but I assure you it works."

Harry nodded and strode to the door, ushering Mary and Silas inside. He mumbled a few words to Tom who, with a feeble smile and a tip of his hat to Olivia, left with them.

"I'll join you in a few minutes," Harry called to them from the doorway. Turning, he paused at her tilted head and creased brow. He cleared his throat. "That was well done, Miss Parr. I believe you possess a valuable skill."

She slipped out of her apron and tossed it in a nearby basket. "My needle is best used to stitch a wound, for I can't sew a monogram on a handkerchief to save my life. I can mix a healing balm but struggle to bake a sweet potato pie. I do the best I can with what God's given me, sir."

"It's a gift, I think."

Her face softened. "Thank you."

"Please, take this—for your time and trouble. I'm grateful." He stepped forward, took her palm, and placed several coins inside, then closed her fingers over them. *They are indeed soft.*

"I won't accept this for myself, but I will save it for Mr. Blake…for the bandages and balm." The money clinked as she dropped it inside a small trinket box.

He resettled himself against the cupboard, watching her poke her pinky finger in and out of the eyelets in her ruffled sleeve. "I'm glad you were here today—at the christening, I mean."

"Glad? Were you really?" she asked, arching one delicate eyebrow. "So glad you forgot I would even be there…?"

Ah, there's the bite of that feisty urchin I found on the trail. He caught himself staring at the rapid rise and fall of her breasts hidden inside her perfect peach bodice. The vision sparked his pulse and reminded him—quite thoroughly—she was anything but a child. He stood up straight and checked his errant thoughts about Olivia, bites and all.

"You make an excellent point, Miss Parr. You humble me when all I really want is to be in your good graces. I am sorry for my behavior earlier today."

She hissed her breath. "Oh, my. Now I must apologize. I've no doubt reminded you I tend to blurt out whatever's on my mind."

"I find your honesty refreshing."

"Truly?"

He nodded once, lifting his chin. "I do. Never apologize to me for speaking your mind."

"Thank you." She folded her hands in front of her, a smile tugging at the corners of her lips. "What I should have said was I'm happy I could help. Tom's a very nice person."

"Is he now?" He walked over and took a seat on top of the long table, a foot away from Olivia and close enough to see the twitch in her delicate cheek. While he hated to see his friend hurt, he was finding this interlude with her exhilarating.

She sidestepped him, reaching for an oblong tray and shuffling the bottles. "Yes, I call him a friend."

"As do I. He means a lot to my family—and to me." He cocked his head and laid his palms on his thighs. "If you don't mind my asking, what do you call me?"

She fidgeted with the kerchief around her neck, then

flashed him a smile. "Hm, I think I call you…Captain."

Her giggle soothed him. *God, I love your spirit.* "May we please dispense with formalities and address one another by our Christian names? I like 'Harry and Olivia' much better than 'Captain and Miss.' "

"But it wouldn't be proper." Her gaze drifted to his bare forearms. Chuckling, he began unfolding his sleeves and buttoning them at his wrists.

"And besides, you're—you're, well, an army officer and old enough—"

"Wait. I'm no Methuselah," he said mischievously. "I can't be much older than you."

"I'm eighteen."

"Twenty-four."

She counted on her fingers in a teasing fashion. "Why, that's a difference of six whole years."

"Olivia…?" He slid off the table, sing-songing her name and closing the four steps between them. "I think we're acquainted well enough—you've shared my saddle, you know. And after all this," he said, his gaze circling the room, "we're practically bound by blood."

"It wouldn't be right, Cap—" He raised his index finger to within inches of her mouth, pinning her with his gaze. The ding of the church bell drifted through the air, and she pressed her lips together for a lingering moment.

"It's 'Harry' you said?" She tilted her head to one side, eyes sparkling. "Then yes, I promise to think about it. So…until we meet again…*Captain.*" She whipped around, giving him a whiff of a smile. "Please close the door on your way out, won't you? I'm late for church."

Harry leaned against the doorjamb while she skirted across the road like a fawn over a grassy meadow. Neighbors who had gathered for the christening were filing inside the chapel. She peeked over her shoulder before slipping inside to join them. He closed the door, chuckling first at Olivia and then at the curious threesome sitting in the wagon.

"And what was that all about?" Mary's tone was laced with motherly love.

He shrugged, never having been so baffled—or enticed—by a woman in his life. "I'm still trying to figure that one out." If he needed a reminder he was not meant to live alone—to shrivel on the vine like some discarded fruit—he had gotten one this afternoon. *Courtesy of Miss Olivia Parr, no less.*

Silas guffawed, clicking the horse team into action and steering the wagon down the road. Harry mounted his horse, falling in behind them, his mind reeling with memories of the day—an unrequited love, a blinding betrayal, and one unexpected earthly angel.

Chapter Seven

Redmond Hill was a place where needs popped up like wild mushrooms. There was fertilizing soil, mending tools, and hoeing dirt to be done. Then there was planting seeds and harvesting. Day after day, the sun rose and set by the ebb and flow of life.

Harry plopped down in his chair, lips twitching at the plate of ham, eggs, and hominy on the table.

Mary poured his drink and set a jar beside the cup. "Silas says you're goin' to town today. Pray bring more of this ointment back for Tom."

His eyes narrowed. "What's he doing with it? Spreading it like butter?"

"Been workin' so good, way I figure it, the more he uses, the quicker he'll mend."

"Of course. Makes perfect sense." He rolled his eyes, swallowing a mouthful of eggs, while Silas chuckled. "I'll stop by the surgery on my way back...if you promise to bake me a blueberry pie for supper." He winked at the roly-poly woman, and she grinned, settling down to her breakfast.

A short time later, staying true to his word, Harry arrived at the surgery, dusting off his boots and shouting out a greeting before stepping inside.

"Be right there," a booming voice called out from behind a curtain.

Harry gazed across the room, noting little had

changed since he was a boy. Same pinewood cupboard filled with clean cloths, and the same black bag, with the snap-close top, that seemed attached to Nigel like a third arm. Harry recalled how he would tease the children saying, "It holds all my secret treasures," before he patched them up and gave candy drops to make them smile. The magic of his bag had comforted him until he turned eleven and his mother fell ill and there was nothing in it to save her. His mother, Abigale, had been the first loss in his life.

"Oh, hello, Harry! How are you, son?" Nigel Blake entered the room, displaying a toothy grin and adjusting his spectacles around his ears. "Come, let me get a look at you." He rocked back on his heels, smoothing his coal-black beard with steady fingers. "By God, you've grown into a man—the image of your father."

"So I'm told." Harry rubbed his knuckles across his jaw, a smile reaching his eyes.

Nigel poured a bit of whiskey in two cups and offered him the chair beside his desk. "Here's to your safe return and a bright future at your Redmond Hill." They drank together. "Olivia told me there was a little excitement here on Sunday." Nigel unbuttoned his vest and leaned back in his chair, revealing the cushiony waistline of middle age. Quite enviable though was the thick dark hair and bushy eyebrows framing a face of unselfish and charitable humor.

"One of my men needed some patching up."

"Well, he was in excellent hands. Olivia's a gifted healer."

Harry traced his finger around the rim of his cup. "Wherever did you find her?"

"She found us—she and her father. They came to

Camden about a year ago. He was pastor at the church—a fine man."

"Was…?"

"Died a few months ago. Weak lungs—pneumonia took him."

His eyebrows arched skyward.

"Yes, so with her left all alone, the missus and I moved her in with us—gave her our daughter's room. Been empty nigh on ten years since she got married." Nigel's lake-blue eyes twinkled. "Say, I bet you didn't know I'm a grandfather now. The lad will be two come August."

"Congratulations. Very happy news indeed." Harry offered a smile, eager to draw the conversation back to Olivia. "So…Miss Parr—she must be grateful to you and Martha?"

"Why, yes, yes—she's a sweet thing." He blushed, a peachy hue spreading above his beard. "Been a huge help around here—goes on calls with me too. Uncommon good at nursing folks. Grown fond of her, we have—especially my wife. Martha's been teaching her about baking and knitting. We will miss her." Harry shot him a look over his cup, and Nigel leaned in closer. "She confides in my wife, she does. Says her aunt has arranged for her to live over there with them—even talk of a marriage."

"Them?"

Nigel leaned even closer. "The Catawba—her mother's tribe."

"Wait. Are you saying we had a Christian Catawba preacher?"

He chuckled, rubbing his beard. "Oh no, no. Her father was a white man who married a Catawba woman.

Few folks ken the details about Olivia's parents, but her coloring makes some wonder. She told me and Martha all about it. Benjamin was an itinerant pastor—moved about the Carolinas before they showed up here. His wife had passed, and he wanted to set down some roots for Olivia's sake—and near her tribe was likely his reasoning. He wanted work, and we needed a pastor, so he stuck around. Pity he didn't live longer—would have been better for her if he had."

Harry blew out a long breath. "Damn..."

Nigel raised both eyebrows.

"Sorry—I meant that's quite a story. But right now, I need—or rather Tom needs—more of this." He reached inside his coat and plunked the jar on the table. "The salve Miss Parr made. I'm afraid he's used it quite liberally and is fresh out."

Nigel examined it, sniffing inside. "She makes it from witch hazel and some of her other herbs. Couldn't tell you for certain." He removed his spectacles so they hung from a strap around his neck. After fetching a new jar and placing it on the desk, he crossed his arms and rubbed his beard meditatively. "Perhaps you'd like to ask Olivia yourself...about the salve, I mean."

He pushed out of the chair, tricorn hat in his hand. "Yes—yes, I would. I'd like to talk with her. Do you know where I might find her?"

Nigel nodded, hooking his thumbs inside his vest pockets. "She mentioned going down by Wateree Creek to gather her herbs and such."

"Much obliged, Nigel." He donned his hat and, tucking the jar inside his coat pocket, sprinted out the door.

Harry skirted the banks of the creek that flowed

beyond the edge of town. Longleaf pines, red oaks, and spicebushes, surrounded by herbaceous skunk cabbage and May apple, dotted the landscape. He touched the knotted bark of a tall pine, arching his body around its trunk, stepping over a fallen branch. Abundant tree foliage created a moist, cool canopy overhead. A rich riparian ecosystem, the creek bed was home to a diverse population of creatures. Chirps, croaks, and plops blended to create nature's melody, but a sound as light as a harp's strings rose above it all. He followed it, spotting Olivia by the creek bank, wearing a buttercream dress that complemented her olive skin tone.

He lingered beside a cluster of sycamores while Olivia bent down, turning over several ruddy mushrooms and holding them up for inspection. With a nod, she dropped them in her basket. He watched her lift her face to the breeze, letting it ruffle her kerchief and billow her hair in waves down her back, then she dropped to her knees on the creek bank. She placed her basket a safe distance from the water and removed her shoes and stockings. Eyes closed and face turned up toward the speckles of sunlight filtering through the trees, she leaned back on her hands and slipped her feet into the rippling water.

"Were you not even going to say goodbye?" Harry stood a few feet away, hands braced on his hips.

Olivia whipped around, and her hand flew to her chest, then she whooshed a sigh of relief. "Well, that's an odd way to say hello." She turned back around, lifting her chin. "Quite honestly, I hadn't given it much thought, Captain."

"Remember you promised to think about calling me by my given name."

"I did." She splashed her toes about, dampening the hem of her dress, and gazed up at him. "You gave me quite a start...Harry."

He stepped closer, grinning down at her while reaching up with both hands to grab a low-hanging branch. "Seems I have a habit of stumbling upon you when you're alone."

"And what brings you here this morning?"

He gazed out over the rippling water. "I've fished along this creek since I was a boy."

"Seems you forgot your pole today."

A warmth spread through his chest. "You've figured me out."

She wiggled her toes, slapping them on top of the water. "I think so."

"Pray, please enlighten me."

Olivia swung around, shaking tiny water droplets from her feet before rising. Stuffing her stockings inside her shoes, she tossed them in her basket. She faced him, petticoat and bare toes peeking out from beneath her skirt.

"You, Captain Harry Fleming, are impulsive, hence you stand here with me rather than tending to your usual business. So...you must be after something." She lifted her hand and rested it on her cheek. "You like to give orders, not take them. And yet I've seen how deeply you care for those who depend on you—like Tom." They locked gazes. "I understand what it is to be sad, and I think something weighs heavy on your heart. Who or what caused the sadness, I don't know—but I recognize the signs just the same."

His heart filled to near bursting, and he pushed the air from his lungs. "God, I love your spirit. Marry me,

Olivia Parr." He blurted out the words without forethought, without preparation. They were borne out of some inexplicable emotion he knew was not love, but something almost as potent.

"What did you—"

"You heard me." Harry inched closer.

"We—um, but—we hardly know each other, sir." Her face flushed a crimson hue.

The corners of his lips turned up. "You summarized me quite well a moment ago."

"You're ridiculous."

He scratched his chin, lips curving into a grin. "No...no, I believe the word you used was *impulsive*."

"Either way, I won't marry you." She ducked under his arm, but his hand found hers.

"Please, Olivia. I don't want you to go away. Stay."

With her back to him, she called over her shoulder, taunting. "Just as I said, 'likes giving orders.' "

He pulled her around, eyes beseeching. "You forgot the part about how deeply I care about those on whom I depend. I believe I could come to depend on you, Olivia—but not if you run away."

"I'm not...running...away." She wrestled her hand free and stepped back.

"What would you call it, then? Nigel needs your help. He and Martha have all but adopted you." Her gaze darkened, confirming he had touched a nerve. "I know everything. I know about your mother and father." His tone softened. "I know the Blakes want you to stay. You have a home with them—or better yet, with me. Tell me, why the retreat?"

"Why does anyone retreat...?"

"Fear." He studied her faraway eyes, pinpointing

frustration and disillusion in their depths. "Are you truly content to go off to your Catawba family?"

"It's all arranged." She lifted her chin, the gentle breeze ruffling the soft cloud of her hair.

Arranged maybe, but not to your liking. "Matters not. Marry me."

"I can't. I-I won't."

"Do you wish to be courted with promises of—" Noting the gash her teeth were cutting in her lower lip, he groaned. "Christ. Of course, you do—all women do."

"No, you're wrong. I'm not silly. I'm aware of my circumstances." She swallowed hard. "It's all set for next week—I'm going to marry a good Catawba man. I need protection, you see."

"You? Need protection?" Harry laughed out loud despite her leveling glare.

"My aunt says it's for the best. I should be with the safety of the tribe—not burdening others."

"You," he said, brushing her cheek with his fingertip, "don't need protection. Companionship, yes— but not protection. You're what my father called a scrapper." He read intrigue in her tobacco-brown eyes and continued. "A scrapper—someone who's smart and strong, clever, brave." He remembered how she challenged him in the woods. "Aye, and steadfast and true."

"You think me all that?" Bewilderment etched her voice.

He reached over to tuck a rebel strand of hair behind her ear. "I do. Which is why I can see you as my wife. We can build a life together at Redmond Hill."

"Redmond Hill...?"

"My family's home. It's just outside of—"

"I've been there. I went with Mr. Blake to check on Silas when he took a fall last winter. It's beautiful…" Olivia ran her trembling fingers along her collarbone, then met his gaze. "You must listen to me. You may think I'm like you, but I'm not. My father was a white man—a common preacher who owned nothing but a horse when he died. My mother left her people to follow him. She died when I was fourteen. I'm not ashamed, but I'm wise about how others see me. I'm leaving so I don't become a burden to anyone. The Catawba are my mother's people, and they accept me. They have to."

Harry listened to her story, her tone telling him what her words could not. When she spoke of her mother, her breath caught in her throat. Her loneliness ran deep, a condition he understood very well. When she finished, her lips formed a firm line.

"Is this your only objection to marrying me?"

She nodded once, and Harry stepped closer, cupping her cheek in his hand, admiring how the sun's rays bathed her face in a golden shimmer. "I'm grateful for your honesty, and I mean no disrespect, but I don't care who your parents were, and I have no qualms about who you are. I have but one requirement in a wife—devotion."

"That's all?" Her eyebrows lifted.

"That's all that matters." He brushed his thumb over her chin. "I won't lie to you about love and make promises I can't keep either. All I know is when I'm with you, I'm happy—and it feels damn good."

She gazed at him. "But what is it you want from me? A wife or friend or partner—I'm not fit to be a lady on your arm."

"I'll have all of you."

Olivia flinched at the raspy edge of his voice. "And what of love?"

He lowered his hands, flexing them by his sides. "What of it? You don't love the man you're set to marry."

"Yes, but I'm asking for you. Don't you want to be in love with the woman you take as your wife?"

"I had love, and it didn't last. I want something stronger." Harry lifted her hand to his lips, kissing her smooth fingertips, emboldened by the pulse racing beneath her skin. "Stay here with me and be my wife, Scrapper."

"But—"

He silenced her with his mouth, his hand curving around her nape, drawing her to his body. She fit him perfectly, soft dewy lips giving in to his in a most trusting way. Her open palms pressed against his chest, and her soft sigh triggered a swarm of thoughts in his head, each one pummeling the other. Loss, loneliness, regret—*you took your eye off the prize*—Zeb's words echoing in his brain. *I'm not letting you go.* When he broke the kiss, he gazed down at her closed eyes and flushed cheeks. She slowly opened them, and in their simmering depths, he found his answer. "Let's go. We can be married by nightfall."

****

Martha Blake swept Olivia into a warm embrace when Harry brought her to their house and shared their happy news. Before leaving to make all of the necessary arrangements for the wedding, he bowed and kissed her hand.

Martha had her house maid draw a warm bath scented with jasmine oil. Once she was alone, Olivia slid into the water, cleansing her body and trying to quell her nerves. *Would I feel like this if I were marrying any man—or just this man?*

A short time later, she stepped out of the tub and dried off, gazing at her reflection in the tall mirror. She let the towel drop to her feet, and as the afternoon breeze from an open window rushed over her body, goose bumps rose on her flesh. She tucked a strand of hair behind her ear and tilted her head. While she had always disliked her longish legs, she favored the gentle curves of her hips, narrow waist, and round buttocks. She paused to consider her feet and hands, concluding they were average.

Olivia stepped closer to the mirror, studying her skin tone. It was a rich, light-tan mix derived from the palette of her parents' very different complexions. *Mix.* A frown pulled at her lips. *Mixed breed.* She was eight years old when a sassy girl with pale skin and freckles first spewed the cruel words her way. Her father had reminded her the Bible said to turn the other cheek to unkindness. *I still wish I'd turned the girl's cheek and slapped it.* She snatched the towel from the floor and wrapped it around her body. She shook off the memory and met her reflection, chin lifted. *Harry calls me his Scrapper, and he's happy with me. I'm very happy with him. Devotion is enough...*

A knock on the door dragged her from her thoughts, and the maid came in carrying fresh petticoats, a robe, stockings, and a pair of ivory leather shoes. She slipped into the robe and sat on the bed.

Moments later, Martha appeared at the door holding an oblong box tied up with a fat, beige ribbon and placed it beside her. "Mary brought it over. It's from Harry."

Olivia untied the bow and lifted the lid. Inside was an ivory linen gown with fine lace edging and tiny ecru rosettes at the neckline of the bodice. She pressed her hand to her throat.

"Abigale's no doubt," Martha murmured.

"It's the most beautiful thing I've ever seen."

"It's as lovely as are you, dearie."

Olivia wrapped her arms around her middle. The waning rays of sunlight streaming through the windowpane danced over her body. "Please tell me I'm doing the right thing."

Martha reached for her hand and held it tight. "Only you can decide what's right for you."

She gazed into Martha's warm mossy-green eyes. "Do you think it's bad he doesn't love me?"

"Love is grand, but a good marriage needs other things. There's respect and caring—oh, and honesty, to be sure."

"Devotion. That's what he said he requires in a wife."

"Well, sounds like a good place to start." Martha gave her hand a gentle squeeze, then there was a knock on the door.

"Sorry to bother you, ma'am," the maid said. "There's a visitor here for Miss Olivia. It's her aunt."

Once they were alone and Waneta was seated in a chair, Olivia paced the room, recounting the tale of the day. Her aunt possessed an even temper and was a harbinger of prudence. After she finished the story, Waneta remained silent for a few long moments.

"Well…? Say something…*please*." Olivia pressed her hand against her throat.

Waneta rubbed her nose and gazed at her with misty

gray eyes. "I think jasmine is a lovely scent for a bride."

Olivia rushed to her aunt's side and linked their fingers. "Should I be trembling?"

"Oh, Olivia. I think you might be in love with your army captain."

She stared at her aunt, mouth gaping. "What...? I-I'm not in love. I couldn't be." She lowered her gaze. "I mean, yes, I care for Harry. He makes me smile and feel...well, all sorts of things." *Did I mention his kiss made my body spark like a rock striking flint?* She swallowed hard, rubbing her fingers over her collarbone.

"Marriage is never easy, but he must care for you or else he would not want to wed you. James cares for you."

"Will James be—or are you—terribly mad? If you can't give me your blessing, then I won't go through with it." She tossed her hair behind her back, straightening. "I-I will go with you. We can leave now—"

"Running from this will do you no good. Just like your mother, the path has chosen you. Don't be afraid to take it but heed me." Waneta tucked a tuft of hair behind her ear, smoothing it back with her fingers. "You may find marriage to a white man captain is not simple. I bless your union because there is no other choice, but be careful." Her aunt lifted a jade stone necklace from her neck and placed it over her head. "And keep this close. It's a gift from me and your Catawba family. And I will stand beside you when you say your vows tonight."

Tears of love and gratitude welled in her eyes, and she fell into her aunt's warm embrace.

****

"What the devil?" Kitt paced his office, then whipped about. "Married to Olivia Parr? Tonight...? You're mad."

"Just draw up the contract and get you and your wife to Redmond Hill by seven o'clock." Harry grabbed an apple from a pewter bowl on the desk and gave him a questioning look.

"Go ahead—eat," he mumbled, waving him off like a gnat.

Harry was ravenous. He had rushed Olivia to the Blake's home and then stopped by the church to summon the parson for the ceremony, followed by a quick stop at Redmond Hill to share his good news. After giving specific instructions to Mary and Tom, he set out to find his best friend. He took a seat and bit into the apple, his lips curving into a smile. Watching Kitt fret was rather comical.

"This is nothing to laugh about. I know you don't give a damn what people say." Kitt stopped, hands flat on his desk. "But do you understand you're entering a legal contract? Olivia Parr will become your lawful wife."

"I understand."

"Zeb won't like it."

"Exactly." He flashed Kitt a leveling glare. "And before you ask—no, I'm not marrying her to spite him, Brandt, or even Catherine. I want Olivia for my wife. Plain and simple."

Kitt shook his head. "You could have your choice of young women in this town. There's more than one Catherine."

He polished off the apple, tossing the core in the wastebasket. "That's just it—I don't want another Catherine. I've no interest in wooing some silly girl. I'm a soldier and farmer, not a damn poet."

Kitt stuffed his hands in his pockets, rocking back

on his heels. "Very well. You're set on marrying an unconventional woman, but what's wrong with courtship? Get to know Olivia before you're bound to her for the rest of your life."

"I don't need it—and neither does she. Besides, I've already proposed."

"But you barely know her, Harry."

"I knew Catherine all my life, and look what it got me."

"But why the rush? Unless she's…?" Kitt cocked an eyebrow.

Reasoning dawned, and he shook his head. "Christ, no. She's not with child. I only just kissed her this morning."

He threw up his hands. "Okay, so again…why tonight?"

"Enough," Harry said, his tone leaving no room for argument. "Stop with the questions. I don't need your examination."

"I'm just looking out for my best friend—only he's not listening."

"No, *you're* not." Harry pushed off his chair and placing his palms on the desk, leaned forward. "Look— a month ago I was a fool on my way home, dreaming about a life with Catherine. All those years I believed she was mine. All I had to do was finish the fight, come back, and everything would be perfect. Well, it was a lie—she was a lie." He could feel the vein in his forehead pulsing, and he pushed out a heavy breath.

"Father died when he was forty-nine. I'm half his age right now." His words stuck to his tongue. "I don't want to live my life alone, Kitt. And I don't care about love—not anymore. You think I'm being rash, and maybe I am." He rubbed his hands over his face, wiping away the remnants of frustration. "I just like being with Olivia. My day's better when she's in it." He dropped back down to his chair with a thud.

Kitt lowered his gaze and sat down in his chair. "Well then. Would you like me to stand with you when you say your vows tonight?" He leaned back, locking his fingers across his chest.

"Aye—nice of you to offer." He snorted. "Need a marriage contract too."

Kitt reached for his flask and poured two shots of scotch, handing one to him. "Hell, I didn't even know you were calling on Miss Parr."

"I wasn't."

"Of course, it makes perfect sense then you'd want to up and marry her—tonight." He gave him a lopsided grin.

"What do you think Father would say?" Harry asked from deep down.

Kitt took a sip of his drink. "Trust your instincts."

"And Mother?"

"Oh, that one's easy. Trust your heart."

Harry detected the smile in his voice and gazed at him over the rim of his glass. "Without hauling me over the coals again, is there anything else you'd like to tell me?"

"Aye. What I haven't said is Olivia is a witty lass and kind to a fault." He leaned forward, elbows on his desk. "She's bonny, too. Something I'm sure you've noticed."

"I have." His lips turned up at the corners.

"What I know of her comes mostly from around church. Aye, you ken her father was our pastor? Our neighbors will expect you at church on Sundays from now on." Kitt gave him a quick wink before continuing. "She's not a bit timid or traditional, so you'll have your hands full to be sure. But I think she has a huge heart like your mother. She'll stand by you."

He choked back a lump in his throat, the enormity of his words hitting their mark. "Thanks."

"Now, off with you—let me get to work." Kitt reached for fresh parchment and his quill. "Surely you've got things to do. You're getting married in a few hours, for God's sake."

Harry beamed at his pal, his heart lighter than it had been in some time.

Part Two

Breaking the Mold

Chapter Eight

On the evening of May 25th, from the porch at Redmond Hill, Olivia placed her hand in Harry's…and secretly gave him her heart. Witnessed by a small assemblage they considered family, the fragrance of wisteria thick in the air, they stood before God and pledged their vows. When he placed his mother's ring on her finger and kissed her, the crowd cheered in unison with the ditty of the barn owl and the coo of the whippoorwill.

Afterward, Harry attended to her, placing her hand in the crook of his arm and leading her across the porch to greet his friends. When Mary served his blueberry pie and Silas raised his glass in a toast, she reassured him her tears were simply a measure of her joy.

Some hours later, Olivia stepped into their bedchamber and closed the door behind her. She leaned against it and breathed in the musky scent of pinewood and leather. With candles illuminating the room from two sides, she gazed at her surroundings. She took a few steps forward, inspecting a bureau stationed in one corner, running her fingers over a comb and a furry rabbit's foot lying in an oblong dish. As she peeked in the top drawer, she spotted a stack of handkerchiefs folded in squares monogrammed with the single letter *F*. A cedar wardrobe stood beside the bureau, wherein she discovered an array of men's trousers, tunics, boots, and jackets. She circled around, discovering a washbowl on a long table by the double window, a cake of soap, and a razor blade alongside it. By the stone fireplace, she found a chair with the *South Carolina Gazette* newspaper lying on the seat. She rubbed her finger over the paper, then set it aside.

Olivia turned and gazed at the enormous bed, covered in a blue and brown stitched quilt, topped with several hefty pillows, and flanked by two short side tables. She pressed her hands to her cheeks and imagined sharing his bed. *No...our bed.* She shook her head. Trying to align her knowledge of human reproduction with marital intimacy was like threading a needle with buttered fingers.

She noticed an empty side table and, guessing it would be her half of the bed, sank into the mattress. Her gaze flickered around the room and stopped at the foot of the bed. *My entire life fits inside one old brown trunk.* Footsteps followed by a light tap at the door roused her, and she blinked back a tear.

"Missus Fleming, may I come in?" Mary asked.

Olivia straightened her back. "Yes, ma'am."

"Beggin' your pardon, but I thought you might be needin' a few things." Mary sailed in with a basket full of fresh towels, more soap, a cup, and a small standing mirror, placing everything on the long table. She pivoted, tubby fists resting on her hips. "Well, now—it's a start. Been a man's room for some time. I'll have Silas get to workin' on your own dresser and chair—oh, and a wardrobe, of course. New curtains would do nicely too." She frowned at the faded plaid ones hanging over the window.

"Thank you." She smiled, rubbing her hands

together on her lap.

Mary waved her hands. "Now stand up and let me help ye with your gown."

Olivia obeyed, allowing her to untie the laces at the back, leaning on her arm to step out of the dress. Mary held the garment lovingly, smoothing it out before hanging it in the wardrobe. "Did ye see how Harry looked at you in his mother's gown?"

She shook her head.

"Aye, well, let's just say he looked very pleased."

"Really…?"

Mary nodded. "Aye, he's an appreciative man. And I knew he'd taken a shine to ye—that evening after you tended to my Tom. He couldn't take his eyes off ye when you skipped off to church."

She sat down on the edge of the bed, hands beneath her thighs, and gazed at Mary.

"It was me who sent him off this mornin' to find ye and bring home more salve for my boy. I reckoned he just needed a little push to start up with ye. Harry always was a quick one—brought home more than medicine today, he did. I'm happy for ye both. He needs a good woman, and he'll make ye a fine husband." They laughed together, but then a hush settled between them. Mary held up a finger and hurried off, returning moments later with a parcel and placing it on her lap.

Olivia unfolded the wrapping and found an ecru nightgown styled with satin ribbon edging over a scooped neckline. Her fingers skimmed over the soft muslin.

Mary helped her into the garment and flashed her an approving smile. "Cap'n Harry bid me fetch you something special for tonight. Fits you just right. I must say it's mighty fine to have ye in this family. I'm happy to serve ye."

"Oh, Mary, I'm still the same girl. I—"

"I know…but just the same, we're all real glad about the marriage." She sniffed a little and reached for her handkerchief in her apron pocket. "I suppose it's time I leave."

"Wait." She touched Mary's sleeve, then the woman folded her into her cushiony arms.

"There, there now, lass. You're just feelin' like every bride on her weddin' night," Mary whispered in her ear. "I held Harry the day he was born and watched him grow, ye ken. He's a very kind man. No need to be afraid—he'll take good care of ye." She gave her a quick wink, then bowed her head and withdrew from the room.

Alone again, Olivia flopped back on the bed and took a deep breath. *I can do this.* Lifting the lid from her trunk, she removed her comb, brush, and Bible and pulled down the bedcovers.

****

The squeak of the bedroom door drew Harry from his thoughts. Mary scurried across the room and lit the lantern on the mantel, squinting her eyes to its citrine glow. She carried it to the kitchen table, took a seat opposite him, and untied her apron.

Harry's gaze flicked from the door to Mary. "Is she…?"

"Right as rain, she is. Looks a bit like a wee mouse staring down the barn cat though." Mary chuckled, accentuating the little dimple in her left cheek.

"She's afraid."

"Not of you, Cap'n. Just the unknown." She folded her hands on the table. "Don't ye worry. Olivia's not your ordinary lass—she'll be fine."

"You don't think she's regretting it, do you?"

"Glory Jesus, no," Mary said, grinning. "Ye may have been the one who done the proposin'—but she was still the one doin' the choosin'."

He felt a smile tugging at his lips, then leaned forward, speaking softly. "I wish I'd had time to get her something special—a wedding gift, I suppose—to make her more comfortable."

"Her eyes lit up when she unwrapped the pretty night rail. And I gave her a few of your mum's little things just now. Never you mind—they'll be lots more times for presents."

He fixed his gaze on the ruby-haired woman he had known since he was in britches. "Thank you, Mary. I'm grateful for all you've done. You're a rare gem."

She blushed. "Well, sir...I think I best be leavin'. Silas will be snorin' like the hogs by now." She rose, picking up the lantern and apron, and in her most motherly tone said, "Give her a little longer before you retire, won't you? And a little knock on the door would be nice."

Harry nodded once and, heeding her advice, stepped out onto the porch. He leaned against the railing, joined by Caddie who, after sniffing his way along the slat boards, dropped down beside his right foot. The sky was pearl gray with only a sliver of moonlight visible through a foggy blanket. The clouds had swept in after dark, dropping but a few dancing pellets on the rooftop at first, then quickly transforming into a sopping rain, drenching the ground and releasing a grassy, resinous smell from the earth. He suddenly felt much akin to the soil, accepting the onslaught of the changes he had made to his life, puddles and all. A chuckle reverberated through his chest, causing the great hound to rise on all fours. He bent down, rubbing the warm, glossy neck resting at his knee. "Come on, boy. It's time."

Harry stood at the bedroom door, holding a carafe of Madeira and two glasses. *Haven't knocked on this door in a long time.* The room had belonged to his parents, and he had claimed it after his father passed, making it his own, yet leaving many of the furnishings untouched. He envisaged Olivia on the other side of the door. *No more lonely bed.* He rapped on the door, relieved when she beckoned him inside.

Harry greeted her, pleased to see Mary had placed tall candles throughout the room, ensuring they would burn well through the night. Everything the light touched radiated a honey-yellow glow, including his wife's demure face. He poured two glasses of wine, then walked across the room, tossing his white neckcloth and beige vest on the bureau. He loosened the top button of his tunic and moved the only chair in the room over beside the bed. Straddling it, he propped his arms on the back rung. He gazed at his bride in a bundle of ivory muslin, sitting on the bed, knees pulled up to her chest, toes peeking out, hands wrapped around her ankles. He grinned and offered her a glass, as pleased as a robin who had snatched up a fat, juicy worm.

"Is your smile meant to comfort or unnerve me?" Olivia's lips curved over the rim of the glass.

"To comfort, I assure you. Simply admiring my beautiful wife." Harry noticed she shifted under his gaze, yet maintained her poised position. "Have you everything you need?"

"Yes, Mary—and well, you of course—have been

most kind."

"We've had one hell of a day, Scrapper." He drank fully, the mellow fruitiness of the wine he had chosen matching his mood.

"We have." She giggled, a blush spreading across her cheekbones.

"Had I more time, I would've seen to your comfort—had appropriate things prepared for you." He set his drink on the night table, then steepled his hands beneath his chin. "I know it's too soon, but I want you to feel at home here—with me—at Redmond. What's mine is yours."

"What's mine is yours, as well." She shifted her gaze over his shoulder. "And sadly, it all fits inside my trunk over there."

He tilted his head, studying the sensual movement of her throat as she sipped her wine. A smile inched across his lips. "You mean it's not filled with silver?"

"You remember when we vowed 'for richer, for poorer,' well…let's just say I've got a good grasp of the 'poorer' part."

A chuckle escaped his lips, but he felt little humor in it. *You're rich in the things I need, Olivia.* He would build a future with her, based on devotion, and settle for nothing less. His gaze met hers, reassuring. "If I wanted to marry a dowry, I'd have done so."

"You could have, I'm sure. And you're not sorry you took me to wife?"

"No. Not in the least. Besides, it's too late for sorry."

"But we've not consummated the marriage yet." Olivia ran her fingers over her collarbone, toying with the jade stone necklace.

"Aye…but we will, Scrapper." He warmed on the

inside when her eyes flickered with awareness. "Say, I've never seen you wear that before. It's striking."

As she rehashed her visit with Waneta, he poured them more wine. It was clear after losing both parents, her aunt figured significantly in her life. From the sound of it, she was a formidable force who had Olivia's interests at heart. With the gift of the necklace and her blessing, he knew Waneta was responsible for their union.

Harry raised his glass to hers. "To family." Her silver ring glimmered in the candlelight, and he took her hand in his. "Perfect fit." He kissed the ring and laced her fingers with his. "Mother's were like yours—firm, slender, and strong."

She met his gaze. "Was she a scrapper too?"

"On the inside? Yes, a good bit. But physically, not so much. God did not bless her with great fortitude."

"I'm honored to wear her ring and be compared to her in any way—even fingers." Olivia squeezed his hand.

He smiled, mesmerized by the candlelight waltzing over her cheeks and neck, and rose from his chair. He sat beside her on the bed, and when she slid forward, he caught her by the waist.

"If you could see yourself as I do, you'd understand why you're exactly what I need in a wife." He untied her chunky braid, unraveling each twist with his fingers, releasing its jasmine scent, until her hair fell loose down her back. He paused when her gaze stopped on the long scar that ran from his right thumb up past his forearm. Though he waited for a reaction, none came. Instead, she rubbed her fingers along the satiny neckline of her chemise, causing the sheer fabric to sway, giving a hint to what lay behind it.

"I tried that this afternoon—after my bath." Her breath hitched. "I-I stood naked in front of the mirror and tried to imagine how you might see me."

Harry's cheek twitched. As an innocent, she could not imagine how such a vision resonated in one particular part of his anatomy. "And what did you conclude?"

"I have no idea of such things."

"Well, it won't be that way for long." He stilled her fidgety fingers, then began stroking the inside of her palm. The candle at their bedside flickered, lightening her eyes to the shade of sweet molasses. Without warning, a pawing and whimpering broke the silence between them.

"Oh, it's Caddie—may he please come in? He's used to sleeping with me—for protection." As her dog clawed at the door, Olivia bit her bottom lip.

"You've a husband for that now." He rose and, quirking a smile, opened the door to the hound. He grabbed a frayed quilt from the bureau, tossed it in the corner near the fireplace, and issued Caddie a command to lie down.

She gazed up at him, lips curving upward. "Hm, did you ever stop to think perhaps I was protecting him?"

He smirked, rubbing his knuckles over his lip. *God, I do love your spirit.* "Oh yes, I've seen you in action— blade in hand—a most fearsome sight." He mimicked her stance that day in the woods, and her giggle drew him back to her bedside. "Aye, were I your devoted dog, I'd also wish to lie by your side for protection in the dark of night...for warmth and comfort. Pray, I may be like Caddie in every way," he said, leaning forward to whisper in her ear, "save one." He allowed his lips to linger where her pulse throbbed in her neck.

Olivia touched his arm. "You will need to tell me more about this one way."

"With your permission, I'd rather show you." He inched closer and kissed his bride, sealing his lips to hers, slowly…softly. He slid his hand up the side of her neck to her nape, angling her mouth to better connect with his. Their tongues touched and teased, and as he drew her to him, something scraped the sheets into a knot. *I can't wait for those fingernails to dig into my back.* He gently broke their kiss, his sixth sense signaling Olivia needed to come to him, to their marriage bed, on her own terms.

"Don't move." Harry stood, stepped back, and pulled his tunic over his head. Then he turned around, unfastened his sable breeches, and tossed them aside. Every hair on his body raised with awareness under her heated gaze.

"You're nervous, Scrapper," he said over his shoulder. "You've been doing too much thinking and not enough exploring. You're a bright and curious healer. Don't you think you should come over and have a look at me?"

The question lingered, fusing the air with anticipation. Every muscle in his body was taut, blood coursing through his limbs. Even from behind, he smelled her jasmine-infused hair. He closed his eyes and with Herculean will, resisted the urge to turn around. *I'll wait for you. You can trust me.* As the bed creaked and feet padded across the floor, he blinked his eyes open, lips curving upward.

****

Olivia glimpsed her husband for the first time, a

warmth resonating deep inside her. Harry had a soldier's body, broad and chiseled at the back and shoulders, lean and firm at the waist and hips. She noted the spattering of scars on his work-honed muscles, no doubt badges of honor from battle. His thighs were as dense as the trunk of an elm tree and sturdy as the flanks of an ox. She bit her lip, her gaze following the outline of tendons and muscles cascading down the length of his back, culminating in two symmetrical dimples above the fit mound of his buttocks. Firm hollows in the curves of those cheeks called to her, and she stepped forward, caressing them with her fingertips. Mindless, she found her mouth poised a mere inch from his back, her breath heavy, so close the heat emanating from his skin met her lips. She kissed the valley made by his straight spine. Her hands squeezed his deltoid muscles, then slid inward, tracing downward, lingering on his hips. Sight, smell, and touch converging in her brain, she barely recognized his voice, his question, bidding her to come around for a closer look.

As she came to face him, the gaze from his indigo eyes prompted a flush in her cheeks. His soldier's discipline enabled him to stand stock-still while her fingers rubbed back and forth across his hips and then upward to where she nestled them in the tawny mass of hair on his chest. Her lips brushed against his nipples, and she turned her cheek back and forth, enjoying the contrast of his furriness against her smooth skin. She continued her tender assault, daring to trace her tongue around the taut flat disk, thrilled when it quivered under her lips.

Gradually, she let her thumbs slide down his hard stomach, sneaking their way inside his navel, stroking the smoothness there. As the back of her hand brushed the rigid shaft pressing against his abdomen, her breath caught in her throat. Her knowledge of male anatomy was enough to make her question how she could accommodate his size. Still wrestling with those images, he swept her hands into his.

"Do you think I might have a look now?" he asked between light kisses to the tips of her fingers.

****

From the open window, the chirping rattle of katydids joined with the quiet thrum of Caddie's snoring. Olivia loosened the ribbon at her neckline and let the gown fall in a pile at her feet. She stepped back, giving him full view of her body. The chorus surrounding them came together in a great crescendo.

"Sweet Jesus...but He did make you a most beautiful woman." Harry gazed at her silhouette defined by opalescent candlelight, longing to caress her smooth lines and curves with more than his eyes. He stepped closer, allowing the light to shift, illuminating her elegant neck, shoulders, and breasts. Her arms rested by her sides, legs steady so only the tiniest sliver of candlelight showed between them. When she shook her head, waves of sable brown hair spilled over her shoulders, and her eyes simmered like black-gold embers from a budding fire. His gaze drifted lower, paying tribute to her untouched femininity, a beacon for his duty to bring her across the threshold to womanhood. His pulse quickened with the thought of bedding a virgin—his wife, no less—and the commitment that entailed.

"Good of you to try, Scrapper—in the mirror today—but you've no idea how I'm seeing you right now."

"You want me, then."

"Oh, aye," he said in a raspy voice. "And before the night is through, I'll have you wanting me, as well." He cupped her chin, tilting it upward, and covered her mouth with his. As he deepened the kiss, he wrapped his free hand around her hip, and when her fingers burrowed into his hair, his fingers ventured lower and squeezed. *Sweet Jesus, what a perfect, round bum.* When she leaned into him, the heat of her breasts searing his chest, he lifted her in his arms and laid her on the bed.

He eased in beside her, planting silky kisses behind her earlobe and down the gentle slope of her neck. She turned her head into the pillow, releasing a light and sensual sigh. Like drawing the bow across the strings of his violin, he intended to release her song. He lingered over her breasts, nuzzling them with tantalizing pecks. He fastened his lips to her nipple, masculine pride increasing with the pitch of her sigh. When he lifted his head, his gaze locked on the vision of her, eyes closed, fingers tangled in her hair. His palm found her flat belly, and he followed it with his tongue, toying with her navel as she had done his. Her skin quivered against his lips, firing his need. Her scent was transforming into a blend of jasmine, musk, and woman, and he breathed it in. When she relaxed her legs enough to reveal her treasure, he released a low groan.

His primal instincts aroused, he raised up on his elbow, returning his attention to her breasts and circling his thumb over her silken nub. She lifted her hips into his touch. *Yes, Liv. Give yourself to me. Take in desire like you would your next breath.* As he drew her nipple between his lips and stroked an ancient rhythm with his fingers, she moaned. Then she crested, her body quaking, and he cradled her through the sheer flood of her long and lingering pleasure. As her breathing slowed, she gazed at him with glassy brown eyes and cupped his cheek.

"You've returned." He ran his fingers alongside her temple, smoothing back damp wisps of hair. In the flickering candlelight, he spotted tiny beads of perspiration on her brow and brushed his lips over them. "Tell me what you're feeling."

"Bliss...and I-I want more." She squeezed his neck muscles, fingernails sinking into their depths.

Harry moved over her, balancing his weight on his elbows, and kissed her parted lips, confident the slickness between her legs would ease the next phase of their lovemaking. His bollocks were aching and tight, but his concern was for Olivia.

He whispered over the curl of her ear. "Keep perfectly still. You understand it will hurt this once?" She twined her arms around his neck, nodding against his cheek. He nudged closer to her entryway, pressing his forehead to hers. "I promise afterward, I'll make it good for you. So damn good."

He gazed into her doe-brown eyes and moved inside her with one swift thrust. She inhaled, stifling a cry, teeth sinking into his shoulder. He began murmuring sweet nothings to her, withdrawing slowly, then sliding in deeper. He repeated the movement, willing his words to dissolve her pain, replacing it with an ardent invitation to join in the cadence of his lovemaking. The blush of her lips beckoned him, and he heeded the call, his hungry lips savoring her plump ones. The rise of her hips gave him hope, and he moved deeper. He pushed himself up on his hands, the soft moans of her passion driving him to the edge. She arched her hips and met his final plunge, and he poured himself inside her. He shook with his release, groaning her name, proclaiming her his wife.

****

In the aftermath of their sensuous storm, Olivia rested her head on Harry's chest, eyelids heavy, but unwilling to succumb to sleep. She was sated, suspended in a place of wakeful drowsiness. His command over her body had been meticulous and vigilant, but the tenderness of this embrace defied definition. His breath moved in and out of his lungs, rocking her head with its steady rhythm. His thumb drifted across the small of her back and alongside the curve of her hip, and her skin tingled. She snuggled deeper into the curve of his shoulder, his sandalwood scent rekindling the memory of the pain and passion infused in their bodies, knowing without any doubt she had never been truly alive—not even for one moment—until Harry.

She blinked her eyes. *Everything's so much...so much lighter than before.* Whether from the spark he ignited inside her or the simple passage of the clouds leaving in their wake a frosty crescent moon, she could only wonder. She shivered.

****

"Cold...?" Harry asked, pulling the quilt over her body.

Olivia kissed his chest, casting her leg across his thigh and rubbing her toes against his inner calf. He smiled and stared at the ceiling, content to savor the intimate touches after their ardent lovemaking. The act had drained his body and filled his mind at the same time, the air still thick with their scent.

He kissed the top of her head. "You're awfully

quiet."

She wiggled herself up, tucking the soft quilt under her arms. He muffled a sigh at her modesty. *And I was so looking forward to the view.* Judging by the arch of her delicate brow, she had something on her mind.

"You said it would hurt."

He caught a curl of her hair and rubbed it between his fingers. "Aye, and I'm sorry. I wish I could've spared you the pain."

"But I think you were mistaken—as was I." Olivia took a sip of Madeira before continuing. "It's just—yes, there was pain. But not at all like I'm used to—cuts and wounds and broken bones and all."

He turned toward her, cradling his head with his arm.

"It was a beautiful pain. I-I wasn't expecting that. I still can't believe it." Her words came on an airy breath. "Was it even real…?"

Harry brushed aside the bedclothes, revealing splatters of dark red on the sheets. "Very real. You've the blood—and I've the marks—to prove it." He snickered, craning his neck around to peek at the scratches and indentations left by her nails. She bit back a frown, and he lifted her chin. "No, that part pleases me—very much."

"I'm sorry. Oh, you know more of this than me."

His eyes softened at the corners. "Aye, and now you do too…a little, at least."

"You mean there's more?" she shrieked, rousing Caddie, who up to this point had slept peacefully despite the rumpus coming from their bed. Her hound shook his jowls and howled a yawn, and Harry threw back his head laughing. She cuffed his shoulder playfully. "You're a fiend, Harry Fleming."

"We've only just begun, my sweet Scrapper. I've much more to teach you." He leaned over and kissed her surprise into submission. When his driving lips released her, she swayed.

"Harry?" she asked softly. "Is it—is it always so...so...stirring...?" She scooted closer, bending her legs, shins pressing against his thigh.

He took a deep breath and eased back on the mattress, folding his hands behind his head. "Like the earth is quaking all around you?"

The rising glow in her cheeks answered him.

He sighed, avoiding her limpid gaze. "It's—well, it's like...uh..." *Steady, man. You've got to get this right.* "Well, as you've already guessed, what happens between a man and a woman is very...satisfying." He regretted the word the moment it crossed his lips because it was a completely inadequate description of the fire she ignited in him. *Damn. How can I begin to explain something even I don't understand?* His fresh virgin bride had undone herself—and him—in their first joining. Acute desire had driven him, but something more than lust fanned it. *Aw, hell.* He reached out and brushed his thumb over her cheek.

"Your question humbles me. I've never shared both commitment and a bed with a woman. This is new for me, as was making love to a virgin." He smiled at the color rising above the edge of the blanket now barely concealing her breasts. "The fact is, you're a beautiful woman...and I'm a hungry man." *But is it something more...?*

Harry raked his hand through his hair, then met her gaze. "We're husband and wife, and you're mine to have and hold. I think that made it more…'stirring,' you said?"

Olivia nodded.

"Stirring." The word passed his lips reverently. He smiled, rather pleased with his summation, until he spotted her knitted brow.

"Did you and the woman you loved ev—"

"No," Harry clipped.

"But you wanted to?" She lowered her eyes, lashes fanning her cheeks.

"Aye. But I loved her too much to take her virtue without the bond of marriage."

He fisted his hands in the sheets to hide his twitching palms. It was no secret his heart had belonged to another, but he did not wish to dwell on it. "Do you want to go down this path right now?"

She shook her head.

"Good. Neither do I." He pulled her down against his body and pressed a kiss to her hair. The jasmine still lingered there, though tempered with the salty-sweet scent of her earlier exertion.

Olivia gazed up at him. "I'm the most lucky of women, I think."

"And I shall do my best to keep that sentiment in your heart." He lifted her arm, letting it rest by her ear, then trailed his fingers from high above at her wrist, down along her inner arm, coming to rest on her waist.

She stirred, turning around in his arms, smiling and sighing all at once. "Is it too soon for more of your lessons?"

"Ah, you read my mind, Scrapper," he said against the curl of her ear, tugging the blanket out from underneath her arms.

Chapter Nine

June 1783

The weeks following the wedding were a blissful interlude for Harry. Muscles once honed for fighting found purpose working long hours in the fields. His mind, at one time fixed on assaults and ambushes, was free to explore his humble agricultural enterprise. His spirit once betrothed to God, Country, and Catherine was finding renewal in the companionship of a new bride.

He was diligent in attending to personal matters and met with Kitt within the week of his nuptials. Over drinks one evening at the alehouse, he found the banter with his best friend a welcome treat.

"I see marriage agrees with you." Kitt raised his glass to him.

"Indeed." Harry rolled his cup between his hands, a lopsided smile spreading across his face.

His friend grinned, slapping his knee. "My mother always said to be happy with what you have, and you'll have plenty to be happy about."

"Aye, but there's more." He paused, shifting in his chair, then leaned forward. "I want my affairs in order—never can be certain what Zeb's plotting. He could seize on anything at any moment, particularly with Olivia and her heritage." A crease formed across his brow. "I won't have anything called into question when it relates to

Redmond Hill and my wife."

"You need a will, my friend. You want the property—with all of your other assets, of course—to go to Olivia and then to your children?"

Harry nodded, hiding his surprise at overlooking offspring as a possible—if not probable—outcome of a healthy marriage.

"What about debts?" Kitt cut an eye in his direction. "Are there any notes on Redmond?"

He shook his head, then steepled his hands under his chin. "There's something else I need to ask. You're my closest friend, and I want you to be my steward—have power over all my legal matters—should anything happen to me...or both me and Olivia together. I want my wife and our workers and their families in trusted hands."

Kitt reached out and shook his hand. "I'd be honored. Come by tomorrow afternoon. I'll have the contract ready for you by noon."

****

The next morning, in the pearly hour of dawn, Harry rode his horse past the junipers on the western perimeter of his property, then spurred him to a gallop. He filled his lungs with the misty air, inhaling and exhaling with the animal's stride, reveling in the poignant song of a new day.

As they approached home, he slowed their pace and scanned the landscape of Redmond Hill. The chirps of robins and thrushes lingered overhead while the cow's mooing vibrated through the ground. He spotted smoke rising from the chimney and licked his lips, imagining the sausage and eggs Mary would have cooking over the fire. The lantern's glow peeking out from the barn door signaled Olivia was busy with the chickens. He dismounted, grabbed his gear, and sauntered inside, greeted by the smell of sweet oats and clover hay. His gaze landed on his wife's familiar figure.

"You're looking well this morning." Harry met her smile with one of his own, then resting the saddle on the wooden post, he leaned against it, taking stock of this most singular woman. Olivia had acclimated to country life, rising early and sharing in the chores before setting off to town to check in with Nigel. Under Mary's fine tutelage, she was learning her way around the kitchen, finding creative ways to blend her herbs with dishes of venison, chicken, and pork.

A gust of wind slipped past the barn door, making it creak soulfully, and it ruffled the kerchief across her neck. She bent down and stretched her arm inside the cubby, finding the eggs and placing them in her basket. He rubbed the amber stubble of hair on his chin. *She looks most fetching—hair pushed back in her kerchief, tresses loose down her back.* In three swift strides, he reached the door and dragged over the latch.

"Almost full." Olivia grinned, scooting around the chicken coop, skirt swishing around her ankles.

"Keep swirling about, Scrapper." He sneaked in behind her, wrapping his arms around her waist, and nibbled at her earlobe. Even if hidden beneath ten layers of clothes, covered with the stench of nanny goats and fresh manure, he would still want her. "Keep fanning your lovely round bum in my face, and I just might…" He trailed his lips along her neck and, feeling the skip in her pulse, took the basket off her arm and placed it on the ground.

Olivia turned to face him. "But what if someone

catches us?"

He gazed at her, smirking. "I'm the master here. No one can catch me doing anything." She gave him a sideways look, but the quivering of her lip gave him cause to hope. "No one will see. I promise—door's locked." He resumed kissing the exquisite curve of her neck. *Christ, I'll promise you the cat, the fiddle, and the cow jumping over the moon to have you beneath me on the hay.* He pulled back, half-wondering if his wife would refuse the pleasure.

"Hm, you are the master..." Olivia began unbuttoning his tunic, exposing his chest and massaging it with her palms. "But even the master has to be careful." On tiptoes, she pressed her mouth in the hollow of his neck. "You've taught me well—so well I might share the power with you now. I can 'catch' you doing any number of things, Captain." She swung out of his embrace. "I can swirl and 'fan my lovely round bum' like so," she said alluringly, "and just like that, I have *mastered* the master." She laughed, a sound as free as the gurgling of a brook, and it pleased him to see her enjoying her role in their mating game.

"God, I love your spirit." He pulled her back to him, squeezing her bottom and burying his face atop her flushed bosom. He circled his nose over one breast, rubbing her nipple through the soft muslin fabric.

"Careful...the last time you said that, you asked me to marry you."

He lifted his gaze, pleased to see desire etched across her face. "And damn glad I did." He stepped forward, taking her with him, leaning her up against the barn wall. His nose twitched. "Do you know what your scent does to me?" Unable to wait for her answer, his zealous fingers found their way inside her skirts. *Thank God she never wears drawers.* He parted her legs, touching her warm center. "Sweet Jesus—you're as slippery as one of those egg yolks in your basket."

"Is that bad...?"

"Not for me." His lips brushed against her cheek. "But for you...perhaps." Her doe-brown eyes softened in curiosity. "For it means I can't wait. I need you. I've got to have you—"

"Now..." She moaned, finishing his sentence on a heavy breath.

He made haste with his placket and shoved her skirts above her waist, lifting her so she could wrap her legs around him. When he slid inside her, a sweet sigh escaped her lips. She clasped her hands around his neck and moved her hips with his, rocking to her climax. They moved in tandem through his thrusts, then he stilled, groaning against her neck until he was spent.

Still heaving from exertion, they gazed at one another, stunned by the spontaneous shock of shared desire. Harry withdrew, eased her feet down to the ground, and fastened his placket. "That was—"

"Stirring." Olivia leaned against the wall for support and took his hand. "It happened so fast, but I wanted you."

"Aye, and that sent me over the edge a little. I behaved a bit like Gordie here when Mena gives him her scent and a saucy swish of her tail." He brushed his fingertip along her jaw. "I'm afraid I'm powerless against thousands of years of feminine nature."

"You actually have a weakness, Captain?"

"Apparently so." He veered closer to her. "But I have my strengths."

"Mm," she said, eyes sparkling. "Now I'm curious."

Harry shrugged out of his coat and threw it over a mound of sweet barley hay. Taking his wife in his arms, he nestled her inside the soft inner lining and moved over her. Supporting his weight on his elbows, he leaned down and rubbed her nose with his. "I think you like my scent too."

Exhaling slowly, she pulled the tie from his queue and wrapped it around her wrist. She ran her fingers through his hair, capturing a rogue strand that fell by his cheek and tucking it behind his ear. "Oh, I like it very much. And so, you were saying something about strengths…?"

He loosened the laces of her bodice and slid lower, wedging his lips between her breasts. "Fingers." He snickered behind a kiss there, delighting in her thrumming pulse. Then he lifted his head, gazing into the brown pools of her eyes. "A strength, you see—to untie laces," he said, nodding toward his most recent act, "or to twist a delightful little button like this." He captured her nipple between his thumb and index finger and stroked it to hardness. He warmed with her soft intake of breath. "If I'm patient and move them just right, they can even pick a lock." He parted her legs with his knee and pushed her skirt aside, running his fingers up her inner thigh. "I can use this one like so." His thumb lighted on her sex, and she quivered. "A few turns to the left…and then a few to the right." He reveled in the smoky haze of pleasure sweeping across her face. "I rotate it round and round," he said, quietly urging, "until the pins…fall…in…place…"

Olivia called his name, whimpering and shattering against him.

Sweet Jesus. He gazed at her, eyes closed, sooty lashes fanned out over her skin, mouth parted. Watching her climax was the most splendid thing he had ever seen. To behold her—in that intimate moment—and knowing he was the one who took her there.

"Christ..." He heaved over her, breathless, pressing his lips to her moist forehead. She purred something warm against his neck as he languished there, incoherent.

"Harry...God, please." Her plea broke his trance, and he shifted his hips for her to open his placket. He fell heavily into her open palms, and she guided him inside her. She tightened her legs around his buttocks, squeezing him with tiny contractions, drawing him in deeper. Flashes of light flickered behind his closed eyes, and he groaned, lowering his lips to hers, tongues teasing. They moved as one, sharing a release that stirred them to their toes again.

By the time they emerged from the barn, the sun had risen above the sloping hills. Olivia had braided her hair, but her kerchief was a casualty from their romp. Harry kissed her flushed cheek, then plucked some stray pieces of hay from the wisps of hair framing her face. She spun him around, brushing off the last bits of oats and grain from his coat, and combed his hair with her fingers.

"Did you see those three new stacks of hickory logs out back?" Harry flicked his head toward the woodshed. "And someone's sharpened the axes and rip saws."

"Mm-hm," Olivia said over his shoulder, smoothing his manly waves into a woven plait.

"Don't recall telling anyone to do those things."

"Believe it was Tom—yesterday after he finished clearing the brushy patch along the short field." She refastened the tie around the blunt ends of his hair, then squeezed his shoulders. "There—all done."

"Thank you." He cupped her cheeks and kissed her nose. "Do you know if he had any help?"

"He and Marcus went at it pretty good at first, but I think it was Tom who finished it up after supper last night."

He inclined his head to his wife while extending his elbow, and she accepted it, wiggling her hand into the crook of his arm. The breakfast bell clanged, and they strolled across the front lawn and stepped inside the house.

"Mornin', Mum." Tom skidded into the kitchen, jerked off his hat, and kissed Mary's flushed cheek before turning to them, tipping his head. "Hello, Cap'n—Missus."

"And what have you been up to, Tom?" Harry held the chair for Olivia and gave her a wink, then claimed his spot at the opposite end of the table.

"Aye, sir, I got right on the brushy patch you showed me yesterday. Thick with briars and scrub oaks, but it's all clear now." Tom sat ready to pounce on his food but waited until Olivia blessed the meal before digging in. "I cut up the hickory wood down by the creek. It's all stacked up the way ye like it. Took to sharpenin' the axes after we finished, then figured the saws needed a might bit of work, so I did them next." He chuckled, savoring a mouthful of warm sausage gravy and biscuits.

Harry gripped his fork in his hand. "All that's finished?"

"Yessir." Tom took another bite of food.

"And your regular chores yesterday?"

"Done, sir." Tom nodded once, then lowered his gaze to his plate.

As the meal continued, the conversation shifted to Mary chattering about shelling beans to Silas, who then clamored on about how Mena was due to see the farrier this morning. Tom kept his mouth busy, sopping up the last bit of gravy with his biscuit before excusing himself.

Harry deliberated, elbows on the table and hands wrapped around a mug of coffee. "Hold on. Come walk with me." He took a final sip, stood up, and crossed the room, Tom falling in line behind him.

When Harry reached the wooden railing around the paddock, he leaned forward, propping his boot on the lower rung. With a swift glance over his shoulder, he spied Tom waiting with hands shoved in his pockets. "Join me, please."

The young man claimed the spot to his left and released a slow breath.

"I have plans, Tom. Plans to make Redmond Hill healthy and prosperous again. To make it happen, I need someone I can rely on, a man who will stand by my side at all times."

"Yessir."

"I need a man I can trust to be the caretaker—who works tirelessly—and is clever and takes action." Harry turned to face him. "Most importantly, this person must be loyal to me—keep my confidence at all costs. I believe you're my man."

Tom removed his threadbare hat, clutching it between his fists, and nodded. "Oh, yessir. I promise I'm all those things. You're the smartest man I've ever known, and I want to learn all I can from you. I won't let you down, Cap'n."

He rubbed his chin with the back of his knuckles. "Tell me, how are you with your lessons?"

"Solid good, sir. I can show you my figures and my writing."

He lifted his chin. "Very good. Let me have a look at them this evening after the upper field is plowed. I'd like to show you my ledgers."

"Aye, sir." Tom shoved his hat on his head, and they shook hands. "Thank you, Cap'n—for believin' in me. You won't be sorry, sir." He dashed off, whistling a tune as he charged up the path to the field.

From the start, Harry had suspected Tom Harkett was the man to whom he could entrust the day-to-day running of the farm. Born on this very soil—eager to please, bright, and most of all loyal—he had earned his respect, and that of the other men. With patience and a steady hand, he would train Tom to keep a watchful eye on Redmond Hill.

Harry turned around to find Silas leading Gordie and Mena from the stable. He grinned at the threesome…and for what he had planned for Olivia this evening.

****

Harry left Silas with the farrier and made his way to Kitt's office. As promised, his friend had amended the property deed, adding language naming Olivia Fleming as his wife and their issue as primary beneficiaries, and had drafted a power document. With the ledgers he brought with him, they updated the statement of assets and liabilities of Redmond Hill. Then Harry put quill to ink, scratching out his signature on the document, and eased back in his chair. A good soldier understood preparation was key to the success of any mission.

"You may be cash poor, but you're rich in property. Zeb can't lay his grubby fingers on you again." Kitt closed his office door, and they stepped outside.

The midday sun glinted off the metal rooftops, and Harry and Kitt lowered the brims of their hats to escape the glare. They walked down King's Street, and Kitt pulled a silver snuffbox from his coat pocket, taking a pinch. As they came upon the mercantile store, Harry spotted two Catawba men, bundles of furs strapped on their backs, in conversation with Reed Barlowe in the side street. Several boxes of liquor and three sacks of sugar lay at the merchant's feet.

Harry stopped and turned to Kitt. "Is Reed a fair trader?"

"Not as much as his cousin. At first, many of the Catawba wouldn't do business with him. When he didn't budge, they caved. Guess they need their vices." Kitt leaned over to use the nearby spittoon.

"Do you know them?"

"Tall one's Nettles. Don't recognize the other. Lots of new faces with the Catawba these days—hard to keep up."

"Aye, market's different from how I remember it. Olivia has family—an aunt and cousins—who trade pottery and blankets."

"Ah, the wife's family, is it? I'd pay good money to see you bantering with them over supper."

"Save your coin." Harry held up his hand, waving him off. "Sitting down for a meal together is a pleasure I've not yet had. I believe they're coming soon, though."

"Pleasure—I suppose that's one word for it. Let me give you a little advice." The corners of Kitt's mouth turned up in a brotherly grin. "Before you meet them, arm yourself with a few belts of scotch. And whatever you do, don't promise them anything."

"Got it," Harry said, tapping his finger on his

temple.

"Been married how long?"

"One month today."

Kitt spit again and smirked. "Honeymoon."

"Aye...and I highly recommend it." Harry winked and, fixing his hat, turned his attention back to the mercantile store. "You know, I think it's time I pay a visit to our favorite merchant." He spied his friend's creased brow. "The wife's sent me to town with a shopping list, is all." He waved a bit of parchment in the air before turning and darting across the street.

A bell jingled when Harry opened the door, and he tipped his hat to a kindly couple as he entered. He made his way to a table filled with an assortment of pelts and knives.

"Good day, Captain Fleming. How may we help you today?" Reed clasped his hands together behind his back.

Harry bristled at the syrupy sweet greeting. "My wife sent me with a list."

Reed took the sheet dangling from his fingertips and, with a snap, gave it to a brown-skinned boy. He took up a position two steps behind him. "And how is the new Mrs. Fleming?"

"Very well." He flipped through several bags of seed. "Are you acquainted?"

"She and her father were some of the first folks to welcome me to Camden—and to a seat in the front row of the church, of course."

A chuckle scraped at the back of Harry's throat.

"Only a simple young woman would befriend a newcomer. But then she was a parson's daughter." Reed rubbed his nose and a blemish to the left of it, stirring up the hairs of his mustard-yellow mustache. "I was speaking to your uncle about this the other day. I imagine a fine soldier with the good Fleming name could have had his pick of genteel young ladies for a wife. Take my Emily, for example." He pursed his lips. "Alas, Zeb could shed no light on this unpredictable turn of events."

Harry flexed his fists, head cocked. "Actually—unlike you and my uncle—predictability bores me. I'm most pleased with my choice of wife." Without a sideways glance at the impudent man, he moved to another table, running his fingers across several rugs and blankets. "Did the Catawba make these?"

"Indeed."

"How do you find trading with them?"

Reed shrugged. "Profitable, but tedious at times. Goods are so plentiful in Charleston. It makes negotiations much easier."

"The back country has its unique qualities." Still admiring the items, he stretched his arm, anticipating Reed's stare.

"Battle scar?" asked Reed, dryly.

"From battle, but not so much a scar." He noted the man's pursed lips. "Pulled one of my men from a burning building. We both came away changed that day."

"You saved him?"

Harry gazed at the warped, tight marks with reverence. "Just doing my duty."

"You're a hero." Reed crossed his arms over his chest.

"I'm a soldier. And what about you? Where were your loyalties in the war?"

"I had no dog in the fight. I was born in Charleston, but I spent most of my life in the Caribbean. I'm a merchant and can strike a deal with any man. Like to think I have a gift for it." He fanned his arms around the storeroom and its furnishings.

"Your cousin ran it well."

"Yes, he made a good start." Reed turned, idly rearranging several cakes of soap in a neat row. "But it's ripe for improvement. My contacts in Charleston will help me turn this little enterprise into something valuable."

As Harry pondered this last statement, the young boy reappeared at Reed's side. With a sweep of his hand, the merchant ushered him to the front counter where his parcel sat wrapped up in burlap and secured with twine. When the doorbell clanged, Reed excused himself and rushed over to greet a woman wearing a plum frock coat. *Bloody opportunist.*

Harry turned his attention to his merchandise. "Fine work, lad." The praise brought a grin and two dimples to the boy's cheeks. As he laid down his money, he spotted a display of wide ribbons in shimmering colors of topaz, emerald, and ruby. He rubbed his fingers across their smooth grain, thinking of Olivia's nut-brown hair. "I'll take two feet of all three colors."

"Very nice gift, Captain." Reed popped up over his shoulder. "I'm sure Mrs. Fleming will be pleased."

Despite the distaste rising in the back of his throat, Harry managed a nod and slipped on his hat. He endured the man's presence to the door and out onto the busy street.

A fair-haired urchin yanked on Harry's sleeve. "Buy some mulberries, sir?"

"Off with you. Scoot!" Reed grabbed the child's wafer-thin shoulders and pushed him away from his storefront. "Don't come back here again." He slapped his hands together, rubbing them as though he were washing away dirt. Their gazes met in challenge. "Have to be vigilant if you want to keep the pests away."

Harry watched the lad trudge off in boots too big for his feet. "He's just poor."

"Yes, and I've just got a business to run."

"And such a *valuable* one it is. Good day, Barlowe." He smirked and, adjusting his hat, sauntered off.

Leading his horse by the reins, Harry found the boy hunkered down at the next street corner, berry stains on his little hands. When he reached in his pocket and handed him several coins, the child jumped up and down. He tipped his hat to the pint-sized peddler, then waved at Reed, who stood with arms folded, the heel of his boot digging into the ground. As he made his way back to Silas and the farrier, he tossed a handful of berries into his mouth and grinned. *Best damn mulberries I've ever tasted.*

On their way home, Harry thought about his father—a man of action, not eloquent words—and the truths he had imparted to him. *Take care of your woman, and she will take care of you.* As he strode toward the house, he felt his father's approval in the sunshine warming his back.

"Supper sure smells good." Harry hung his hat on a nail by the door and inhaled an aroma of roasted chicken, carrots, and onions. His gaze lighted on the width of table set intimately for two. Their fine Holland tablecloth covered the space, and a pewter cup holding fresh blooms of zinnia and marigold served as a centerpiece.

"The missus has been workin' on this all afternoon. She even added rice to the stew, just the way you like it. A fast learner, she is." Mary heaved, lifting the cast-iron pot from the fire and bringing it to rest on the hearth beside a basket with cornbread and apple butter, and a crusty blackberry cobbler.

"Then I shall be very appreciative." He produced a square box, wrapped in starched white linen and tied with a satin bow.

"Aw...you remind me of your Pa. He was always surprisin' your mum with gifts." Her cheeks resembled summer strawberries. "She'll be very pleased."

A lighthearted song drifted through the air, and they smiled at each other. "Thank you, Mary. I'll take over from here."

Harry walked into the bedroom and shut the door. He spied his wife in the oversized tin bathing tub with her back to him. Long ebony tresses spilled over the edge, shining with traces of white suds.

"Oh, Mary—thank goodness. I've not much time. Will you please rinse my hair?" Olivia sat up straight, hair clinging to her slender back while she waited for the drenching. "The water's over here." She waved her right hand at a tall jug on the floor.

Harry closed the three steps between them. *I'd like to do more than rinse you.* He gazed at her, willing her eyes open.

"You should have made yourself known, Harry." She flashed him a coy smile.

"And miss all this?" he asked, grateful she had not slipped back into the depths of the water. He liked the view very much.

"But I wanted to surprise you—to have your favorite things ready for you."

"You've already succeeded, I assure you." He kissed the pouty wrinkle on her forehead, finding her shower of attention comforting. "You may have your way with me tonight, my wet Scrapper...surprises and all. But first, I have something for you—in honor of our first month as husband and wife." He placed the box on the stool beside her.

"What's this?" Olivia leaned forward, and he wiped her hands with a cloth, drying each finger one by one. She pulled up her knees until they poked through the water, and he placed the gift in the palm of her hand. "I'm unused to such things."

"Then I shall have to remedy that. So...open it."

The bow on the box gave way with her gentle pull. She removed it and the square linen cloth and placed them on the stool, as though they were treasures as precious as what lay inside. She wrapped her fingers around the slim amber bottle and blinked her misty eyes. "It's too much, Harry."

"Is a gift for the wife not also—secretly—a gift for the husband? Here, let me." He removed the cork stopper and held the bottle under her nose.

She lowered her gaze, lashes black as coal against her skin. "Mm...lavender."

He added a drop of the fragrant oil to the jug and swirled it around. The stream of water trickled through her hair, filling the air with the floral scent.

"It's heavenly," she murmured, taking his hand and stroking the patch of marred skin stretching from his thumb to his forearm.

"Why haven't you asked me about it?" Wonder colored his voice.

Olivia lifted her gaze, lashes damp. "It's your story to tell. I'm content to wait until you're ready to tell it to me." She kissed the scar with moist lips.

Harry kneeled beside the tub, massaging her shoulders before picking up the cloth to wash her back. "It's strange. Sometimes it seems the war was a lifetime ago. And then, when I stretch out my thumb like this," he said, pointing to the fully extended skin, "it's still painfully very much a part of me."

"You carried every bit of yourself into battle. It's only natural you'd come back changed, both inside and out."

Her insight tugged at his heart. "The fire happened before dawn. One of our men got a little careless with his torch during a raid, and before he knew it, the Tory barn was in flames—remnants of powder inside fueled it fast." He rinsed his wife's shoulders with more water, letting the droplets trickle over her skin. "I almost missed his cry for help, but I found him—pinned under a beam—grabbed him up as best I could, but not before a blaze whipped up around us. He took his marks alongside his ear—and well, you see mine."

"He owes you his life."

He squeezed out the cloth and draped it over the side of the tub. "He would have done the same for me."

"I'm sure he would have." Olivia eased back, eyelids slanted, wrapping her hands around the rim of the tub, water licking up over her breasts. "But you—you're exceptional."

Harry rose, shedding every piece of clothing from his body, and gazed into her dark whiskey eyes. He eased in the opposite side of the tub, sloshing water over the top, and took her foot in his hands. As he massaged tiny circles into her arches, her shoulders drooped, and her eyelids fluttered shut. "And you're intoxicating."

"I think it's the lavender." She leaned her head back

languidly.

He lowered her foot to the bottom of the tub and held out his hand. "As I said, it's a gift for me."

She took his hand, gaze traveling toward the door. "But our supper…"

As he fixed her astride him, her knees flush against his hips, her giggle turned into a soft moan. Blood coursed through in his veins from a hunger only she could satisfy. "Pray, unlike me—it'll keep."

****

Hours later, with nothing but a bisque half-moon casting shadows over their bed, Olivia slipped out from under Harry's arm and lowered her feet to the wood floor. She shimmied into his tunic, which lay in a bundle atop the blankets, letting it swallow her curves, hanging down to her knees. Caddie moved, tail swishing, and took his place beside her. From the bedside table, she stacked their stew-stained bowls onto the plates and balanced them in her right hand while catching their empty glasses between the thumb and index finger of her left. She moved cat-like, placing the remnants of their twilight supper on the tray by the washing table. Then she swiveled about, picking up his sable breeches, pressing them smooth against her belly before placing them in his wardrobe.

She scooped up his neckcloth and pressed it to her nose, then twirled around to sit at her dressing table, gazing into the round mirror. A sigh escaped her lips. For her, matrimony mirrored the healing power of the human body. Her promise to love, honor, and obey had become the tonic wherein she poured all her energy, nurturing their mutual conditions. Harry was the heart and she the blood, going wherever he sent her, making them stronger and healthier…together.

"Come back to bed." Harry's command dragged her from her woolgathering, and she looked up and smiled at his reflection in the mirror. Even in a scant bit of moonlight, his square jaw, rakish grin, and straight teeth stopped her breath. She complied, scampering over to the bed, tucking her knees under the expanse of his shirt, resting her chin on top.

"For you." Harry placed a square of muslin in her hand, and she made a little O with her mouth. "When I saw them, all I could think of was how beautiful they'd look in your hair."

She slid her fingers inside the folds of fabric and uncovered three hair ribbons. She dangled them from her hand, the satin slick against her skin. She cast him a thank-you smile, turning around and shaking her hair down the length of her back. He slid the emerald ribbon underneath her mane, pulling it around and tying it in a simple bow. She tilted her head to one side, revealing the arc of her neckline, and he kissed her there.

"Forgive me if I don't say it enough, Scrapper…but I'm most content with you." His words vibrated against her flesh, sending tiny tremors straight to her heart.

"And I with you." She turned to him.

Harry scooted back on the bed, the mattress creaking and sagging with his weight, and rested his head atop a feather pillow. A warm current swept through the open window, rekindling the scent of his sandalwood, her lavender, and their glorious lovemaking.

He gazed at her, hands folded behind his head. "I've had more peace in this one month with you than I ever have in my lifetime."

"Aye—but it all scares me a little." She tucked her

hair behind her ears. "Everything has happened so quickly—and I've none of the graces fine ladies have. I truly hope you don't have any regrets."

Harry lifted his arm, and she fell into his open embrace, intertwining her legs with his, resting her head on his chest. He stroked the ribbon in her hair, then gave her shoulders a squeeze. "You're what I need."

She clung to his reassuring words, the sound of Caddie's heavy breathing mingling with her husband's, until sleep came to them all.

Chapter Ten

July 1783

Tranquility filled the morning air, drifts of fog
veiling peaks of orange sunlight. Brandt strode from the
house toward the barn and found Eli hunkered down in
front of the wooden pens. He turned his good ear toward
the bird trainer who was communicating with the
splendid gamecock using light, cuck-cooing sounds.
Once freed from his wire-encased nook, the bird paraded
on elongated legs in the dimly lit confines of the barn,
stirring up dirt and hay with his claws. His lean, ebony-
feathered body, marked throughout with streaks of
indigo and alabaster, extended to a husky neck, powerful
beak, and claret plume.

Brandt recalled seeing Eli in action when he was a
lad and would peer at the spectacle of the cockpit from
dark corners of the barn. Eli had been his grandfather's
birdman, and he had prowess with training gamecocks,
though it had been a decade since his skills had been in
use. He watched the old codger lead the bird through its
paces.

"Menacing fowl." Zeb stepped up to the fence post
beside him, puffs of smoke lifting from his pipe.

"Bandit's his name." Brandt dug the heel of his boot
in the dirt, then propped it on the railing.

"It's a visceral sport."

Brandt lifted and lowered one shoulder. "Not every man has the stomach for it."

"Nor the stupidity."

"Well, that's a fine way to talk about Grandfather. Must you always disparage people you don't understand?" Brandt raised a wary finger. "Never mind—don't answer that. I don't want you souring my day."

Zeb sat down on a nearby stool. "You share his infernal lust for the wager. I hope you manage it better than he did." He gazed up at him, smacking the lip of his pipe, coaxing the last bit of tobacco to simmer. "I have no doubt you can tell me ten things about your bird and how old Eli is handling him." His eyes narrowed behind his spectacles. "Can you say the same about your wife?"

Brandt turned and met his gaze.

"A good shepherd counts his sheep, son—never lets even one go astray." Frustrated, he rose to his feet, dumping the spent tobacco on the ground. "Catherine's your property—a lamb you don't want to let wander."

"She's a mother and expecting our next one come winter. She'll not stray."

"Never underestimate Harry," Zeb said, sputtering.

As his father succumbed to another of his spells, Brandt dug inside his coat pocket, found a handkerchief, and passed it to him. "Tell me, has Nigel looked about that cough?"

He slowly regained his breath, loosened his neckcloth, and unbuttoned his coat. "Bah! Nigel's seen more parts of me than I care to mention."

"And?" He spotted a shadow in his father's eyes. *What are you hiding?*

"Nothing his tonic won't cure. I'll have a swallow

of it after breakfast." Zeb rejoined him at the fence rail, chewing on the inside of his rather liberal cheek. "Now, back to what I was saying about Harry—"

"Stop right there." Brandt shot him a look. "You're stirring up trouble. He's married now—to the resourceful mixed breed. Pitiful, but he's gone and done it, hasn't he?"

His father scowled like he had been stuck with a pitchfork. "Harry has an appetite. She fills it. Doesn't mean he's happy—or satisfied. He's always dogged me like a damn beagle on a rabbit."

He threw his head back, scoffing. "Perhaps he married for love and not to vex you."

"You're a fool if you believe that. He's only ever loved one woman."

Brandt pushed off the fence, bracing his hands on his hips. "Yes, and we all know who's to blame for how things turned out."

"You'd do well to have a care—for your wife…and yourself. Mind your sheep." With a glare of consternation, his father turned, shoved the stool out of his way with his boot, and stormed off.

Brandt stared at his father's husky frame silhouetted in the morning sun. Even with only one functioning ear, he could hear the litany of curses rolling off his tongue. *What the hell did Harry ever do to deserve your wrath?*

A crow on route to the barn rafters flew by, and Brandt shrugged deeper into his coat, hands stuffed in his pockets. When the stable hand arrived with the morning feed, a restless black mare whinnied and stomped her foot. The gamecock cawed and clucked inside the game pen. *Damn. Is Harry right? Am I his lackey?* He cared deeply for Catherine, but he would not have taken her—

or any other woman—as his wife. All he required was a steady diet of whiskey, tarts, and wagers. He had wanted no woman by his side after Margaret died. *Christ, I can't go there—not anymore. I married Catherine, and it's over.* He shook his head, his thoughts simmering, not for his wife or from his father's warning, but for the glorious creature before him expanding its wings in territorial dominance. Brandt pivoted and strode away, images of them triumphant in the ring bringing a smile to his face and goose bumps to his flesh.

Chapter Eleven

Harry shielded his eyes from the relentless summer sun, the heat-laden air around him stifling. Cottontail rabbits cooled themselves with flicks of their long ears in the shade of the trees. The men and mules worked in the fields, resting when perspiration beaded and glistened on their skin. Caddie panted while he lounged under the branches of the great magnolia. Marcus doused the soil in the pen with buckets of water, turning it into a muddy-brown bath for the hogs. Moisture cloaked the air until tiny wet beads turned one's shirt into a second skin.

"If hell had a twin sister, it'd be the back country on the last day of July." Harry wiped away the line of perspiration trickling down his neck with a towel.

"Did you see that?" Olivia leaned forward on her knees, pointing at a pile of large stones. "The lizard over there—he slipped right into the crack."

"Christ, that's not the only thing slipping into a crack." He pried his sweaty breeches from his backside and settled into a chair. "How is it you're so unaffected by the heat?"

She hid a giggle behind her palm, placed a bowl of juicy muscadines on his lap, and helped herself to a mouthful. "Well, for starters—my body's not a kiln. You're always hot."

"Thank you." He smirked as she pinched his thigh, then closed his eyes.

"I simply imagine cool and pleasant things."

"Such as...?"

"Mm...the obvious is snow, though I've seen it only a few times. But my feet on the floor first thing in the morning—that's always cold. Sometimes I think about the clear night sky. Then there's tiptoeing across stones in the creek bed. Oh, and what about sticking your toes in the mud there and wiggling them around? Very chilly."

"You're a most singular woman, you know that?"

"Thank you," she said, grinning. "I suppose the best of all is being in the water."

He opened one eye. "You like that?"

"Of course." She wiped a dribble of berry juice from her chin. "I love the water. Papa taught me how to fish too."

"Liv."

"Hm?"

"Want to ride out to Saunders Creek?" Harry warmed at her smile. "You could pack some food. I've got fishing poles. We could swim if you'd like."

"Could we...? Right now?"

With his nod, Olivia ran inside the house, filling her satchel with provisions. She met him by the kalmia bushes, and he settled her in front of him on horseback. With Caddie falling in behind them, they slipped past the curious gazes of the workers taking their midday rest. He tipped his hat to Mary, who stopped to mop her brow and give them a hearty wave.

Magnificent crepe myrtles were in full bloom, the tiny fluffs of magenta marking the path to the creek. It was quiet, no sounds present other than those of Mother Nature. A lingering breeze brushed up against beds of fragrant phlox growing in the damp earth near the trees. They made their way to the creek's edge, thick with woodland sedge and hazel alder, and he tethered his horse to a nearby tree branch before wading into the water.

They found good fortune with fishing, Olivia squealing when a fine-looking striper snapped her bait and a hefty trout swallowed his. She was radiant, sunshine licking her cheeks and nose, and sporting tan breeches soaked up past her knees. Having caught what they needed for supper, they slipped out of their clothes and into the freedom of the cool water.

Harry emerged sometime later, her admiring gaze making him feel like Poseidon himself. He fetched a towel from his saddlebag and, after extending his hand to help her out, used it to dry off their bodies. While he slipped back into his breeches, she scooped up his tunic and wiggled into it. He gazed at her speculatively.

"What...? You don't need it. I prefer you bare chested. Besides, I like the way it flounces and swishes around me, see?" Olivia twirled around in a circle, the long tail of it licking her thighs.

"You ken what happens when you swirl your bum around—and it bare." His hands landed on her hips, gently squeezing her curves, and she stopped mid-swirl.

"You want me, then...?"

He gave her a devilish wink. "Oh, aye—but we've had a mere handful of muscadines since breakfast. I'm damn near starved. I need sustenance before I take you, my love."

"By all means."

The smile that sprang to her lips tugged on his heart. The endearment had slipped out without thinking, and it was a first. *My love? Where the devil had that come from?*

Harry started a fire with the abundance of branches around them while she dug through her trusty satchel, producing a skillet, platter, knife, and a long-edged fork folded up inside a leather wrap.

Squatting on his haunches, Harry blew over the budding flame. "Got your bandages and ointments in there?"

Olivia gazed at him, tilting her head. "Yes, and you should be thankful I keep my bag well-stocked." She tucked her feet underneath her bottom and began scaling and filleting the fish.

"You're a good one to have around, Scrapper."

When she brought him the fillets, he dropped them onto the iron skillet nestled in the coals and listened while they sizzled and popped with great fanfare. She sliced a tomato, squash, and cucumber and placed the pieces on the platter beside the grilled fish. Then they sat knee to knee on the grass—sipping from a bottle of wine he had squirreled away in his saddlebag—and ate with their fingers.

Afterward he spread out his blanket under the billowy cover of the live oak tree, and they lay down together. With her hair spread out in soft waves framing her face, they remained quiet with nature's song of ruffling leaves and trickling water.

Harry leaned on his elbow and gazed down at her half-closed eyes. His palm found her belly beneath the flounces of his tunic, and he stretched his fingers out, touching both her hipbones. A passing current brushed his nose, bringing with it her bouquet of woman and honeysuckle. His fingers ghosted downward, caressing the downy hair adorning her entryway. He smirked, realizing how drawn he had become to his wife, as comfortable tracing the lines and curves of her body as he was his own—but with infinitely more pleasure.

Olivia shifted under his touch, parting her thighs a little. He opened them farther, sliding his tunic up over her hips, easing down to rest his cheek on her silky inner thigh. Unencumbered, he teased her soft folds with his breath and reveled in her immediate response, lifting her hips to meet him. As she grabbed clumps of grass between her fingers, he proceeded to douse her with a meticulous tongue bath, intent on ensuring her pleasure.

Only after she shuddered, tasting her nectar between his lips, did he look up and see her unabashed glow. His chest swelled with a primitive pride and an unquenchable desire to possess her. *What are you doing to me...?* He kissed her stomach and laid his head there to rest.

"I could stay here forever," Olivia said sometime later, lacing her fingers through his hair.

"Nice to leave the world behind sometimes, no?" Harry pushed up, scooted back, and leaned against the tree, stretching out his legs and crossing his feet at the ankles. With a passing breeze cooling his bare torso, he plucked a blade of grass and slid it in his mouth.

"I wonder how old it is..." She stared up at the live oak tree's dense spray of leaves.

"Been here my whole life. Father brought me here to fish when I was a boy."

She leaned up on her elbow, cheek mushed in her palm. "Are you very much like him?"

He chewed on the slick blade and stared off in the distance. "Father fought and loved hard. He was very tough, brave, and brute strong. He had no fear." Then he shifted his gaze back to her. "Except of living life without Mother." Her warm, brown eyes gave him silent encouragement. "Her heart," he said with outstretched arms, "was so big—it'd swallow you whole. She'd melt him with one smile. His aim was steady with her by his side."

Olivia sat up, resting her chin on her knees, arms hugging her legs. "And after she passed?"

"Lost. The light in his eyes never came back." Harry reached out and plucked a fresh stem of grass. "For a while, it was the three of us—then my sister Josie married Hugh when I was thirteen. They moved to Charleston—his family's in the indigo trade. And then it was just the two of us. That's when I became more like my father, I think—took me with him everywhere." Olivia patted the ground, inviting Caddie to join her, then he continued. "Father was one of the early Regulators in these parts. I cut my teeth with him on back country skirmishes—shooting, hunting, and tracking. And he saw to my education—so I could take over Redmond one day. Nothing as fancy as a university, but I had a tutor and spent a year in Charleston at their academy. I was eighteen and had just come home when his heart gave out in his sleep."

"On your own at eighteen…like me." She walked on her knees to his side.

"That's why I was so keen about you." He brushed his fingers under her chin, lingering over the softness there. "You were me six years ago—smart and strong and alone—but I was a man. I had an inheritance. I could shoot, be a good soldier, enlist, and fight. You must've had dreams—ones that didn't include marrying any man."

Olivia ran slim fingers through her hair and began braiding it. "We never settled anywhere for very long. We mostly got by on God's grace and the kindness of others. Waneta and Betsey—the entire tribe—gave us food and shelter. Elan had gone off with other Catawba men, fighting in General Sumter's militia. My cousin's a skilled tracker and scout, very canny and brave." She pulled a small band from her wrist and tied off the blunt ends of her hair. "I learned about healing from Mama— she always did what she could to help others. I've been to the ocean, but I've never seen the mountain tops. Papa would tell me about them, though. I wasn't ready to be alone. I'd never had even one suitor—and no wonder, with no dowry or real home. But there was naught to do about it. Nothing's much fair between men and women." She stretched out her legs, with palms flat on the ground beside her, letting Caddie lick her toes.

Harry swallowed hard. "I took off half-cocked but committed to freeing the colonies—following our dream. I wanted to take charge of my life and make Father proud. Didn't stop to think how things would change in my absence. I didn't think about the cost."

"And what was the cost, Harry?"

He rolled onto the quilt, extending his hand to her. She joined him, her head on his chest, snuggled in close. His heart thrummed while the words ricocheted in his head. *No. No, no, no. I can't open my heart again.* Many quiet minutes passed with nothing more than the sound of their breathing and the chickadee's song between them.

Olivia pointed at a gaping hole in the trunk of the live oak. "Do you suppose it will die? From that hollow there…?"

"That's actually its way of protection, getting rid of something dead and fortifying the rest of the trunk by forming the hollow." He stretched out his free arm, pointing. "See how the tree's spread out long and wide—the bottom branches skimming the ground? We climbed on them as children. It's had plenty of room to grow, and I expect it'll be around for a long time."

"Remarkable…"

Harry pulled the tunic up over her exposed shoulder, and she moved with him, always edging in closer to his body…and perhaps even his heart. He was impulsive by nature, but in this matter, after enduring the loss of Catherine, caution won out.

"I'm sorry I can't talk to you about the cost of my actions." His voice hinted of regret.

"It was a silly question." Her breath felt warm against his chest.

"No, it's not. You deserve an answer, and I promise you'll have it when I'm able. But for now, I'll tell you this," he said soberly. "I have holes. I think maybe you have some too. And the way I see it, we're a little like the tree. We fill the holes in one another, sealing away the dead parts, healing…to keep on living." He kissed the top of her head. "I found you, Liv. Only God knows how, but I found you—and I'm grateful."

Harry hugged her closer, overcome with the realization she had become something his first love was not. *Real.* Her body was flesh and muscle. She was mouth, hands, tongue, and fingers. *And she's devoted to me.*

Olivia moved atop him, his tunic slipping down with the movement, exposing the crescent shape of her breasts. The heat at the juncture of her thighs radiated over the taut laces of his breeches. A rush of wind blew through the tree limbs above them, and his shirttail ruffled, giving him a glimpse of her backside.

"You're right. My dreams didn't include marrying any man." Olivia untied her braid and shook her head, freeing her long locks. "Only marrying you—the man I love."

He fought to quell the surge of emotion racing through his body, placing his hands on her hips and squeezing her soft flesh.

She tilted her head, gazing down at him. "Do you remember the time you asked me what I would call you and I said—"

"Captain...yes, I remember," he said in a gravelly voice.

She bent down and whispered against his ear. "It's still true. But now you're mine, Captain. Not hers." She unfastened his placket, releasing his aching cock. "Mine."

Olivia pushed herself up on her knees and slid onto him, surrounding him with her warmth. *Sweet Jesus.* She thrust her hips forward and took him deeper, casting his shirt aside and offering him the most exquisite view of her breasts. His hands slid up the sides of her waist, pausing to caress her nipples to pebbly points.

"I love you, Harry Fleming." Her voice was airy and urgent. "I'm going to fight for us because I know you're not yet able." She kneaded his chest, her massaging hands punctuating her pledge. "And because I know one day you'll do the same for me."

He eased himself upright, keeping her cleft tight around him, claiming her lips. Her mouth molded to his, soft and giving, and his need for her grew exponentially.

She pulsed over him rhythmically, and he inhaled her scent, glorying in it. He pulled back and gazed at her—cheeks flushed, lips swollen—and hardened more. "You're mine, Scrapper."

He lifted her, withdrawing so he could lay her gently on her back, keeping her head cradled with his hand behind it. As he plunged inside her again, she sank her fingers into his buttocks and drew him in to the hilt. With the scent of honeysuckle and juniper in the air, their bodies illuminated in twilight shades of lilac and pink against the sky, they crossed a new threshold together.

Chapter Twelve

August 1783

Olivia liked pork and bean soup, and she particularly liked fried cornmeal cakes. But today, all three left her stomach feeling like the sticky, stringy innards of an over-ripe pumpkin. Her skin was cool with no sign of a rash. There was no pain in her head, though in the past ten minutes, a wave of dizziness had descended upon her while shelling green beans.

"You still look puny." Mary flipped the cakes in the greased skillet.

Olivia dropped three more beans in her bowl. "I don't understand it."

"Well, I sure do."

She gaped, then screwed up her mouth, shaking her head.

"You ain't considered it?" Mary shuffled over, wiping her palms on her apron before resting her hand on her shoulder.

She resumed her shelling, working her fingers faster. She hunched over, blinking back tears.

"Your belly aches—smells are makin' ye faint. Even took a nap after breakfast today, ye did." Mary snatched a handkerchief from her pocket and passed it to her. "And now you're sobbin' for no good reason."

"I haven't," she said hiccupping, "I-I haven't bled

since the first of June."

Mary patted her shoulder, her wide girth shaking merrily. "Well, there ye have it. It's your wee one growin' inside—lettin' ye know he's in there."

She dabbed her eyes. "What'll I do...?"

"What kinda question is that? Why, tell Cap'n Harry, of course. He'll be so happy." Mary shuffled across the kitchen, grabbed a basin from the cabinet, and placed it in her hands.

"You think so?"

"Why do ye doubt it?"

"He rather likes me the way I am. What if this changes things?" She clutched the bowl over her middle. "What if it's too soon?"

"Shush your silly talk. Ye didn't get in the motherly way on your own. I bet he's halfway expectin' it, the way you two get on and all." She gave her a reassuring wink. "He's got a heart of gold. You can tell him after supper."

Olivia nodded, staring at the beans in the bowl, trying to ignore the queasiness in her stomach. In no time she turned aside, heaving what little she had eaten for lunch into the empty basin.

****

After supper, while attempting to work the yarn through her knitting needles, Olivia's gaze drifted to Harry. Seated at the opposite end of the porch swing with his ankle crossed over his knee, he balanced his newspaper on his thigh. For a moment, she imagined him with a toddler on his lap, making faces at his strapping son or delightful daughter. She scratched her teeth over her bottom lip, hedging. Before happiness could bloom in her heart, she needed to tell him her secret. "You were quiet at supper tonight."

"I was thinking the same about you. All you ate were Mary's hoe cakes. Then you took off without any of her apple fritters. Hardly like you, Scrapper." Harry folded the newspaper in his hand and tapped it on her knee.

She sighed and made a mental note to add "annoyingly observant" to her list of his character traits. "Oh, I just needed some fresh air. Caddie likes it when I sit on the porch with him." When she spoke his name, her hound lifted his sizable head.

He lowered his paper and rubbed his knuckle over his lip. "I've been thinking about the harvest. I was going over the math this afternoon."

"Anything I can do to help? I find no poetry in numbers, but I'm happy to try."

A smile reached his eyes. "You're sweet, but my figures are sound. Just can't predict the weather—and wish we could've gotten the third field planted in time. If I'd only been able to get home sooner."

"You saw to your duty first, then came home. That's who you are." She clutched the needles in her hands. "Besides, I've got a good feeling about the yield. It may be smaller this year, but any harvest is better than none at all." She shifted and refocused on her knitting, biting the corner of her lip.

Harry leaned over and squeezed her toes poking out from beneath her cornflower blue skirt. "May I hold you to that?"

She bobbed her head, winking over her handiwork.

"And from where do you get this assurance?" With a sweep of his hand, Harry cast their things to the floor and drew her close to his side.

"The Lord." Smiling, Olivia lifted her gaze out over the grassy lawn and breathed in air laden with the fragrance of summer hay and honeysuckle. "He's all around us."

"I have as much faith as you, yet none of your confidence."

She arched her eyebrows playfully.

"Aye, I pray. Though maybe not as often as you."

"Oh, Harry, I can tell when you're fibbing. You get this little wrinkle on your forehead." She pointed, lips pressed together. "That one right there."

"And you figured this out all on your own?" He laughed, lifting her onto his lap. "My wife is indeed a fast learner."

"I am." Olivia wrapped her hands around his shoulders, tracing the curves of his muscles with her fingers. "And what's more, I think I could beat you at a game of twenty-one—yes, I can play." She bit into her lower lip. "You already know I can catch and clean a fish. And ride a horse—not sidesaddle either. Um...and chop wood and—"

"Stitch a man's bleeding arm," he added while rubbing small circles at her nape with his thumb.

She nodded her head against the tingling sensation, scrambling for another example. "And I can break a chicken's neck, too. Oh yes, Mary taught me that one last week."

"Is there not anything else I can teach you, Scrapper?"

The glimmer in his blue-lagoon eyes made her heart leap and thoughts soar. *It's now or never.* She shifted deeper into his embrace. "You're a most attentive teacher—and you've taught me many things. But you can't know *everything*." She gazed up at him, tracing her finger across his firm square chin.

"No?"

She shook her head.

"Tell me."

Olivia took a deep breath. *I'd rather show you.* She moved his hand from her waist to rest on her stomach. She held it there, her palms clammy, and waited.

He flexed his fingers, squeezing her belly, then his gaze sought hers. "Are you...?"

She nodded, trying to decipher his darkening eyes. "Is it okay? Surely, we knew it could happen what with—"

Harry placed his finger to her quivering lips. His mouth twitched into something akin to a smile, but more abstract. "You're with child." She thought his tone sounded like the preacher's when he said "amen" after a prayer. Then he cupped her cheeks in his hands and pressed their foreheads together. "This—this is wonderful."

"Are you certain? I mean—I'm so happy, but I wasn't sure if..."

He brushed a wisp of hair behind her ear. "Yes, I'm very happy, Scrapper."

Harry hugged her, and she molded her body to his, casting aside all doubts, uncertainties, and ghosts. Under the shelter of the front porch, wrapped in his arms, it was just the two of them, their loyal hound, and their child growing inside her womb.

Chapter Thirteen

September 1783

Harry had few memories of autumn that did not include his uncle's barbeque at Glen Laurel. Postponed by the war, this year's gala promised plentiful food, drink, and sport, a celebration to unite neighbors and strengthen alliances.

It was a serene afternoon, the sun perched high in a cloudless, azure sky. Harry emerged from the carriage first, offering his hand to Olivia. Aware of the importance of her first official appearance as his wife, he had gifted her with a bronze taffeta gown with fitted sleeves and a split front that revealed an underskirt of white lace. Other than the two smooth plaits pulled away from her face, the ruby ribbon he had given her woven through them, her hair fell loose down her back. With her heirloom jade necklace resting at her throat, she was regal in look if not pedigree.

Tom held the door for them. "Ye look mighty pretty, Missus. The Cap'n did a fine job pickin' your dress. The color matches your eyes."

Olivia smiled at Tom, dressed in tall boots, gray breeches, and a woven shirt that months ago would have hung off his shoulders. Despite a little fraying around the edges, his dark coat was a rather smart addition to the outfit. His old hat rested comfortably over his brow.

"Your sharp eyes and honey words are spot-on. I couldn't agree more." He smiled at his wife, then turned to Tom. "Go on ahead. Join the others around back and enjoy yourself, eh? I'll send word when we're ready to leave."

Tom smiled, touching his finger to the brim of his hat, and dashed off.

Harry placed his hand over his wife's fingers crooked around his arm. "Even in gloves, your fingers are cold."

"I'm afraid." She gazed up at him.

While the gown gave her a superficial shell of composure, he imagined inside her stomach was in knots. "I realize this is all very new for you. My family is a mixed bag of tricks, but it must be obliged on such occasions. Rest easy—some here already know you."

"As the parson's daughter or Mr. Blake's helper," she whispered into his shoulder. "Not as your wife. I'm not sure I can do this."

"I'm proud to call you mine, and you look beautiful. Trust me." He kissed her gloved hand, then they took the wide, curved staircase leading up to the front door.

Zeb's grandfather constructed Glen Laurel after the turn of the century. Situated on a sloping hill, flanked by a handsome fishpond and some ninety acres of fertile soil behind it, the brick house was a two-story with four fireplaces at the corners of the structure. The living areas—entryway, great hall, dining room, study, and kitchen—were in the middle with a massive, two-sided stone fireplace as its focal point. Separate wings for expanding families were at the four corners. Glen Laurel had a smokehouse, roasting pit, and slave quarters on site, as well.

Harry entered the great hall and, hearing his name chanted from various directions, made his rounds, introducing his wife to his friends. A myriad of tables, both inside and out on the lawn, featured favorite foods like barbeque shoats, buttered onions, and apple tansey. Folks filled their bellies with food and spirits and greeted each other with open arms. The Grant twins—stout and strong as a couple of tree stumps—meandered around the great hall with their signature dark hair, light smiles, and hearty handshakes.

"Harry, I'm damn glad to see you," Jimbo Grant said, a bit of frothy ale on his upper lip.

The taller twin, Willie, stepped forward, hand extended. "It's been too long, Bulldog. How have you been?"

"Can't complain." Harry grinned at the use of his old nickname. "Olivia, allow me to introduce you to the Grant twins—Jimbo and Willie. Gentlemen...please greet my wife."

"James Beauregard, ma'am, but everybody calls me Jimbo." In kissing her gloved hand, he all but erased the traces of foam from his lip.

The corners of her mouth curved into a smile. "Very nice to meet you, sir."

"Willie here told me you got married, but I had to see it to believe it. Now I understand why." Jimbo propped his elbow on his twin's shoulder.

"Pleased to meet you, ma'am." Willie bowed his head.

Harry grabbed two glasses of port from a servant's tray and offered one to Olivia. He sipped his drink while reacquainting himself with the twins. At one point, he glimpsed his wife, fair and wide-eyed, fixed to his arm.

She had garnered more than a few appreciative gazes from gentlemen in the room, though to her credit, she showed no clue of it. Unlike other flirty, chatty women in the room, she was both grace and innocence.

"Harry and Jimbo are like a clump of sparks on dry wood." Willie's breezy charm shone through an unassuming smile. "When we were boys, they'd get themselves into the biggest messes. Why I remember one time they—" Willie spied the squint of warning from his twin and assumed a lopsided grin. "Well, ma'am, let's just say boys will be boys."

Olivia nodded. "Yes, how right you are, sir."

"Well, as much as I'd like to stick around with you two, my wife and I have some family matters to attend to." Harry hated how his words stole the smile from her face.

"Must we…so soon…?" Her voice trailed off.

"It's time, Scrapper." He kissed her hand, then steered them across the room to his intended target, the man with whom he had clashed for most of his life.

"Uncle." Harry noted the man's timeworn hand still rendered a firm shake. "As always, you host a delightful affair."

"I was beginning to think you'd disappoint us, but alas, you're here." Zeb's aged but sharp emerald eyes met his. "And who's this attached to your arm?"

"You must be slipping in your old age. You know Olivia. But of course, she's now my wife." He raised his chin.

His uncle attempted a smile. "Welcome to Glen Laurel."

"I'm honored, sir." Olivia's curtsey was flawless.

"I trust you find Redmond an adequate home," Zeb

said, waving for a fresh drink. "Harry certainly has his hands full with the restoration."

"Yes, sir, I'm most comfortable. I try to help Harry any way I can." Olivia returned her hand to Harry's arm.

"But of course, you come from hard-working stock, d-don't you?" Zeb stifled a cough and, fumbling in his pocket for a handkerchief, wretched until he dislodged a pink-tinged mucous plug. Brandt appeared at his father's side, a crease forming between his brows. Zeb scowled, wadded up the cloth, and shoved it in his pocket.

With his fist over his mouth, Harry cleared his throat and met Olivia's gaze. "Actually, Uncle, the better description would be resilient and resourceful."

"Indeed." He gave him a curt nod over the rim of his glass.

Brandt stepped closer to him. "At first, I didn't believe the old gossips about your marriage—and such an impromptu one. But you've always been fast to the trigger."

"Just going where my heart and spirit take me…unplanned and unexpected." His muscles tensing, he leaned into Olivia's steady shoulder.

"But we forget ourselves." Brandt quirked a brow, rubbing his chin, turning his attention to Olivia. "May I have the pleasure of a dance with my new cousin?"

Though her fingernails dug into his arm, Harry did not flinch, giving her a quick wink instead. "My wife's both graceful and light on her toes. Are you up to the task?"

"Absolutely." Brandt extended his arm to Olivia and led them toward the fiddler's music.

Harry dodged his wife's heated glare. He hated to let her go, but there was no point in putting it off. It was time she ventured into the Fleming swamp.

As Harry looked on and sipped his drink, he detected a familiar scent wafting over his shoulder. It sent him backward in both time and step. He could neither escape nor ignore the delicate smell of gardenia, so he responded as any gentleman would. "How are you today, Mistress Fleming?"

Catherine came around to his arm, fixing her gaze upon Brandt and Olivia. She tilted her head to one side. "I'm well—but perhaps not as well as the *other* Mistress Fleming."

He pressed his lips together. "I've never seen her like this."

"You'd scarcely seen her at all before you up and married her."

"True." His eyes widened at the notion. "I find I'm enjoying the discovery in our relationship. No expectations. No disappointments."

She turned to face him, her hair coiffed to perfection, tiny ringlets framing her magnolia-white face. "Why did you marry Olivia? She's...well, she's not...?"

He noted Catherine's figure was untouched by motherhood, still fit and curvy, but her tongue had developed an unfamiliar, unwelcome bite.

"Not you too." He scrubbed his hand over his face and exhaled. "No, I did not compromise Olivia. I'd have thought you knew me better, Cee." A faint scowl shadowed his face. "I'm not a fan of abstinence, so a wife seemed the logical solution."

"Hm, how practical you are—and choosing such a robust woman too. The war changed you more than I ever thought possible." She wore the expression of someone who had just emptied a chamber pot.

Harry straightened and turned to her, shoulders square. "It seems we've both changed. Truth is, Olivia caught my attention, and I took a fancy to her. She's like no one I've ever known." His fingers flexed by his sides. *Devoted and loyal...to me.* "When I found out she was going to go away, run off to her Catawba family—well, I couldn't let that happen. I married her because I need companionship in my life. I need a friend...and a lover."

Catherine raised her glass to within an inch of her mouth. "Why, you're her Lancelot. Without you, she'd be alone, and God knows where."

"It's fitting. I don't do alone so well."

"Do you think I could forget? I was there, remember?" She sipped her drink.

His heart pinched his throat. "Yes, and when everyone in my family had either died or moved on, I trusted you to wait for me. I carried you with me in my heart, Cee. Every. Single. Day."

She wound her fingers through the curl skimming her cheek. "No need to be hateful, Harry. While this marriage was not my doing, I agreed to my father's wishes. And now we have Peggy, and soon—"

"Yes, you've made a nice family for yourself. It should have been us—but you threw it all away. I promised I would come back to you." He reached inside his pocket and pulled out her blue hair ribbon, shoving it in her palm.

Catherine blinked, then her eyes softened at the corners. She rubbed the ribbon between her thumb and index finger, a shaky smile forming on her face. With an audible sigh, she placed it back in his hands, closing his fingers on top of it.

"You're a man, Harry. A brave man, full of conviction and fire...and you don't understand at all what it means to be a woman. Do you think only a man can be duty-bound?" When he tried to turn away, Catherine yanked his sleeve. "Do you believe a sense of honor is only for a soldier?" She dropped her hand, casting a furtive glance left, then right. "You can save your accusations. I simply fulfilled my duty to my family."

She stormed off, and Harry clenched his fists, swearing under his breath. He shoved the ribbon in his pocket as Brandt and Reed appeared on his left.

"Seems you and my wife were discussing something much more interesting than the weather." Brandt's gimlet eyes narrowed as he lit a cheroot. "I don't like her being overtaxed, Harry. She's delicate. Reed and I are traveling to Charleston next week, and I don't want her distraught."

Harry nodded his agreement, then arched a brow. "Are you trading in goods or flesh this time? And you're prime to get on the tables at some of their best clubs, eh?"

Reed stuffed his hands in his pockets, rocking back on his heels. "I have connections, Captain. Perhaps you'd like to come along, join us in a few wagers?"

Brandt cast a sideways glance at his mustached friend. "My honorable cousin lacks the constitution for gambling, and he prefers to bear the burden of his fields on his own back—and on those of a handful of hired hands. Neither he nor his father understood the labor needs of our economy."

"Surely such thinking limits both the fruit of your land and your prosperity," Reed said dubiously.

"Ah, but Harry—he stands on the side of humanity.

Prosperity be damned." Brandt took a drink and swished it around in his mouth.

"I'll take my chances any day on a man who stands with me over one shackled to me." Harry bowed his head. "Safe travels to you both."

****

Olivia found her female friends the warmest company she had encountered all afternoon. They were gathered by the refreshment table, swapping stories and sharing advice, when a chorus of cheers sailed through the air. A spirited tune filled her ears, and she watched as couples clapped, hooking arms with one another and dancing in a large circle. She lifted on her toes, craning her neck.

"Why th-that's Harry. He's playing?" Olivia tugged on Martha Blake's arm while her husband moved about with ease, bending the bow across the violin strings. "I truly know so little of him."

Martha clasped her hand. "I remember when he was his father's shadow around Redmond—working, riding, soaking up the good green earth. Harry attracts people like fish to warm waters. It was Abigale's gift too. I sense she and Joseph were with you on your wedding day. I'm sure she's looking down from heaven, comforted her son found love."

"You remember what I told you—I'm not his first love." Doubt laced her words.

"Not all of us can be someone's first love. First doesn't mean better."

Her gaze softened. "Oh…you mean Mr. Blake?"

"No. Me." A grin spread across Martha's lips. "Nigel wasn't my first love, dearie. He's much more than that."

Olivia covered her mouth.

"Don't be afraid of what's in his past. You're Harry's wife—not an illusion—and you're here with him in the flesh." She wrapped an arm around her shoulder. "Memories of first love are powerful but lose their strength day by day. Trust me."

The song ended, followed by applause for the musicians. As Harry took a bow, their gazes met from across the room.

****

Harry winked at Olivia, pleased to find her nestled in safe company. As he made his way past the crowd on the dance floor, the memory of his recent interaction with Catherine niggled him. *Olivia deserves better. I must give her better.* He hauled in a series of breaths as he approached her, the rising pink in her cheeks guilting him right down to his toes.

After exchanging pleasantries with the women, Harry took Olivia's hand. "Ladies, if you'll excuse us, I wish to dance with my wife." With a bow, he led her to the dance floor and swung her into his arms.

"I watched you with Brandt earlier. I'd no idea you danced so well." His hand found its home at the small of her back as he took the lead.

"Hm…then why did you say I was graceful and light on my toes?" She tilted her head, lips pursed in challenge.

"You are in everything else—why not dancing too?" He gave her a suggestive smile and drew her to him, a blatant play at softening her rigid spine.

She bristled. "And why do your friends call you Bulldog?" She lifted her chin a little higher. "And how could you forget to tell me you play an instrument, hm?"

Harry twirled her under his arm to dodge her feisty glare and was bombarded by the scent wafting up from her neck. *You're all lavender and sweet simmering heat.*

He grunted to clear his throat and proceeded to mitigate the damage. "So...Bulldog's a youthful nickname. I'm sure you won't have any trouble guessing how that came to be." He sneaked a peek at her before continuing. "And the violin—well, it's the most civilized skill I possess. Mother taught Josie to play, of course. Then she insisted I learn. Turns out I was a natural." His expression softened, and he rubbed the inside of her palm with his thumb. "I apologize. I should've played for you first."

They danced across the floor, and when her lips softened, Harry leaned down and whispered into her ear. "We must have more song and dance in our home. Babies enjoy music, I think." When her shoulders dipped, he relaxed into a smile. *That's my Scrapper.*

"I think we should dance as much as possible before I become big as a watermelon, and you won't be able to twirl me around anymore." Olivia gazed up into his eyes, soft tendrils brushing across her cheek.

"Suppose you're right. There will be no dancing, no lovemaking. What shall I do with you when you grow very large with child...?" he cajoled. "Wait—I have an idea."

The corners of her mouth turned down, and she stiffened in his arms. "You'll like me still, won't you, Harry? Even though I'll most surely blow up like Fannie."

He met her troubled gaze. "Our cow...?"

She nodded, lips pressed in a thin line.

"Good God." He snorted a laugh, and as the song

ended and a slower tune ensued, he corralled her in his arms. He placed her hand on his chest. "Do you know who I have to thank for this? Every day your belly grows larger, so does this feeling in my heart." As the sparkle returned to her eyes, he squeezed her hand. "Aye, Scrapper, I'll still like you even when your size rivals our sweet Fannie." His smile spread. "I'll still want you, I'm afraid, so I merely had a notion of what I might do with you when the time comes." *Will I ever tire of teasing her?*

"What?" Olivia nibbled at her lip. He continued to sway with her in his arms, delighting in her sweet torment. "Harry…" she whispered loudly at him.

His lips brushed her ear as he spoke the words, then he gazed down and spotted the silent O of her mouth. "Hm, I thought you might like it."

Chapter Fourteen

October 1783

There be three things which are too wonderful for me, yea, four which I know not: the way of an eagle in the air; the way of a serpent upon a rock; the way of a ship in the midst of the sea; and the way of a man with a woman. Proverbs 30:18-19, KJV

Olivia treasured the tender break of dawn when sunlight sprayed over the rolling terrain and kneaded the world to life. It was Harry's ritual to have an early ride on horseback, and of late, he had taken her with him on these communal journeys. The robin's birdsong would drift above them, fallen leaves in hues of rust and gold their cushion beneath the cotton quilt, his thigh a perfect pillow for her head. While the air was resinous with earthy smells of damp pine bark and cedar fronds, she never felt chilled. The blanket tucked around her, combined with his heat warming the back of her neck and shoulders, was all the insulation she needed. Intertwined in a benediction with nature, he would open the book to wherever they had last left Robinson Crusoe—washed up on the virgin island beach or transformed into a sailor and merchant—and read aloud to her. She would close her eyes, resting her palms over her rounded abdomen, lulled by his baritone voice.

Harry's study, a room with an entire wall dedicated to books of history and science, stories of adventure and amour, and volumes of poetry and philosophy, piqued her interest. There she had found the English dictionary, looking up new words every day and regaling him with her discoveries. She could read and write, but being in the company of so many books—not just the Holy Bible and a book of Shakespeare's sonnets, both of which her father had treasured—brought her indescribable joy.

As he had promised at the barbeque, Harry brought music and dancing into their lives, his mother's violin a welcome friend in the evenings after supper. Their families would gather on the front lawn around dusk, men dabbling in whiskey, while mothers chatted, pestered by youngsters scampering about the yard like piglets, slippery and hard to catch. Around the fire pit, Tom would play lilting tunes with his recorder, with Marcus keeping time brushing two wooden blocks together, and Harry playing the violin. Spirited melodies were favorites, coaxing them to dance. She had enjoyed the spectacle, many times in the hands of a lad who, on tiptoes, head lifted high, took her for a turn. Often Harry scooped up curly-haired Polly, Ian Murphy's five-year-old daughter, and gave her his best two-step, her feet planted atop his.

When the hour drew late and they were alone in their bed with nothing but silver moonlight over their bare bodies, skin still glowing from shared pleasure, she would cradle Harry's head down low. She would twirl her fingers through his hair while he sang a lullaby to their child growing inside her belly. In these moments, Olivia knew she might never fully know the way of a man with a woman, but the fullness of her new life left her in awe of the wisdom of God for first giving Eve to Adam and then her to Harry.

Chapter Fifteen

Olivia came to town on a mission. She helped Mr. Blake at the surgery for an hour, cutting cloth strips and preparing remedies, then made her way to the trader's market. She passed by many Catawba—their magnificent furs, salted meats, baskets, and pottery on display—while looking for Waneta.

Her gaze flitted about, then landed on Elan. Her cousin was a formidable man, tall and muscular, clad in suede, a muslin tunic, and a brilliant beaded vest. Standing beside their covered wagon, he conversed with a stout man who came only as high as his elbows. He lowered his head to him in conversation, then stepped back and shook his hand, exchanging pottery and pelts for coins. Elan's black hair hung down the center of his back in a smooth coil, and it moved with him as he hoisted another box from the wagon.

"There you are. I've been looking for you." Olivia stepped forward, gently clutching his arm.

Elan scooped her up, feet dangling in the air, and planted a kiss on her cheek. "What do you mean? You can see me anytime you want—you know where home is."

"And you me."

His copper eyes shone bright, and he arched his eyebrows. "The likes of me and Waneta at your big house uninvited—no, does not suit me." He resumed his work, methodically unpacking the box.

She shrugged deeper inside her shawl, as though it would hide her from the truth. "I-I'm sorry. You're right. Relationships require communication to keep the flame alive, and I've been remiss. We're all family. I would very much like for you to visit us at Redmond."

"Redmond?"

"Redmond Hill. Harry's—I mean, our home."

Their gazes met, then Elan pivoted, checking her profile before crossing his arms, mouth fixed in a solemn line.

Waneta emerged from the wagon, walking between them, giving voice to his thoughts. "You're with child."

Olivia's throat constricted, and she licked her dry lips. "Will you—can you—be happy for me?"

"Dear girl, you have my blessing." Waneta fanned her arms wide. "Why do you doubt it?"

As tears pooled in her eyes, she fell into her aunt's embrace, pressing her cheek to her bosom. Waneta smelled of hickory smoke and pine, and her arms, while slim and aged, were strong.

"Your husband—he treats you well?" Elan asked with purpose.

Olivia lifted her head, wiping her nose with the handkerchief she had pulled from her pocket, nodding profusely. "Yes, yes. He's a good and kind and generous man. My life, it's changed so much," she said, unable to find words equal to the task. "I am well."

He crooked his arm around her neck, pressing his lips to her forehead. "Very good, then. Way it should be, eh?" She heard the smile in his voice and hugged him.

"When's your time?" Waneta's gaze fixed on her low, round bump.

"March, we think."

"Same month you were born." She grinned. "Well, there is much joy in this news. Get us the brandywine, son."

They enjoyed a drink together on the wooden bench inside the wagon, sharing news of Catawba family, healthy harvests, and promising trading. She recounted stories about Harry, their friends, and working on the farm. To their surprise and delight, she practiced some of her Catawba words while they chatted. The warmth spreading between them had little to do with the wine.

"I will come to your house soon. I should see this fine life for myself." Elan winked at her, lips turned up at the edges.

"I'd like that."

Elan escorted her back to the mercantile, where she met Mary and Tom for the ride home. She waved goodbye to her cousin, and he disappeared into the flurry of people in the marketplace.

****

Shortly after they arrived back at Redmond Hill, with the wind rustling over her shoulders, Olivia found it difficult to concentrate. Harry followed her directions, remaining still while she worked. The steady thumping of Caddie's tail stirred up the dirt in the yard. Polly squatted beside him like a frog, knees sticking up from underneath her skirt, fingers hidden inside the dog's furry coat.

"The missus cut my hair last week, Cap'n. See how nice she done it?" Polly asked.

"Did it," Harry corrected kindly.

"Yessir." She nodded, scratching her knee. "See how nice she *did* it?"

He glanced up from his newspaper. "Yes, your bouncy blonde curls are the envy."

Olivia glanced down at the girl's scrunched up nose and translated. "He means everybody wishes they had your pretty curly hair." She gave her a wink. "Now, tell the captain, 'Thank you for the compliment, sir.' "

Olivia placed her hands on Harry's shoulders and nudged him. He looked up and into her communicative eyes, laying the paper on his lap.

"Thank you for the cuplemit, Cap'n, sir." Polly flashed him a sunny smile.

He met the child's precocious gaze. "You're welcome, lass."

"Now, will you please go tell Miss Mary I'll be in soon to help with supper?" Olivia waited for the girl's nod, then watched her dart off toward the house, the hound in playful pursuit.

Harry reached over and touched her hand. "I'd be most happy with a little lassie like that one."

Olivia bent and kissed the top of his head. "She would steal your heart. And what if it's a boy?" As she resumed combing his hair, she imagined his smile was stretching even wider.

"A lad—he ought to come with a special warning like, 'Beware, I want to ride my horse too fast, play all day in the dirt, traipse through creeks…and make presents of frogs and lizards to the women I love.' "

She stopped cutting, mouth agape. "You didn't."

"I did. Even Brandt too, sometimes. You can ask Mary," he said, laughing. "I remember once—when I was very small—I put a frog underneath my Granny Red's butter churn. Christ, I got the switch that day."

"Please stop," she said, giggling. "I want to finish

your hair before dark."

"Oh, sorry." He leveled his shoulders, holding his head steady again while she alternated combing and snipping. "She was a kind, sturdy Irish woman. Grandfather was a Scot, of course."

"Mm…and I suppose she had red hair?"

"Oh, no. Her maiden name was Redmond—so we called her Granny Red."

"Ah…your grandfather must have loved her very much. Redmond Hill's quite a legacy." She ran her fingers from his scalp to the tip ends of his hair, crouching down to see if both sides were even. "You share the same last name, but how are you related to Brandt?"

"Our grandfathers were brothers, our fathers were cousins, and we're whatever cousins come next. I'm also kin to the Cantey family on Father's side and the Rosses on Mother's."

She stopped cutting. "How far back can you trace your family?"

"About six generations, give or take." He opened the newspaper again and held it level with his eyes.

Remarkable. She rubbed her stomach, comforted their child would have Harry's lineage.

"Are you about done?" He brushed her thigh with his knee.

"Hold still now—one…more second." She lowered her gaze, judging her handiwork. Satisfied, she stood back and held up the hand mirror. "What do you think?"

Harry quirked his brow, turning his head back and forth. "Not one nick, and no snip gone awry. I'm impressed. Can it be you're as skilled with scissors as you are a needle?"

She snipped the scissors in the air. "It's a brave man who teases a woman while the clippers are still in her hand." Air latent with his smell of soap and sandalwood tickled her nose. Harry nudged his knee against her thigh again.

"Oh, I'm brave all right. I'm married to a scrapper, you know."

The gleam in his eye sent a warm shiver up her spine. She set the clippers and comb on the stool and took her place on his lap. With her head tucked underneath his chin, her fingers found his chest, and his wandered to her belly. *Safe and comforted in his arms is all I want for the rest of my days.*

Chapter Sixteen

November 1783

Olivia welcomed autumn's telltale chill when the air became lighter and thinner, having squeezed out all the moisture from summer. Days grew short. Brilliant red maples dotted the landscape, branches heavy with foliage transformed into a palette of crimson, orange, and gold. Chipmunks foraged for odd bits of pecan shells and twigs for nesting. The hedgehog skimmed the forest floor, consuming every morsel of fruit and nut it could find, bulking up its layer of fat for the winter ahead. In the quiet pre-dawn, one could hear the flight calls of thrushes and wood warblers as they passed over the Wateree. It was the season of mellow fruitiness where titian gourds and pumpkins hid beneath a carpet of prickly leaves, and apples in shades of vermilion hung from branches, ready for picking and pressing into cider and jam.

Olivia had kept her cloak draped around her shoulders all day. She usually enjoyed being out in the frosty air making house calls with Mr. Blake, but she found it unsettling today, unable to keep warm. While riding Mena back to Redmond Hill, sweat beads popped up on her brow, yet her ears and fingers were cold. Marcus greeted her at the stable, and she handed him the reins before turning toward the house. Then her breathing came uneven. She pinched the bridge of her nose, head down, as she climbed the front steps. *I think...Oh, Lord, I'm...* As a hazy blur filled her head, her knees buckled.

****

With the thud of footsteps outside the bedroom door, Mary jumped to her feet.

Harry stormed into the room. "What happened?"

"Don't know, Cap'n. Marcus saw her fall and carried her in." Mary clutched a handkerchief in her hand.

"Where's Nigel?"

"On his way, sir."

He pressed his lips to her hot, damp forehead. "Liv. Olivia...can you hear me?"

She moaned and pressed her hand to her temple. "My head...hurts." Mary covered her brow with a fresh cloth, casting a grim look at Harry.

"Shh, Scrapper..." He edged in beside her, stroking her cheek.

Her thin lips managed a smile. "Will you stay with me a while?"

"I'm not going anywhere."

Olivia fell back to sleep, her breath airy and shallow. Like trying to row a boat with no oars, Harry drifted, smoothing damp hair from her forehead one minute to caressing her tummy the next. *Sit tight, wee one. I'm going to take care of you both.*

Soon Nigel swung the bedroom door open and rushed to her side, checking her pulse, heart, and breathing. He probed around her head and lifted her hair to inspect her shoulders and back. He touched her forehead and then pressed his fingertips over the swollen glands in her neck. After unfastening the hook of her blouse and raising both arms, he froze. "There it is. Look at the little bugger."

Harry peered over his shoulder and spotted it—a fat, purplish tick anchored behind her left armpit.

"And there's a rash all down her side." Nigel pointed, then reached for tweezers, grease, and alcohol. "He's not too big, thank goodness." His able fingers took over, lubricating and then removing the tainted mite, depositing it in a jar, and tightening the lid. He cleaned the area with alcohol and covered it with a clean bandage, calling over his shoulder, "We need fresh tepid water, Mary—as much as you can get your hands on."

Mary dashed out of the bedroom, and Harry watched Nigel yank off his spectacles and press the heel of his hand to his temple. Though it had been more than a decade since he had lost his mother, the memories threatened. *Not again. Not Olivia.*

Nigel reached out and touched his arm, grounding him. "We need to get her fever down, son. Gather up some towels—and sheets and a few more blankets too—and bring them to me. Go on now."

Minutes stretched into hours with Harry at Olivia's bedside, helping her sip water when she awakened with pangs of thirst. Nigel stayed the first night and into the next morning, until Harry pushed him out the door, accepting his promise to return by dark.

Despite Harry's vigilant routine of tepid wet cloths pressed to her body, Olivia's fever continued into a second and then third day. He held her hand, stroking her palms, whispering indiscernible words as he marked the rise and fall of her chest with bleary eyes.

Mary slipped inside the bedroom and placed a bowl

of chicken and vegetable stew on the nightstand, the aroma wafting near his nose. "Please eat, Cap'n. It's nigh on supper time. You're doin' her no good starvin' yourself." She plunged her fists deep in her apron pockets. "Neighbors brought the stew and cornbread. There's ham and a cobbler, too. Good Christians all..."

Harry sighed and gazed at the woman, her knitted brow always his undoing. *Damnation.* He grabbed the bowl and swallowed a big spoonful, wiping a dribble from his chin with his thumb.

She beamed, patting his shoulder. "I'll be back in a jiffy, sir."

He made quick business of the stew, sopping up the remnants of broth with the savory bread. He poured a finger of whiskey and gulped down the liquid heat, thinking it much akin to Olivia's skin. The door creaked open, and he spoke over his shoulder. "You were right, Mary. The stew was—"

"Harry...?"

He closed his eyes. *No. Please not her. Not now.* There was no need to turn around. "Why have you come, Cee?"

"I-I brought food. I'd like to help."

"A good Christian...of course." He pinched his fingers on the bridge of his nose.

She crossed the room and stopped at the foot of the bed. "You must remember Olivia's strong and healthy. She's a fighter. We've got to be patient and give her time to heal. I'm sure Nigel has—"

"Look, I know you're trying to help, but will you just stop? Please...? To the devil with Nigel—with all of this." Harry pounded his fist on the night table, and the lantern rattled. "Damn it, she just lies here. Sometimes she cries out, but I can't help her. She drinks water, but she won't eat. And the fever doesn't stop."

Catherine placed her palm on her hip. "When's the last time you slept?"

He stiffened, shaking his head.

"Now you listen to me, Harry Fleming. You need rest to keep up your strength. Let me sit with her for a while."

"No. I'm not leaving them." He glared at the flush of understanding rising in Catherine's cheeks.

Her gaze faltered, and her fingers fluttered over her silken kerchief. "Of course. I-I didn't know. Perhaps I'll be of more use at prayer. I'll light a candle for them both this evening." She cleared her throat with a light cough. "And think about getting some rest. If not for your own sake, then Olivia's."

He whipped around in his chair, eyes imploring. "Cee? Please pray for her and the baby. Pray hard. Pray God doesn't take away the one person who loves me."

She closed the steps between them, turned him around in his chair, and placed her palms on his shoulders. He softened, selfishly soaking up the comfort until after some long, agonizing moments, she made her way to the door. When it clicked shut, he groped under the quilt for Olivia's hand and steeled his resolve for yet another night of relentless fever.

****

Bacon crackled in the iron skillet, the salty aroma blending with the scent of sweet molasses and biscuits, signaling the dawn of a new day. Olivia's nose twitched with the familiar smell. Papa loved bacon. She breathed again, and with it came an image of him leaning over an open fire. She blinked heavy eyelids, slowly at first, until she could open them, soaking up her surroundings like water to parched roots. *Wait…Papa's gone…but Harry?*

She sighed, warmed by the comforting weight of Harry's arm sprawled across her middle and raising it gently, rubbed her palms over her noisy stomach. It moved again, only not from hunger this time, but a kind of fluttering deep inside. She had noticed it a few times recently, and she kissed her fingers, pressing them on her belly, sending her little one some love.

She eased onto her side, a trifle stiff and achy, but desperate to see her husband. Sprawled out on his stomach, she smiled at the half of his face she could see. She observed his sleep, eyelids fluttering, breathing uneven and labored. Never able to be close to him without touching, she let her fingers travel from his brow, past his closed eyes, to linger on a dense growth of facial hair.

Harry awoke with a jolt, rising on his elbows, blinking at the sunlight illuminating the room. Amid a deep sigh, he stopped stone cold, jerked his head around, and gazed at her. He placed the back of his hand to her forehead and neck and then found the pulse in her wrist. He tilted his head toward the ceiling, a smile of half joy, half relief etched across his weary face.

"You scared the hell out of me, Scrapper. Don't ever do that again."

"I-I won't." Olivia rubbed her fingers over his jawline. "Didn't know you fancied beards."

"It's what happens when you don't shave for—I don't know, some five days." He hid a smirk behind her knuckles, holding them against his lips while he kissed them repeatedly. "How do you feel?"

"Like Mena stomped her hooves all over my head.

But otherwise, I'm fine. What happened?"

"A tick. Thank God you reacted to it so quickly, before it got too big. You had a raging fever and—" He stopped, peering over her shoulder and down her back. "Good. It looks like the rash has faded."

"A rash …? Oh, good Lord." She sighed, rubbing her temples, and caught sight of Caddie sprawled on top of their bedcovers. "Well, hello, boy—and what are you doing up here? Your papa won't like this." She cast Harry a tentative glance.

"I was actually grateful for the companionship. Too many dark, lonely hours. I was afraid for what might happen to you…if the fever didn't break." He rubbed the hound's furry neck, an unmistakable grin appearing on his floppy pink-brown lips. "We never left your side, Liv."

A knot gathered in her throat, and she blinked away the tears lurking behind her lashes. "I knew you were with me…and the baby. I didn't want to let go."

Harry corralled her in his arms, hugging her with a force that nearly had her gasping. Light-headed from hunger—and the notion he had feared for her life—she snuggled deeper in his embrace. Only when her stomach growled did he pull back, kissing her cheek and the top of her tummy before darting off to get them some breakfast. When he returned, in between small bites of porridge and sips of water, he told her the tale of the past three excruciating days.

Chapter Seventeen

Harry followed Nigel's instructions and kept Olivia under his close watch for the next few weeks. She milled about the house, helping with meals and tending her herb garden, having promised him she would not exert herself. They spent quiet evenings together and finished *Robinson Crusoe*. He promised to read her Thomas Paine's *Common Sense* next, a book that had influenced his—and his father's—philosophy about colonial independence.

With the sun barely breaching the horizon, he awakened, tucked the quilt around Olivia, and eased out of bed. He made speedy preparations and within an hour, bounded out the door to see his best friend.

"Just in time." Harry removed his hat and claimed his seat at the corner table inside the alehouse.

Kitt gestured to the basket of warm biscuits and honey, licking a drop of the amber sweetness from his finger. "You're looking much better." He motioned to a serving girl to bring them coffee, then lowered his voice. "No offense, but you looked like hell last time I saw you."

"I was in hell." He cocked his head. "Which reminds me—I don't recollect thanking you and Sarah for the food you brought."

"It was the least we could do. From the looks of your kitchen, many folks had the same idea."

"Well, I'm humbled." Harry smiled his appreciation to the girl filling his mug with coffee.

He folded his arms on the table. "You were missed at the town meeting, but not forgotten."

"My place was with Olivia."

Kitt nodded, welcoming the two plates of eggs and meat to the table. "I believe Barlowe planted a seed in your absence—with the help of your cousin. They raised concerns about the discord with what remains of the Wateree. Most have joined in with the Catawba, but a couple of bands are still at odds with one another…and with us at times."

He gazed at him with narrow eyes. "And what does Reed suggest as a remedy?"

"It's more what Brandt proposed you might find peculiar—forming a local militia."

"Militia?" His voice was louder than he would have liked, and he lowered his shoulders. "What the hell does Brandt know of militia? He left that duty to those of us who could do the fighting."

"He thinks a show of unity will dissuade any rogue elements from rising up—trespassing on our lands and livelihoods."

"What did Zeb have to say?" He cocked his head with interest.

"He wasn't there."

Harry held up his fork, inspecting the bite before swallowing it. "Then my uncle was surely missed…but not forgotten."

"Brandt said his father was all in. Reed and his cronies supported the move too." Kitt wiped his mouth with a woven cloth before tossing it to the table.

"It's Zeb's plan, for God's sake. They wouldn't

make a move without him." He shook his head, his brow creased. "He's stirring the pot."

"Aye, and many Catawba fought with us. Promises were made—but you know how things go once the smoke settles."

Harry swallowed the last bite of his eggs, then folded his arms and leaned back in his chair. "You said I wasn't forgotten—any voices of dissent?"

"Mine, of course—and McClellan and Coxe voiced a strong no. Jimbo and Willie don't want any provocation either." Kitt polished off his coffee.

"That's good to hear. With any luck, this won't go any further—and pray they don't make any trouble with us first."

They lingered over their coffee, engaged in lively conversation, and sometime later stepped outside to the sound of the smithy's hammer and rattling wagons harkening the passage of the morning.

"Might I have a word?" Kitt rubbed his hand behind his neck. "Be careful. You're so damn open with your emotions, which may put you at a disadvantage this time. Reed's a shrewd bugger. He already has Brandt in his pocket with his high-stakes gambling. But make no mistake—Reed has fixed his aim on you. I can't figure out why, but be wary. Don't let him make his mark."

Harry mounted his horse and gave Kitt a nod. As he moved into an easy trot, his mind wandered back to a time when he and Brandt were not just family, but close friends. Though his cousin outranked him in education and social standing, Harry was clever and personable in his own right. *At least I don't hunger for a bet like Brandt does.*

But in truth, Harry had never been good at hiding his

emotions. *You're like an open Bible on Sunday morning, Mother always said.* He turned up his collar, then spurred his stallion to a canter, taking to the trails to clear his mind of troubling thoughts.

In time, Harry approached Redmond Hill and spied Tom with his head down, pacing in front of the paddock, chewing on a long stem of straw. Harry tossed the reins to Marcus, who scooted off without looking him in the eye. Harry took the porch steps two at a time and reaching the door, spotted a path of ruby-red blobs between the swing and his feet. He burst inside and found Silas hunched over in a chair sharpening his knife. He marched over to Mary who was fidgeting with her apron strings and bouncing her knee.

Mary met his gaze, sniffing. "The poor missus. She's so brave, sir."

Harry barged through the bedroom door, and Nigel looked up, his lips in a flat line. "I need a few more minutes."

"You will tell me—"

Nigel slid his spectacles down his nose. "Wait outside, and I will be there as soon as I can, son."

Harry withdrew from the bedroom, dropped into his chair at the kitchen table, and pointed. "Whiskey."

Mary obeyed, filling a glass, frowning when he finished it in a single gulp.

"Another."

She obliged again, exchanging a painful look with Silas who then returned to filing his blade.

Harry grabbed the bottle himself the third time, pouring yet another shot, the fiery liquid burning into his gut.

The wait was maddening.

He could bear a great deal of pain himself and had proved it in battle. But this—Olivia's pain and him powerless to stop it—wrenched his soul. *God in Heaven, keep her safe.* He pulled at his neckcloth, yanking it off and tossing it across the table. Mary leaned over and laid a plump freckled hand on his arm, squeezing it tight. He looked at her and, seeing that knitted brow once again, dropped his head into his hands.

The house remained silent for some time, save for Tom who had set to work with a bucket of water and soap to clean up the bloodstains on the wood planks. Silas no longer labored but sat in his chair by the fireplace. Mary folded towels, hands pressing creases in them with each turn of the fabric.

They gazed at Nigel when he emerged from the bedroom, sleeves rolled up the length of his arms, perspiration soaked through his shirt. He carried a covered basket in his hand.

Harry jumped to his feet, sending his chair crashing to the floor behind him. "How is she?"

"Lost a good bit of blood, but she'll be all right. I took care of everything. I gave her some laudanum to help her sleep." Nigel removed his spectacles, age lines fanning around his misty eyes. "The baby—he didn't make it, Harry. There was nothing anyone could've done. I'm sorry...so sorry."

Harry froze, his limbs numb. Out of the corner of his eye, he spotted Tom leaning on the doorframe, staring at the floor. His ears detected Mary's wretched sobs, her outburst tightening the knot coiled inside the pit of his stomach. *Our child—a boy—is gone. Sweet Jesus.* He remained quiet, a muscle flexing in his jaw.

"It's just God's way of taking care of these things,"

Nigel said, breaking through his thoughts.

"Was it the sickness, the fever?" Harry asked, his brow furrowed.

"We may never know for certain. Olivia's been through an ordeal, but she's young and healthy. Next time will be different." He placed the basket on the floor.

He corralled the storm raging inside. *Be strong, damn it. For Olivia's sake.* He squared his shoulders and heaved a heart-wrenching sigh. "I can't think about that now. I must bury our child."

"I'll help, sir." Tom stood ready by the door.

Relief flooded him when Nigel offered to stay with Olivia.

"And ye don't need to ask me, Cap'n. I'll be right by her side." Mary wiped her eyes with the frayed edge of her apron, then patted his arm and disappeared into the bedroom. Silas moved to stoke the fire, adding a few fresh logs, then grabbed another shovel and took off out the door behind Tom.

Alone in the room, Harry's thoughts drifted like dandelion seeds in a blustery wind. A prickle of dread passed though him before he released his breath and, without looking back, took hold of the precious basket and followed the men up the hill to his family's cemetery.

Chapter Eighteen

The Lord is nigh unto them that are of a broken heart; and saveth such as be of a contrite spirit. Psalm 34:18 KJV

Olivia's features clouded with the passage of each day, no loss or sorrow too great to suspend time. The first sad days turned into sad weeks, but life at Redmond Hill moved on even if hers seemed chained to that dark day of loss. From the porch steps, she would stare on while Harry oversaw the repairs to the barn roof, and Mary, with little Polly straggling behind, tended to the sage and thyme recently planted in the herb garden and two hives of honeybees. When sitting idly on the front porch swing, her gaze would follow Tom and Marcus while they seeded the fall cabbage and turnips in the lower field, and Silas as he tended the livestock.

One evening, the screech of the barn owl lifting through the air, she walked over to the window in the study. She peered out, seeing naught but Harry, slinging the ax over his head, slicing it through the birch wood. Even at dusk, she could make out the lines of his muscles, his shirt clinging to his skin from exertion. Fog etched on the windowpane foreshadowed a chilly night ahead, and she wiped it clear.

"Harry should put on a dry tunic if he's going to labor on," Olivia mumbled to the empty room. She retired to her chair by the hearth, flanked by her hound, and resumed her stitching of a torn sleeve. She drew in a shuddering breath to stave off the ever-present lump lurking in the back of her throat.

Within the hour, Harry stepped inside, crossed the room, and poured a large glass of water. He downed it handily, then refilled it. His gaze turned her skin to gooseflesh, and she bowed her head to focus on the needle in her hand. He finished his drink and with a shake of his head, disappeared into the bedroom. He reemerged a short time later in a fresh tunic, wiping his neck and brow with a clean towel.

"Damn." Olivia pressed her middle finger to her lips but not in time to stop several drops of blood from landing on her skirt. She dropped her sewing on the floor.

Harry frowned and offered her a cloth. "Here— don't soil your dress."

She snatched it from his hand, winding it around the puncture wound. *I've never been good at this—or anything else womanly*. She stood and gazed down at the droplets that had spread wider, leaving a garish stain on the cotton material drooping in loose folds over her middle.

"This is the second dress I've ruined in two weeks. Doesn't matter—it's too big for me now. Shouldn't even be wearing it." Her tone matched the hard mask she wore to disguise her sadness.

With one swift stride, Harry rushed in behind her, encircling her with his arms, resting his chin on her shoulder. "Stop this, will you? Please…?"

Her shoulders sagged, and her breath caught in her throat, hiccupping. "I can't. I-I can't do anything right."

"That's not true. Talk to me, Liv."

"It is true. Bearing children is the one thing a woman should be able to do. And I-I've failed."

"You're hurt, and your heart's broken. You'll feel different about it in time." He smoothed a strand of hair behind her ear and kissed it tenderly.

"Will I?" Olivia jerked away, head cocked. "Will you...?" She pressed her palms over her stomach. "Our baby was growing inside me. He fluttered around—even burped once." Her voice cut razor sharp. "I was a whole woman."

"You still are."

"No. No, no." She shook her head, hands curled at her sides. "I've a hollow hole in me. I'm empty—like that old tree by the creek."

He corralled her in his arms. "The tree's alive, Olivia, and you know it."

I know nothing except I wasn't able to keep our baby alive. She twisted against him, and he tightened his hold. A cry started in her stomach, wrenching inside her, until it sprang forth in jagged gasps. Caddie jumped up on all fours, the hair of his brindle coat rising with her sobs. She drove her fists into Harry's chest, over and over again, and when the ache in her arms matched the one in her heart, she slumped forward and buried her face in his chest, weeping. With her head tucked under his chin, he rubbed his hands over her back and shoulders, whispering soothing words against her hair.

In time, the tears slowed, and she regained her voice. "Oh, Harry. Perhaps you're right. Maybe the oak lives on—but not rightly so."

"Are you questioning God now? He just took away the part of the tree that wasn't healthy, so it might live on." He lifted her chin and gazed into her eyes. "You've the strongest faith and purest heart of anyone I've ever known. You must—nay, we both must accept God's hand in this."

She pressed her cheek to his chest again, holding her breath for some agonizing seconds, his words resonating in her mind. "But my heart—it aches so much. And what if there's never another baby? If I can't—"

"I don't believe that...and you shouldn't either." Harry pressed a kiss to her head. "I've never told you this, but my parents lost a child—my sister Drew. She came between Josie and me." She glimpsed his throat, his Adam's apple rising as he swallowed hard. "They said she had a headful of golden hair—just like Mother—but she was born early, and her lungs were small. She passed the following month, buried in our cemetery. Life goes on, Liv. My parents had me the following year, and we had a good life, even if it was short. We will have children. I believe it, and so must you."

She hugged him close, soaking up his strength. "Will you maybe take me tomorrow to the live oak tree? And to his grave?"

"Aye."

"We should give him a name. I was thinking Gabriel, like the angel."

"That's perfect. I'll have Silas get to work on a marker straight away." Harry rocked her in his arms.

"And would you maybe...?" She shifted, gazing at him with bedroom eyes.

"Aye...I've been missing you," he said wistfully. "But are you sure you're well enough?"

She brushed her lips over his, parting them for him. His response was tender, his hands sliding to the small of her back, fitting her to his body. Passion stirred between them, and he lifted her in his arms, kicking open the bedroom door and placing her amongst the bedclothes.

Harry undressed her by golden candlelight, but she refused to dwell on the loose-fitting dress he had cast to the floor. *He's got the right of it. Perhaps God will bless us again. Maybe even tonight...* She released a breathy sigh as he shed his clothes, and when they were fused together, skin against skin, she cared only for him. For the way he grounded her in his strength, for how the curve of his smile made her knees weak, for the way he caressed her in both body and soul. When he settled over her, his eyes shaded in the muted light, she gave herself to him completely.

Chapter Nineteen

December 1783

Harry spent the month preparing the farm for the onset of winter. Silas and Marcus slaughtered the hogs, smoking and salting the meat to preserve it. He and Tom oversaw the livestock, caring for newborns and purchasing another milk cow to go along with Fannie. Mary schooled Olivia, along with the other women of Redmond Hill, in the elaborate processes of stocking the cellar and pantry for the harsh days to come. Pumpkins harvested in recent months were stored, ready to become pies or soup. Apples were treated similarly, with some mixed with butter and even more into sauce and jam. Oats and grain were bagged and stored, and peppermint and spearmint were dried for seasonings and remedies. He greeted each morning with his wife by his side, finding purpose in the home they were strengthening together.

One evening after supper, Harry reclined on the sofa, flipping through the pages of *The Gazette*, his brandy still half-full. He peered over his newspaper, gazing at Olivia as she stuffed the table linens in the cupboard, plunked down in the rocker, and propped her heels on the footstool. She closed her eyes, resting her head on the back of the chair, then snapped her fingers to gain Caddie's attention. The hound scooted closer, and she ran her fingers through his dense coat.

Harry chucked the paper and took a long drink, swirling it around. "Might I have a bit of that?"

"Hm, perhaps later." A smile played on Olivia's mouth.

"That's good to hear...because I saw Brandt in town today. Asked me to join him this evening. Appears he has a new gamecock in the ring."

She opened her eyes. "Wants to drag you neck-high into that sinful thing he calls a sport."

"He'll not suck me into it. He just wants my backing, I think. Maybe it's his way of trying to reconnect with me. I don't know, Scrapper—men are foolish." He moved to the floor and, sitting across from her, placed her foot in his hands. He massaged her arch with his thumbs, pressing into the firm flesh.

"Lord, that's heavenly. Mm...if you're trying to soften me up for your little night out, I think it's working."

He chuckled and went to work on her other foot.

She sighed, eyelids fluttering closed again. "Well, Brandt might consider reconnecting with his wife. It will be her time again soon. Bringing a child into the world is no easy business."

His shoulders stiffened at her declaration, finding it near impossible to imagine Catherine laboring through childbirth. *She hated even the slightest bit of perspiration on her brow. Is her constitution up to the task a second time?*

He rolled his neck to shake off the disquieting thoughts. "Which is why God entrusts womankind with the task. He's given her the strength for it."

"Not all womankind." She opened one eye, and his

fingers stilled.

"Your courses…?"

She nodded. "This morning."

Harry held out his hand, and she accepted it, crawling onto his lap and into the curve of his arm. "Aye, this is disappointing news, but not the end of the world. Besides, the cycle begins anew each month, and therein lies the hope…the possibility…and don't forget the pleasure we can give each other."

She wiggled up, meeting his gaze with consternation. "How can you speak so?"

"Because you're my wife. And I want to make love to you every day—multiple times whenever possible." He kissed her nose. "Every week of every year." He pecked her chin and then skipped to her soft earlobe, nipping it with his teeth. "Even when we are wrinkled and hunched over, surrounded by a herd of our children and grandchildren, I'll still want you."

"You're quite convincing." She pressed an open-mouthed kiss in the hollow at the base of his throat. "Ah, but you must go out tonight…so it will have to be much later."

"Keep our bed warm," he said against the curl of her ear.

"Pray take care, will you? Brandt seems in need of you, which might not be a good—" She halted with the rapping at the door, and Caddie jerked up.

"It's Tom. I'm taking him along for good measure." He winked, helping them both to stand. "Rest easy, Scrapper." He kissed the soft skin between her knuckles. "And Caddie—watch over your mistress until I return."

He gulped down the last of his brandy and met Tom at the door. Hat in hand, he blew his wife a kiss of promise and shut the door behind him.

****

The carriage moved along at a steady clip despite the drizzling rain. Inside, sitting on the bench across from his cousin, Harry scoffed at his misplaced optimism this outing might reunite them. He feared too much had passed between them to ever bring them back to normalcy.

Brandt rested his arm on the window frame, legs crossed, drawing on the cheroot he held between curled lips. "Your fellow Tom seems smart enough—most attentive."

"He's a good man." Harry sat up straight, feet planted on the floor.

"Glad you could join me for the entertainment tonight. We've spent little time together since you got home."

He shrugged, settling his coat down over his shoulders. "We're hardly boys. We've both got responsibilities now."

Brandt scowled, brushing a bit of fuzz from his sleeve before fixing his gaze back on him. "It's time we clear the air. You do remember I was in love with Margaret—set to marry her?"

"That's rather beside the point."

"Not really. My love for her lingers, as does yours for Catherine." He inhaled and released the smoke slowly. "Granted, it must cut a little deeper for you, seeing Catherine at family gatherings and such."

"It slices my heart in half." He muttered several expletives against his fist. "What the devil are you fishing for?"

Brandt leaned forward, elbows on his knees. "A

truce. You're my cousin, and I don't like being at odds with you."

"You should've thought of that before you married the woman I loved."

"We both were cheated, Harry. Me by God, and you by Zeb. We were powerless to control it."

"But why? Why does he hate me so much?"

His eyes simmered a jaded green. "He was in love with your mother—to my own mother's detriment." He fell back on the seat, crossing his arms and drawing on his cheroot. "But there's got to be more to it, after all he adores your sister."

"She's the image of Mother, and of course, I'm the 'spit of my father.' " His words dripped with venom.

A single line formed on Brandt's brow. "Zeb's a complicated, calculating force. He gets what he wants, and at the time, I didn't have the will to refuse him. I may not be in love with Catherine, but I care for her very much. I see to it she has everything she desires." He toyed with a silver button on his vest, rubbing his thumb back and forth over the smooth finish. "You know what I mean. You've done the same thing with your wife."

He swallowed hard and cranked open the carriage window, letting the damp frigid air wash over his face.

Brandt reached out and cuffed his knee. "Enough with this foul talk. Say, do you remember when we were kids, and you'd be my ears? You'd punch the first clod who teased me without my knowledge."

"Jesus, what's your point?"

"May I be your ears for once?" Brandt rubbed his knuckles under his chin. "People are talking—about you and your wife. Everyone thinks you married Olivia because you got her with child. I mean, a Fleming doesn't just up and marry some stray Catawba."

Harry simmered, hands balling into fists beside his thighs.

"And your farm hands—you consort with them like they're your friends. Even this simpleton Tom is too close to you. And this appeasement you favor with the Catawba—you're acting a fool."

"Again...your point?"

"You're throwing away your good name and potential to prosper. You've a place in the order of life here if you would stop long enough to see it." Brandt tapped the heel of his boot on the floor. "We don't have to make the same mistakes our fathers did—to let a woman come between us."

"My mother had a choice, and it wasn't Zeb. Catherine had none."

"That's where you're wrong. Catherine chose duty...and took me for her husband." Brandt crossed his arms over his chest. "Respectfully, with the miscarriage, let Zeb take the legal steps to end this marriage—seeing to it your wife's needs are met. Olivia is a kind, skilled young woman, but she's a mixed breed. Marry a suitable young woman, partner with Zeb and me—with Reed— to grow and protect your assets. Put the past behind you and make a smart future for yourself." He eased back in the coach seat, hands folded.

Harry snorted, something between a cough and a chuckle, and glared into his cousin's eyes. "All right, Brandt—now it's my turn. Word is you're a bit off your mark—that you've become sloppy with so much focus on your...shall we say 'pastimes'? Your lust in the gambling ring is fodder for the gossips. Some think your mind is becoming dull from these expensive and addictive pursuits." He rubbed his palms together surreptitiously. "So…while I appreciate the consideration you've given to my marital and financial conditions, might I urge you to mind your own?"

Their gazes met in a silent duel. After the carriage lurched to a stop, they emerged, coat collars raised and hats on, hoofing through puddles toward the old barn.

****

A line of black crows roosted in the rafters of the tobacco barn. It was not a grand building, but with its sturdy log construction and central fireplace and flue for curing the leaves, it functioned well. On game nights, they exchanged old wooden slats and drying racks for rope lines and stools, arranged in a circle for betting. The cock-fighting ring was win or lose, live or die, leaving room for little else.

While Tom was out scouting the premises, Harry leaned against a wooden post not far from a makeshift bar. Six iron lanterns hung from black hooks on the walls, their glow diffusing through the smoky haze of cigars. The air reeked of whiskey and ale. The hum in the barn, infused with cawing and crowing, hollering and snorting, bespoke the stakes of the evening.

A short time later, Harry spotted Tom cutting the corner and walking toward a young woman pouring drinks. Harry crossed his arms and fixed his gaze on her. Hair as coarse and lush as a horse's mane framed a bronze, heart-shaped face with cinnamon eyes. She had lithe arms and legs, moving through the tight space with purposeful motion.

The woman filled his cup, and Tom rubbed his hand over the brim of his hat, leaning close to whisper in her ear. The woman stilled and shook her head. Then she bit her lip and grinned, and Tom nodded his head like a damn woodpecker. *Holy hell.*

Harry uncrossed his arms, and when Tom turned around, hands stuffed in his coat pockets, their gazes met. Harry waved him forward, and Tom crossed the space between them.

"So...have you learned anything about the bets for tonight?" Harry asked.

Tom scratched his cheek. "Yessir, there's about two dozen men here—lots of fine horses and carriages. Bets passin' round quicker than a jug of moonshine."

"The stakes?" Harry arched his brow.

"High—and not just for money. There's papers with fancy writin'."

"Who's got birds in the fight?"

"Outside of your cousin, just two others I heard of." Tom paused, flicking his head. "Pudgy fellow by the bar with the oily black hair—missin' a tooth, he is—goes by name of Knox. And then a man named Ramsey."

"Any new gamecocks in the ring?"

"Aye, sir. I heard of one—they call him Kratos."

"Did you get a look at him?"

"No, sir. That Knox fellow is keepin' him hid." Tom's gaze strayed to the young woman.

Harry gave him a nod. "Good to know. Stay on your toes now."

"Yessir."

"And you best stop gawking at that girl." He shifted his gaze toward the comely serving girl. "You ken she belongs to Reed Barlowe, right?"

"Yessir." Tom bobbed his head, then licked his fingers to smooth back the hair around his ears.

"Why don't you take another walk around the place

before things get started?"

Tom repositioned his hat and took off toward the door.

In need of escape from the rowdy crowd, Harry stepped outdoors and welcomed the frigid blast on his face. His breath made swirls in the air, and he propped his boot on the fence rail and whipped out his pocket watch.

"Got somewhere better to be?" Brandt rambled over, claiming a spot beside him.

Harry flicked a brow. "Actually, I do. When the hell does this thing get started?"

"Relax. It won't be long now." The fence railing creaked under the weight of his arms. "Hey, see that moon?" He lifted his gaze. "It's a waxing crescent moon—means it's growing. Spiritually it means a new beginning—a commitment to intentions."

Harry fixed his gaze on the white sliver perched high in the cloudless sky. "The moon controls the tides…it's akin to a woman's cycle…but destiny? Are you a celestial philosopher now?" Impatience colored his voice.

"Maybe I am. There's wisdom in the heavens." Brandt rolled his empty whiskey glass between both hands. "My bird's been unbeaten for months. Eli's got him trained right. I think maybe my luck is changing."

"You've been spending too much time behind your telescope. Quit contemplating the stars."

"The moon's not a star."

Harry smirked. "You know what I mean. You're already damn lucky. Keep pressing and you'll be fortune's fool." He cupped his hands over his mouth, blowing his warm breath in them.

"You've seen him. Bandit's a devil in the pit."

"Devil or no, he's only as good as the next bird he fights. Just thinking about odds, that's all."

Brandt cocked his head. "Did you place any bets?"

"I've got some coin on your bird. Enough to make it interesting."

"Good. Conservative, but good." Brandt shrugged deeper in his coat. "Now thanks to you, my arse is frozen. Let's get inside."

A short time later, amidst hoots and jeers of eager gamblers, the gamecocks battled in the ring. The bout was decisive, a tactical assault of muscle, beaks, and claws. The one called Kratos, like his namesake from Greek mythology, was sheer brute strength and power. Harry had never seen such a menacing fowl. He matched Bandit in height but outdid him in the circumference of his chest. Besides boasting a torso of slick jet feathers, he had a broad neck surrounded by a spiked saffron fringe.

At first taunting, his cerise beak clamped down on Bandit's shoulder like the jaws of a snapping turtle. They went airborne several times, igniting raucous cheers from the half-drunk crowd. Then the cocker Eli got down on all fours, goading his bird while he pricked his opponent's left wing with sharp brass spurs. Harry spied Brandt gazing at the combatants with crocodile eyes, his body stone-still save for the occasional upward thrust of his right fist, in unison with Bandit's lunges.

The fatal blow came from a swift spur at Kratos' neck, leveled amidst violent squawking and hammering wings. Blood soaked his brilliant golden neckline, then he convulsed, falling limp to the ground. A collective moan rippled across the room, a show of respect for the valiant winged gladiator. Eli scooped up his victorious bird, praising and cooing him, and flashed his master a buck-toothed grin.

Brandt pulled out a fresh cigar, lighting it, smacking it between his lips. He slapped Harry on the back, emerald eyes dancing. "Do you believe me now? The moon knows."

Part Three

A Kind Heart

Chapter Twenty

Air heavy with anticipation—*or perhaps dread*—met Harry on the doorsteps at Glen Laurel. On Christmas Day, they always gathered to celebrate with family and friends. The war had taken its toll, and at those times, bereft of money, security, and loved ones, people honored Christ's birth as best they could. Harry spent the last four with his company, ensconced in the rugged hills of the Carolinas, at times bitterly hungry and cold. He shivered, half-wondering if he would not prefer another Christmas freezing in snow to one steaming in deception.

Despite the rift between their families, Harry wanted the day to soothe the sadness still lingering in Olivia's heart. She stood beside him, neck long and graceful with her hair pulled back in two ribbon-threaded combs, and he helped her out of her woolen cloak. Her pale blue linen gown, free from the fussy finery some women adored, hugged her lines and curves perfectly. With her hand snug in the crook of his arm, he reaffirmed his duty they come away from their first Fleming Christmas together unscathed.

Boughs of green pine and red-berried holly graced the entryway, and a wreath of mistletoe hung at the entrance to the great hall. Cinnamon, orange, and pecan aromas permeated the air, which was warm and dry from the abundance of logs burning in the fireplace. A pair of Orange Belton English Setters sat by the enormous fireplace, surveying the myriad of guests. The spirited tune of the fiddle, mixed with stomping and clapping, flowed through the house. When the mistress of Glen Laurel turned toward them, she revealed a large belly.

"Harry, Olivia—Merry Christmas. We're so glad you're here." Catherine extended her hand for his kiss, then turned to Olivia. "Please forgive my waddle." She smoothed her hands down the front of her dress and over her mound.

"You're as graceful as ever, Cee. The babe is clearly at one with you." Harry instantly regretted his sentiment. He watched his wife's gaze fix on Catherine's rosy cheeks and motherly stance.

"What's this about graceful and my wife? Daresay those two words don't belong in the same breath." Brandt chuckled, then recovered under Catherine's glare. "But then, who said anything about childbearing being graceful, my dear? Any woman would be just as awkward were she in your condition."

Catherine stiffened, fidgeting with the white lace on her sleeve. As the dinner bell chimed, she pinched her lips in a bow.

"May I?" Brandt offered Olivia his arm, and she fell in step with him. Harry placed Catherine's hand in his and gave it a reassuring squeeze.

The oak dining table stretched the length of the room, at least a dozen chairs circling it, with two large candelabras down the center. Platters of beef royal, braised lamb, and salt-cured ham were the stars of the feast, flanked by hefty platefuls of steamed oysters, poached fish, and smoked venison, and bowls of carrot puffs and stewed squash. Jars of brandied peaches, dates, and stuffed mince pies rounded out the fare, alongside an abundant array of whiskey, rum, and port. After Zeb blessed the food, merriment erupted, everyone eating, drinking, and talking all at once.

"Harry, what plans have you for spring planting?" Zeb chewed, waving his fork with each word.

"Much as I can afford. We'll have all our fields ready for seeding this season."

"Fertile soil is a must. This new year will mark another milestone for Glen Laurel—in harvests of many kinds." He grinned at his daughter-in-law. "A toast to my wee grandchild due next month."

Zeb raised his glass, and others echoed their good wishes. Catherine bowed her head and smoothed back the soft tendril beside her cheek, trembling fingers toying with the curl.

Fertile soil? You insensitive brute. Harry tossed back his port to mask his resentment, gazing at Catherine's profile, the delicate curves of her nose and chin drawing him in. As she turned her head, he detected her airy scent of gardenia. Memories of his fingers gliding through her silky tresses, her soft mouth submitting to his, assailed him. After some moments— how many, he was unsure—he blinked, breaking the spell, woefully unprepared for Olivia's watchful gaze. *Damnation.* He managed a feeble smile for her, feeling as poached as the trout eyeballing him from his plate. Then signaling to the steward for a refill of wine, he recovered and immersed himself in the mundane conversation around him.

****

Glen Laurel was bustling in full Christmas regalia, still thrumming with music and dancing after the lavish meal. The entertainment extended outdoors under the luminous midday sun, grounds fit with tables for card games, lanes for horseshoes, and a circular pit for cockfighting behind the barn. Children ran about playing tag and leapfrog, filling the air with squeals and giggles, safe under the watchful eyes of their mothers. Meanwhile, a throng of men kept vigil over a couple of slow-roasting hogs on the spit over an amber fire.

Alone on the veranda, Olivia found a respite, lifting her chin, letting the arid breeze blow her hair away from her face and behind her shoulders. It was brisk and refreshing, carrying with it the aroma of succulent pork and charred fat. Gazing at half the town scattered across the endless lawn, she figured there were more here than in the pews on Sunday morning.

Catherine appeared beside her, hands bracing the iron railing. "Quite the show, isn't it?"

"A Christmas for everyone." Olivia formed a brittle smile. "I'd no idea any of this existed."

She masked her surprise when Catherine locked arms with her, leading them down a series of steps onto a granite stone patio. They strolled past the merriment, past the long barn and cockpit, then behind a string of broad cedar trees. A mere quarter mile away from the big house was a reciprocal scene. When she peered through a patch of sparse cedar fronds, she saw families with skin tones ranging from wheat to ebony, frolicking to merry tunes from a fiddle and a makeshift drum. Men and women danced in a big circle while children skipped along, shaking small bells in a matching rhythm. Those not dancing were leaning over iron kettles or minding pigs cooking over a mound of hot coals.

"You're right. Christmas is for everyone around here." Catherine nodded once, eyes bright. "As it should be. The house Negroes will join them after our guests leave. Zeb will give the families gifts of sweets—and new coats, clothes, and shoes."

"That's good of him."

"Zeb takes pride in all celebrations—particularly now the war's over. He likes things big—to be the center of attention." Catherine turned to face her. "Not exactly your custom?"

Olivia shook her head, forcing a smile she hoped disguised her disgust of slavery.

"Well, you're a Fleming now, so you must learn to put up with us—the good and the bad."

"Forgive me. I meant no—"

Catherine shook her head with a tsk, then smiled and hooked arms with her again.

The servants and field hands continued their preparations, undisturbed by their presence. Catherine waved at several little tykes dashing by in a game of tag, and Olivia spotted Tom with a group of lads sitting on a porch step. He was laughing, loose pieces of his russet mop peeking out from the sides of his long hunter hat—a fine piece she knew he had just purchased. *Quite smart*, she mused, as he stood up and tipped it to a young woman. He moved closer to her, his smile splitting his face and freckled cheeks growing round. She swayed as they conversed, her expression warm and inviting, then he offered her his arm. Olivia smiled behind the back of her hand, detecting more in Tom's expression than common cordiality, raising the question in her mind who she was—and to whom, if anyone—she belonged.

As they strolled back toward the main house, she gave Catherine a sideways glance, imagining her smooth alabaster skin, slender nose, and expressive bluebell eyes were what had given Harry a pause at dinner today. She gave an inward sigh, unable to deny it. Catherine Fleming was a singular white dove in a world full of gray pigeons.

Catherine came up short, rubbing her belly with her free hand. "Olivia, dear, I'll need you again—soon, I think. I cannot imagine doing this without you. May I rely on you?"

Ashamed of her envy and woolgathering, Olivia squeezed her arm. "Yes…it'll be just like last time with Peggy. I'll be there with Mr. Blake to help you."

"I'm grateful to you." They closed the distance to the house and walked inside.

****

Harry stood in a circle with Kitt and several other men, drinking and swapping stories, when he glimpsed Olivia and Catherine entering the great hall. With a quick nod, he excused himself, making his way across the room to where his wife stood alone.

"Was wondering where you were, Scrapper." Harry snaked an arm around her waist and kissed her knuckles. "You're freezing."

"Just my fingers…and nose. I had my shawl. It started out as a breath of fresh air but turned into a walk around the grounds with Catherine."

He arched a quizzical eyebrow. "Aye, a walk. And how'd that go?"

"Well, I think—oh, thank you," Olivia said, accepting the glass of sherry he placed in her hand. "She's got a lot of energy, considering how far along she is."

"Yes, but she should be careful, though—like you say about women in her condition."

"Mm…I think—"

"Harry! There you are—c'mon, the cockfight's about to start." Brandt squeezed between them, arms across their shoulders, scotch sticky on the corner of his mouth. "Trust me," he said, whispering thickly. "You don't want to miss Bandit."

"I'll be there in a minute." He gave him a dismissive wave and turned to Olivia, the heat of her glare scalding him.

She slid out from underneath Brandt's arm. "If you'll both excuse me, I think I'll go find Mrs. Blake." She strode off, skirt swishing around her legs.

Brandt nudged him in the side, his snickering laugh filling the air as he bounded out the door.

Harry rolled his eyes heavenward, dragging his hand across his prickly warm neck, then gazed at Zeb, perched at the front of the room alongside his setters and the stone fireplace. Always comfortable at the center of things, his uncle hovered like a haggard vulture scouting for tasty scraps. The old man leaned over, heavy in his handkerchief in another coughing fit—one of many he had noticed today—but came up recovered, washing any trace of it away with a gulp of scotch.

Reed slithered in beside him. "A tough and clever old codger, your uncle."

"A Fleming family trait."

"Ah, Harry, how advantageous to have familial connections."

He laughed, astonished. "And you have none?"

"Sadly, I'm poor in that regard." He slid his hands in his pockets, rocking back on his heels.

"So…you seek advantageous friendships in place of it."

Reed cocked his head. "Is that wrong?"

He thought of Olivia, bereft of family through no fault of her own, and his eyes narrowed. "Well, no, I don't suppose so. As long as it's done with honest intentions."

"And have I given you reason to think mine are not such?"

Harry pulled out his flask and took a healthy swallow. "Not yet."

"I'm an ardent admirer of your family." Reed fanned his arms outward, palms open. "The Flemings have accomplished much in three generations."

He recapped his flask and tucked it inside his coat pocket. "If you like things on a grand scale, then yes, Glen Laurel is a rare pearl. I'm from a lower branch of the tree, so our purse is smaller, but I think Redmond Hill is a gem."

"Redmond could surely shine a little more—rival this estate, if you had a mind to do it."

"Well, now that's the difference between you and me. I think it already shines." Harry stepped closer, his jawline unyielding. "My wealth increases by leaving the trees standing tall in my woods, preserving the creek beds for all of God's tiniest creatures. My wife makes her healing medicines from the herbs and flora growing there. Our children will play in the grassy patch under the shade of the live oak. They'll learn every trail, every hiding spot at Redmond Hill like the back of their hand." He pointed a cautionary finger at the man. "That's how it shall always shine."

"You paint a serene picture." Reed stroked his mustache. "Believe me when I say I have nothing but respect for your homestead. If only something so grand was mine… Oh well, if you'll excuse me, I'm late for the games." The wiry-haired man sauntered away, coattails swinging behind him. Harry jerked on his lapels, muttered a curse, then turned on his heel. *I need fresh air. Now.*

A flock of snow geese flew by, showering guests with their boisterous honking, their silhouettes dark against a tangerine sky. Harry lifted his gaze to the ripples of lilac-blue clouds drifting southward along with the birds. He blew out his breath. Nothing about this day had gone as he had hoped, and after his exchange with Reed, his insides were twisted tighter than a monkey's tail.

"Achoo!" Catherine stood at the far corner of the patio, shivering. She untied her sleeves and pushed them down to her wrists, buttoning them. She sneezed again.

"Still catch a chill at the slightest change in air—and you're never prepared for it," Harry scolded, removing his coat and draping it over her shoulders. "And dragging Olivia all over Glen Laurel this afternoon?"

"It was a perfect afternoon for a walk, I assure yo— you. Achoo!" Her head bobbed, and as she recovered, she took the handkerchief he offered. "Suppose you're right. I'm quite unlike your wife." She dabbed at her pink nose. "Can't imagine any crisis for which she'd be unprepared."

He answered her with a proud smile.

"I must rely on her again to help bring this child into the world." She smoothed her hands over her belly. "It's difficult for me to admit, but she's remarkable, Harry. She's a good soul. She really is."

He turned around and leaned on the railing, arms crossed over his chest. "Olivia is a lady of great abilities.

You, my dear, are simply a great lady."

"More ornament than substance. That's how I feel most of the time."

"So says the swan," he said, half-chuckling. Then he spotted her finger twisting inside the curl by her cheek. "Cee? Tell me what's bothering you. Please."

"Let's say I wish my husband would take a fancy to me more often than to just leave me with child." She crumpled the handkerchief in her fist. "I have a mind. I can listen and think and talk."

"Yes, I know that."

A frown swept across her face. "But he doesn't see me the way you do."

He looked away absently, rubbing his knuckles under his chin. "You care for him—more than I thought." He bristled, digging deep for words—honest words—to give her comfort. "What can I say about Brandt? Pressures weigh on a man—family, money, business—and he would never want to burden you. He cares for you—he does." *Damn it all to hell, but it's the truth. He told me so.* "My cousin's always been a fortress. Whatever he carries inside, well…he just doesn't want to worry you."

"Yes, I tell myself that. But he has another fancy."

His eyebrow arched to the sky.

"No, the fancy's not a someone—at least I don't think so—it's a something. Gaming and drinking—it's the way of men, he tells me, though I've never seen my father thus engaged." There was a fair amount of censure in her tone. "Nor you."

He dragged his hand over his face and cursed the wounded look in her eyes. "Brandt enjoys his whiskey and a wager—always has. Surely you knew his vices before you married him."

Her soft intake of breath was his answer. "I'm sorry, Cee. I don't like seeing you unhappy. What about Zeb? He can make him listen."

"I used to think so. But not lately. He's rather peeved with him too." She slipped out of his coat and placed it over his arm.

He clutched her hand. "If you need my help, you have it. Just say the word. I'll never stop caring for you." She responded with a hint of a smile, then bowed her head and turned away. His gaze followed her until she disappeared around the corner.

****

Inside the great hall, the mantel clock chimed four times. Harry took off down the hallway, scanning every room for Olivia. Above the clamor of iron pots and skillets in the kitchen, he heard a child's giggling squeal and inched closer. As a serving girl toting a bucket of dirty dishes pushed through the door, he spotted his wife bouncing a toddler on her knees.

Harry approached her from behind, laid his hands on her shoulders, and whispered in her ear, "There you are...I've been missing you."

Olivia reached for his hand as the boy slid off her lap and wobbled over to his mother. "Please take me home."

****

Harry and Olivia celebrated Christmas with the families of Redmond Hill that evening with a hot supper and dancing by the outdoor firepit. Light on frills, but heavy in kindred spirit, it had been a cherished time with those he held most dear.

He walked over carrying a lantern in one arm, a

woolen blanket in the other, and joined Olivia on the porch swing, careful to avoid stepping on Caddie's tail. "You sure you're not too cold?"

"Not with you to keep me warm." She snuggled under his arm, and he tucked the wrap around her body. "Everyone loves you. And not just for your gifts and generosity."

"We don't have much this year, but I hope the little extra helps our families."

"You amaze me."

He swallowed at her unabashed praise, then recovered. "And you, Scrapper," he said, planting a kiss on the back of her hand, "make me a better person."

Stillness expanded between them, soft and low, only crickets chirping in the distance.

"You've given me everything, Harry. It makes me cry sometimes. I wanted to give us a child, but I made jokes about getting fat. A good wife wouldn't have such ideas." She drew up her feet, tucking them underneath the blanket, and slid deeper inside the shelter of his arms. "When I lost Gabriel, you gave me your strength, and I gave nothing in return. I've been beastly selfish."

He breathed in a hint of lavender from her hair, rubbing his thumb across the stiff wool blanket covering her shoulder. "You're not selfish, Liv."

"But I am. Catherine looked so radiant today." She pushed up, pressing her palms on his shoulders. "She asked me if I would be there again—during her confinement." She slumped back down, burrowing into his chest. "Where is her husband in all of this, I'd like to know—consumed with gambling, he is." Her hand curled into a fist on his thigh. "And just how did he lose his hearing?"

"A childhood fever made him deaf in his left ear. It was hard, but he was such a smart lad—he overcame it. We all worried for him when his mother died, leaving him alone with Zeb. Raised by a tyrant, for God's sake."

Olivia relaxed her fist.

He nudged her shoulder. "Just remember what you told me—nothing to do with family is ever easy."

"Well, I wanted to say no to Catherine today—to throw every hateful thought in her direction because she's with child...and I'm not." She wedged her bottom lip between her teeth.

"But you didn't." He patted her arm. "Like I said. You're not selfish."

"And you—are you content with me?"

"Most content, Scrapper."

He kissed her nose and shifted to his right, retrieving a small box from his coat pocket. Eyes sparkling, she lifted the lid, and he fastened a silver and pearl bracelet at her wrist. She turned it around, admiring it in the lantern's glow, then kissed him soundly on the lips.

"I love it. There's your goodness again. You're too kind to me."

"I'm happy you think so. Father told me different—said there was no such thing as a good man." He answered her quizzical look, rubbing his chin. "A good woman, a good scotch, aye, and a good dog and horse. But not a good man." His jaw tightened. "He was right."

"I mean no disrespect, but you're living proof he was wrong."

He gave her a lopsided smile. "You're a good woman—and devoted."

"That is what you asked of me. But I want to do better—give better—as your wife. I want to cherish you more." She turned, framing his face in her hands.

"And I you. All the days of my life." His tone was laced with naked emotion. *I want to wring my heart of Catherine and open it to you. I am trying, Scrapper.* He sought her lips, allowing his kiss to tell her what his words did not. She responded with a similar urgency, and he scooped her up in his arms, making her laugh in a way he had not heard in weeks. Once inside, after Caddie scooted into their bedchamber and curled up by the fireplace, he closed the door and made love to his wife.

Chapter Twenty-One

January 1784

Aside from the routine of keeping livestock thriving and reproducing, the first few weeks of the new year meant fortifying Redmond Hill and preparing its fields for spring planting. Harry invested in timber and posts, supervising repairs to fencing all around his property. Tom put his mind and hands to work by day, supervising the clearing of all three fields, ridding the soil of dead roots and debris, and mixing in fresh compost. At night Tom took inventory of equipment and tools, assessing their viability, sharpening and repairing what he could by the light of a lantern. Amidst the cows' waffling snores, Harry lifted the latch to the tool shed and stepped inside.

"Oh, good evenin', Cap'n." Tom donned a grin, accentuating his dimples. "What ye got there?" He peered at the basket in his hand.

"Your mother sends food." Harry placed it on the worktable.

The lad lifted the cover and peeked inside. "There's plenty, sir—please dig in." He swapped his wrench for a rather large, meaty chicken leg. He bit into it, his face awash in satisfaction, chewing hungrily. "Mum thinks of everything."

"She hasn't let me down yet." Harry helped himself

to an apple fritter, licking the stickiness from his mouth with a flick of his tongue.

They ate in silence for a time. Harry uncapped two bottles of ale and handed one to his mate.

"Mum says you're a wise and brave man. I know it's true." Tom took a drink, wiping the foamy bubbles on his upper lip with the back of his hand. "If you don't mind me askin', what was it like fightin' in the war? If I'd been a little older, I could have joined."

"I'd have been proud to have you in my regiment. You're strong and smart, and most of all, you never give up—you always find the good in things. That's maybe the hardest part about soldiering. A man can press on with just a wee bit in his stomach, but he's as good as dead if his heart and soul are empty."

"And the battles—ye were at King's Mountain and Cowpens, no?" he asked, pop-eyed.

"It's not as glorious as you think. I could tell you things you probably haven't heard about before—like sickness. Terrible bouts of fevers and dysentery came around every summer. Plagued us—and thankfully, the Brits too." Harry took up an empty chair and sat down, elbows on the table, bottle in hand. "You can't imagine all the planning that goes into a battle. So much happens before even the first musket fires—unless it's an ambush, and then all hell breaks loose."

Harry swigged his ale, then wiped his mouth with his sleeve. "All of it's bruising to your body and your mind. Once things commence in a battle, your heart races like a wild animal. Can't think about anything but the fight in front of you and following orders. And afterward, Christ, every emotion hammers you all at once. Then you thank God for sparing your life, get up, and help those not as fortunate. That's what I'm talking about with you."

Tom's face shone with the compliment.

"Sometimes a man has to dig down deep to find the good. To you, it comes naturally."

"Hm, people have told me that before."

He raised an eyebrow. "Besides your mother and me—and my wife, no doubt—who else?"

"Oh, it's nobody, sir." He shrugged, taking a bite of an apple fritter.

He watched the lad's ears turn a faint pink. "You got something on your mind, Tom? Spit it out already."

"Sir?" Tom sputtered, mouth full.

"Not your food." He bit back a smile. "I meant spit out what's on your mind."

After a moment, Tom swallowed his food, nodding. "Oh, yessir. Well, there's this girl, and I've been wonderin'—how did ye ken, Cap'n? About Missus Fleming, I mean. How she was the one."

He halted mid-swallow and coughed, trying not to choke.

"You're happy, no? And she's always smilin' at you when you're not lookin'. You seem to rub along real good." He slurped his drink between bites. "Seems ye found the right woman, sir. I'd sure like to know how ye knew."

"You don't have something on your mind. You've got someone on your mind—and that's no small thing."

"Yessir—and I canna talk to my mum." His chin lowered a bit. "Would be all wrong."

Harry pulled a flask out of his jacket, shaking it near his ear, and judging its weight to be equal to the task, set it on the table. He propped up his feet on the workbench and leaned back, striving for his best brotherly tone. "Help yourself. And then tell me about this girl."

****

Oliva awakened to the sensation of a warm, wet tongue. It began with a lick or two, thick and bumpy across her knuckles, and then it quickened and moved to her dangling fingertips.

"Um...morning, Caddie." She rubbed his muzzle in a reciprocal greeting. Only a scant bit of daylight shone through the window, but it was morning. Her hound shook his jowls and released a yawn. "I agree." She forced her eyes open, stretching her legs, toes pointed. Then she curled up in a ball and gazed at the long, muscular body sprawled out beside her.

She had missed Harry last night, sheets cold and stiff in his absence. Though the hour was late, she had melted when he fixed himself behind her in spoon-like fashion, her buttocks nestled against him. She smiled with the memory of it. *My Lord, he is a glorious man.*

Now save for the blankets wadded up around his knees, he lay on his back, one arm above his head, the other over his chest, body as bare as the day he was born. Even in winter, he never seemed to chill. His skin was a warm, creamy beige, except above the waistline where the sun had kissed his beautifully brute torso. His tawny blond hair was long—thick and lustrous by a man's standard—something not everyone knew since he wore it smoothed in a queue. She gazed in wonderment at the curves of his chest, his hand rising and falling with steady breathing, stomach flat and hard. She leaned on her elbow, her gaze fixed on another, most precious part of him that was also hard. She remembered her surprise when he informed her men awakened in the state of "morning glory." Now, being most appreciative of this condition, she slid closer, resting her head on his firm abdomen, and he stirred. She shook her hair, sending its scent wafting upward.

"Lavender..." Harry half-chuckled, and the sound reverberated in his chest.

"Mm," she said, her nose rubbing, teasing the part of him that was wide awake.

"It's a gift for me." He massaged her head, fingers circling round and round in the heavy mass of her hair.

"You are my gift." She parted her lips and took him in her mouth. She pulled the fan of her hair to the side and moved closer, paying tribute to his cock with each pass of her tongue. She engulfed him in a shower of wetness, her lips sliding up and down his length.

"Come here, Liv." Clasping her hips between his hands, he swung her around to straddle his chest. With a direct line to his manhood now, her breasts brushing his abdomen, she continued her delicious assault. With exquisite skill, he lifted her up so the heart of her femininity was mere inches from his lips. She gasped when he sucked it like a cluster of sweet grapes dangling from the vine, teasing her bud with his rolling tongue. She moaned against him, their worship of one another's bodies perfect, and they gave their release to each other in shared ecstasy. After they recovered, she circled around and rested on top of him.

"Fascinating..." Olivia murmured, smoothing a lock of hair from his brow.

"I couldn't resist."

"I had no idea we could kiss each other like that—in those places—at the same time."

Harry inhaled, burying his face in her lustrous hair,

and nipped her earlobe. "I believe my lessons are now complete, Scrapper. Anything else we have the urge to do, we will figure out together."

"Promise?" she purred, certain he could hear the smile in her voice.

"You have my word." He pressed a kiss on the slope of her neck and moved over her body again.

Sometime later, damp and breathless, Olivia molded her body to Harry, her arms and legs like malleable clay, mind soused from their coupling. With violent tenderness, he had carried her with him, diving deep into her sweetness, unleashing his need multiple times. Like the churning of cream brings forth butter, he transformed her every time they made love.

With her back pressed against his stomach, Olivia relaxed into the seamlessness of skin against skin. "You stayed a long time with Tom last night. I stayed awake as long as I could."

Harry sighed. "Turns out he needed a lot more than supper."

"You helped him with his chores, then." She pulled his hand close, tucking it under her chin, and kissed his knuckles.

"That would've been a lot easier. No, he's of a mind to take a bride."

Olivia's eyes flew open.

"It's Lucie."

She wiggled around, facing him. "I saw them together—at Christmas, at Glen Laurel. They looked rather sweet talking together, but I didn't—"

"Nor did I." He rubbed his chin reflectively. "Well, I mean—I'd caught him staring at her a few times—all dreamy-eyed, but good God, marriage?"

They remained still for several minutes, then Harry pushed out a heavy breath. "Tom comes to me with this predicament last night, asking for my advice. I can increase his salary to support a family—add on to his cabin when need be—but I can't help him wed this girl. She's not—"

"Free."

"Aye, she's Reed's property."

"But if they're in love…"

"Love or not, it'll pass. In time, he'll come to understand—learn from it, and move on."

Brays, clucks, and moos lifted from the barn, morning sounds bringing the farm to life. Olivia scooted over, pressing her face into the smooth hollow of his neck, his chin brushing the top of her head.

"You're right. There's more to happiness than first love." Martha's words echoed in her mind. *First doesn't mean better.* Was there even the smallest part of Harry still wondering about his own spoiled first love? Did he want Tom to suffer the same fate? *Could he buy her freedom?*

"I know what you're thinking, Scrapper—and it's romantic—but no, I can't. Reed's price would be too steep."

"I feel bad for her—and Tom. But at least he's a free man."

"Aw, hell." Harry raked the loose strands of his hair away from his face, fist landing on his forehead. "Let me think on it."

She smiled, his inherent goodness at work again, as inseparable to his nature as energy to a flame.

He cupped his hand behind his head. "Which reminds me, Liv…I received a letter from Josie last week."

Her brow arched speculatively.

"She's eager to meet you." He winked, his lips turning up at the corners. "I've got business in Charleston—need Tom with me, might even do him good to get away for a while. But I was thinking you could come along too—meet my sister and her family."

Her heart leaped, then it skidded to a halt. She reminded him of the promise she had made to Catherine to be there for the birthing, which could be any day now.

"You're right, of course. Nigel relies on you." He lifted her chin from where it lay drooping against her chest. "Tell you what—we'll go in May. We'll make it an anniversary trip. We can spend some time with Josie and Hugh—her boys are real sprouts, especially Sean. And we'll have some time alone for us." His simmering gaze made her tingle deep inside.

She sat up refreshed, consoled by his promise, locking her hand with his. "I love this plan. And...I also love your fingers." She rubbed each sturdy digit from base to tip.

"Even the calluses?"

"I love them most of all. Reminds me how hard you work to take care of all of us."

"And will you miss me while I'm gone?" Harry asked, brow raised. "You're so capable on your own. I rather like thinking you need me, at least a little."

"I'll miss you." She leaned over, kissing him on the cheek. "And I'll miss you this afternoon too. I've got food to fix for church." She sucked in a breath. "Oh, and Mrs. Coxe, I promised to check in with her first thing this morning."

She scurried off, swaddled in a blanket, taking a seat

at her dressing table to brush her hair. "She's still recovering from that dreadful distemper—oh, I made her more elderberry tonic. I mustn't forget it."

Harry laughed. "Aye, you mustn't forget me either. What if I need my wife?"

Olivia gazed at him through her mirror, half-smiling at his mock indignation. "God created me, Harry Fleming. He didn't create 'my wife.' She's a concoction of your own making," she teased, tying off her ponytail, folding her arms on the table.

He jumped up and, never one to be shy about nakedness, strolled across the room to stand behind her chair. He leaned in behind her ear and whispered over the curl of her ear. "And a damn good job I've done. Wouldn't you agree?"

She answered him with a smile reflecting all the love in her heart. "Trust me, Harry. 'My wife' will be back as soon as she can."

Chapter Twenty-Two

Damnation. The one word summed up Harry's frustration. He stole a glance at his pocket watch while keeping Reed Barlowe in his periphery. The rascal stood at the window in his storeroom office, fingers drumming on the windowpane. *Christ, will you stop preening already?* He maintained his rigid posture while he clocked Reed's steps back to the table.

"Lucie?" Reed chuckled, reclaiming his seat. "Why no—no, my little Lucia Jeanne isn't for sale, but I know of some others you—"

Harry lifted his chin. "I'm only interested in her."

"She's a treat—perhaps we can come to some kind of arrangement." He pursed his lips. "I must admit, I hadn't pegged you as the type."

"I'm not the type. I want to buy her freedom."

"Freedom…?" He smirked, raising his hand and holding up two fingers.

Lucie promptly brought them two shots of an amber scotch. He noted how Reed's lecherous gaze tracked her every move.

"What the devil would a charming little thing like Lucie do with freedom? She has everything she needs with me." Reed eased back in his chair, arms crossed, and spit in a tin cup.

"I'm willing to be quite generous."

"You're doing this for your Mr. Harkett. Aye, don't

think I haven't noticed him nosing around my property."

She's a person, not a damn horse. His jaw tightened with loathing. "Your price—please."

Reed pulled a paper from his vest pocket and walked to his desk. He dabbed a quill in ink and after a few moments, scribbled something on the sheet and returned to his chair. He dropped the note on the table.

After glancing at the note, Harry pushed it aside. "I said give me your price—not your dream."

"They're the same."

"Impossible."

"Playing cupid doesn't come cheap, Harry." He cocked his head. "And to be clear, Lucie's more than a piece. She has skills. She's a virgin—not a nun, mind you—but she's never been rutted. I protected her for a reason—increases her value exponentially."

He grunted a snort, producing a parchment of his own, laying it on the table.

Reed perused it. "Mr. Allington's handiwork, I see."

"It's all legal—including the fat price I'll be paying you."

Reed leaned aside, spitting a hunk of tobacco into the cup. He sipped his liquor, swishing it around in his mouth, then spit again. "I'll stick to my original price."

"Twenty acres? You're a madman."

"I've been called worse." He pretended to rub a smudge off his vest, then met his gaze. "Fact is, I have something you want. Think how happy Tom and Lucie could be—and you, their hero."

His hands hit the table with a force, shaking their glasses. He stood over the menace, his glare stark and stone-cold sober. "You're playing a game with people's lives, Reed. A dangerous game." His words hissed between his clenched teeth. "You'll never sow not one seed of grass on Redmond Hill land, nor lay claim to a single pebble in its soil—you hear me, you sick swine?" He slapped the man on the back in reiteration. "Not. One." Pulling on his lapels with both hands, he straightened his coat and strode out the door.

Harry stewed in his juices for the remainder of the day and into the next morning. The vile man—with his sick dissertation about Lucie—was reprehensible. He intended extortion, for Christ's sake. *And he's a friend to Brandt and stepfather to Emily Wakefield?* He shuddered, adjusting his neckcloth in the mirror on his wife's dressing table, thinking Kitt had been right about Reed all along—the man had his sights set on him and Redmond Hill.

"What's this...?" Olivia asked in wonderment, picking up the long hair ribbon from underneath his wallet and weaving it between her hands. "It's beautiful." She ran her fingers along its silky grain and velvet edges. "What a pretty shade of blue—a little faded in some spots," she said, examining the delicate treasure, "but altogether lovely. Did it belong to Josie?"

With hooded eyes, Harry gazed at her through the mirror, his mouth twitching. A prolonged silence lingered in the air. The usual warmth in the room vanished, swept away by a dubious current. He walked toward her like a convict taking his final steps toward the noose. He opened her hand and pulled the ribbon free from her fingers, clutching it in his fist before turning away.

"Stop. Don't you dare." Olivia pinched her lips into a bow.

He assumed an erect stance, a natural defensive

tactic honed through years of soldiering.

"Tell me who that belongs to."

He peered over his shoulder. "Let it go." *Don't make me say it. I don't want to hurt you.*

"Tell me. Now."

He pivoted, willing himself to ignore the tears pooling in her eyes. "I believe you can guess."

She wrapped her arms around her middle. "But why do you have such a thing? What is it to you?"

"It belonged to—" *Catherine? Christ, I can't tell you that.* "—to the woman I loved. I'm not even sure why I keep it anymore."

"Stop talking in riddles, you...you gutless bastard." She lunged at him, fists pounding on his chest. Her wailing brought Mary to the doorway, her face bone-white, mouth gaping at Olivia. He silenced Mary with his glare, and she backed away from the door.

Olivia pushed him away and stumbled backward. "All this time. How could you? How could you be such a liar?" Her voice dragged the lowest note, and she slumped down on the bed.

Silent moments stretched into silent minutes, and he sensed the divide between them growing deeper.

"Say something, Harry. I don't give a fig what—just speak."

He buried his expression in the hard lines of his face, lips thin. "It's all I have left of her. She gave it to me—and I kept it safe through storms and filth and fire...battlefields." He raised and lowered one shoulder, lifting his chin. "It's a part of me, I guess."

"She's a part of you."

"I understand you're angry but—"

"Angry? Is that the best you can do? How about

betrayed, abandoned? Livid? Jilted!" Olivia coughed a laugh cloaked in a sob.

"Christ, will you stop using those words? You're not a damn dictionary." He pressed the heel of his hand to his brow. "You're making too much of this."

"Am I? Prove it. Toss it in the fireplace. Right now."

He studied Catherine's ribbon, a simple object given in token of her love and affection. Over years of separation and travail, it had morphed into a being all its own, redolent of the precious times and promises they had shared. In his hands was his memory of her—he had neither the will nor desire to destroy it. He searched Olivia's eyes for a flicker of understanding.

"You can't do it. You. Can't. Do it." Olivia pressed her fingers to her temples, squeezing her eyes shut. "Martha was wrong. Memories of first love...they don't...they don't lose their strength..."

"What are you babbling about?" he snapped, dragging his hand across his neck.

She straightened her back. "There's no room for three in a marriage. A ghost love was bad enough, but now she's practically living and breathing in our bedroom."

"You deserve better but—"

"Then give me better, Harry."

The words stung. He wanted to give in to her command and rid his heart of the lingering pain. *I-I just don't know how.* He stepped backward, leaving a vacuous space between them once more. Shoving the ribbon in his pocket, he resumed packing his saddlebag.

"Go on, then—let her warm your bed," Olivia spat.

He glared at her, fists flexing at his sides. "I've never lied to you. I've been faithful."

"And all the time with that *thing* next to your heart. There's more than one way to cheat, Harry."

"We," he said, waving an accusatory finger, "had an understanding when we married—aye, you remember, Scrapper? It was a mutual decision. We spoke of devotion—not love."

Olivia drew her knees up under her chin.

God, I'm an arse. Like she needs a reminder I never courted her, never vied for her affection. He kneeled before her. "Please, Liv. I don't want to leave things like this."

She rubbed the back of her hand under her nose, sniffing. "How should we leave it, then?"

"Anything but this."

Olivia sighed and gazed at him with misty eyes. " 'Let not the sun go down upon your wrath,' Ephesians, chapter four, verse something. I don't remember."

He took a deep breath, longing to hold her, but thought better of it. *No. Space. We need space.* The muffled sound of Tom's voice outside the door signaled it was time to leave. They had miles to cover and needed to make the most of the daylight.

"That'll have to do. But know this—I harbor no wrath, only regret." He gave her hand a gentle squeeze. "I'll be home in a fortnight. I'll miss you."

He stood and crossed the room, grabbing his bag and easing into his riding coat. He glanced at Olivia—who wore a perfectly painful expression—then left, closing the door behind him.

Chapter Twenty-Three

Olivia's first day without Harry had been the longest day…ever.

Mind and body aching, she leaned on the windowsill and gazed across the lawn stretching out to the barn. She smiled, spying the old mouser cat traipsing around the bushes on the hunt for a snack. Fog had appeared on the window, cozy warm air inside clashing with the frigid blast outside. She pressed her nose and forehead against it, the damp chill mirroring the one in her heart. *Does Harry miss me? Or are his thoughts only for the one with the blue hair ribbon?*

The dry wood Mary had added to the fire popped, jolting her from her doldrums. The bedroom was redolent of Harry, his woody sandalwood and musk scent teasing her nostrils. Her gaze traveled around the room, noting the usual evening amenities, fresh water in the basin and towels folded in a stack alongside it. Mary had only brought one glass of port, though, and there was no *Gazette* waiting on the table by his chair. Unwittingly, her mind reverted to the first moments she had spent in their bedroom, alone and anticipating his arrival on their wedding night. *Has it only been eight months?* In no time, they had transformed the room from a foreign island to an intimate oasis. Her cheeks warmed with the memories of their lovemaking and the precious moments of unspoken language shared between them.

As she settled into bed, blowing out the candle and snuggling deep beneath the quilts, she had but one prayer in her heart. *Please God, bring him back to me.*

Olivia awoke the following morning with a start, scrambling out of bed and into some semblance of normalcy. She arrived at the barber-surgery before nine o'clock with a basketful of herbs, welcoming the satisfaction that came with helping folks. She needed a lifeline to survive the empty days until Harry returned.

"Oh good—you made more." Nigel stood in front of the cupboard, counting the jars. "This white willow bark tea blend has improved Mr. Barlowe's gout considerably. He'll be by for more soon, I think."

Olivia gave him a smiling nod, then began cutting the stems off the peppermint, chamomile, and coneflower she had gathered on her morning walk. The dead of winter promised fevers and coughs, so she prepared tonics and teas with the herbs. They would consider themselves blessed if they did not see smallpox this season. The dreaded disease had decimated thousands of Catawba, including her mother, and countless more fighting men during the war.

Nigel's voice lifted in greeting, and she cast her gaze toward the front door, craning her neck for a closer look.

"Olivia, dear—come, come." Nigel beckoned with one hand, his other braced on his hip, gaze intent on the young woman's foot. He slid his spectacles down his nose. "Lucie, I can see you're in pain. Did you fall? Sprain your ankle?"

"Oh no, you're imaginin' things." Lucie stood still, feet steady.

"But your face just now." He gave Olivia a sideways glance. "Wincing, she was. No mistaking it."

"Thank ye, sir, but I'm well. I've come for Massa Barlowe's medicine."

With a frown, Nigel slid his spectacles back in place and strode into the next room.

Olivia watched Lucie standing with her shoulders straight and hands clasped behind her back. With her hair combed back into a low bun, she displayed a slender neck and small, flat ears.

"If you'd like me to have a look, I can." Olivia's gaze traveled through the empty room. "No one will see."

Lucie followed her gaze, then her lips thinned into a flat line. "I'll be all right in time. Mighty kind of you, Missus. I heard about your goodness."

Olivia gave her a quizzical look.

"From Tom."

"Do you see him often?"

"Sometimes. I like talkin' to him."

Is she aware of Tom's intentions, and Harry's attempt to free her? "Would you—" She hushed when Mr. Blake returned with two jars.

"Here you go, Lucie. This should do the trick." Nigel placed them in her basket. "Tell Mr. Barlowe to follow the same instructions as last time."

"Yessir."

"And Lucie," he said hooking his thumbs in his vest pockets. "Come back, won't you? If you don't get any better."

"Yessir. Thank ye." She shrugged deeper inside her coat, tucked the basket under her arm, and walked out.

They watched the slight figure disappear down the street. Pulling his spectacles off, Nigel placed a tip in the corner of his mouth and held it there. "I know what I saw, Olivia. What's she trying to hide? And why?"

Chapter Twenty-Four

Even after enduring nine hours of labor and delivering a healthy baby boy, Olivia thought Catherine still looked like a damsel from a fairy tale. With arms and legs flailing, the child came into the world on the last day of January. The mother nursed her infant, his lips seeking her milk-rich breast upon arrival. At the end of her travail, Mr. Blake remarked how her generous hips were fit for childbirth. When Olivia left the bedroom sometime later, Catherine and her son were asleep.

Glen Laurel hummed with the joyous news. Olivia burrowed her way through the throng of well-wishers in the great hall while cigars, scotch, and congratulatory handshakes circulated throughout the room. She made haste, slipping out the back of the kitchen. Once outside, a cold wind stung her cheeks, and she leaned back against the closed door. Tears escaped from the corners of her eyes, streaming down her cheeks. She let them flow onto her kerchief, dampening the muslin, making the fabric cling to her chest. It made no difference, though, for the load she bore inside—deep in her heart— was more than enough on its own.

Olivia noticed a familiar weight drop on top of her boot and looked down, Caddie's sizable paw nudging it back and forth. She sniffed and wiped her nose with the least soiled sleeve she had. She stared into his clear brown irises—like she had done the day her father first placed him on her lap almost five years ago—and found refuge in their depths. He was now some fifty pounds heavier, standing up to her hip, but his eyes were unchanged.

She rubbed behind his ears and looking up, glimpsed the silhouette of Marcus framed against the ashen sky, nothing visible but the scarlet glow from the tip of his cheroot. He stepped forward in acknowledgment, bringing behind him their two saddled horses. She dragged her hand over her forehead and bit back a laugh, embarrassed she had forgotten all about them. They had both waited for her while she fulfilled her promise to Catherine.

Suddenly, she was acutely aware of the loose strings of matted hair glued to her temples, dried bloodstains scattered across her arms and apron. She bent down to sniff her underarms, the aroma redolent of salty sweat. Another cold blast ripped past her, and she sucked in her breath, a stark reminder that just a few miles down the road was Redmond Hill, where she longed to be soaking in a warm bath and crawling into a clean, if not overly cozy bed. She gave Marcus a wave and, staving off the tears, rose to meet him, Caddie close on her heels. As she approached, he clamped his hat over his chest, then helped her swing up into the saddle and led them home.

****

Harry gazed at the brilliant stars shining bluish white in the winter sky, grateful for their light in the moonless heaven above. Several hours ago, expecting the business meeting might extend into the supper hour and beyond, he had sent Tom ahead to inform his sister he would arrive after dark. As he neared the Sutherland home, he tempered his sadness about Olivia with thoughts of his sister and her three rambunctious sons.

Her children never ran short of mischievous ideas or the energy to execute them. Yesterday, the middle boy, Clyde, convinced the youngest he had squashed a large, plump ant—which was an erstwhile blackberry—inside a napkin. When he pulled it out, dangling it above his open mouth, he swallowed it whole in front of the lad who flew off, wailing "Ew" at the top of his three-year-old lungs. Never to be outdone, the eldest, Sean, swapped the jar of sugar for salt night before last, turning his mother's sweet cakes into a pungent, briny mouthful, which Greer spit out onto his plate. As the youngest of the Sutherland brood, Greer would bear scars from the torment—until, of course, he came of age and could concoct devilish pranks of his own. With three such clever and inventive lads under one roof, Harry had turned to Josie and Hugh, doubled over in laughter, to ask what more they could ever want. The couple had exchanged a glance, looked him calmly in the face, and replied, "A little girl."

Harry hung his coat and hat on the rack by the door and took up a chair at the oblong table. He stretched his arms in front of him, then pulled them back in, pressing his forehead on top of his clasped hands.

"What's troubling you?" Josie rubbed his shoulders, kissing the back of his head.

"It's nothing." Harry pulled himself upright, his gaze softening. "Sorry I missed supper."

"Nonsense—it's still warm." She grabbed a small pot from the hearth, filled with lemon-broiled shrimp, cod, and whiting, along with a basket of biscuits, and placed them in front of him. He spooned hunks of meat into his mouth and sopped up the broth with the flaky bread. To his delight, she presented him with a bowl of Carolina rice pudding, and he slipped her a half grin.

"You've turned into quite the cook. I bet Tom ate his weight in this stew. Hugh's a lucky man. Where is he anyway?"

"Aye, I am, and yes, he did. And Hugh's both fortunate and dead asleep—as are the boys." She unfastened the small hooks holding up her sleeves, and they fell loose around her wrists. "And you're still good at changing the subject. Now, I've left you alone for three days—time's up. I'll ask you again—what's troubling you?" She brought over two glasses and filled them with a dark liquid, then took the seat across from him.

"What's the cure for being a damn fool?" Harry swallowed, smacking his lips in appreciation. "Best thing about Charleston has to be the quality of the liquor. Hard to get your hands on the good stuff in the back country."

"Stop hedging. Now, you're a lot of things, but 'fool' is not one that comes to mind."

A crinkle formed across his brow. "Perhaps, but marriage changes a man."

"Either you did something—or wish you had. Which is it?"

"The former."

"I see." She threaded her hands into a single fist. "Tell me about your wife, Harry."

"Olivia...? Uh," he said, scratching his chin. "Well, she's about your height, with long dark-brown hair and deep chestnut eyes. Her skin's this beautiful olive tan—oh, and very smooth. She's slender, but she has a healthy constitution—and firm hands too," he said, shaking his own two for emphasis.

"Good Lord, I'm not trying to sketch her portrait." Josie squared her elbows on the table and leaned toward him. "I asked you to *tell me* about your wife."

"Oh, well make yourself comfortable. Throw another log on the fire. And you'd better hang on to that bottle. We're going to need it."

Over the next hour, Harry spared no detail, telling his sister all about Olivia.

Josie's chin dropped in a most unattractive way. "You mean you left her like that? 'I'll miss you?' "

"Aye." He rolled his glass between his hands.

"Hm, you are a damn fool."

He grunted something unintelligible under his breath and walked to the fireplace, spreading the embers into an even layer with the iron poker. He had been feeling like a reprobate for days, but in hearing his sister's blatant confirmation of it, he clamped his hand around the rod with a vise-like grip.

"You've got to leave all of this—the deceit and betrayal—in the past. Do you hear me, Harry? What Zeb did to you was horrible. I don't understand why he hates you so much, but it's over—been over for years now."

He scowled at her summation and took a seat in the rocking chair, hands folded in his lap like a preacher waiting for the pulpit on Sunday morning. Her cat had stretched out on her lap during his lengthy retell and was sound asleep. The hush between them was deafening.

"Please, Harry—please don't think I'm judging, but the fact is Catherine married our cousin when she could have said no—duty or not. I would never have agreed to such." Josie shifted in her seat. "Did you ever think maybe…possibly…the commitment on her part was not as strong? Perhaps things for her changed after you left?"

"She put duty before her happiness—I know it. Christ, I hate Zeb with all my heart. He stole her away to spite me and ruin my life." He kicked a small stack of logs with his foot, sending them rolling across the floor.

"They're married. She's the mistress of Glen Laurel, for God's sake." Josie leaned forward. "They have a child—probably another one by now. Trust me—they change everything." She blew out a heavy breath. "Like it or not, they're a family. Those children need their parents. You can't go on wishing things were different— you're throwing away your life if you do."

He gave her a leveling glare. "Then I'm a stubborn damn fool."

Josie roused her cat and set him on the floor. She shuffled over and kneeled by his knee, placing her hand over his. "You've always taken control of your life. Zeb took that away from you once—don't let him do it anymore. Live your life—love this bright woman who carries your name. Olivia's right—get rid of the ghost."

He scrubbed his hands over his face, trying to wash away the self-loathing he felt inside. *Olivia's a ray of sunshine. Would it be so hard to live in that light...leave my storm clouds behind?*

"You're right. No one's ever loved me the way she does. I don't want to lose her."

She squeezed his hand. "Then don't."

Chapter Twenty-Five

February 1784

Olivia snipped her wildflowers and weeds, separating them into bowls, while Lucie waited on the bench inside the barber-surgery. The girl's inquisitive gaze scanned the cupboard, table, and chairs along one side of the room before landing on her.

"Beg your pardon, Missus, but where'd you learn how to make your potions?" Lucie tilted her head, hands folded in her lap.

Olivia picked up her pestle and began grinding. "They're not magic, if that's what you've heard." *That's what Reed would call them.* "My mother taught me the ways of the Catawba and their healing remedies."

She lowered her basket to the floor. "Whatever it is you mix up, it sure is helpin' Massa Barlowe's gout."

Olivia smiled a nod and returned to her preparations.

"I've seen you with Cap'n Fleming, too. I watched him open the door for ye...holdin' your hand." Lucie sighed wistfully. "Why, ye smile like the mornin' sun when you're with him. I ain't never seen much of that before. The massa ain't that way with his wife."

Olivia dropped her pestle and gazed into her tobacco-brown eyes. "I've never met Mrs. Barlowe. Where does she live?"

"They got a single house near the water in

Charleston. She stays there with her daughter, Miss Emily, most times. The girl came for a visit last spring, though."

"His stepdaughter…yes, I saw her at church with the Allington's." She wiped her brow with her sleeve and resumed her grinding. "Does Mr. Barlowe have many folks like you?"

"Slaves, ye mean. Yes, two stay with Missus Barlowe. Then Massa's got me and Grady, his errand boy. We stay in the rooms above the store. It's tight and noisy sometimes, but it's not so bad."

"Have you been with him long?"

"Since I was fourteen. Never knew my mama or my daddy. Massa Barlowe takes care of me."

"I'm sure he does." Olivia pointed her finger downward. "I see your foot's still bothering you. Do you think he'd mind if I had a look?"

Lucie slid her feet as far back as she could behind her skirt. "It's not so bad no more."

"Good, I'm glad. It's just—well, maybe I can help ease the pain. Like you said, I make that herb tea that helps Mr. Barlowe's gout."

Olivia reached for a few more stems, gazing at Lucie from beneath hooded eyes. She returned to work, humming while she crushed the flower blooms. The scrape of boots sliding over the wood floor reached her ears. *That's it, Lucie.*

Olivia laid down her pestle, wiped her hands on a rag, and went to her side. Kneeling, she unlaced Lucie's left boot, and amidst the girl's stifled cry, exposed a sock stained purple and red around the ankle. Gently peeling it away from the skin, Olivia exposed a deep gash, part of it scabbed, but other parts moist with green mucus.

There was bruising too.

Olivia spoke in a hushed tone. "Is the other ankle like this one?"

Lucie's head bobbed up and down.

"I need to tend to it. It'll hurt, but I promise to help make it better. Now you must tell me how this happened."

Olivia began applying her healing salve while she listened to Lucie's tale. Her stomach churned, bile slowly rising to her throat. *What kind of demon straps a woman's ankles to the bedposts?* Lucie described how Reed sometimes held a candle to the bottoms of her feet until she would scream from the heat of it, tearing deeper cuts into her ankles from the restraints. *Curse him!*

"This is not right." Olivia fisted her hands by her sides. "He's sick, and he can't just make up for this cruelty by feeding you and giving you a room with a bed. Or little gifts, you said?"

Lucie nodded. "He gave me a pretty new scarf after…after this." She flicked her gaze at her feet.

"Well, it's wrong. All of it. Dead wrong."

The girl withered into a lump on the chair, and she grabbed her hands. "Oh, Lucie, I'm sorry. I don't mean for you to think you've done something wrong. It's not your fault he does these things—truly it's not."

"Even if I believed what ye say, it don't change things. I have to keep him happy. If I don't, then what'll happen to me? Really, most times he's nice—just sometimes not."

Olivia sat back on her haunches. "I wish there was something—anything I could do."

Save for their breathing, the room was silent.

Lucie pulled her socks and boots back on her feet,

wincing mildly. "You done good. Thank you for the ointment, Missus."

Olivia dropped the jar in her basket. "Keep it. Rub it on every morning and night until you've healed."

"Would you maybe pray for me? I think when I die, I'm going to hell. God can't overlook the things that go on sometimes—"

Olivia suppressed the urge to vomit.

"—I think I'm soiled real bad. I'll never have no husband. A good man like Tom wouldn't want me if he knew the truth. And the Massa wouldn't let me go no way."

"I take it you know my husband tried to buy your freedom?"

Lucie nodded. "He's mighty kind. But I know what I am, and I know my place. Maybe God will have mercy on me when my time comes." She pulled herself up straight and hugged her middle.

As a child, Olivia had wondered about angels. As she beheld this defenseless young woman, enslaved to a sadistic monster, forced into submission and depravity, she saw everything she had imagined an angel could be—only her halo was on the inside.

Chapter Twenty-Six

Reed scraped his boots on the grooved stones at the entrance to Glen Laurel and removed his hat before stepping inside. The old butler, moving at the speed of a caterpillar, led him into the study bright with sunshine from the late morning hour. He removed his coat, tossed it over the chair, and sat down.

"You here to blind me with your shiny feathers, you damned peacock?" Zeb propped his elbows on the desk and drew on his pipe, deep and full, blowing the smoke in his face. Reed held his breath behind a stiff smile until the haze dissipated. He glimpsed a bowl filled with several oranges—one already pulled apart into sections—and smirked.

"Good morning to you too." Reed cleared his throat. "Why so cross? Citrus not agreeing with you?"

"Ever since Nigel announced I need to eat the damn fruit, they put them in front of me every time I turn around." He shoved the dish across his desk.

"They're good for what ails you—perhaps even improve your humor."

"Humor—ha!" He pulled on his pipe. "And what ails me is my son—out gambling and carousing every other night with the likes of you."

Reed pursed his lips.

"Aye, you're drowning in it. Hosting your games and women and parties—my son should be more concerned about his home and family."

For as brilliant as Brandt was, he was also a cocker and a dicer, neither of which rubbed along well with domesticity. Reed sighed, willing to make this concession and keep Zeb in his corner. "Perhaps you're right. I can bring things down a notch or two. We have been running a bit thick lately."

"Like a damn swamp."

"Consider it done." He smoothed his mustache with one finger. "And besides, I have another matter to discuss with you. Something else we have in common."

Reed remained still, content to wait for him to nibble at his line. Since making Harry's acquaintance, Reed had quickly deduced the man was a brave fighter, clever and headstrong. Common folks liked his steadfastness to simple ideals—a regular champion of the people. But the way he paraded his mixed-blood wife around good Christian folks gnawed at his gut.

Zeb cocked his head. "What are you cooking up this time?"

Reed crossed his hands on the desktop. "Well, being such good friends with Brandt, he's shared with me your concern about Harry's wife. She is a bit of a rotten limb on the family tree, albeit from a lesser branch, of course. Way I see it, his marriage to her is a direct jab at you." He delighted in the darkening of Zeb's gaze. "I've a plan that would rid you of the half-breed and install in her place a genteel young woman, deserving of the Fleming name. And afterward? Why, there'd be no end to what both families might accomplish together."

His eyes narrowed like a fox on a rabbit. "Who might this genteel young woman be?"

"My stepdaughter, of course."

He puffed on the tip of his pipe, leaned back in his chair, and guffawed. "Emily...? You're mad. Ballsy...but mad."

Reed raised a questioning brow toward the bottle of scotch and, after receiving a nod, poured two glasses. "Don't dismiss me so quickly. Here's what I've learned about Harry." He leaned forward on his elbows. "He'll move heaven and earth for those in his care, like his foreman Tom. Tried to buy my Lucie from me for thrice her market value—thrice!—all for the young man's happiness." He chuckled wryly. "Why, with his pride, there's no telling the lengths he would go to protect his wife and ensure her safety. She may be nothing but a crow...but she's *his* crow."

"And this plan of yours?"

"Already in motion. If you agree, I'll take it to the next step at nightfall—while Harry's still gone."

Zeb steepled his hands under his chin. "To be clear, I'm rid of the half-breed tart, and you will—through marriage—get your hands on Redmond Hill. As long as there are no slip ups, of course."

"Without boring you with the details, yes, that sums it up."

He stared into the depths of his glass, swirling the liquor around. "I will require your influence with Brandt—he must curb his excessive appetites. Bring him around to see his place as the future head of this family."

"Of course, I'll make every effort on your behalf." He sipped his scotch, gazing at him over the rim of his glass. "So...may I rely on your support with getting rid of the crow?"

The old man smacked on his pipe, shifting in the comfort of his favorite chair, then raised his glass in silent salute. They sealed their pact with a drink and a handshake.

****

Olivia retired after cleaning and drying the supper dishes, preferring the solace of the bedroom to chatting with Mary. With Harry's absence, she found it difficult to present a cheery face, especially in the evenings.

Seated at her dressing table, she unwound her hair and pulled the brush through it. She closed her eyes and breathed in the smoky aroma of the hickory logs on the fire. Silver moonlight joined with the candle's flame to illuminate her reflection in the mirror. She glimpsed the dark-hued circles under her eyes, a testament to the unsettling dreams that had been invading her sleep. She leaned in closer when a pounding knock sounded from the window.

Olivia and Caddie jumped to their feet. As she reached for her knife, he released a low growl, white teeth showing between brownish-pink gums. There was a brushing of leaves followed by another thud. She opened the window and peeked out.

"Help me, please! Missus—help!" a voice whisper-screamed.

Olivia's gaze dropped to a figure huddled in the shadows of the kalmia bushes. "Lucie…? Is that you? What are you doing?"

"Please, Missus, I need your help. I'm runnin' away, and I—please, will you help me?"

Olivia shimmied out the window and planted her feet on the ground, clutching the girl's arms. "Oh God. Did Reed hurt you again?"

"Yes, and I-I couldn't take no more. I took off runnin', and I dunno what to do—where do I go?" Her voice trailed off.

"Listen and do as I say." Olivia pushed her to the ground. "Stay low—here in the bushes. I'll be right back." She saw the whites of the girl's eyes gleaming in the darkness, then climbed back through the window.

Olivia landed on her feet, and Caddie jumped up to meet her. He followed her while she stuffed her knife, a flask, and coin purse inside her satchel. She rifled through her trunk and found pants and a couple of woolen tunics, jumping into them and sliding into her black coat. She heaved on her boots and strapped her bag on her back but halted at the anxious face staring back at her.

"No, boy—you stay here." Olivia rubbed her dog's ears, pressing her cheek to his. "I'll be fine." He let out a whining yowl, shifting his weight from side to side, then she ducked out the window into the pitch of night.

Olivia found Lucie curled up in a ball. "Put these on—be quick about it. Dogs won't be looking for my scent."

Lucie stared at the garments, then followed her instructions. She gazed at her blankly. "Thank ye—for helpin' me."

"Don't thank me yet. What were you planning? Where is Mr. Barlowe?"

"Entertainin' some of his friends. Told him I was sick with my courses. He don't come round me much when it's that time."

"Did anyone see you?"

Lucie shook her head.

Olivia pursed her lips. *Where can I hide you? Dear Lord, what will he do when he finds you gone?* She shook her head, banishing the image from her mind. "Maybe I can hide you here until we figure out what to do."

"No, he'll find me." She folded her arms around her middle, rocking back and forth.

"Okay—I guess the farther we get from here, the better. I don't—wait! Wait, I've got it," she exclaimed, squeezing the girl's arm. "Stay right with me, okay? Do you understand, Lucie? Don't leave my side."

"Where we goin'?"

"To get my horse."

"No!" Lucie squealed. "I'm scared of horses. Please don't make me get on one."

"Ugh! Lord, come on." Olivia pulled her cap from her pocket and shoved it on her head, gazed left and right, then focused on the woods ahead. She grabbed Lucie's trembling hand and led them away from Redmond Hill.

They crept through the woods, a miserly bit of moonlight all they had to guide them along the path. It cast eerie shadows through the boughs of the pine trees, beams of light touching them like an old man's crooked fingers. Lucie yelped and jumped with every night sound that popped or whirred around them.

Off in the distance, Olivia heard the bay of an animal rising from the cusp of a chilly breeze. Her heart skipped a beat. "Come on!" Frenzied, she led them onward, skirting their way along the path, dodging roots and low-hanging limbs.

"Ow!" Lucie yelled, a branch scraping across her cheek.

"Keep your head down." She scanned the area for a place to hide, the barking coming closer.

The girl jerked back. "Oh, Lord! Dogs!"

Olivia dragged her over to a fallen log. "Dig down and stay low. In the leaves—now!" As Lucie sobbed and tunneled into the underbrush, Olivia took a position behind the trunk of a large maple. The barking and baying descended upon them, and she unsheathed her knife, praying.

The blathering pack of fiendish men approached, torches blazing, and Lucie shrieked when one of them yanked her up by the hair. Olivia stepped out of the shadows and lunged at the man, making a direct cut in his arm. He yowled, cursing, and as she whipped around to advance again, a cracking thud radiated from the base of her skull. Ears pounding, eyeballs rolling backward in their sockets, she buckled, and the last thing she saw was the wart on Reed's grubby cheek and a blinding white flame.

Chapter Twenty-Seven

Harry held open the door for Tom with his foot, both men damp and bedraggled from the sleet that had fallen during the past hour. The lad skidded past, dropping their saddlebags on the floor by the kitchen table, and came up short.

"Cap'n? What's Mr. Allington doin' here?" Tom motioned to the man covered up on the sofa.

Harry removed his hat and shook his head. He stepped forward, practically stumbling over Caddie. His quizzical gaze drifted from the hound to the open bedroom door.

"Kitt!" Harry's voice thundered as he strode across the room.

The man bolted upright, mumbling a few unintelligible words.

"You all right, sir?" Tom came around to the end of the sofa where Kitt's feet dangled off the edge.

Kitt rubbed his eyes with his coat sleeve. "I must have drifted off. The last thing I remember was Mary giving me a dram of whiskey and this wool blanket. God—what time is it?"

"It's nigh on morning, sir." Tom clutched his hat in his hands. "We been ridin' all night."

Harry stormed back in the room. "Where is she?"

"That's why I'm here." Kitt pushed himself up, bracing his hands on his hips. "Olivia's in jail. Come

235

on."

They arrived at the alehouse within the hour. Harry sat rigid in a chair, hands cupping his knees, cold glare hiding the fury brewing inside him. He held up his hand in refusal of any drink and watched Reed sink into his cushioned chair. Kitt sat an arm's length between them.

"Quite the conundrum your little wife's gotten herself into. Trifling with the law is no small thing, Captain. Considering what she did to my Lucie, I believe my offer is fair. Agree to my demands, and she goes free." Reed chewed on his bottom lip.

"And what's your proof?" Harry's tone drew blood.

He snapped his fingers, and Lucie came forward. "Recognize these?" He pointed at the tattered pants and tunic in her hands. "Your wife's rags. She forced her into them to keep the dogs from tracking her scent." He gestured with a flick of his head. "Look at the scrapes the tree limbs left on her cheek. Frightened, cold—why, Lucie didn't even know where she was taking her."

His brow creased. "And how did she come to be with my wife?"

"Aye, my Lucie's a sensitive little thing." Reed touched the cuff on her dress sleeve, rubbing it between his fingers. "An easy target for a crafty potion-maker like your wife—filling her head with nonsense. She's such an innocent."

He seared Lucie with his gaze, and she shifted her feet. *Innocent, my arse.*

"Somehow the girl got the crazy notion I wasn't caring for her as I should. Never was a problem before your wife stuck her nose where it didn't belong." Reed spit tobacco juice into his cup. "My Lucie took off two nights ago and ran to your wife for help. She should've brought her back to me at once."

"You admit Lucie came to Mrs. Fleming for help?" Kitt leaned forward in his chair, calculating.

"I do." Reed drummed his fingers on the desk. "But that doesn't change the fact the woman absconded with my property, took off running with her in the dead of night, going God knows where. The change of clothing proves she intended to throw off her scent and escape the law."

Harry lifted his chin. "How did you come to find them, then—clothing aside?"

"Good men with good dogs can sniff out a runaway. Tracked them down about a mile from your property, and your wife fought back." Reed wagged a finger in the direction of the jail house down the street. "Even stabbed Jake Dobbs in the arm."

Kitt scrubbed his jaw. "Rest assured, Jake knows Captain Fleming will make amends in every way."

"Well, good golly, Mr. Allington," Reed said, mocking. "And will the bigwig captain be making amends to me, too?"

"Hell, no." Harry slammed his fist on the table.

Reed chuckled, and the squirt from his mouth fell short of the cup, a trickle of brown juice running down his chin. He whipped out a fresh handkerchief and dabbed it dry. "Content to let the little troublemaker sit in jail a while, are you? Maybe teach her a lesson?"

"You bastard. Olivia's innocent—you're using her to get at me and my homestead."

"Innocent? You're quite sure of that, eh?" He folded his arms on the desk and leaned in. "We caught her red-handed with my slave—my property—on the run in the woods under the dark of night. Even assaulted a man.

You understand what happens to lawbreakers—even ones as pretty and sweet as your wife?"

Harry spotted a tiny twitch in Kitt's cheek. Their gazes met, both knowing the situation was grim. Should Reed choose to charge Olivia with a crime, neither ignorance nor naivety would save her from his wrath. He scrubbed his hands down his cheeks and blew out a breath.

"You're doubtless tired from your journey. And then to come home and discover your wife's foray with the law." Reed tsked, rubbing his knuckle over his mustache. "You should take a day or two to consider my offer, Captain. Old Jake will see she's kept comfortable in jail while I decide whether to press charges."

Harry pushed out of the chair and stormed out of the room. Outside, songbirds chirped a greeting and he bristled in response. He strode down the street and sat at the end of the raised walkway, back flat against the wall, arms hanging over his knees. He closed his eyes against the throbbing in his temples, his mother's words creeping into his thoughts.

"You're a good lad, Harry." Abigale cradled his head, caressing his thick blond waves with her fingers, and he curled up on her lap, a frown pasted across his face. With his ear pressed against her breast, he shut his eyes tight. "Aye, you're only six years old, but you must remember actions matter. They can hurt you and others. You see, Harry, if you cut a rose from the plant in the garden, you can never put it back on again. You can't stick the stem back on with glue. You can't sew it back on with a needle and thread. You've cut it from the plant and at best, it will sit in a vase and give you the last bit of its beauty...until it fades and droops and finally

*withers away. You may even wish you hadn't cut it at all,
realizing it a grave mistake—only it's too late. A grave
mistake indeed for the rose—its life ended so soon, and
all because, in haste, you wanted to take the flower with
you."*

Harry cut a sideways glance at Kitt when he took a
seat beside him. "It's my fault—all of it." He held up his
hand in a defensive gesture. "No, let me speak. I'm so
damn selfish. Would you even think twice about giving
in to Reed's demands? To free Sarah?" He pressed a fist
against his lips. "There's something wrong with me. My
mother knew it." Kitt arched a questioning brow, and he
nodded. "Aye, she did. Told me so when I was a boy. I
thought I shouldn't have to choose—I should be able to
have it all. Keep the rose for myself…"

"You're rambling, Harry…and you're exhausted."
Kitt nudged his shoulder. "Go see your wife. Then go
home and eat and clear your head. We'll figure
something out."

He nodded, though not entirely sure he shared Kitt's
optimism, then pulled himself up, dusted off his coat, and
made his way to the jail.

Once inside the building, Harry followed the guard
down a short corridor and came up short. He gazed at
Olivia, his heart falling to the pit of his stomach, and
spoke her name softly.

Olivia jumped up and rushed over to the iron bars
separating them. "Oh, Harry, I'm sorry. I was trying to
help Lucie. You must be so angry with me." Her voice
was small, breathy.

He despised her apologetic tone, especially when he
was to blame for the rotten situation. He had left her
alone and confused, a target for a cad like Barlowe. He

intertwined his fingers with hers around the bar, tracing his thumbs over her wrists, inching upward.

"We'll have none of that, Captain." The young guard stood in the doorway, hands on his hips.

"You will stand down. Leave us." His command effectively sucked the energy from the room, and the fellow trudged off.

He fixed his gaze on Olivia, hating the bars preventing him from scooping her up in his arms and planting her on his lap. "I could never be angry with you. I shouldn't have left you the way I did. I'm so sorry. Please forgive me, Scrapper."

"Oh, Harry. How I've missed you calling me that. I've missed everything about you—about us." Tears filled her eyes, and he cursed his stubborn pride.

He brushed away her tears with his thumbs. "Shh, don't be afraid." He scanned the dank confines of the small cell. "I promise this'll all be over soon."

She quivered, her breath uneasy, and he motioned for them to sit at the two stools. She leaned her forehead against the bars, eyes downcast. He pushed his hands between the bars and held her hands.

"I'm sorry. I was only trying to help. Reed—he hurts her, Harry. He abuses her body, her mind—he's violated her time and again. He's Satan in the flesh."

"Aye, it's very sad. She may have wished to be free of him, but she'll never be able to let go. She's enslaved to him on a much deeper level." *It was all an act, Liv. Reed wants my home and my life. But that's not a story for today.*

"She begged for my help."

He nodded once. "Tell me, were you taking Lucie to your family?"

"It was the safest place I could think of. Elan is so clever, and I thought he might know what to do."

Because your bulldog husband was nowhere to be found. His need to console her outweighed any correction of her good, albeit misguided, intentions. His grip tightened around her hands. "You did what you thought was best. You were very brave."

Olivia withdrew her hand, fingers scraping across her collarbone, and gave a bitter laugh. "But none of that matters, does it? Reed says I've broken the law—called me a thief. What's he...what's he going to do to me?"

"Nothing." Harry brushed a wisp of hair behind her ear, caressing her lobe. "Trust me. I'll have you out of here in no time."

"Really? Back home?"

"Aye, you've my word." Urgency filled the air between them, and their lips sought one another, obstructed by the iron, but locking in sweet promise. He was reluctant to part from her, the taste of her tears a reminder of life's uncertainty. *But there's one thing I can set straight, by God.*

"Wait," he said, reaching into his coat pocket, placing the blue hair ribbon in her palm. "Hold this tight between your hands."

Olivia complied, her eyes widening as he lifted his hands and cut the threads with a quick swipe of his blade. Then he took the two halves, matched them between her hands again, and made another slice.

"Now, get rid of it please."

She nodded and tossed the remnants in the wastebasket by the cot. He kissed her once more, then turned to leave.

Chapter Twenty-Eight

As Catherine closed the door to the nursery, a feverish discourse reached her ears. She took two steps down the stairs, careful to remain hidden, and peeked around the half-walled stairway. She spied Brandt pacing the length of the study.

"Father, this is horseshit. Harry needs our help, and he'll have it."

"Bah! You wanted rid of the chit as much as me," Zeb said in rebuttal.

"Not like this—bloody scheming again. Will you never change?" Brandt stopped, then he blew out a groan. "We could have reasoned with Harry and taken Olivia back to the Catawba—not see her ransomed by a wolf. And what of Redmond Hill? He'll get his hands on his home."

"And you think I can control Barlowe? The cad has his own agenda."

"He'll see to it she's arrested and found guilty—there are no boundaries he won't cross. God knows what her punishment would be."

"And that's somehow my problem?"

Catherine detected the heavy clap of Brandt's boots walking across the floor again, then there was silence.

"No, but you've got dirt on every man from here to Charleston. You must have something you can use against him."

"I don't," Zeb said caustically.

As the front door burst open, Catherine sucked in her breath and ducked farther behind the wall. She remained still for a few moments, then inched forward again. She spotted Harry entering the study, coattails swinging.

"Please, Zeb." Harry's voice broke, frenzied like a cornered animal. "If you ever had a care for me—or if you did once love my mother—you'll help me. I-I can't fight Reed alone. You have connections—resources, friends at your disposal. You must help me stop him from stealing my wife and Redmond Hill."

Suddenly Zeb entered her field of vision, his greedy green gaze turning her skin to gooseflesh.

"Must...?" Zeb spat. "Must? Why, none of this would have happened if you had any wits, boy. You exposed yourself, and Reed spotted your weakness— defying your moral obligation to the Fleming name and marrying a mutt."

Catherine cupped her hand over her mouth.

"You're the one who stole Catherine from me and gave her to Brandt. What did you expect me to do?"

"Same old story, boy. You live to spite me—always have."

"Christ! Why can't you believe I didn't marry Olivia to spite you?"

"Damnation, but you are just like your father. You're a selfish, cocky, conceited jackass."

Catherine craned her neck, catching a glimpse of Zeb rounding his desk.

"You bastard!" Harry spat.

Catherine winced, the sound of glass crashing on the floor, books slamming to the ground, and heaving men making her bite into her knuckles. *Stop this! What's Harry talking about? Zeb stole me and gifted me to Brandt?*

"Do you think Joseph loved your mother? Do you…?" Zeb hissed.

"Of course, he did."

"No. No, he didn't. Because if he had, you wouldn't be here. You should've never been born, and if Joseph had had a care for someone other than himself, he'd have never allowed it to happen. We almost lost Abigale in childbirth with Drew. Afterward, she felt obligated to give your father one more child—one more try for a son."

The thundering echo of Zeb's voice sent fear spiraling through Catherine's body.

"You killed her, Harry. Sure as sunrise, your birth brought about her death—you made her weak. But that son of a bitch—he got you, yes, sir. Joseph got his precious son. And I lost the only woman I ever loved, and my reason for living."

An interminable silence permeated the air. From where she was perched, Catherine spied her husband collapsed in the high-back chair, head down, hands clasped behind his neck. The rasp of Zeb's breathing, labored and haggard, lifted in the air.

"Good God. It all makes sense now. My whole life I've wondered how I wronged you, but the truth is you hate me for my very existence. It's why you destroyed my relationship with Catherine. You wanted to deprive me of my love, just like you were all those years ago. You hate me so much you'd stake your own son against me." Harry let loose a string of curses that stung Catherine's ears. "And when I did marry—someone you deem an embarrassment—then by God, you plotted with the devil himself to destroy me yet again."

Catherine spotted a servant approaching the door to the study, likely alerted by the ruckus, but the lad turned back. *Smart boy.*

"I don't want your help, Zeb. I'll take care of Reed myself. Everything from you is bloody cursed, rotten to the core."

Zeb muttered something, then sputtered in an attempt to tamp down another of his coughing fits.

"And I hope *that* kills you, old man."

Booted feet stomped across the floor, pausing at the doorway of the study. Catherine shrank deeper into the shadow of the stairs.

"Harry, wait—don't go." Brandt tugged at his arm. "I'll help you. I'll talk to Reed. I can make him see reason."

Catherine peeked down to where her husband and Harry stood face to face in the doorway. A prickly sensation coursed up her spine.

"Did you know what possessed him when you agreed to wed Catherine?"

"No. I didn't understand the depth of his hatred until now." Brandt squared his shoulders. "I was in a very dark place after Margaret died, and I-I didn't…damn!" He slammed his fist against the wall.

Harry jerked Brandt's sleeve. "Did you love Catherine, even a little? Do you now…?"

Catherine clamped her mouth shut for fear of crying out. *Oh, Lord. Please, Brandt. Say it—say you love me.* She watched her husband turn and disappear into the study, and tears pooled in her eyes.

"Christ, I don't even care anymore. Your marriage

is your own damn business." Harry blew out a savage breath, then turned toward the two men in the study. "I'll never forgive myself for leaving Olivia alone. Her place was with me in Charleston these past weeks, but she promised *your* wife she'd be here for the birthing." He jabbed his finger in the air. "And I want nothing from you, Zeb. That bastard can take Redmond Hill, but I'll not end my marriage and marry Emily—ever. You and Barlowe may extort my birthright, but never my heart and soul. Then, old man, I will never lay eyes on you again. I'll leave with my wife and take my chances on my own, far away from this swamp. My only regret is I won't be around to see you die. I hope you rot in hell!"

Catherine held her hand to heart as Harry stormed off. She flinched as he slammed the door, mind reeling. *Dear God. Brandt doesn't love me—it's all been a lie. And poor Olivia has no idea about Reed's plot.* Without hesitation, she gathered her skirts, pulled herself upright, and raced down the back staircase. Her mind set, she called for her carriage and set off to Camden.

****

Olivia listened as Catherine retold the scene from Glen Laurel in grisly detail, raw emotion etched in her every word.

"It's awful. Absolute evil is all around us in the men we thought we could trust." Catherine removed the hood of her cloak. "It can't go on, I tell you. We must stick together, which means you can't be left in the dark. Men always think they know what's best for us—as if we don't have the ability to process anything more taxing than a sonnet." With gloved hands fisted by her sides, she paced the length of the cell bars between them and turned, revealing a ribbon tied in a bow around the base of her chignon.

Olivia jumped to her feet. *No. No, no. It can't be...* She clocked the steps until Catherine paused and whipped around again. She ran a shaky hand over her collarbone, then stilled, lifting her chin. "That's a beautiful hair ribbon, Catherine. Wherever did you get it?"

She paused and touched it gingerly. "This...? It's rather old, but I've always liked the color—matches my eyes."

Olivia formed a curt smile before striding to the waste pail filled with discarded strands of the same ribbon. She snatched them up, walked back to Catherine, and dumped them in her hand. "Tell me why you're wearing this same ribbon."

Catherine ran her fingers across the threadbare pieces, her eyes cloudy.

She grabbed the cell bars and shook them. "You heard me. Harry carried this with him everywhere—every day for the past four years—until this afternoon when he cut it into these pieces. Tell me why you have the same ribbon. Tell. Me. Now."

Catherine scooted back. "Please. Calm down." She untied her bow and held it—and the tattered shreds—in her palms. Her head began to shake. "Dear Lord. Oh, Olivia. I knew Harry still had it, but I had no idea he kept it close. Truly, I didn't. You must believe me."

She braced her hands on her hips. "I'm such a stupid fool. You all must have had a great laugh behind my back. Silly girl who marries the man everyone knows is in love with Catherine the great."

"Did he not tell you...?"

Olivia's gaze sent a scorching reply.

Catherine moved in closer, seething. "This proves my point. They've all lied to us. Harry should have been honest with you."

"But how could you break his heart and marry Brandt? He loved you—he still does."

She clutched the bars between them. "Everyone lied to me, Olivia. I obeyed my father and trusted Brandt. I thought he loved me, cared about me. But that's not even the worst of it. Zeb plotted the whole thing to spite Harry—to crush him."

"You're all mad. You're a wretched bunch." Olivia turned away and plopped down on the squeaky cot.

"That's why I'm here—to tell you the truth. You need to know what Reed's asking in exchange for your freedom. He wants Harry to end your marriage, marry his stepdaughter, and give him the deed to Redmond Hill."

"What?" Olivia jumped to her feet, aghast.

"It's true. Then I heard Harry say he would hand over Redmond Hill, but he wouldn't abandon you. He wants to take you away with him—somewhere far away."

"My Lord, I'm nothing but a pawn. Reed's blackmailing him with me." She covered her mouth with her hand, fearful she might cast up her lunch.

Catherine wound her finger through the curl by her cheek, frown lines creased around her eyes. "Honestly, I assumed Harry had told you about our past. I never mentioned it because there was nothing to hide. It was a youthful infatuation. Harry's always been so exuberant and impulsive, but I admit, I like living comfortably. I'm not hearty and resilient like you. You're what he needs in a wife, whether he realizes it or not. But regardless, please believe me. I never meant to cause him—or you—any pain."

Olivia approached and met her at eye level. "My aunt warned me about marrying into your world. I don't understand your ways—half-truths and greedy, jealous games—but I thank you for telling me the truth. You've given me a lot to think about."

"Please don't fret. I'm sure Harry will give Reed what he wants. You won't be here long."

Despite the iron bars separating them, they clasped hands in a kind of secret pact. She stared at the floor, eyelashes flat against her cheeks as the great Catherine Hastings Fleming, the living, breathing ghost in her marriage, strolled out of the jailhouse.

Chapter Twenty-Nine

With the afternoon's revelations fresh in her mind, Olivia devised a plan based on her observations in the jail over the past two days. She lingered over her supper, having coaxed Caleb McElroy, the young night guard, to eat with her. His oblong ears and chin gave him a sweet, awkward visage, and together with a snaggletoothed grin, he was most endearing. They conversed easily after their meal, which made what she was about to do even more difficult.

She thanked Caleb for the company, and as he lit the wall lantern and walked down the corridor, she kneeled by the cot and prayed. No scriptures came to mind—no recollection of Jesus to which she could cling. She knew only one thing. She would not stay put and be the puppet in Reed's game. She had decided devotion to Harry meant action. If the puppet vanished, there would be no deal to strike and no reason to sacrifice Redmond Hill. Harry would keep his home, protect their tenants, and start a new life. He had lied to her from the start about Catherine—and had never even once said he loved her. *There's simply nothing left.*

Olivia prayed to God for protection and forgiveness—and whispered, "Amen."

****

"What is it? Missus, what's wrong?" Caleb held his lantern up so the light illuminated her face.

Olivia stood, screeching and fretting on top of the cot, hair disheveled in a flurry around her shoulders, the curves of her breasts visible, she knew, in the lamp's glow. She bounced again, crying for help. "Oh, Caleb! Caleb, please—don't leave me. I heard it first, but then I saw it!"

"What did you see?" Caleb's voice lifted in urgency.

"Oh…oh, it's a rat! Horrid black thing—its eyes so beastly. Please, please don't leave me!"

He hung the lantern on a nail and fumbled with the keys on his belt loop. "I won't leave. I'll help you." He swung the door open, and she tumbled into his arms, sliding down the length of his body. His hands clung to her gently sloping hips. She sighed, worrying her lip.

If I've judged it right, I can slip my arm behind my back and reach the bedpan. She pressed her breasts against his chest, then gazed up into his eyes…and clobbered him with the heavy dish in one mighty blow, sending him careening to the ground like a fallen sapling. She stared down, cupping her cheeks. *I'm so sorry, Caleb.* She scampered into her coat and slid alongside the wall toward the back door of the jail. Her pulse thundering, she cracked the door open, slipped around it, and planted her feet on the ground. She never looked back and raced home to her Catawba family.

****

Harry and Tom woke early, ate their breakfast in relative silence, and set off for town at first light. Within minutes of turning onto King's Street, a breeze brushed past a line of white pine trees, filling the air with a chill. They tethered their horses outside of Kitt's office, but before they could reach the door, he emerged, hat pulled down low over his brow. He corralled them around the corner of the building, gazing over his shoulder for onlookers.

"What the hell—" Harry shook him off, in no mood for dramatics.

"It's Olivia. She's gone." Kitt leaned closer. "Did you have anything to do with it? Don't lie to me."

He braced his hands on his hips. "Christ, what do you mean she's gone? She's in jail. Where is there to go?"

He pulled back. "All right, I had to be sure you weren't a part of it."

"Part of what?" Apprehension laced his voice. "Damn it, Kitt—where's my wife?"

Wordlessly, Kitt led him to the jail and into a hornet's nest.

Jake Dobbs, Camden's pudgy, middle-aged marshal, pounded the fist of his good arm on his wobbly desk. His other arm still bore the bandage from Olivia's dagger. "Captain, I'll tell you this much—our Caleb is lucky to be alive. Your wife bewitched him, then clubbed him on the head with a bedpan for Christ's sake. She's a vixen, that one."

Harry stood beside Kitt and scratched his four-day-old beard. His eyes ached from sleep deprivation while his mind grappled with the notion Olivia had escaped her confinement. He sized up the young jailor who was leaning against the wall with a slab of beefsteak over a pumpknot. *Bewitched and clubbed him—lucky that's all she did.*

A gust of frigid air rushed in with the opening door, a dark figure silhouetted against the bright morning sun. It leaned over and spit into a tin cup.

"What the hell kind of jail you running, Dobbs?

Prisoners breaking out?" Reed tipped up his hat with the back of his hand.

"The young woman was under our watch, yes—but she was never charged with a crime now, was she? I told you that when you first dragged her in. Fact is, what we have here is a missing person, not an escaped prisoner." Dobbs fidgeted with his holster, chin jutting forward.

Reed scowled and exhaled, his nose twitching. "You had something to do with this, Fleming. I smell a rat."

"You're the damn rat." Harry advanced, but Tom interjected his body between them.

Kitt strolled forward, hands behind his back. "Your accusations are baseless, Mr. Barlowe. Olivia Fleming was never a prisoner. She's left the premises, and with no charges on record, this matter has reached its conclusion."

Reed pointed his bony finger in Kitt's face. "Save your horseshit talk. Christ, I've got better things to do than mess with you two. This ain't over, Captain." He spat on the jailhouse floor and stormed out the door.

The room turned deadly quiet for several moments before Harry slapped his hat on his head and walked over to Dobbs, his brow speckled with tiny sweat beads. He placed several coins on the desk. "This should cover the damages here—for the both of you. You have my apology."

Harry made his way to the door, holding his hand up in refusal to Kitt and Tom as he passed by them. He swung up into the saddle, kicked his heels, and spurred his horse into a gallop. With his body leaning forward and into the crackling wind, he blinked back the wetness pooling in the corners of his eyes. In all the ruckus, the torment of his encounter with Zeb, the accusations and maneuvering in the jail, there was one distinct fact no one—not even his friends—had acknowledged. Olivia was gone.

Chapter Thirty

Harry eventually slowed his pace, his mind fogged. He lifted his gaze heavenward and found neither sun showers nor clouds. The mid-morning air was bland and tepid, like ale poured in a glass and then forgotten. He heard no chirp from the pine warbler in the distance, and there was no song from Olivia to look forward to at home.

As Harry led his horse onto his property, he came upon a mule hitched to a wagon beside the magnolia tree and spied a broad-shouldered Native sitting on his front porch steps. Noting how far his legs stretched out in front of him, he judged his height to be more than six feet. He wore breeches and tall boots made of a brown hide, and a blue tunic and tan vest covered his rugged torso. The man's skin resembled a melted blend of topaz and copper. His ink black hair was slick against his skull, palm oil combed through the length and woven into a thick waxy braid. Dark eyes, sober and steady, locked with his cold blue ones. After he dismounted and tethered his horse, the impressive-looking visitor rose to meet him and extended his right arm.

"As master of Redmond Hill, seems I should be the one waiting to greet you. You must be Elan." Harry shook his outstretched hand.

"I thought it best I come quick, even if it meant waiting. I spoke to your people and told them my purpose."

Harry took the porch steps by twos and held open the door. Elan stepped inside, taking a seat at the kitchen table. He claimed his usual spot, gaze traveling the room, satisfied Mary was hiding but within earshot. Caddie walked over, toenails clicking on the floor, and lowered himself beside his boot.

Elan clasped his sizable hands together on the tabletop. "I bring news. Olivia is well."

His stomach turned a flip. *Thank God.* He kept his jawline firm, revealing nothing of his inner turmoil.

"But she is not so much well on the inside." Elan placed his hand over his chest.

"She's been through a great ordeal."

"There's more, Captain." He expelled a heavy breath. "Olivia has made up her mind. She wants to stay with us."

Harry leaned forward on his elbows. "But she's my wife."

"Her actions brought trouble to you and your Redmond house. Barlowe is using her—says she's done a crime, yes? He wants to take this place from you because of her."

A deep crease formed on Harry's brow. *How in hell does he know about Reed's blackmail attempt?* He straightened his back, hands flat on the table. "He accused my wife of breaking the law, but I was prepared to give him what he wanted in exchange for her freedom. I was on my way to see her this morning when I learned she'd fled."

"Olivia will not let you give up your land. It's all a man has."

He cut him with his gaze. "I don't give up Redmond

Hill easily, but I would do it for her. We will start over somewhere else."

"No. Her father had no home, and she knows how sad that is. A real home is all she's ever wanted, and she has it with the Catawba. She does not want to be your wife. Your heart is split." He gestured, separating his third and fourth fingers like a fork. "You love another woman."

"I will speak to my wife."

He frowned, pulling a folded note from inside his vest, and placed in on the table.

Harry ripped it open.

Harry,

When I learned what Reed was demanding in exchange for my freedom, I couldn't let you pay such a steep price. Redmond Hill is your family's home—your past and your future. With me gone, there is no bargaining to do. You keep your homestead by default. Reed Barlowe will give up his plan, and I'll soon be forgotten.

Do what you will about his stepdaughter—and Catherine. Cannot say I was entirely shocked when I figured out about the two of you. You always had such a softness for her. I should have realized sooner you were in love with her.

I believe I lived up to my end of our deal. I did my best to give you devotion. By leaving you now, I'm doing the most devoted thing I can—preserving Redmond Hill for you and those you care for.

Olivia

Harry refolded the note and tossed it on the table. *How did she learn about Catherine? I should have been the one to tell her. But I can make her understand.* He twisted the lid off his flask and drank a swallow of scotch. "You may tell my wife this is not her decision to make."

"Olivia's not coming back here."

He stood, palms planted flat on the table, and leaned forward. "Then I will go to her."

Elan rose to meet him, hands flexed at his side. "She said you were stubborn."

He smirked under his breath. "Then she must have also told you I don't take orders—and I'm impulsive."

"She did. But I speak to you now as man to man—soldier to soldier." His taut cheeks softened. "I believe this marriage was wrong. A white man may have fathered Olivia, but her mother nurtured her and taught her our ways. She has our blood—Catawba blood. We can protect her in ways you cannot understand. Can you say the same for your people? With you, she has been sad and hurt—a way for Barlowe to get to you and your land. She's not safe with you. If you care for her, you will leave her be."

Harry rubbed his knuckles across his stiff whiskers. "She told me you were brave and canny—I'll give you that much. But you forget Olivia is my wife, and we share a bond."

"Shared." The word echoed through the room, dark and forbidding. "You forget I know about the child you lost. Even your God knew your union was not right."

"And your Catawba man—he'd have been better for her?"

"Yes." Elan huffed and reached into his pocket, placing a small silver object on the table.

Harry picked it up with dumb disbelief.

"The ring is yours. I am here for her trunk and the

dog." Elan tilted his head in Caddie's direction. The hound shifted uneasily, ears pricked up. "He was a gift from her father."

Harry kicked his chair to the floor and walked away, needing distance to keep from strangling the man. He turned the ring over in his palm, trying to fit it on his pinky, but it would not go past his knuckle. *It would appear I'm not fit for much—least of all you, Scrapper.* He stuffed the ring in his pocket and turned about, head erect. "Take what you will—and get the hell out of my house."

Elan untied Olivia's blouse from his waist belt and rubbed it over Caddie's nose. On his knees, he met the dog at eye level, rubbing his smooth coat and whispering in his ear. The hound yowled and whimpered, lifting one paw, then the other in protest, wiggling when Elan fit the lead around his neck.

Harry remained immobile, gazing forward, his body as hard as salt stone. He never flinched as Elan left with Olivia's trunk and her dog. A few hours ago, he knew his wife was gone. Standing alone and cold beside a simmering fire, he realized it was so much more. Olivia had said goodbye.

Part Four

Brave in Reflection

Chapter Thirty-One

April 1784

Olivia stepped backward, eyebrows creased. The oblong dish wobbled on the table, the beveled edge fatter on one side than the other. Perhaps the crafting of clay pots in the Catawba tradition was not one of her gifts.

"Do not worry. You'll get better with practice." Waneta placed an arm around her shoulder.

"You said the same thing after my fourth pot. I'm on what—sixteen now?" Olivia stepped away and wiped her forehead. "It's so hot in here." Her hands went to her neck, ready to twist her hair up into a bun, but her fingers came up short. They found only her cropped hair, still thick and lustrous, but cut to within a few inches of her scalp. With the new haircut, simple breeches, and always a loose-fitting shirt designed to cover any hint of her bosom, she looked every bit a boy. That was the intent anyway.

Betsey exchanged looks with her mother. "Hm, maybe it is a little warm today. The sun's out—let's go for a walk. Can we? Please, we won't go far—promise."

Olivia grinned, excited about something for the first time in months. It was spring, and the sun's rays were warming the earth. Weary of being cooped up inside—disguised, lying low for her safety and that of the tribe—she was desperate for fresh air.

"I suppose so—but take your little cousins with you." Waneta crossed her arms over her chest. "You'll look more like a group playing together and not a courting couple."

She and Betsey looked at Waneta, then at each other, and burst out in laughter.

"What?" Her aunt chuckled with them. "I just think you'll draw less attention, is all."

"Whatever you say, Aunt," she said overtop a giggle.

When they reached the meadow, Olivia reclined on her back, shielding her eyes with her hand against the sunlight. "This is nice." Puffy clouds pranced across the sky, and she stretched her imagination, making little pictures with them in her mind.

Betsey gazed at the youngsters playing nearby. "It's good to see you smile."

The scent of snapdragons and lavender blossoms filled the air, tickling her nose and rousing images she would rather forget. She had scarcely allowed herself a passing thought of Harry these past few months, much less a full-blown memory. She rolled over, resting her chin in her hand, and propped up on her elbow.

"Is it hard to talk about?" Betsey plucked a red clover from the grass and rolled its stem between her fingers. "Elan told me not to ask you about him."

Betsey was fifteen, a bit young for marriage in the tribe, but old enough to have a notion of such things. Olivia wanted nothing more than to let everything spill out—each laugh, every whisper, endless looks they had shared—but she would stand by her decision. She would keep every precious memory with Harry locked away in the quiet recesses of her heart.

"Elan's right. I love Harry more than anything else in this world, but that part of my life is over."

"Do you think you will ever see him again?"

She shook her head. "I don't think he would risk coming here, knowing what Mr. Barlowe might do if he found out where I was."

"That man put you in jail—he could've killed you. Don't you worry he'll come after you again?"

Sadly, Reed haunted her dreams. Elan had told her he and some of his old toads had come around soon after her escape, but the tribesmen held them off. Elan assured her even if he kept sniffing around, he would find no trace of her.

Olivia shook her head. "I think the more time passes, if I'm careful and keep to myself, I'll be fine."

Olivia warmed with her cousin's reassuring smile. With fawn-brown eyes and long straight hair, she was Elan's younger sister by five years. She was a skilled potter, obeyed her mother without fail, and always made time for simple pleasures with her friends. Since their father's death some years ago, Elan bore the mantle of their family. With a care for Betsey's happiness and safety, he would no doubt see her promised to a strong, well-respected tribesman.

"I'm glad you're here now. I am sorry for all the bad things that have happened to you—living with those people."

"That's just it, Betsey—I'm half 'those' people." She sat up tall and noted her cousin's scrunched-up nose. "You see, the world gets a person whose skin is white or black or brown—even if it doesn't treat them fairly. It can handle absolutes, and each one has its own place— but it can't decide what to do with a mixed breed."

"What a bad word."

"It is. It's hard being different. I never belonged much anywhere. I was afraid Harry would regret marrying me."

"Well, you fit in here. I look at you and think you're like me."

Olivia smiled, grateful for her sentiment.

"Oh, no. Come back here, you two!" Betsey hopped up and ran after the children. Caddie barked at the threesome, enjoying the revelry.

Olivia turned on her side and stretched out, arm curled under her head. Their unbridled joy reminded her of afternoons last summer at Redmond Hill—little Polly and the other children dancing around, playing tag games under the shade of the trees. She rolled onto her back, slamming her eyes shut and shoving her fingers in her ears. She began to count in her head.

"What you doing…?"

The question was muffled by her fingertips, but it was discernable. She opened her eyes and gazed into a pair of mud-brown three-year-old eyes. The boy wrinkled his nose as she pulled him to her chest and squeezed tight. He giggled and squirmed with delight, sitting up, straddling her chest with his chubby legs. With his hands cupping her head, he planted a fat kiss on her cheek.

"You taste funny." The child smacked his lips together.

Tears have a way of doing that. "Well, so do you." She laughed, growling and biting at his neck, pretending to gobble him up. He squealed louder, and before she would even think about letting him wiggle away, she hugged him one more time—for no other reason than the warmth it brought to her empty heart.

****

Harry hated goodbyes. He had already been through the first one at Redmond Hill less than a week ago, a gathering of his tenant families and closest friends. In a fortunate turn, Kitt and Sarah shared news they were expecting a child before the end of the year. For Harry, it was a stark reminder that amidst sorrow in life, there were always pockets of joy. He had no doubt his best friend would make an exceptional father.

The hardest thing was leaving Tom behind. He had grown reliant on his loyal companion and had found in recent weeks they shared the even deeper bond of loss and dissolution. The lad bore a terrific burden for his involvement with Lucie—and how she and Barlowe had preyed on Olivia's good heart—and spent much of his time telling him so. After reassuring him he held him blameless in the whole wretched mess, Harry asked him for a favor. He was entrusting the day-to-day operations of Redmond Hill to Tom, increasing his wages and giving him the position of overseer. Kitt would be there to support him in every way, transacting any legal and financial matters during his absence. Tom's somber face and old floppy hat were the last things he saw as the coach pulled out, destined for the coast.

On the docks at Georgetown, Harry was exchanging farewells again, only this time with the Sutherland crew. His nephews considered his departure an adventure. Clyde was especially jealous of the excitement he imagined he would encounter at sea, and Josie and Hugh hoped it would be a safe journey to clear his head and heal his heart.

Harry carried Greer in his arms, grateful for the

toddler pressed close to his heart. "You're blessed, Josie." He kissed the boy's feather-light curls before placing the child in Hugh's open arm.

"Take a wee bit of time to enjoy Bermuda, eh? Bigham's a good man—he'll take care of you." With the little boy squished between them, Hugh gave him a hearty embrace and strolled on ahead.

"You'll be dodging pirates, you think, Uncle Harry?" Clyde asked, tugging on his coattails, eyes wide.

"I hope not." He stooped down to meet his nephew's precocious blue eyes, touching his pistol reverently. "But a good soldier is always prepared."

Clyde gazed up at his mother, pulling on her skirt. "I want to be a soldier when I grow up."

Josie tousled his auburn hair. "Is that so? And last week you wanted to be a fisherman."

His gaze softened with recollection.

"Be off with you, son," she said, grinning. "Go catch up to your papa."

They watched him gallop along, scooting in alongside Hugh.

"Now that one's going to gray my hair." Josie stuffed her hand through Harry's arm, fingers squeezing his muscle. "He reminds me of you."

He gave his sister a half-smile and kissed the top of her head.

Up ahead they spied Sean sitting on a bench, hands on his knees. Though he was just ten years old, he had feet like his father—two long narrow boats. He shifted under the weight of his tan twill jacket and flipped his collar up against the sea breeze.

"Time to say goodbye to your uncle." Josie tilted her head to one side. "Sean…?"

Harry gazed at the lad, then gave his sister a level look. She walked on, giving a wayward glance over her shoulder at them. He took a seat beside the boy and leaned back, breathing in the salty air.

"I heard Mama and Papa talking yesterday," Sean said, squinting against the sunshine.

"Did you now?" Harry turned toward him, resting his arm over the top of the bench.

"Yup." He bobbed his head once. "Said your head was broke and your heart—um…they said your heart needed clearing out."

He coughed a laugh. Though backward, the lad had the gist of it.

"How come? You seem fine to me."

Harry rubbed his knuckles across his upper lip. "Sometimes a man needs to be on his own so he can figure out what's become of his life. I hope taking this trip—and helping your father with a bit of business— will help me fix things in my head…and my heart."

"Why didn't you bring Auntie Liv with you? You promised you would on your next visit. Is she not well?" His nephew kicked a pebble with his foot, and it skipped over the wooden walkway.

"She's well—but things are difficult for us at the moment."

Sean crossed his arms studiously. "You're a soldier and a farmer, right?"

He nodded.

"And married last year?"

"Yes."

"And you've a nice big house called Redmond?" He stopped to scratch his nose with his coat sleeve.

"Redmond Hill. Yes, I do."

"So…isn't that what your life is? Is there much to figure out?"

Harry could not help but chuckle at his simple wisdom. He searched his mind for a plausible illustration—and finding one—nudged the boy's shoulder.

"You've got a point, Sean. Maybe this will help. A great American patriot named Thomas Paine—lives in New York, you see—put it this way. 'I love the man that can smile in trouble, that can gather strength from distress, and grow brave by reflection.' Let's say I'm going off to work on the 'brave reflection' part."

Sean's blond hair blew with the wind, the ends curling up in a cloud around his shoulders. He turned his face upward, revealing fair cheeks with a dusting of light freckles. "I think maybe I can work on the 'smiling in trouble' part. Sure seems like I find enough of it. It might make Mama happy if I took to smiling my way through it."

He gave his shoulder a gentle squeeze. "You're a good lad, Sean Sutherland. Let no one tell you different."

"Yes, sir." He leaned in and hugged him tight around his middle.

The move caught his breath, and he shifted, enveloping the boy with his arms.

"You'll be back to see us soon, Uncle?"

"You can count on it."

Farther down the dock, Harry spotted Hugh and Clyde jousting playfully with two tree branches while his sister strolled their way, Greer's body slumped over her shoulder. She stopped in front of them, and he gazed into her eyes, damp with tears she had hastily wiped against her son's curly hair.

"I will miss this one, Josie. You've got much to be proud of in him." He tousled Sean's hair.

She opened her free arm to Sean so he could stand with her.

"Goodbye, Uncle Harry. I wish you safe travels. Good luck on growing brave in your reflection." The boy gave him a spirited wave.

"And here's to smiling in trouble, aye?"

"Aye," he said, laughing, running off to join in the jousting game.

"What was all that?" Josie asked.

"I'll let Sean tell you." Harry squeezed her hand and gazed at the ocean over her shoulder. Soon he would have the tides, white-tipped waves, and space he needed to think. He was ready to be off but stopped short and turned to face her. "Keep the deed I gave you in a safe place. I want you to hold on to it for me. I'm alone again, and the fact is I may never have children of my own. Redmond Hill would become Sean's after I'm gone."

She shifted her sleeping son higher on her hip. "You're not thinking clearly. It's your home—Olivia saved it for you."

"It's nothing but a target on my back, men using it against me—gave her the excuse she needed to desert me." He averted his gaze, squinting into the sun.

"So bloody stubborn." She craned her neck, pushing Greer's head gently to the side with her cheek and with her free hand, removed her necklace. "Here, I want you to have this—it was Mother's. I helped Father pick it out for her birthday. He gave it to me after she died." She looked at him through misty eyes. "Keep it with you— think of her and me. You won't be alone."

He secured it around his neck, tucking it away under

his shirt and neckcloth. He leaned in to hug his sister, acutely aware of just how well she understood him.

"I love you, Harry."

He pressed his lips to her sun-kissed cheek. "I love you, too."

He gave her one last smile and, rubbing the sleeping child's back, proceeded to the dockside office, Sutherland's bills of lading for the indigo shipments in hand. It was time to board the island-bound sloop and make his first ocean voyage. With any luck, he would grow brave in reflection—and somehow mend his broken head and clear out his heart.

Chapter Thirty-Two

May 1784

Olivia found leading a nomadic life had its advantages. *Roots or wheels—you can't have both*, her father often said. Early on, she learned to rely on herself. Friendships were few when moving from place to place. Dressing each morning was simple with but a handful of garments to pick from, and fewer clothes meant less time spent washing and drying them. No matter where she had called home, she busied herself with supper preparations—and today, that meant shelling sweet peas.

Since Olivia had always lived light, her belongings carried special meaning. She had her father's Bible, mother's satchel, and most recently, the necklace Waneta gave her on her wedding day. The only living thing she had ever called her own was Caddie, a gift from her father the first Christmas after her mother passed away. Her faithful hound had been the one constant in her tumultuous life, following her around as amicably as the springtime sun. Now, if Waneta's observations were correct, she would have another living thing in her life before too long—this one a gift from Harry.

Her recollection of the last time they made love gave her solace. She often went there, deep down to her heart's light, when she was alone. That had been the morning he promised to take her to Charleston for their anniversary. Though the calendar said May, there was no longer any marriage to celebrate. She was a nomad once more, only this time, a pregnant one.

Olivia sat on a chair outside her family's wood and bark-framed house, shelling peas in a basin on her lap, gazing at several youngsters playing games under a sunset pink sky. As Elan approached and swung down from the wagon, he hoisted crate after crate on his shoulders and unloaded them inside the shed. She scowled, imagining the sizable collection stacked against the back wall, all filled with pottery and blankets refused—for the third time in the past few months—by Reed Barlowe's mercantile.

Olivia gazed into his grim eyes, her anger rising like steam. "Again? Same as last week?"

"It's clear Reed Barlowe doesn't want to do business with us. He's gotten others on his side. People walked right by me at the market."

"Ugh, so he's shunning you—because of me. Isn't there something we can do to stop him?" She broke the next pod and tossed the pea overhanded, watching it land near his foot.

Elan stared down, crushing it into the soil with his boot. "No. Nothing peaceful anyway."

"And he's going to keep on doing this?"

"He won't forget so easy. He means to make you pay for what you did—or tried to do—with his property."

"She has a name, Elan—it's Lucie. Her name is Lucie, and he's a disgusting little wart-faced...grub worm."

Elan squatted on the ground beside her, back against the wall.

"You're too quiet." Her gaze grew dark. "There's

something else, isn't there...?"

He dragged a stray twig through the dirt, tracing little circles with it in the soil. Finally, he took his palm and erased the scribblings. "It's the captain—he's gone."

Olivia turned away. *Gone? Gone where? Why...?* A wave of nausea swept over her, and she lowered the basin to the ground.

Elan clutched her elbow. "Have you eaten?"

"Yes—and I've kept most of it down...until now." She covered her mouth with her palm. "Give me a moment."

Waneta pulled up a chair beside her and patted her arm. "You should eat little bits all day long—make time to fill your belly."

Olivia took several deep breaths, then complied, pulling an apple from her pocket and taking a noisy bite out of it.

"Did you know? About Harry...?" she asked between mouthfuls.

Waneta cut her with a look of cool indifference. She picked up the bowl and took over the shelling.

"I can finish that as soon as I 'fill my belly.' "

"You need to calm yourself." Waneta's gaze darkened. "We have more important things to deal with than your rantings. And yes—Elan already told me. I asked him to give me a day before telling you."

The news of Harry disturbed her, but why did it matter to Waneta? *What are you hiding, Aunt?* The plunk of peas dropping in the bowl was maddening.

Betsey came around the corner and stopped short, smile fading. "Supper's almost ready."

"We won't have these peas tonight." Waneta tilted the bowl in her daughter's direction. "Let's keep them for tomorrow." She kept to her task, the three of them watching as though she were snapping open pods of gold.

A limpid smile washed over Waneta's face, highlighting her cheekbones, and she gazed at Olivia. "I loved my big sister, and I never wanted to stand in the way of her happiness. But the path she chose was hard. Benjamin knew it, but together they moved forward and made it work. Then you came along, and they took you right along with them—never missed a step."

Waneta popped the last two peas out of their shell and passed the bowl to Betsey. She pulled out a brown leather wallet from her pocket. Elan scooted forward and sat with his legs crossed, gaze fixed on his mother. Olivia shifted forward in her chair.

"After your mother died, Benjamin came to me and bid me give you this upon his death—but only if you ever found yourself in something he called an 'ill pickle.' " Waneta sighed. "You made a match for love that has left you alone, with a broken heart and a child on the way. Your actions—and the captain's too—have left us in danger."

"What do you mean?" She struggled to decipher her aunt's expression.

"Reed Barlowe hasn't forgotten you're just a few miles away. I think he is using you and this trouble against us. He threatened Betsey last week—won't be long before he moves on to others."

Olivia whipped around to Betsey. "What? He didn't hurt you, did he?"

"It was in his store—trying to scare me. Elan took care of him." Betsey gave a stiff satisfied nod.

Elan looked away, eyes hooded. "Men like Barlowe

find out things—and use them to their advantage. We can do nothing against him without raising tensions. The tribe does not want it, but he is pushing me too far. First you, then my trade—and now my sister?"

"I'm so sorry. Th-this is all my fault." Olivia hung her head, anguish clouding her voice.

"I believe now is the ill pickle your father was talking about." Waneta laid the wallet in her hands and motioned with a flick of her head for her children to leave.

With clumsy fingers, Olivia opened it. A man's signet ring, engraved with a strange seal, dropped into her lap. She pried a piece of folded parchment from the crease inside the pouch and opened it.

Dearest Daughter,

If you find yourself reading this, my heart—though long since stopped of its beating—will be mired in sadness. It will mean you are in a dire circumstance, an ill pickle, as we used to say, and I cannot help you.

For all you knew of me, and for all the many sermons you heard pass my lips, I fear I have been a Pretender of the highest order. I have not lived as I have asked others to. I have lied to you about your family. My name is not Benjamin Parr. I am Benjamin Parr Evans, son of Oren Allen Evans and Annie Lee Drummond.

I turned my back on my kin when I left home, aged twenty years, and traveled the back country preaching the gospel of our Lord. Made my way on my own in this world and never looked back. How selfish of me to deprive my Evans family of knowing and loving you—the kindest, sweetest heart set on this Earth. I pray you will undo this wrong now, as you are hurt or harmed, and make your way to God's majestic mountains. You need to bear nothing but my ring, and this letter, should you desire it, to my relations in North Carolina. Waneta will see you (and should you still have the wee hound Caddie at your side) get there safely. She has sworn her promise to me on this. She is a woman of her word, pledged to her sister's honor.

Consider my words carefully. They come with the greatest of apology, my sweet daughter. My family will welcome you into their fold.

Pray on this, the lasting gift of my kin to you. I am eternally your loving father and pray for you from Heaven above,

Benjamin

"Have you read this?" Olivia waved the letter in the air.

Waneta shook her head, hands folded in her lap. "No, but Benjamin told me. You have two families, but which is best? There is much uncertainty with both. You must think about what's safest for you and the baby."

"And for you and the tribe." Her hands fell to her stomach, the child's presence not yet visible. She gazed at her aunt. "Do you think they would accept me though—like Papa said?"

"I trusted Benjamin. I think they would. He also left you this." Waneta reached into the wallet and pulled out a separate pouch.

She ran her fingers through the pile of silver coins. "Where did this come from...?"

"He did not say, and I did not ask. But I can tell you it was very important to your father you have everything in here." Waneta tapped her index finger on the wallet.

"Should I go...? I must decide before I get too far along. And how would I even get there?"

"Elan has already offered to take you. He has vowed to not leave your side, not ever. You will not be alone, I promise. He will protect you with his life."

"Oh Lord." Her head and voice dropped in unison.

"The decision is yours, child. I had to keep my word to your father. Given your situation, I could not keep this from you any longer. Whatever you decide—stay or go—I will do my best to take care of you both."

"I never meant for any of this to happen. I have caused you so much trouble." She fell to her aunt's knees, laid her weary head on her lap, and wept. Waneta rubbed her hands over her back and shoulders, infusing comfort with every stroke. Regardless of her choice, her future would be precarious.

Chapter Thirty-Three

June 1784

Where the remote Bermudas ride
In th'ocean's bosom unespied,
From a small boat that rowed along,
The listening winds received this song:
"What should we do but sing His praise
That led us through the wat'ry maze
Unto an isle so long unknown,
And yet far kinder than our own?"
Excerpt from *Bermudas* by Andrew Marvell, 1621-1678

The conditions on board the *Amelia* were as Harry had expected. The men in the tavern at Georgetown apprised him of her history in the waters between the South Carolina coastline and Bermuda. In this voyage, filled with cargo of grain, indigo, cocoa, and brandy, she moved with surprising speed and agility through the sometimes stormy, sometimes fair waters of the southern Atlantic. The gaff-rigged sloop, built from rot-resistant Bermuda Cedar, had been at sea for eight days.

The vision of ocean meeting sky was visible from any vantage point on deck. A cascade of silver white clouds often blanketed it, the albatross and petrel soaring high above them. By dusk, a halo of crimson and gold would surround the setting sun, clouds etched in watercolor hues of orange and pink on the horizon. Pelicans swooped past the deck in the afternoons, scooping up fish in their handsome beaks. A plethora of fish and schools of dolphins skimmed by them daily, engulfed in the vibrant waves of the sea. By God's grace, Harry had not found himself overcome with seasickness—just the churning waves on the first day had sent him flailing and heaving for the nearest bucket.

Harry dug deep into his emotional reserve to survive the nights. Though he dabbled in drinks and card games in the evening, he would retire to his room only to find sleep elusive. With only the moon and stars for company, he was like a lone firefly captured in a jar—alive and breathing but confined.

He moved light-footed in his room this morning, packing his bag with ease, eager to disembark at St. George's Port—shortly before noon, according to the ship's captain. He scanned the meager furnishings around him and, satisfied he had all his belongings stuffed in his bag, made his way up to the deck.

Relief washed over Harry's face when he planted his feet on the Bermuda sand. The temperature and humidity reminded him of home. An incoming breeze carried the smells of citrus, salt, and rum in the air. A smile reached his lips as he made his way through the flocks of traders lining the cobblestone streets. The vendor carts were spilling over with prickly skinned pineapples, ruby pomegranates, and round melons. The sound of children's laughter lifted from the alleyways, and the smell of fresh grilled fish and gingered ale spilled out of various taverns. He slipped through the door of one called The Gilded Lantern, ducking around a buxom young woman clad in a translucent lemon-yellow gown—the outline of her breasts visible through the bodice's sheer fabric. *Some things never change.* He gave her a polite nod, then he made his way across the room.

Harry climbed up on a stool, meeting the gaze of the fellow working behind the bar. "Scotch please."

The man had smooth, acorn-brown skin and black hair hanging in long locks down his back, tied off with a scrap of white muslin. His eyes matched the color of his skin, and he gazed the length of the bar, taking care of each customer's needs.

Harry dropped two coins in the barman's hand when he came back around with his drink. "I'm looking for Sam Bigham. Supposed to meet him at—" He read the scribble on the paper once more. "Slug's Tavern."

"Ah…Big Sam, you mean." The barman gestured with a tilt of his head. "It be about three corners down from here—an eatery and such—on the left."

Out of nowhere, a girl popped up beside the man, her brown eyes peeking out above the counter. She tugged on his apron, and when he bent down to meet her, she cupped her hand and whispered into his ear. Harry watched the secretive exchange with interest. With a pat to her head, the child jumped up and down and took off skipping, but not before flashing Harry a sweet smile.

"You made her happy." Harry circled his finger around the rim of his glass.

"She's a little monkey." The man shook his head, smirking. "You've any of your own?"

Harry drained the last of his drink and adjusted his hat over his brow. "No, I don't."

"Ah, my mistake. I thought I saw it in your eyes.

Seemed like you knew something about a brown-eyed lass tugging on your heart to get her way." He chuckled, extending his hand to Harry in a firm handshake. "I'm Tobias, by the way. That moppet over there is my daughter, Eliza."

"Harry—pleased to meet you." He tried to quell his uneasy thoughts. *I had a brown-eyed lass once, but she left me.*

Raising the bottle in the air, Tobias flashed a pearly grin. "Will you have another?"

"Maybe later." He arched an eyebrow. "Say—who do I see about getting a room?"

"That'd be the man standing by the stairs—tall fella with the mustache."

Hoisting his bag on his shoulder, Harry went to secure his lodgings and find Sam Bigham.

****

After an hour and several pints of ale, Harry and Sam reached an agreement. They sat at a whitewashed table outside Slug's Tavern, deep in negotiation amidst the seagulls and longtails scattered around the docks. In Charleston, his brother-in-law had informed him about the Sutherland's longtime business relationship with Sam Bigham, a Scot by birth, but a man who had lived most of his life on the island. His ruddy red hair and beard complemented his round husky face. In fact, he judged the Scot's shoulders wide enough to hold one of the great green herons perched on the railing beside them. With a burly handshake, Sam took receipt of the load of indigo Harry had delivered, and six caches of rum and multiple bags of ginger and cinnamon would travel back with him to South Carolina next week.

"Why the delay?" Harry asked, smiling at the

buxom barmaid swerving around him. She placed two bowls of seafood stew and a basket of bread on the table. He imagined her pointed gaze was turning his neck pink beneath his collar.

"*Amelia's* just in need of a few repairs. She'll be fit for sailing in no time." Sam spoke between large mouthfuls of Johnny bread.

"Oh, it's fine by me. A welcome turn of events, I think."

"You sound like a man with none too many cares in the world."

"Oh, I have them—I just don't have a clue what to do about them."

Sam guffawed, half-choking on the stew. He lifted his cup in the air and, with a cheery grin, summoned the barmaid back to their table. "You look mighty fetching today, Annabelle."

"And a very good afternoon to you, Big Sam." The young looker topped off their cups with ale. "Who's your new friend?"

Sam performed the usual introductions peppered with his own raw but endearing language. His sea-blue eyes had a glint to them, and he sat up tall as he spoke, fists the size of cannonballs resting on the tabletop. Though his brackish words made Harry wince and Annabelle blush a crimson that matched her hair, the fellow seemed to be the honest, good-humored merchant Hugh had described.

"First time in Bermuda, Captain?" Sam asked.

He nodded, dropping his spoon into his empty bowl and wiping his mouth with a checkered towel.

"Well then...you must sample a bit of her flavors." Sam winked, ruddy cheeks rising to meet his eyes.

"There's nothing a cool pint and a warm lass can't fix in a man, aye?"

He smiled and brushed his knuckles over his lip, planning how best to dodge the invitation. "Aye, but first—Christ, I could use some cleaning up." He fanned his dingy tunic and quirked an eyebrow.

Sam wrinkled his nose. "Ah, you do reek, my friend. Go see to it—then meet me back here at six."

Harry gave him a nod, then made his way to the door.

****

Within the next two hours, rinsed clean of salty sweat from scalp to heels, Harry donned the last fresh shirt and breeches from his bag, slipped into his gray vest, and headed out the door. As his feet landed at the bottom of the staircase, he spied Eliza sitting on a stool by the bar where her father served drinks. Her eyes were droopy, body flopped over like a rag doll. She met his gaze and lifted her little fingers in a wave. He responded in kind, noting an odd tingle radiating through his palm. He could not help but hope the perky girl would soon return.

He met Sam for supper, sampling several native dishes, from curried ginger chicken to tangy pineapple cake, accompanied by a frothy amber ale. They talked of Scotland and America, trade between the colonies, and the condition of slavery in both. It seemed the commercial trader was as comfortable in these surroundings as a bear in his den.

After the meal, like Hugh had predicted, Bigham sniffed out the best entertainment, booze, and female company in the house. Harry enjoyed the first two immensely, finding fair good fortune in both the deck and his high ball glass. He put his skill at billiards to the test with a few of Sam's friends, the games ending all square.

As the hour grew late and the fiddle player's hands tired, Harry watched his red-haired companion's gaze wander from the cards in his hand to the swaying hips of his favorite curvy barmaid. They had not seen the looker Annabelle tonight. No, Sam's gaze followed a ripe, seasoned woman—quite comely, she was—endowed with the generous pear shape of maturity. She sat down on the Scot's lap, wiggling her arse against him. Sam grunted his approval.

Harry smiled and sat up a little taller in his seat, placing his cards face down on the table. "Fold."

"Oh now, you needn't rush off, Captain. Louisa here has a darling young friend I think you'd fancy—a racy little blonde with—" Sam held up his hands around two imaginary voluptuous breasts but stopped short as Louisa cuffed him on the arm.

"Perhaps another time." He bit back a grin and stood up, reaching in his pocket for some coin.

"You're my guest tonight—you can cover me tomorrow." Sam waved an indifferent hand in his direction, his other one already busy working its way up Louisa's ruffled bodice.

Harry cleared his throat and excused himself, stepping out into the street, welcoming the salty breeze rushing across his face. He guessed the quarter mile walk back to his lodgings would be suitable for some brave reflection.

Chapter Thirty-Four

Harry spent the next few days exploring the vibrant streets of St. George's. He spent hours walking around the markets, discovering row after row of native goods and wares. This morning, he bought a few gifts for Josie and his nephews from a persuasive old peddler and gave him a wink—and an extra coin for his trouble—after a vigorous but altogether enjoyable negotiation.

By the time he strolled into The Gilded Lantern for lunch, he found it in chaos. The innkeeper was behind the bar, sleeves rolled up past his elbows, bottles in both hands. Flushed and disheveled, the man used a bar towel to wipe perspiration from his brow. A mob of thirsty men had gathered around the counter, each one barking out his order a little louder than the last.

Harry slid in behind the bar and leaned toward a squatty man with a slick brown mustache. "What can I get you, sir?"

"A shot of your best rum."

He turned around to the shelves behind him. *Damn.* There were no less than three bottles of rum staring him in the face—and not caring which one was which—he started pouring, setting the cut-glass on the counter and stuffing the man's money in his pocket for safekeeping. He chanced a quick look over to his partner, who shrugged and gave him an appreciative smile.

They worked elbow to elbow for another hour,

serving the busy midday crowd until their numbers dwindled. Harry leaned back on the counter and stretched his neck muscles, rolling his shoulders in a circle. "What the devil's going on? Where's Tobias?"

"Not here." The fellow poured two mugs of a frothy ale and passed one to him. "You have my thanks, Fleming."

While they ordered two meals and ate their fill of seafood chowder and corn cakes, Harry learned Tobias' daughter had taken ill last night, and her fever had spiked. Sadly, there was no one else but him to care for the child.

"What'll I do in a few hours? The night's busier than this." The man stared blankly over his mug.

"Do they live nearby?" Harry asked, swallowing his last bite of chowder.

"Upstairs—third room on the left."

"Don't worry—I'll be back before the night crowd shows up." He winked, draining his ale and emptying his pockets of the money he had collected serving drinks. "I believe this belongs to you, my good man."

Harry located their room, and after knocking on the door, he entered. He found Tobias sitting on a chair beside his daughter's bed, his gaze rheumy and fatigued. Across the room there was another single bed, three tall-backed chairs, and a square table with a washing basin.

As sunlight streamed through the window, casting a saffron glow over the sleeping child, Harry's breath caught in his throat. Dark shadows plagued his mind, memories of Olivia's fight with the tick fever still close to the surface.

Harry took a step closer, relieved when he saw her shift under the quilt. "How is she?"

"The old midwife's been by, but not much she can do. Fever's got to run its course, she says." Tobias spoke with none of the spirit he had shown yesterday.

Harry arched his brow, securing his approval to pull up a chair. He leaned forward, arms on his thighs, recalling how Nigel treated Olivia's tick fever. "Have you some tepid water and clean towels? And a cup? She needs to drink water—lots of it."

Tobias nodded, scurrying off, slinging the door behind him.

Harry reached over and touched the velvet softness of the child's forehead. Her eyes were sunken, half-circles the color of smoke etched beneath them. Her cheeks were hot, and perspiration beads dotted her upper lip. She moaned, shifting her head to the side, then turned her face toward him.

"Hello there." Harry fastened his gaze on the child.

"I-I remember you," Eliza whispered.

"And I you." He smiled at her, turning about when he heard the door close behind him. Tobias set the items on the table and followed his instructions, holding his daughter's head up so she could take short sips of water. Harry stood, pouring some of the water into a basin, then dipped a towel in it and squeezed out the excess. He gave it to Tobias who placed it on her forehead. They repeated the process, putting the next cloth on her neck and chest, then he held the cup to her mouth once more.

"How do you feel?" Harry asked.

"My head...hurts," she said, closing her eyes.

He wrenched his gaze away from her as Tobias stroked her cheek and flipped over the towel on her forehead. With encouragement, she lifted her head to let the cool water pass through her lips.

Tobias shook his head. "I'm no good at this. My wife took care of such things."

"I'm sorry, friend."

"She died about this time last year."

Harry exhaled a long breath.

"They told me downstairs how you helped out today. I'm grateful. But the night crowd's a different story." Tobias lowered his head.

"I proved my bar skills well enough. Tonight will be no different."

"I couldn't ask—"

"You're not. I'm insisting. This is what's important right now." Harry pointed a finger at the wee girl.

Eliza stirred as her father removed the chest towel, dipped it in the water, and put it back in place. She shivered, pulling the edge of the blanket up closer to her chin.

"Will you stay with me a while?" Eliza asked her father.

Harry shook his head, dazed, leaning on the wall again for support. "Scrapper...?"

Tobias looked dismayed. "You all right, Captain?"

A breeze slipped through the open window, and every hair on his arms stood on end. He came around and fixed his gaze on the girl, blinking away the dream.

"Please...? Will you stay?" Eliza asked again.

Tobias leaned in closer so she could see him, patted her hand, and kissed her button nose. "I'm not goin' anywhere. The good captain's working my shift for me tonight. Hush now."

Harry watched their exchange, then slumped over in the chair by the table, his hands clutching both knees. He had complete control over his faculties, he was certain of it. He saw what he saw and heard what he heard. Yet from deep within the hollow of his subconscious, cloaked in idle darkness, he sensed Olivia's presence in the room. Bonded in their vows—*in sickness and in health*—he had never left her side.

"You all right?" Tobias' urgent words broke through the veil blurring his mind. "You look like you saw a ghost."

"I believe I have." Harry gazed down at Eliza, her countenance so angelic despite the grip of the fever, then turned to her father. "She'll be fine—trust me. Don't leave her side, not even for a minute. Give her plenty of water and let her sleep. I'll have the maid bring you some supper."

"How can I ever repay you?"

"Don't worry, my friend. Let's just get her well." He gripped the fellow's shoulders before making his way out the door and away from the unsettling spirits.

****

The hour was approaching midnight and the sky black as tar when Harry settled into a chair on the dock. He stretched his achy legs out on a wooden stool, drew in a deep breath, and stared up at the heavens. He loosened his neckcloth and turned his neck back and forth, releasing the tension from hours spent working the tavern bar. A chair skidded across the wooden planks, and he lowered his gaze.

"You searching for answers in the stars?" Sam eased into the chair.

Harry shrugged. "Asking questions, seeking answers. What's the difference?"

"Oh—aye." He gave him an understanding nod. "I thought I might find you here. Nothing like the briny sea air to ease a man's bones." He drew on his cigar. "Heard you were a big help tonight at the tavern."

"I know the plight of a mother bird now." His proclamation produced a puzzled look on Sam's face. "A nest of babies squawking with their beaks wide open. Thirsty men are demanding fowl."

The crusty brute roared with laughter, hitching up his waistband, legs sprawled out in front of him. He mashed his lips around his cigar. "So...there's something I'm right curious about. What brings you to our island? You're nothing like the men Hugh usually sends my way."

He gave him a questioning look.

"You've got a keen mind and a knack for figures. I saw you doing it all up here the day I met you." He tapped his pointer finger on his temple, then continued. "You're uncommon kind—helping out Tobias while his child's sick. Aye, and I'm happy to report the girl's improving."

Harry sat up straight, a trifle uncomfortable at his appraisal, and planted his feet on the ground. "Thank God."

"So...why did you really come here, eh? You're eight hundred miles away from something—or someone." He flashed him a teasing wink. "I'm bettin' it's a brown-haired lass you fancy. Has to be—how else could you have turned down little red-haired Annabelle last week, and not to mention the racy blonde with the two—"

"How indeed." His blue eyes softened.

"Unless I missed it, you've been dodging all the lasses...which can only mean one thing." Sam smacked his lips around the stogie.

He rubbed his knuckles under his chin. "My nephew said I had a broken head and needed to clear out my heart."

He let out a throaty hoot. "Well young Captain—why don't you kick back and tell Big Sam all about it."

"It's complicated."

"Complicated is not so bad. Nothing worth having is ever simple." Sam pulled a flask from his coat pocket, took a swig, and passed it to him.

Harry swallowed, the rum burning his throat and firing his internal battle. *Where do I begin...?* He rubbed his tongue on the inside of his cheek as the words took shape in his mind.

"Well, it started when Olivia and I got married last year. Perhaps it was rushed and unplanned, but we were happy." Harry took another sip, wiping his mouth with his shirt sleeve. "Then I disappointed her and hid the truth from her. Then she ran off, trying to save my homestead, but I didn't need her help. I had a plan—I needed her to trust me, damn it." He slammed his fist on the table. "What's a man supposed to do with a stubborn, willful—"

"Devoted and independent wife?" Sam straightened his legs, crossing his feet at his ankles. "Don't know—depends on how much he enjoys being alone, I suppose. Pride won't keep a man warm at night."

Harry slumped forward, forearms flat against his thighs.

"You're a bright strapping fellow. You can go anywhere you please—travel any place you like, for as long as you like. But the only place worth staying is with the one you love."

Harry cut him a shadowy gaze. "You ever been

married?"

"Aye. I had a great love—and she had me." He snorted, scratching his beard. "And then she went away to the angels."

The corners of his eyes creased. "I'm sorry. You must miss her."

"Like soil misses water."

He scratched his head and sighed. "Do you ever think you might marry—"

"No. Now I'm not going live like a monk…but no, I could love no one the way I loved her. Nor would I want to." Sam shifted in his chair, leaning back with his stogie lodged between his teeth. A smile inched up his face, and their gazes met. "You know, Harry, my granny had an old saying. She said, 'If ever in love, don't be daft, flirtin' and teasin' to make it last. Nay, waste ye no time, no kiss, no tear. For if ever in love, to make it last, love ye dear.' "

Sam inched forward in his seat. "Time's the only one you should ever quarrel with. She gives, aye, she does. But she always gets the last word. Tell me—how would you feel if you never saw your Olivia again?"

"I can't imagine it." Harry shook his head. "No. No, not ever. Even now, I want to be with her. She's all I think about. But it's been months, and I've wasted so much time."

"It's only wasted if you come to the wrong conclusion."

Harry gazed off into the darkness.

"Are you going to fight for it, man? Do you love her or not?"

"I-I heard her, Sam." His voice took on a dream-like tone. "My wife—in Eliza's words this afternoon. I can't shake it off. It was like Olivia was here…reaching out to me."

"Maybe she was. The Lord works in all kinds of ways—even through a sick little girl." Sam reached for the bottle and took a long swig. It passed between them a few more times before he exhaled sharply. "Damn, but you are stubborn—so I'm going to ask you again. Do you love Olivia or not?"

They held one another's gaze in silence for several moments before Harry lifted his face toward the sea breeze. He expelled a shaky breath, so very tired of hiding from the truth.

As understanding began to bloom in his heart, memories of Olivia—his truest friend and sensual lover—softened its tattered edges. *God's honest truth?* He missed her sweet songs filling the air. He missed her beautiful, capable hands stained with dirt and berries. *I miss* her*!* He shook his head realizing it was more than that.

I'm in love with her!

Harry rolled his shoulders, the weight of regret and denial lifting. With eyes closed, he prayed to every saint in heaven he was not too late. He turned to Sam, fumbling around the knot in his throat, and spoke with conviction.

"I'm in love with her, Sam."

"Aye, then—there it is." Sam puffed on his cigar, folding his hands over his plump middle. "Took you long enough."

Harry leaned forward on his elbows, knuckles folded under his chin, a small grin spreading across his face. "I love her. My wife. Sweet Jesus, it's such a relief to say it out loud. I love Olivia." He shot him a look.

"I've got to get home to her…and fast."

"You're in luck. Just so happens the *Amelia* is set to sail with the tide tomorrow." Sam grinned around his cigar.

He tilted his head toward the heavens. "Thank you, God. I'm going home to get my girl."

Sam raised the flask. "So…I'd say your heart's all cleared out now. How's about that head of yours?"

Harry cuffed him on the shoulder. "Thanks to you, my friend, it's on the mend."

Chapter Thirty-Five

July 1784

The *Amelia* landed at Georgetown, South Carolina, eight days after setting sail, wind whipping through her massive sails, a burnished sun hanging low against a violet sky. Harry had been one of the first to disembark the sloop. He spent the night with his family in Charleston, recounting tales of his adventure. He and Sean said prayers at his bedside, and the boy told him about his efforts to face his troubles with a smile. Harry reciprocated, reassuring his nephew he had improved the condition of both his head and heart while in Bermuda. The grin on Sean's face had stilled his heart and strengthened his resolve to waste no more time.

Harry arrived at the Catawba village two days hence, and upon seeing Waneta—still a formidable woman packaged in a compact body—he gazed at her blank expression. Her home smelled of buttered corn and molasses, the scent of sugar-cured ham heavy in the air. Judging by the slant of her eyes and the fixed line of her mouth, he imagined the aroma would be the only sweet thing about this encounter.

Waneta sat at the end of the table opposite him. "You don't look well, Captain."

"I've come a long way. I didn't have time to shave."

"Why are you here?" Her eyes narrowed.

"For my wife."

"You don't have one." The way she held her chin in a strong uplifted line reminded him of Olivia.

"We're still married." His tone was pointedly low.

"Elan returned the ring. Your law means nothing to us." She clasped her hands on the table. "Olivia released you from your bond. She wants you to keep your ancestor home and live long and happy."

Harry pressed his palms together, his gaze locked on the woman. "I respect you—and Olivia respects you. I know you care for her a great deal, but I really must see my wife now. I have to tell her how much I love her."

"You cannot. She's gone from here to a place where she will be safe."

"What...?" He leaned forward, glaring. "What the devil do you mean she's gone?"

Waneta met his gaze. "Olivia was not safe here with that snake Barlowe around all the time. He threatened her—all of us. So...she went away to her father's family."

He shook his head. "But she never spoke of his family. Did she go alone?"

"No. My son took her."

"I want to see him immediately."

"Your orders mean nothing to me, Captain."

Harry suppressed the urge to throttle the woman and rephrased his request. "I would like to speak with Elan now, please."

Waneta reached for her braid and rubbed the end of it between her fingers. "He has not returned. I hope to see him soon, but he promised to stay with her—by her side—for as long as she needs."

Trapped in a silent ambush, Harry mulled over her

words and found himself unsettled both by what she said—and had not said.

"And before you say anything else, I have an order for you."

Harry whipped his head around at her brazen command.

"I will not tell you where she is…ever." Waneta rose, hands on her hips. "Go back to your white man's life and forget you ever got your claws into my niece." She walked to the door and waved her hand in invitation to leave.

Hearing his horse's loud snort outside the door, he grabbed his hat and moved to within a foot of her, seething. "I will find her, Waneta. I can promise you that. Without your help, it will just take longer."

"Do what you must. I will do what I must."

Harry stormed off toward his horse. *Damn the meddling woman.* He checked his saddlebags, already calculating the provisions he would need for his journey, and prepared to mount.

"Sir, please don't go." A hand touched Harry's arm, and he turned around to a small-framed girl with doe-brown eyes. She shifted her feet back and forth, peeking over her shoulders. "Are you Mister Captain Harry Fleming?"

"I am."

She took a tentative step closer and placed a folded letter in his hand. "I'm Betsey. My brother is Elan. He said to give this to you if you ever showed your face, and he was not here to talk to you himself." She spoke carefully, then smiled, undoubtedly please with her recitation.

He ripped open the seal and scanned the note.

Moments later, he gripped her arm, his face awash in relief.

"I know where she is." He gasped. "Thank you, Betsey. I'll find her and bring her home."

"But no—she's not safe here. You must not."

He came up short. "I'm sorry, please forgive me. It's an expression—home can be anywhere, so long as Olivia's with me."

Betsey wrinkled up her mouth. "You love her, then?"

"Yes, I do. Very much."

"When you find her, will you stay with her no matter what? Elan will not leave her side."

Harry groaned, sure there was something amiss between their languages. "Your mother just said the same thing to me. What do you mean 'he won't leave her side?' "

"Elan loves her and will not ever leave her alone."

He took a moment to process her words, which were contradictory to the letter he had read. "Tell me, does Elan have a wife?"

The girl's gaze turned dark. "He did, but she died giving birth to their child. They're both gone."

"What kind of love does he have for Olivia?" Harry could only hope the young woman understood his meaning.

"Elan is very smart and good and strong. He takes care of us. He promised to love Olivia and be sure they were safe with her white family before he would come back. If it's not good there, then he will stay with them and make a life together—far away from Reed Barlowe."

"Who are 'they' and 'them'?"

The girl's eyes grew round, and her voice hitched.

"Oh, I mean Elan and Olivia, yes, them—is that not how you say it in English?"

He studied the soft lines of her face. There was something hidden in her words, but he shook it off.

"Listen, Betsey—I'm grateful to you for the letter. I don't care what you're saying about your brother right now. I'm going to find my wife and God willing, I will be the one never leaving her side again."

Two dimples popped up with her ear-to-ear smile. "Goodbye, Captain. Go find Olivia, yes."

Harry swung into his saddle and left town by following the path of the river. The letter gave Evans as the name, and they lived in the White Oak region of the Appalachian Mountains. Rural, rugged terrain to be sure, but nothing he had not encountered before. He touched his mother's necklace pressing against the hollow of his throat and rubbed her wedding ring. He meant to keep them both close to his heart until he found Olivia—and find her he would.

He filled his lungs with fresh air. His commitment knew no boundaries, and no distance or obstacle would deter him. He had nothing to lose, for living without Olivia was unthinkable. With the breeze at his back, he thought of Sam and took assurance from his words, vowing to waste nothing—no time, no kiss, no tear—ever again.

Part Five

Heart and Home

Chapter Thirty-Six

August 1784

Dying was nothing like Zeb expected. The Fleming men left the world much the way they lived in it, unapologetically bold, decisive, and direct. He would have preferred heart arrest or an apoplexy in a single deadly blow to the months he had endured coughing up bloody mucus in a bedside bucket. He had had his fill of probing by family and friends, all well intentioned, but woefully inept in navigating their true opinions about him against their Christian duty to love thy neighbor.

A man of influence, Zeb had more adversaries than he could count on both hands. In contrast, the count of loyal friends barely filled one. Did he have any regrets? Not especially, but he held on to hope he might resolve one matter before it was too late. While physically confined, but mentally unencumbered, he meandered through his days, sowing what seeds of promise he could in his purgatorial existence.

He studied his reflection in the mirror on the nightstand. His green eyes had a filmy look these days, cheeks gaunt, his once coarse beard having turned thin and patchy. The one thing left inside him with any strength was the rumbling, raw cough consuming him on the hour. He scooted back, propped up against the headboard, and swapped the mirror for a cup. The watered-down scotch was as pleasing as leftover gruel. He reached under the pillow for his flask, fortified the drink, and formed a smile as it passed over his wrinkled lips.

As he took a few more sips, his thoughts strayed to Catherine. She had chased off after his granddaughter some time ago, leaving her embroidery rings strewn on the chair by the window. He was weary of looking at her grim, white-lipped face. She hated him for orchestrating the marriage bargain and spoiling her future with Harry. While her notions were foolish, he had to admire her spunk, finding her anger at him infinitely more palatable than pity.

Zeb's thoughts drifted to Brandt, and he blew out a beleaguered breath. That his son had stayed with him every night for a month meant two things. First, he was staving off gamecock fights, cards, and the liquor that accompanied them. He shook his head, beyond weary of hearing stories about him seated at a game table, stroking a deck of cards with one hand while fondling the pert derriere of a nameless vixen with the other. Second, he was not sharing a bed with his wife. The latter unsettled him, for keeping a prize like Catherine happy demanded attention. He had talked with Brandt at length last night about his wife, two healthy children, and the rich life they could have if he got his priorities in line. *The gambler's spirit runs deep in you, son. Beware the cost of letting down your guard.* Only time would tell if he had made an impression on his son.

Zeb put his flask on the nightstand and crossed his arms over his chest. He pictured Reed Barlowe—the proverbial polecat in the chicken coop—in his tired brain. Olivia's jail break had not been in Reed's sights, and that rankled the man like a rotten tooth. The clever woman disappeared into the darkness of protected tribal lands, thwarting his plan to take charge of Redmond Hill. He sighed, confident the time had come to press his advantage against Reed.

Zeb bent over into his handkerchief, clutching his gut with his free hand, and convulsed several times. When his breath returned, he straightened up and pulled out another little gem from underneath his pillow. He opened the pocket watch and pulled back a damask lining, revealing an image beneath it. Despite the faded brushstrokes, he saw what he always had...*perfection.* The blue of Abigale's eyes matched the hyacinths in his summer garden, her lips the color of pink peonies. His fingers rubbed the edges of the paper, frayed much like his heart. She had rejected him in favor of his cousin Joseph some forty years ago. Though he had moved on, marrying well and securing his legacy at Glen Laurel, his true love ripped a hole in his heart long ago, and it had festered ever since.

A breeze ruffled the muslin drapes, lifting the scent of magnolia through the room. The fragrant flower was ever present in the magnificent trees surrounding Glen Laurel. Zeb's lungs might be little more than mush now, but his eyes, ears, and nose missed nothing. He chuckled, appreciating what he could from a body that had stood the test of fifty-nine years.

Zeb leaned his head back and, with eyelids closed, focused on breathing. He did not care if he lived another day or even weeks, if his one last wish would come true. When Brandt told him Josie had come to Redmond Hill upon learning about Harry's disappearance, he sent her a missive. As he dozed off, he hoped Josie would come before it was too late.

Chapter Thirty-Seven

"Zeb," Josie whispered, nudging his feeble shoulder. She had not seen her uncle since her father's funeral seven years ago. The man lying still beneath the quilt bore little resemblance to the brooding, shrewd patriarch she remembered. Though she no longer lived in Camden, she knew the havoc he had wreaked on her brother and his wife.

"Zeb? Can you hear me?" Just as she was thinking his end had come, she spied a slight rise in his chest. "Well, suppose I can sit for a while." She grabbed the tall chair by his nightstand and took a seat. She studied his face and noticed the flicker of his brow. Slowly, the corner of his lip turned up in recognition.

"Ah, little Josie Fleming. I knew you wouldn't keep a dying man waiting, lass." Zeb's mouth curved up in a smile. "Come here and let me get a look at you."

She pulled the chair around and leaned into his line of sight. "You've always been impatient. Some things never change. And I'm Josie Sutherland now."

"Bah—you're a Fleming first and always. I do hate waiting, but that won't trouble me too much longer. Dear God, it's like I'm seeing Abigale again." Zeb blinked his eyes, lips quivering. "But don't fret, my mind knows it's not true."

Josie knew that while the curve of her jaw and firm chin were Fleming features, the rest was all her mother.

She pursed her lips. "Mother's been gone a long time, Zeb."

"Not a day goes by I don't think of her. It's the reason I asked you to come. I wanted to see the light of her once more—in you—before I die. Right sure I'll not be joining her in heaven."

She hid the tingle shooting up her spine with a pasty smile and withdrew her hand, frowning down at her feet. "You're missing the bucket, you know."

"Do you think I give a damn about where those filthy rags fall, my dear?"

"Obviously not. But you must give a damn about something." Josie leaned back in her chair and folded her arms. "Why am I here?"

He dragged his hand across his beard, gazing into her eyes. "I need to right something with your brother before I'm gone."

"To which of the many wrongs against Harry are you referring? Sounds to me like you're trying to squeeze your way through the pearly gates after all."

"Bah! The marriage between Brandt and Catherine, well…it's done. There's no changing it. I did what I thought best for my son and for what I knew would bring Harry pain. But this business with Reed and Redmond Hill and the Indian girl—"

"Show some respect. She's not some Indian girl. Olivia is his wife, and she has our name." She muttered a few more foul words behind her hand.

"All Harry needed to do when he came home was accept his fate and fall in line with the family. I bested him, and he couldn't stand it. Vexed me, he did—and married her on the spot to embarrass me and the Fleming name." Zeb lurched over, covering his mouth with a rag.

Josie shook her head, waiting until the coughing spasm passed. "You've only yourself to blame. This whole calamity is at your feet. For a man who supposedly loved my mother, you've made it your life's work to punish her son, her own flesh and blood. She would have hated you for it. Harry was her heart."

"And she was mine! Abigale went much too soon because of him."

"Mother was never so strong as you remember—even before Harry was born. She was not meant to live such a long life. And you always forget one nagging little detail—she loved Father." She gazed at his sallow, unreadable face. "Think what you will. Honestly, I can't take much more of this, so please—what do you want with me?"

Zeb turned on his side. "Josie, please—I want to give you something that will hopefully make amends for the recent situation. Hand me my box." He pointed to a wooden container on the nightstand. He opened it and, riffling through a few papers, pulled out an envelope, sealed with red wax and his initials, and placed it in her hand.

"When I die—and not a minute sooner, mind you—take this to your brother. He will know what to do with it. This information about Reed Barlowe will help him get his wife and homestead back."

Josie glared at him.

"It's not a joke. You have my word. Take it and do as I say. Promise me."

"You're still the most confounding man I've ever known," she said under her breath. "Very well. I promise. It's just—right now, it seems—no one knows where Harry is. He came back from Bermuda and took off to find Olivia. He left for their village, and that's all we know. It's been over a week now." She waffled, waving the letter. "You see—your words here may mean nothing, the damage done. It may be too late…"

Her heart tightened in her chest, and her palm twitched. Zeb scooped up her hand and squeezed it, and his eyes brightened to a forest green.

"Now you listen to me, Josie Fleming. Don't you go soft. You know Harry well as I do—whatever has detained him, he's on top of it. There's nothing that stops your brother from going after what he wants."

"You did."

"I didn't stop him—not really. He made it easy, racing off to war like he did. Never considered marrying Catherine before he left…and he could have."

"She was all wrong for him." Josie averted her gaze. "Indeed?"

She nodded. "Yes, but it still doesn't forgive your behavior. It's just—well, I think he needs someone who can match his spirit and strength. I never even got to meet Olivia…"

"You will. And when you do, I will rely on you to convey my apology to them. I don't ask for forgiveness, and they shouldn't give it. I will face my Maker on all counts of my life and own every one of them."

She watched his eyes soften, and a faraway look settled in the pools of his eyes. Zeb was boorish and brute—hard and crusty as a blue crab—and she disliked him enormously. Listless in the bed now, his earlier animation having zapped his strength, she considered him a test of her faith, amazed even a sliver of Christian charity lingered in her heart.

"If you're telling me the truth, and you have

something here to help Harry, then I'm grateful." She rubbed the seal on the note with her finger, trying to settle the edge in her voice.

"Thank you, my dear. Now, I know I don't deserve it, but I'd consider it a special gift if you'd sit here with me for a while—till I drift off. I feel uncommon good and tired right now." His body relaxed, and with a gentle smile on his lips, he succumbed to sleep.

****

The next morning, Josie received a missive from Brandt and read the words scrawled on the page. *Zeb passed away during the night.*

Josie made haste in finding Kitt Allington and gave him the envelope from Zeb to lock away for safekeeping. By noon, they were gathered with their closest friends— Mary, Silas, Tom, and Jimbo Grant—around the kitchen table at Redmond Hill. They listened as Tom recounted his morning at the trading market. While his efforts to pry information from Waneta had come up short, her daughter had sneaked away and told him about Harry's visit to their tribal village. She explained how she had given him Elan's letter, and then he took off on horseback to North Carolina to find them.

Tom leaned forward on both his elbows. "Seems Olivia's father has family there. She called it Gilbert Town, White Oak Mountain."

"I went through there during the war," Jimbo said to the group.

Tom clutched his hands together on the table, speaking with a certainty beyond his years. "I want to go find him, Mr. Allington. You can't do it—your place is here."

"He's right, Kitt. You need to stay put and take care

of your wife and watch over Redmond Hill. I'll go with him." Jimbo gave a nod in Tom's direction and ran his hand over his chin. "Makes the most sense. Truth be told, I'm loving the idea—be an adventure." He flashed a handsome, swarthy smile to the group.

Confident the two men were more than equal to the task, Josie smiled, humbled by their devotion to her brother. "Thank you both. I'm so grateful for your help."

"Let's get to it, then." Jimbo slapped his hands together and turned to Tom. "How soon can you be ready?"

Tom stood, hands on his hips. "First thing in the morning suit you?"

"I'll meet you here at dawn." He reached over and shook his hand, then turned to Josie. "I promise we'll find them. I know those hills good as Harry—the trails to take and ones to steer clear of. He's fine. Me and Tom will be too."

With her heart hammering in her chest, Josie grabbed the oak of a man and hugged him fiercely. She pulled back, then reached for Tom, gifting him with a similar embrace.

The following morning, Josie gazed at the two men as they rode off on horseback—taking with them ample provisions, money, a map—and a letter from her relating the news about Zeb and his evidence against Reed.

Chapter Thirty-Eight

After leaving Gilbert Town at dawn, Harry rode at a steady pace, grateful each time he located one of the landmarks the local innkeeper had described to him. He turned onto the White Oak Path, fields of goldenrod cascading over hills of oak. Hickory and short-leaf pines dominated the terrain. He spotted a small skulk of red foxes on a shady slope, a peregrine falcon perched on a crooked branch above. With a click to his horse, he approached a clearing with a sizable house, barn, and fields. Children played chase on the lawn, and a few men milled about the barn. He ventured closer to a man shading his eyes with the back of his hand. *Christ don't let one of them shoot me on the spot.*

"Good afternoon, gentlemen. Sorry to trouble you, but I hope you might tell me if I am close to the home of Mr. Oren Allen Evans. I'm a friend who's come a long way." Harry held on to his breath for what seemed an eternity before he got a reply.

"You found it. I'm not Oren—I'm his son, Kyle. Who're you, friend?" The man was no slouch and stood rock-steady with his pitchfork in his hand. Two younger fellows of similar size took up a position at his back. Harry dismounted, keeping his hands in sight and a charitable grin pasted on his face.

"Harry Fleming, sir. I'm from South Carolina, but I spent four years in these foothills during the war. It's good to be back."

"Which side you fight for?" Kyle cocked his brow, chewing on his rather fat bottom lip.

"Continental Militia, Mecklenburg regiment. I was captain, sir."

"My son, Stuart, was a patriot." He flicked his gaze over his shoulder. "He fought at Ninety-Six and Cowpens."

"I was at Cowpens. Honored to meet you—all of you." Harry squared his shoulders.

"Fleming, you said?"

He took another step forward. "Yes. I'm looking for my wife and her Catawba cousin. Her name is Olivia. She's the daughter of Benjamin Parr—I'm sorry, I meant Evans."

The man broke into a toothy grin. "Looks like you boys owe me a bottle."

The man called Stuart cuffed his father's shoulder with his hat, chuckling.

Harry arched a quizzical brow, rubbing his chin. "I beg your pardon?"

"I bet my sons that Olivia's husband would be round for her soon enough. So…the next bottle of whiskey is on them."

"Christ, she's here?" He clutched his hat in both hands.

"Yes, Captain. I hadn't laid eyes on her since she was a babe and, well…surprised the heck out of me to see her again—and that cousin of hers too. Knew it was her even before she showed me my brother Ben's letter and ring."

"Is she—"

"Safe and sound." Kyle crossed the space between

them and shook his hand. "You look like you could use a shot about now."

"Aye." His throat constricted, something between a choke and cough. "But first—may I please see my wife?"

****

Olivia pulled a bedsheet from the basket and threw it over the rope tied between two hickory trees. She waddled from one end to the other, spreading it out and watching it billow with the breeze. Hands on her hips, she breathed in and exhaled. The mountain smells were dense and earthy, laced with a hint of the cleansing sweetness of cedar and fir. Hickory logs burned every day for their heating and cooking. The first harvest of apples would come in another month or two, and if their look and aroma meant anything, it would be a fine, healthy crop. She bent down, scooped up a tunic, and slung it out in front of her releasing a spritz of water droplets. Caddie shook his head, jowls jiggling, and she laughed. She hung up the garment and bent down for another.

"You're not humming. I don't think I've ever seen you work without a song in your heart."

Olivia froze. *Oh Lord, oh Lord.* She slammed her eyes shut, trying to ignore Caddie's tail thumping in the dirt. A current brushed her shoulder, causing strands of hair too short for her ponytail to tickle her cheek, and teased her nose with Harry's musky scent of sandalwood and pine.

"Sweet Jesus, Liv. I can't believe—" Harry's voice sounded parchment thin.

"How did you find me?"

"It wasn't easy."

She released a shaky breath. "What do you want?"

"My wife."

She forced her eyes open, feeling betrayed as her hound jumped up to greet him. She gritted her teeth and staved off the wetness in the corners of her eyes. "You won't find her here."

"You once told me 'my wife' was a concoction of my own making, and you were right. But she is you, and you her. You're the only woman for me—you are my love."

She envisaged Harry behind her—surely standing but a few feet away now—and pressed her palms on top of her sizable tummy.

"I'm so sorry, Liv. Please, can you forgive my idiocy? I love you."

Her knees caved, and she swayed, grabbing hold of the clothesline for support. His arms encircled her in one mighty swoop, and she drooped back against his chest.

****

"Sweet Jesus." Harry quaked beside her ear, his senses awakening with the intimate aroma of her hair and skin. As he slid his hands lower, his fingers stilled over her belly. *Oh, sweet*—he pressed his eyes shut— *sweet Jesus...*

With gentle circular motions, he palmed the perfect mound, then without breaking contact, turned her around in his arms. He opened his eyes and dropped to his knees, pressing kisses on the folds of the skirt covering their precious child. He stirred when her fingertips slid through this hair, soft pads kneading away the fear and longing that had clouded his mind for so many months. A ripple swelled and rolled against his face.

"I love the sensation of the baby moving on the inside. I wish I could feel it against my cheek." Olivia's voice was weak, but her words genuine.

He rose and pressed a kiss to her forehead. *My Scrapper.*

"Well, well. The sea voyager has returned." Elan spoke with a glacial tone.

Harry turned, gaze honed on the man who had severed Olivia from his life. He reached behind his back, found her hand, and squeezed it. He brought her around to his side, motioning at her pregnant belly. "And just in time it would appear."

"That child," Elan said, gazing at the same spot, "is the only reason I left you a letter. It was the right thing to do, but I didn't believe you would ever read it. I never believed you would come for Olivia."

"I know my actions forced her to flee in the first place, but you—you took her away from me. I was completely lost." Harry swallowed what felt like a fistful of sand. "I came as soon as my ship docked. Waneta was no help...but your sister did as you asked and gave me your note. I'm grateful."

Elan stepped forward. "You should be. But that doesn't mean I'm going to let you snatch her up again." He turned to Olivia, and his voice softened. "Are you well?"

Her gaze shifted between them, and then she nodded to Elan.

"You don't have to talk to the captain. Would you like to go inside and rest?"

"No. No, I'm fine." Her fingers fluttered over her collarbone. "It-It's just such a shock." Her tone dipped to a level not meant for his ears, and she leaned toward her cousin. "A letter, Elan...? You left Harry a letter?"

He nodded, and before she could ask, he added, "He

deserved to know he fathered a child…but only if he sought you out first. I'm sorry for not telling you sooner." He took her hands in his.

Harry monitored their exchange with growing acrimony. *Slide your hands up her arms, and I'll lay you out flat.*

"I understand, and it's all right." Olivia glanced his way, no doubt seeing his shoulder muscles flaring, hands fisting. "Thank you, but I don't need to rest. Harry's come a long way. I need to hear what he has to say."

Elan huffed a sigh and glowered at him.

Reciprocating with a laconic gaze of his own, Harry wrapped his arm around his wife.

****

They came inside the house, apologizing for the interruption to the family meal. After introductions, Olivia found her aunt had placed portions of Cheshire pork pie, buttered corn, and pumpkin pudding on a platter. With a motherly smile, she insisted they retire and take their supper in her room.

She followed Harry as he carried the tray into the bedroom and placed it on the dressing table. She warmed inside when she spotted his familiar saddlebag propped up against her old trunk. Caddie circled twice before snuggling into his blanket beside the bed.

Harry gazed out the curtained window. "Elan makes himself useful with the horses, I see."

"Yes." Olivia took a bite out of a muffin. "He's kind to everyone. I don't know where I'd be without him."

She shifted under his assessing eyes, then moving the tray to the bed, used the trunk as a bench and took a bite of corn. He poured her a glass of water from the pitcher on the nightstand and took his flask from his bag.

As he sat down beside her, Olivia knew something greater than miles separated them. Perhaps crossing the physical divide was the simple part. Months of emotional isolation cast a shadow over them in the room. She leaned into a bite of the Cheshire pie, but a loose strand of hair fell across her jaw and into a bit of broth at the corner of her mouth. After dabbing it with her napkin, she groaned and yanked the rest of her hair out of the haggard ponytail. Let him see the state of her mane—she could not care less. *That's a lie. I care. A lot.*

Olivia ate in silence, lost in the valley between them. She had always loved Harry, but he had had to learn to love her. That was an enormously different thing. Her thick brown locks kept brushing against her chin as she ate, reminding her just a few months ago, Waneta had chopped it all off in a boyish cut to confuse Reed Barlowe. It had helped somewhat, but disguise was never the solution to her problem.

Harry's thigh grazed hers as he leaned over her belly for his flask, and the corner of his lip curled up. He touched his bottle to her glass of water. *Is he actually flirting with me?* She sipped her drink, wishing it was Madeira and it was their wedding night again. Embarrassed, she cleared her throat, hoping once their stomachs were full they might empty their hearts.

Chapter Thirty-Nine

Harry lit the candles in the room while Olivia slipped off her shoes, loosened the laces of her bodice, and stretched her arms over her head. He watched her climb onto the bed, cradle her tummy, and ease down on her side. He fluffed the pillow under her head and tucked the quilt around her knees and feet. He brought a chair up beside the bed and straddled it.

"You're sitting like you did on our wedding night." Her lips curved into a smile.

Harry beamed with the memory of it. "All we need is Madeira."

"Afraid you won't find any of that here."

"Says who?" He hopped up and pulled out a bottle from his bag.

"Where did you—"

"From home—before I left to find you in the village."

Harry filled two cups and tossed his neckcloth on the dresser. He straddled the chair again and opened his heart to his wife. He spoke of his fear for her safety after her jailbreak and an all-consuming rejection when Elan returned her wedding ring, leaving Redmond Hill with Caddie on a lead. He admitted his guilt over hiding his past, confessing had he just told her about Catherine from the start, the hold of first love would have broken sooner. His impulsivity—and fury at Zeb's betrayal with her marriage to Brandt behind his back—had soured his heart to love. He acknowledged the ribbon was more a symbol of his survival than an expression of love. Only his stubborn pride kept him from realizing it.

"When you married me, you promised devotion, and you gave me that—even when you left. I see that now. I'm sorry I didn't always give you the same." Harry's voice hit a low, dull note of regret.

Olivia slid her hands between her cheek and the pillow, and she sighed. "I think I was in love with you that evening you saw me on the steps at church."

"You wore that lovely peach dress and your little brown shoes." He dropped his chin on his hands. "Did you know I hung back behind the trees and watched you humming and sweeping before I ever showed myself?"

Her mouth dropped open. "You didn't."

"Did too." His chest swelled with pride.

Olivia raised up on her elbow and sipped her wine, her nose twitching with its fruity, mellow aroma. "It was when you were about to leave—when you were turning around—and I called out your name."

"Actually, you called me Captain." A smile reached his eyes.

A blush colored her cheeks, then she continued. "But I had this huge lump in my heart, afraid I might not see you again, so I blurted out about you coming to the christening. Lord, I was so desperate."

"From the moment I found you in the woods, I thought you were singular and remarkable...and altogether the most exceptional woman I'd ever met." He rose from his chair and walked over to the window. He cranked it open and breathed in the mountain air. "I knew I was in love with you that day at Saunder's Creek. Do you remember?"

"Every moment."

He circled around, half-sitting on the edge of the dresser, making his breeches pull tight across his thighs. When he heard her soft intake of breath, his heart swelled. "Making love to you that day—Sweet Jesus, I remember the need to make you mine hurt so bad it was almost joyous." He raked his hand through his hair. "I knew you made me the happiest I had ever been in my life."

"I told you I loved you that day." She smiled and grabbed a pillow to wedge between her knees.

"Aye. It changed my heart. You said you'd fight for us because one day I'd do the same."

"And here you are."

As their gazes met, he sensed their shared urgency, both needing the same reassurance. She lifted her hand to him, and he crossed the room and fell to his knees, face down in the covers.

"Oh, Harry. I'm still yours—we both are." She pressed a kiss on the top of his head. "Will you hold us?"

He waited a beat before lifting his head. "Of course, but there's something I have to do first."

She tucked her hands under her chin again. He unfastened the necklace and let the precious ring fall in his palm, then slid it on her marriage finger.

"Please never...ever...take this off again." His lips touched the ring, sealing it with his kiss.

Confusion creased her brow, and she blinked her misty eyes. "Does this mean...you want to be...with me?"

Canny, resourceful, and independent she was. Secure and confident in him, she was not. He was responsible for this burden on her heart, and he would see it lifted. He covered her hands with his. "Yes, Olivia. You're my wife, and I've come here for you. I love you, and I'm fighting for us—now and forever. You are, and will always be, my home."

Harry came around behind her and slid under the quilt, wedging her soft body against his. When she tucked her bare feet between his, toes rubbing his ankle, he relaxed in a way he had not in months. He breathed over her ear, causing the short pieces of hair to brush her cheek, but he smoothed them away with soft, damp kisses. "I have so much to tell you, Liv."

She laced her fingers with his and squeezed tight. "I do so want to hear everything." Then she flipped around—quite deftly, despite the sphere of her belly—and they touched noses. "Oh, Harry. I've missed you so…"

"Come here," he said, grinning, rolling onto his back, letting her snuggle in close. She pushed her skirt aside and slid her leg up on his thigh. Her head fit into the curve of his shoulder, and her palm rested on his chest. So long as he lived and breathed, he vowed she would never be alone again. "I love you so much, Scrapper."

****

Olivia and Harry spent the next few days together. She found comfort in watching him chop wood for her uncle and tend the horses while she pruned herbs in the garden. Seated at the dresser, she gazed in the mirror and pulled the brush through her hair. *Busy days make for restful nights*. From outside, the hoot of the barred owl mixed with the tremolo of the loon, their sounds drifting through the evening air from the half-cocked window.

She looked up and smiled at her husband's reflection in the candlelight. He was reclined on the bed, long legs covered in fawn breeches extending down the length of the mattress, bare feet crossed at the ankles. His shirtsleeves were rolled up, exposing firm, tanned forearms. She watched his gaze travel the lines of the newspaper and bit her lip. *No, I couldn't. I shouldn't dare...*

She eased open the dresser drawer and gazed at the satin ribbons Harry had given her last year. She hoped soon she would have hair long enough to wear them again. Then her gaze drifted to something else he had gifted her many months ago—a treasure she had always kept for him. She held the amber bottle to her nose and closed her eyes. The bows might have to wait, but not this. She dabbed the stopper at the hollow of her neck and then behind both ears.

Olivia closed the space between them, crawled up the bed on her knees, and wiggled into her spot, his thigh her personal pillow. "Do you miss your *Gazette*?"

"Eh, the North Carolina one's equally good." Harry folded it in half and dropped it on the nightstand. His hand traveled to her tummy. "How are you two tonight?"

"Hungry all the time." She took an apple slice from the bowl on the nightstand and bit into it. "Waneta told me to always keep something in my stomach—keeps the baby happy." She held a piece to his mouth, and he devoured it with a smile.

"How about I fetch you something sweet? Your aunt's gingerbread was delicious. I think I saw some in a basket on the kitchen table."

She flipped her hair away from her neck and, grabbing his hipbone, pulled herself a little closer.

"Delicious, hm?" She opened her mouth for him to feed her another slice of apple, slowly sinking her teeth into the fruit.

"Not as delicious as you, Scrapper." She nuzzled deeper into his groin and flicked her hair again. He smiled wolfishly. "What are you doing?"

"Oh nothing," she said, lips pouty. When his finger trailed over them, she sucked the tip into her mouth.

"Lavender's a gift for me. You saved it all this time?"

She nodded, biting his finger softly.

"Sweet Jesus," he said in a gravelly voice.

"Yes, He is. And so am I. You just called me delicious." She sank her teeth in a little deeper.

With an earthy groan, he took back his finger, placed her head on the pillow, and moved over her. He ran his nose along the line of her jaw and nuzzled her ear. "Oh, Liv. I've been waiting—praying you'd come to me." Resting on his elbows, he caressed her cheeks with his thumbs. "I want to make love to you. I promise I'll do nothing to hurt you or the baby." He slid back on his haunches. "I only want to lay eyes and hands...and my mouth on you."

****

A gentle smile tugged at her lips as he eased her up, lifted her arms, and pulled the chemise over her head. He knew he had not imagined the increased fullness of her breasts, but seeing them with his eyes, healthy blue veins visible through her shiny skin, he drew in his breath. He longed to worship the two exquisite globes. Completely bare, feet and legs tucked around her, she sat with her back straight and hands curled into the folds of the quilt. She had never looked more radiant. He drew in his breath again, gaze simmering, recommitting every inch of her body to his mind.

He moved behind her, massaging her shoulders, burning kisses behind her earlobes. His fingers waltzed over the sensitive skin of her inner arms, lingering at her wrists before perusing the hollows of her palms. As he sank his teeth into the softness of her shoulder, he brought their hands to rest on the baby, rubbing the mound lovingly. She wiggled against him, the length of him hard against the small of her back. He thumbed her nipples to hard peaks.

He shifted, laying her in the blankets and fluffing the pillow behind her head. He tossed his tunic to the floor and shadowed her with his body. He followed her gaze as it traveled down the line of hair that began on his stomach and disappeared behind the flap of his breeches—arousal stretching his laces to the point of popping.

"Close your eyes, Scrapper."

He pressed his lips to the arch of her foot, and then his tongue traveled over her anklebone and up her shin. He sensed a shiver spreading through her body whetting his appetite for more. His breath licked her inner thigh, and when his gaze lighted on her exquisite womanhood, he inched closer and parted her folds with the tip of his nose. Her heady scent left him dizzy and aching. *God, how I love you.* He could not ignore his desire, his lips seeking and finding her silken bud. She moved to the rhythm he set with his tongue—never missing a single beat—until he heard her inhale sharply. She lifted her hips in his hands, the tiny ache of her voice his reward, and flooded him with her pleasure.

He laid his head on her thigh and met her glassy gaze

with a steamy one of his own. "I wonder how that felt to our baby."

"Like frolicking in the water, I think." She stuffed another pillow behind her head and scooted backward.

He pressed a multitude of kisses across her stomach. "And where do you think you're going? I'm nowhere near finished with you." She giggled with such exuberance he pulled himself up on his elbows.

"But fair's fair, Captain. Perhaps I have a little something in mind too."

****

With both hands, Olivia pushed up from the mattress and wedged herself between his thighs. She refused to keep him corralled inside his breeches one minute longer and made haste with the laces. His erection sprang free, and she touched his smooth head with her thumb while wrapping her hand around his length.

His head fell back, and he took a steadying breath. "You don't have to. Tonight is about you. I only want to pleasure you."

"And my lips on you will pleasure me greatly. Now, please stand for me." He complied, and her hands worked feverishly to meet her ends, pulling his breeches past his hips until they pooled on the floor. A single look at his virile handsomeness—honed stomach, lean hips, and bare feet—sent a chill up her spine.

"What is it?" Harry asked.

She met his smoldering gaze, biting her lip. "Am I wicked for wanting you so badly? Am I wanton?"

"God, I hope so." He leaned in with a long, slow kiss threatening to unravel her further. With the flat of his palm, he teased her nipple to a point.

She came up for air and gazed at him through dark

smoky lashes. "Must you know me so well?"

"Same as you know me, Scrap—"

His words died in his throat, replaced with a feral groan when she slid him between her lips. He dug his fingers in her hair, massaging her gently, while she reacquainted herself with his cock.

Lord, he is so beautifully endowed. She cupped his bollocks, judging each one warm and incredibly full with his seed. She rubbed them reverently and felt them tightening. She changed her angle to take him deeper— if that were even possible—and welcomed the tremor rising in his loins. Then he broke free, baring all, giving her his very essence, and she consumed everything he had to give. The intimacy stirred her heart and left tears pooled in her eyes.

Chapter Forty

Harry awakened, his wife encircled in his arms, her back flush against him. He laced their fingers together, curving their joined hands beneath her womb while the baby frolicked inside her belly. *I love you, Scrapper.* He kissed the back of her head, and she snuggled closer, clearly undisturbed by the baby's rollicking at such a wee hour.

A short time later, he slipped out of the bed, shrugged into his clothes, and strode across the yard toward the stable. He heard clanking from within, the sounds of a new workday dawning, and pushed the door open wide. His footsteps roused the stable boy and a few of the horses. Finding the one he loved best, he unlatched the door, and Gordie whinnied, opening his mouth for a fat carrot.

Harry took pride in caring for his mount, feeding him what remained of the vegetable—leafy green top and all—and gathered up the grooming tools. He began with a currycomb, brushing it in a circular motion to loosen dirt from his neck. The animal's ears twerked, and he looked up, waiting until the creaking of the wooden steps ceased.

"Good morning." Harry dipped his head, working the comb through the horse's hair.

"Good morning." Elan stood at the workbench and lit another lantern. He stretched his arms high above his head, turning his neck left and right until it popped. With his hair long and smooth, shoulders squared, he turned around and leaned back against the bench. "He's a fine animal."

"I agree." Harry walked around his horse, continuing the grooming. Silent seconds ticked by, reminding him he no longer wished to harbor grudges. *Not where Olivia is concerned.* He stopped mid-stroke and cleared his throat. "I want to thank you. You have my gratitude for caring for Olivia in my absence and leaving me your letter."

"You are welcome." He offered him a basket with apples, but he shook him off.

He gazed at him over the horse's back. "But I do have a couple of things on my mind."

Elan bit into the fruit and chewed with his mouth open. "As you should."

"Why did you do it—give me your location? I begged your mother for help, but she refused." He braced his hands on Gordie's back. "She told me to forget I ever got my claws into her."

He smirked. "Waneta owed you nothing. She gave her niece to you once—over another man who would have made her a good husband—because Olivia loved you. And then you ruined her life."

His nostrils flared. "Then why help me?"

Elan finished his apple and, with a rather pointed glare, tossed the core in a bucket. "I decided if you ever came looking for her, you should know where we were headed. If you followed, it would be because you loved her, not because you had fathered a child." He wiped his chin with the back of his hand, then crossed his arms. "I was never going to seek you out. My plan was to tell you myself if I ever saw you again. Before we left, I saw to it my sister would act in my place."

"And what if I'd never come to the village looking for her?" Harry switched to a stiff brush, using it to remove the loosened debris from the horse's tail. "What if I'd taken you at your word? You returned my ring, remember? Said she was through with me." He moved stealthily, working his way down each flank, his stroke taking on the mood of his growing ire. "You would be here with her now—my child in her belly. What then?" He raised his brow.

"I would be with her. I'd make a family with her here...or someplace else." Elan spoke with the metronomic tone of a preacher reciting scripture.

Harry snorted. "What—as her husband?"

"Yes. I would want to marry her."

His hand froze. He leaned over Gordie's back, gaze simmering.

Elan pushed away from the bench, his stance wide, arms crossed. "Had we never seen your face again, I would have taken Olivia as my wife. You should thank me for that."

"*Thank* you?"

Elan shook his head, chuckling under his breath.

"You're daft." Harry resumed his brushing. "Don't bother waiting for my thanks."

"You speak with so much pride. For once, can you try to think with something besides your cock?"

He froze again.

"Tell me, Harry. If you weren't here, what do you think would become of Olivia, a beautiful woman with a fatherless child?" His copper eyes narrowed to slits. "She might stay here...and become a drain on her uncle. Or go out on her own, telling everyone she met she was a widow and begging for food and shelter. But then how long would it take before some snake lured her into a marriage for her *protection*—all the while angry her bastard eats all his food?" Elan picked up a knife and drove it into another apple, cutting it in half. "Or," he said, chewing savagely, "she might not even be so lucky. She could wind up flat on her back every night, trying to keep them both from starving."

Elan inched closer, pointing his finger. "Believe this—I care for Olivia and would have never left her side. I would have protected her, this child—and the others we might have made together—with my life." He advanced and fed the horse the other half of the apple, rubbing his sleek neck. "Would she have loved me like she loves you? No. But ask yourself—would I have been best for them? I say yes. Again, you should thank me."

"Does she know about any of this?" Harry spoke with a flint-like tone.

"Yes, but not in such detail."

He threw down the brush, picked up a towel, and began rubbing his horse. A crow cawed in the rafters above them, slicing through the tension in the air. "I made mistakes, Elan, and I've learned from them. I'm a better man now."

"She lost everything because of you—her name, our family's safety...her freedom. What did you lose? Not even this Redmond Hill. She saved it for you." Elan turned to leave, then paused, the corner of his mouth curled. "You might want to take it a little easy there. Rub him any harder and you'll wear the hair right off his ass."

"You can believe this—I'm not going anywhere without my wife and child." He clutched the towel in his fist and took a step forward. "Are you sorry I came for her?"

"I stand by my decision. I only fear you'll hurt her again—but it's too late. She let you in her bed…and she wears your ring again."

"You would do well to remember that."

"And you this. I will not be leaving soon, if that is one of the things on your mind. I want to trust you. Doing so would make Olivia happy—but I cannot." He pivoted, his hair a whipping torrent of smoke, and left the stable.

****

Olivia slung her satchel over her shoulder and headed toward the garden, woodland flora on her mind. She spotted Elan sitting under the hemlock tree, head bowed, arms dangling over his knees. Over their many weeks together, she had grown accustomed to his calm resolve and ready adaptability to life's twists and turns. *What has you in such an ill-pickle, cousin?*

Olivia approached, brushing the toe of her shoe against his foot in greeting. "I'm surprised to find you here. Why aren't you out with the others?"

His dark gaze met hers, then he shrugged.

"What is it? Elan?"

He folded his arms across his chest. "I've been waiting for you." He blew out a heavy breath. "I had words with Harry this morning."

"What kind of words?"

His lips turned downward. "The not very nice kind."

Elan helped her to the ground, and she sat down, tucking her legs under her skirt. She gave him an encouraging smile while he recounted their heated exchange in the barn.

"You didn't. You told him to stop thinking with

his…?" Olivia bit her lip. "Lord, such a remark would have sent the old Harry swinging."

"Old or new, I don't care. It's the truth—makes him act a fool." His tone dripped with vinegar.

She shifted her weight and sighed. "He's no fool. I'm sure when he thinks about it your way, he'll be grateful you would have taken care of us if he'd never come back."

Elan sat up taller. "But there is more. At the right time, I would have made you my wife. Don't look at me that way." A crease formed over his brow. "I care for you—that should not be a surprise after all we've been through together."

Olivia rubbed her fingers over the jade stone of her necklace. "Everything you've done—well…you saved me. That you love me enough to marry me, given my condition…" She looked down, laying her palms on her tummy. "You are a blessing."

"I told you I would never leave you, and I meant it."

"I don't want you to leave my life, but I sense God's hand in this—all of it. Harry is committed, and he loves me."

"How can you be so sure he won't fail you again?"

"This." She lifted her hand, her wedding ring glinting in the sunlight. "I was wrong to take it off—terribly wrong. Running away, leaving him…it hurt him deeply. We made vows to each other, and now we've renewed them in our hearts."

Elan reached for her hand. "In marriage, I knew you would not look at me the way you did him, nor would I look at you as I did my wife. But it would have been good and right. I had peace with it."

"I would have been grateful, but we're not each

other's great love. The Lord will bring you another wife to love and protect—and children too. You are the best of men, and you deserve a love equal to you."

Elan grabbed a twig, bending it back with his thumb...then it snapped. He tossed the pieces aside, and their gazes met. "My faith—I'm not sure it's so strong anymore."

She shook her head. "You're wrong, Elan. You have great faith and strength, and you saved my life. I love you and will never forget all you've done for us."

A small smile tugged at his lips, and he cuffed her knee. She giggled, and a rather large bump rolling across her stomach caught her breath. He helped her to her feet, and she hugged his neck.

"Thank you for telling me what happened today. I never want there to be any strangeness between us."

He laughed, inclining his head toward her belly. "Well then, you'd better do something about the strange pumpkin you're growing in there."

"I promise to take care of that in just a couple more months." Olivia winked at him, then followed the path to the garden.

****

A short time later, Olivia sat on a front porch chair, and her cousin Sadie strolled toward her, wiping her brow. "Ma sent me to help you with the corn."

"Oh good. There's plenty of it." Olivia gestured to the large brown sack by her feet.

Sadie sniffed a stem of sassafras from the basket on the table, then joined her on the swing. "I can't wait for you to show me what we can make with your wildflowers, too."

Olivia had bonded with Sadie over the past months,

sharing a love of flowers, gardening, and music. Sadie was long-legged and tall, able to walk the half mile from the house to the pond in no time. With laughing hazel eyes and curly brown hair, she owned the role of youngest child—and only daughter. Olivia liked her cousin, and having had few friendships in her life, she cherished this one.

"Ma was thinking we could do a little singing tonight after supper." Leaning forward, Sadie ripped the green husks and silks from the corn and scrubbed the ear with a stiff brush. "Good heavens—would you look who's coming and just in time for supper?" She pushed up, hands on her hips, and stepped over the sack. "Isn't that...?" She planted her hand on the rail and raised up on her toes, then relented. "No, not who I thought it was. The skinny one with the floppy brown hat reminded me of Redd Turner—he's sweet on me, you know."

Olivia laughed at the gregarious girl, remembering another man who wore a floppy brown hat. "Oh, my goodness." Her chin dropped. "But no—it can't be..." She dropped her ear of corn and stood, knees wobbling. Her hand flew up to her chest.

"What's wrong?" Sadie wrinkled her nose.

Olivia rushed to the steps, taking each one carefully, and when her feet hit the ground, she gathered her skirt and ran as best she could. "Tom? Tom Harkett, is that you?"

"Good Lord, it's the missus!" Tom urged his horse forward, then jumped to the ground and into her open arms. His eyes grew wide at her increased size, and she gave him a sheepish grin. "Aw, Missus Olivia. I'm so happy to see ye—and there's so much of ye."

"There's a bit more of me nowadays, to be sure."

She nodded, then waved her hand. "Mr. Grant, it's a pleasure to see you."

The robust man swung down from his saddle and kissed her hand. "You remember, please call me Jimbo. Boy, I'm sure glad we found you."

Sadie scooted in close and locked arms with her. Olivia made the introductions, pleased to see her cousin warming to her two friends.

"Please tell me you've seen Harry," Jimbo said.

Olivia nodded.

His chest rumbled with a deep sigh. "Thank you, Jesus. We've got something to give him."

She lifted her hand to her brow, shielding the afternoon sun. "How did you find us?"

Their gazes focused on Tom as he recounted the story at the trading market.

Olivia beamed. "Harry's working with the others, but they should be home soon. He'll be so happy to see you—and hear your news."

"Now, you gentlemen must be tired and thirsty." Sadie looped arms with her. "Why don't you come on over to the porch and tell us about your trip?"

Following Sadie's lead, they sat together on the porch, listening to their stories about cascading waterfalls and sleek bobcats spotted up high on the hillsides. It seemed the more family joined them, the more Jimbo enjoyed himself. A natural-born storyteller, the lilt of his voice transformed with each tale. The ever-respectful Tom made a perfect sidekick, interjecting the occasional quip for dramatic effect.

"Now what's all this? Seems every time I turn around, there's another new face on my doorstep." Kyle guffawed, scraping his boot on the edge of the bottom step and wiping his brow with a handkerchief. Sadie skipped to her father's side, all too happy to provide introductions.

Olivia made her way across the lawn to watch for Harry, and before long, she spotted his silhouette against the golden afternoon sun. She flashed him a smile—certain it would thrill him to see his friends—and tried to ignore the prickling at her nape.

****

After supper, with their stomachs full and singing voices spent, folks turned their thoughts to sleep. Jimbo and Tom insisted on bunking in the stables with Elan, preferring the outdoor air for sleeping. Harry escorted Olivia to their room, helping her onto the bed and taking a seat in the chair.

With her hands enclosed in his, he told Olivia about his confrontation with Elan. He confided that while the waters between them were cold, like a river fraught with joints and spurs, they would move forward as one on her behalf. He had apologized to her cousin for his arrogance and thanked him for his devotion to her—for that he owed Elan a great debt. She squeezed his hands, grateful for his honesty.

Then he pulled the envelope from Jimbo and Tom out of his pocket. He asked Olivia to break the seal and read Josie's letter aloud, which she did three times over.

"He's dead. I can't believe it." Harry dragged his hand across his face, then wrapped it around the back of his neck.

Olivia folded the note and slid it back in the envelope. "I didn't know your uncle for long, but I believe he was a very sad and troubled man."

"As always, you're too kind. Zeb was a greedy,

manipulative...arrogant, jealous bastard. It was bad enough he took out his hatred on me, but to go along with Reed's scheme, hurting you to get back at me? It's unforgivable."

"What about Josie? She's at Redmond Hill. She must be so worried."

"I never thought to send word back home. All I could think about was finding you." He kissed the back of her hand. "From what Jimbo and Tom said, she believed Zeb when he told her the information would bring us back safely to Redmond Hill. Whatever he's given me will stop Barlowe. Thank God Kitt is keeping the evidence safe for me. But can we really trust Zeb? Nothing would please him more than to stick it to me again from the grave."

"He must have changed at the end—prolonged illness can do that to a person. If we believe in him, it will mean being able to go home."

"Home is wherever we are together—the three of us." Harry paused, placing his palm over her belly. "I'm not a wealthy man, but we have enough money to make a new start. There are so many opportunities, now more than ever."

He stood and began regaling her with his ideas. Certainly, he could purchase some acreage from Kyle, or perhaps they could travel farther west, securing a land grant deeper in the Blue Ridge Mountains. He concluded there was always Charleston where he could join Hugh in his plantation and trading enterprise.

"So...what do you think?" Turning on his heel, he found his wife with shoulders slumped, tears streaming down her cheeks. "Oh God, Liv. I didn't mean to upset you." He hugged her to his chest.

"I'm sorry. I-I don't know what's wr-wrong with me." She hiccupped, trying to recover.

"I've thrown too much at you is all. It's new to you, but I've had these ideas floating around in my mind for days—trying to think of where to make our home—believing Redmond Hill lost to us. Come here." He lifted her in his arms and placed her on the bed. "What you need is rest."

She sniffled, nodding as he bared her down to her chemise. Then, securing the quilt around her, he undressed and joined her, loving the press of her cheek against his chest and the baby snuggled against his side.

"Don't worry. The answer will come to us." Harry waited until she found the stillness of sleep before he closed his eyes.

****

Being with child, Olivia woke up at least one time during the night for the chamber pot, the baby weight making it impossible to wait for sunrise. She eased out of bed and went behind the privy curtain, then returned to bed.

Olivia lay on her side with hands curled into fists under her chin and watched the pearlescent moon shadow dance across Harry's bare chest. It was a fine one, simultaneously firm and forgiving, most often a cushion for her head, but sometimes a pillow for her to punch in anger. It had a curious way of beckoning her, becoming the haven of solace she needed whether she was happy, sad, frustrated, resistant...or passionate. She remembered the first time she laid her palms on it—the day he proposed to her—when he held her in his arms and kissed her for the first time. Then on their wedding night, it was a different sensation, her cheek touching warm naked skin, toned muscle, and soft tawny hair. She had known even then she wanted shelter there for the rest of her days. With her arm cradling the baby, she slid over and into her cherished spot.

Harry pulled her in close, lowering his chin so he could kiss the top of her head. He pulled the quilted coverlet up over her shoulder and smoothed it down.

"Thank you, Harry."

"For what?" he murmured.

"For loving me and for caring for me...and for giving me your child again. I could not be happier."

"Just when I think I can't love you more, you say something like that, and I come undone a little."

"Well, I'm undone a lot." She slid up on her elbows and kissed him square on the lips. "I want to lay flat on top of you the way I used to...but I can't." She rubbed her hands over her tummy.

"True. Neither of you would find that comfortable, but you'll think of something."

She sat up, brown hair in a tumble above her shoulders, and with his help, straddled his waist. When he gazed at her with those blue lagoon eyes, she imagined she was Venus herself in her white cotton shift, the outline of her breasts visible in the moonlight. His hands slid underneath the cloth and covered her belly.

She massaged the heels of her hands into his firm chest. "This may well be my most favorite part of you."

"It's yours forever." He squeezed her hips. "So...what's on your mind at this wee hour of the morning?"

"Just grateful...and thinking how I love you in the strangest of ways." She gazed at his furrowed brow. "Like the way you covered my shoulder just now, the way you smooth my tummy, keep me sheltered with your body. My comfort matters to you. I love it when you read to me—"

"And I promise I haven't read one word of *Gulliver* without you—he's right where we left him in Lilliput."

She smiled her thank you. "You may be stubborn and impulsive, but you saw something in this awkward girl—with her dog and knife and satchel filled with bandages and ointments—and you married her. You traveled such a long way to find me, too."

"How could I not come after the woman I love?" Harry laced his fingers with hers. "I fought for you this time—like you did for me when I wasn't able."

She squeezed his hands. "I said it in our wedding bed, and it's even more true today. I'm the luckiest of women. I love you, Harry Fleming, and all I want is to lie with you anywhere, so long as it's on your beautifully brute chest, for the rest of my life."

"Come here, Scrapper." He eased her off his body and drew her close. She cuddled into him, the small of her back sealed against his hard abdomen, and his arm cinched around her. "We're in complete agreement. The three of us will be together always."

"Where we live doesn't matter to me."

"Nor to me." He gave her a reassuring hug.

They lay coiled together, still and quiet, a chorus of crickets and hoot owls drifting through the open window. The low glow of the lantern cast their single curved shadow against the bedroom wall.

"Harry?"

"Mm?"

"Remember the morning by the creek when you asked me to marry you, and you wondered why I was retreating?" His nod rubbed against her cheek. "Fear is not a good reason to flee."

"I agree. It's better to face it than to run from it."

"I don't want to retreat. We shouldn't run off out of fear about what Reed might do. I'm not afraid of him so long as you're with me, and I should've known that from the start. Kitt's holding the evidence for you. I think God was with Zeb in his last days, and he wanted you to use this information—to stop Reed once and for all—and come home."

Harry let out a lengthy sigh. "I suppose any path we choose comes with risk." He grabbed her hand and squeezed it. "You know I'll protect you with my life, right?"

She nodded and kissed his knuckles.

"Are you sure, Scrapper? Truly, is your wish to go back to Redmond Hill?"

She wobbled around to face him, her warm brown gaze mingling with his cool blue one. "It is—more than anything in the world. I want to go home."

"Well then...it's decided."

"Really?" Her voice hitched. "Oh, goodness. When can we leave?"

He ran his finger down the curve of her jaw. "Are you well to travel with the babe?"

"Oh, he's tucked in good and tight for another two months." She patted her mound. "Besides, I promise to ride and rest under the cover of the wagon."

She clasped her hands under her chin, wiggled her toes against his calves, and gazed at him. *How is it even when bathed in moonlight, his face fills my heart with sunshine?*

"Very well, my Scrapper. We'll tell Elan and begin

preparations at first light."

"Oh, thank you, Harry!" She leaned up and kissed him sweetly on the mouth, and as she withdrew, she gave voice to the love filling her heart. "Hm...but whatever shall we do until morning?" She traced her index finger down the slope of his neck, sliding it along his shoulder and over his bicep.

"I am rather awake now." Harry stretched and brought his free arm in to cushion his head, the corners of his lips curving up. His gaze drifted toward the hearth at the fireplace. "I ought to clean my gun before we make the journey. Perhaps I could sharpen your blade for you?"

She tossed a pillow at him, and he ducked, doubling over in mirth. She tilted her head, marveling at his unbridled laughter—a most rich, robust, joyful sound to her ears.

He leaned down, pulling *Gulliver's Travels* from his leather bag, and waved it in the air. "Or there's this?"

"Oh, now that's very tempting." She inched closer until her breath was warm on his chest and her chin brushed his nipple. "Don't start without me. Let me get my pillow back—"

"You'll do no such thing, Scrapper." He flashed her a devilish grin, covering her in one stealth move, his tanzanite eyes smoldering. She arched into his body as he planted tender kisses along her collarbone, lips blazing a trail down to the mound of their baby. He nuzzled there, and she gazed down at him, the vision stealing her breath.

"Sweet Jesus, I love you so much. I thank God for bringing you to me, and I am never, ever, letting you go." His words vibrated over her skin, nearly sending her over the edge.

Olivia reached for him, needing him in a most serious way, and he moved over her. Cupping his cheeks, she drew his face close to hers. "I love you, Harry. You'll comfort and keep me forever?"

"Yes. Always, love. And I'm taking you home. Home to our Redmond Hill, where I'll keep us safe until we're wrinkled and hunched over—"

"And surrounded by a herd of our children and grandchildren." She giggled, the warmth of the memory filling her heart.

He kissed her, then eased onto his side.

"—And I'll still want you, Liv. Remember that. It's always only you."

The book poked out from between the sheets, and she took it in her hands, nibbling on her lower lip. "Read to us, won't you? Like old times."

Harry scooted up and leaned back on the headboard, and she laid her head on his lap, tilting her chin up to the ceiling. His voice warmed her like sunshine on still waters, and when he placed his palm over the baby, a peace came over her. No more surviving ill pickles, no more melancholy. *Wait. That's not true.* She lifted his hand to her lips, kissed his palm, and lowered it to her heart. *Because every day is filled with challenge and joy...heartbreak and promise. As it should be.*

Olivia's heart thumped with a new speed, to a rhythm strengthened by their unending love.

Epilogue

October 1784 ~ Seven Weeks Later

The high-pitched squeal of a newborn pierced the air...then cheers erupted around the family room at Redmond Hill. Seated at the kitchen table, his face awash in the brilliant morning sunlight, Tom whooped a holler and whacked a grinning Silas on the shoulder with the brim of his hat. Harry's knees buckled for an instant, and he grabbed hold to the mantel above the fireplace. Elan stoked the fire, then rose, casting him a reassuring nod. Kitt shook his hand and clapped him on the shoulder, and Brandt gave him a back-slapping hug that nearly stole his breath.

The bedroom door swung open, and Harry whipped around. He dragged his gaze from Mary's flushed cheeks and rumpled apron to the noisy bundle cradled in her arms. Mary crossed the room and sidled up to him, the baby squirming inside its swaddling. "I held ye the day ye were born, Cap'n. Now, it's my honor to do the same for your wee daughter."

Harry's heart soared clear to the moon. He rubbed his daughter's tiny fist with his thumb while she let loose a chorus of happy-to-be-alive cries. A grin of unbridled joy broke across his face. "She's perfect, Mary. Is she not? Absolutely perfect..."

"Why there's none finer than this little lassie." She

cooed to the infant, blowing a puff of air over her brow, making her bangs flutter. "She's a bonnie one. Good and strong."

Just like her mother. Awareness struck him like a lightning bolt. "Sweet Jesus. Is Olivia…?"

"Don't you fret. The missus has the strength of ten men." Mary clutched his arm, leaning in close, head bowed. "And she's gonna need it 'cause there's another."

A shiver crawled up his spine. "What d'you mean? Another…another *what*?"

"Another baby." Apprehension colored her voice, and they locked gazes.

"You mean…twins…?"

Mary bobbed her head. "Olivia can't nurse this one just yet, and the wee lass is fussy about that."

Harry steepled his hands over his mouth and blew out a long breath, ticking through the signs in his mind. Her belly had grown into the watermelon she predicted. *Explains the nonstop kicking—two babes dueling in a tight space.* And her breasts? *Like a pair of cantaloupes.* He scratched his head, his knowledge of anatomy and physics telling him there was but one way to bring a child in the world—through one expandable, yet rather narrow canal. *And she's already spent…exhausted.*

The baby squalled, lips quivering, and Mary rocked her gently in her arms. "Cap'n, maybe we—"

Olivia interrupted, releasing a long, heart-rending cry, followed by several hiccupping sobs. The sound upended him, and the room of people fell silent.

Mary's face paled.

"Harry!"

His wife's scream ripped his heart open at the seams, and without looking back, he sprinted from the room.

Harry slid in behind Olivia on the bed, wedging her between his thighs. Her jaws immediately unclenched, and her breathing stabilized, and she fell slack against his chest. He threaded his arms through hers, pressing kisses against her temple and the perspiration-soaked kerchief tied around her head.

"The baby—she's well, yes?" Olivia croaked, and Waneta stepped forward, holding a cup to her lips. She sipped, water dribbling around the curve of her smile.

"She's perfection, Liv." He nuzzled her earlobe. "You're extraordinary, you know that? You're so strong, and I love you so much it hurts."

She rubbed her hands over her belly. "I love you, too. I-I can't wait to see the other life God created w-with our love." With the rising contraction, her eyelashes fluttered, and her eyes rolled back in her head. He tightened his hold around her.

Nigel wrapped a towel around his neck and waved them forward. "Come closer, Olivia. Back to the edge of the bed. All right now. Let's bring this child into the world. Steady now." Nigel met his gaze, then turned his attention to Olivia. "On the count of three, my girl, I want you to give me your best push. One, two…three!"

****

Sometime later, Harry dropped onto the chair across from Olivia, arms on his thighs, head bowed while Nigel cleansed and restored her womb. Waneta tended to her next, bathing her with warm water, patting her skin dry, and covering her with fresh sheets. Save for a log crumbling into embers in the fireplace, silence blanketed the room.

He gazed at his wife nursing their daughter, and his

lips softened at the corners. He dragged his fingers through his hair, reflecting on the events of the past few weeks, days, and hours, and for a beat, he floundered. *How could I have been so damn stubborn?* He scrubbed his hand down his face. With his seed planted in her belly, Olivia had nourished two lives with her body and blood for nine months—at least half of them without him. His gaze settled on her thick braid of hair—falling below her shoulders these days—and her dark lashes fanning over her peach-hued cheeks. His heart hammered in his chest, Big Sam's words echoing in his mind. *If ever in love, to make it last, love ye dear.* He closed his eyes, pledging a silent oath to Olivia and God. *I'll love you dearly until my dying day.*

Olivia's gentle voice dragged him from his thoughts, and he eased in beside her. He cupped his palm around the crown of his daughter's head, brushing her downy blonde hair. As she released her mother's nipple, a slip of air passed between her lips, a trickle of milk rolling down her chin. He met Olivia's gaze, whispering the words "I love you, Scrapper," and she blinked back tears.

Outside the bedroom, the voices of their family and friends lifted in conversation. As the door creaked open, Caddie lifted his head in acknowledgment. Mary strolled in, taking his baby girl in her arms and patting her back.

Waneta came forward and, dropping a strong maternal hand on his shoulders, placed a small, quiet bundle in his arms. "It's time you meet your son, Captain."

****

By the time Harry shuffled into the kitchen, the room was quiet, and the afternoon sun hung low in the sky. He inhaled, the scent of buttery chicken pie and roasted squash still warm on the hearth making his mouth water. He lifted his arms in a stretch, the flex and pull of muscles drawing a grateful sigh from his chest. Mary looked up from the stack of folded sheets on the table. As she made her way to the cupboard, pulling out a pair of plates, he hugged her a thank you and walked outside.

Harry braced his hands on the porch railing, admiring the gold and crimson autumn hues blanketing Redmond Hill's landscape. The leaves rustled with the breeze, the rush of cool air fortifying his soul. *I'm a very lucky man.* Last week, he received a letter from Josie confirming she had arrived safely back to her family in the Low Country. Tom remained his strong arm, yoked to him like a trusty mule, committed to their future prosperity. He furnished an available cabin for Waneta, Elan, and Betsey for their extended stays—complete with new rugs, curtains, and a stockpile of fresh pine logs on the porch. Their visits brought the kind of smile to Olivia's face that made his heart leap with joy.

Harry bristled at the shrill bark of a red fox in the distance, and Reed Barlowe's face flashed through his mind. The day after his homecoming at Redmond Hill, Harry had confronted him in the back room of his store.

"Don't test me, Reed. I will use this evidence and ruin you. Your name—as pathetic as it is—will be worth less than a horse turd. You'll be shunned in the street, cut by every man in this town. No one will do business with a sick, twisted, thieving liar."

"So, to keep my conviction secret, you want me to promise to leave your little wife alone?"

"Let me be clear." Harry stepped forward, his voice

like the edge of a very sharp blade. "Set one foot on my property—or come within ten feet of my wife or family—and I will cut your balls off and happily watch you bleed out."

Reed swirled the liquor around in his glass. "And in return for leaving you alone, you'll keep this evidence to yourself?"

"Agreed."

He arched an eyebrow. "Who else knows?"

"That's none of your concern. No one will ever speak of it." Harry took a step backward and crossed his arms over his chest.

Reed smirked around the rim of his glass. "Agreed."

His gaze snapped back and nailed him. "I will have your word."

"Thought it was a horse turd."

"It is. But it's all you've got, and I will have it."

Reed rubbed his fingers over his mustache, then fixed his mouth in a flat line. "Very well. You have my word. I'll do no harm to your family."

At that, Harry had quit the room without a sideways glance. Reed slithered out of Camden the next day—thankfully taking Lucie and Grady with him. He lowered his chin to his chest and breathed in chilly evening air. *You're like a bad coin, Barlowe. And I'll be ready if you ever turn up here again.* He pushed out the breath, tilting his head heavenward.

A chair clunked on the wood floor, and Harry glanced over his shoulder.

"It's in moments like these I believe in God." Brandt settled back in the chair, crossing his leg, ankle over his knee. "How a woman grows a life—*two* in your case—and brings it hollering and kicking into the world." His voice trailed away, and he shook his head, dark creases shadowing his eyes.

Harry succumbed to a smile and, with his hands in his pockets, rocked back on his heels. While a surge of masculine pride rushed through his veins at having sired twins, he reined in his thoughts. "Aye, Olivia humbles me. She's an extraordinary woman. I don't deserve her, but I thank God for her. Every day. I'll never be apart from her again."

Brandt withdrew his flask, and they shared a few swallows of scotch. They reminisced over their childhood—following animal tracks along Black Creek, skipping stones over the water, and sneaking into Granny Red's snuffbox when she was napping.

Brandt gave him a wry smile. "Would you believe I used to confess my sins to Peggy when she was a babe? I'd prop her against my knees and spill my guts. Much easier to have a tell-all with my child in my lap than traipsing down to Mother's grave." He covered the hitch in his voice with a dry cough. "My Peggy was all eyes and ears—and no mouth spewing out advice or ultimatums. God, what a blessing that was."

Leaning back on the porch rail, Harry surveyed his cousin with quizzical eyes.

"Fathers and sons are so different—my father was, anyway." Brandt shifted in his seat, stretching out his legs, feet crossed. "I wanted to believe in Zeb—so much so I ignored his machinations. Told myself to trust his intentions were good." He lifted his flask to his lips and took a swig. "God, how I envied your relationship with Joseph. Your father was as real as a wart on a toad's back—no pretenses, no shades of truth. Tell me, did you ever catch him in a lie?"

"Never," Harry said without hesitation.

He scooted forward to the edge of his chair, brow arched. "Was he faithful to Abigale?"

"Always."

Brandt fell back in his chair, pointing a finger at him. "You sound just like him with your 'never' and 'always.' He wasn't one for bluster either. In my family, we floated around words like 'perhaps' and 'coincidentally.' " Brandt heaved a sigh. "Zeb's character was as curved as a sickle. Joseph's was like a straight steel blade."

"Your father was the greatest adversary I never knew I had—and I understood the least. Zeb never gave a damn about me, but his hatred—that day when Olivia left, and I came looking for his help…?"

Brandt pinched the bridge of his nose. "It's hard to forget the day you learn your father's not only a selfish, cunning tactician, but he's also a jealous, vengeful bastard—and all in the name of loving Abigale. Christ, what my mother must have endured in silence. No wonder she went to an early grave." He averted his eyes, gazing off in the distance.

A solemn silence stretched between them.

Harry shifted against the porch railing, crossing one foot over his ankle and his arms over his chest. No man lives his life without some measure of sorrow and regret. Flesh, muscle, and bones heal, but the soul is the great equalizer. *It needs forgiveness to survive.*

Brandt straightened in his chair and stretched out both arms in front of him, cracking his knuckles. Their gazes met. "I owe you an apology, Harry. If I'd only said no to Zeb and refused to marry Catherine…well, all our lives would have turned out differently. It was his plan, but I agreed. I'm sorry for the pain I caused you."

Harry nodded. "I've already forgiven you, and yes, our lives would be different. I'm a stubborn man—and I had to go down a very lonely, painful path to realize it— but Catherine's not my great love. In truth, she never really was. I am deeply in love with Olivia, and I know that now."

He bit back a chuckle. "I envy you. You've managed to make something wholesome out of something rotten."

"Aye, but I stewed over my circumstances for too long." Harry gripped his hands on the railing by his side and leaned forward. "Have you ever considered you've done the same thing? Perhaps your romantic dream of Margaret has kept you from falling in love with your wife?"

Brandt steepled his fingers under his chin and looked at him through hooded eyes.

"Just listen to me." He let go of the railing, palms open at his sides. "Catherine and I grew up together, and I know her to be bright and caring. She wants the protection of her husband—the way Jon cared and doted on her as a child. Her constitution is genteel and dependent on certain comforts, you might say." He rubbed his knuckle over his lip. "With her beauty it's easy to think her shallow and disinterested, but I think you know she's not." Their gazes met. "And while she did what her father asked in marrying you, there is no way I believe she agreed for that reason alone. Some part of her—even if she didn't realize it—loved you, Brandt. Hell, she can convince her father of just about anything, so she didn't have to marry you. Catherine loves you—I know she does." He stepped forward. "She'd make you a damn good wife. You just need to set your aim on becoming a shipshape husband."

Brandt cleared his throat and rose from his chair, fisting his hands around his coat lapels.

"Those are my thoughts anyway. Just think about it, Brandt."

"I will. On my ride home." He fixed his tricorn on his head and extended his hand.

Trusting his gut, Harry threw his arms around him and spoke into his good ear. "Love you, cousin." He felt the stiffness in Brandt's shoulders soften, and he smiled on the inside.

"Take care, Harry. We'll come calling in a few days."

With that, Harry watched Brandt swing onto his horse and ride off for Glen Laurel. The door creaked open, and he smiled at Mary over his shoulder.

"Olivia's eaten her supper, Cap'n. Time you got a bellyful, too. Need to keep up your strength for the bairns, ye ken."

He strode over to Mary and gave in to his gut again, pulling her into a hug. "Is Silas afoot?" He pulled back. "For that matter, where's Tom?"

"Sent them to town for proper wood to make a second cradle. They'll be back soon enough." He praised her quick thinking and, with a kiss to the top of her head, led her back inside.

Carrying a plate of chicken pie and biscuits in his hand, Harry strolled into the bedroom. Candlelight flickered over Waneta's face when she looked up from the cradle. He joined her, listening to her croon soft words to the twins, wrapped in their swaddling and tucked inside the one cradle. He swallowed a bite of food, a smile tugging at his lips. *Suppose you two will have to make do with close quarters for a few more days.*

He gazed at Waneta, a woman small in size, but great in stature. *A bit like Olivia.* "I'm grateful you're here with us."

She tilted her head. "I am happy to be here with Olivia and the children…and with you, Captain."

He paused, his spoon inches from his mouth. "You can call me Harry. We're family, you know."

"I will. When I'm ready."

He chuckled, swallowing his food while the women exchanged knowing smiles. Waneta made her way across the room and closed the door behind her.

Harry shoveled a few more bites in his mouth and made his way to the bed. He sat beside Olivia, offering her a spoonful. She opened wide, swallowing and licking a drop of gravy from her mouth. The smooth skin of her throat rippled in a sensual way, firing his senses, and he was lost—wholly and completely—to this amazing woman, his wife and mother of his children. He kissed away what remained of the gravy on her lips.

"Waneta likes you. She just likes tormenting you." Olivia snickered, dragging the quilt up to her waist. "And what about baby names? We agreed a son would bear your name, and we'd call him Henry. He looks like a solid, serious Henry."

Harry smirked. "He had to be, sharing the womb with his commanding sister. You liked Alice for a girl, or Felicity?"

She folded her hands in her lap, chin lifted. "I think she looks like an Alice. Strong…and like you said, commanding."

He gazed into Olivia's coppery-brown eyes, captivated by their beautiful intensity. She opened her mouth for another bite. *Oh no, I have other plans for your tongue.* He placed the dish on the nightstand and inched closer, his thigh pressing against her hip.

Harry bent into her lips, brushing them softly with his, sharing her breath. Her hands wrapped around his biceps and traveled upward, circling around his neck.

"I. Love. You. Olivia." He punctuated each word with a kiss on her lips. As he nuzzled her neck, she sighed his name. "Oh, my sweet Scrapper. The things I'm going to do to you when you're well and recovered," he whispered in her ear and pulled back, admiring the blush dotting her cheeks.

"Oh, Harry."

"Say it again."

She dragged her fingertip along his bottom lip, sighing a smile. "Harry…"

"I'll never stop loving you. Ever."

Olivia rolled back the sheets, and he slid in beside her. A warmth spread through their bodies, stoked by feathery kisses and hushed words. He made love to her with his gaze. Their hands met, fingers intertwined, thumbs stroking the sensitive curves in their palms. With Henry and Alice blissfully asleep in the cradle beside their bed, their world—the one before, the one in this moment, and the one tomorrow—was right, renewed by an honest and vulnerable love. Together forever, they loved each other as dearly as two people ever could.

A word about the author...

Ann enjoys spending time with family, trying out new recipes, and relaxing on her back porch to read and write. She's a member of Heart of Carolina Romance Writers and Low Country Romance Writers. She loves watching television dramas and always has a great romance book in her hand. Connect with Ann at http://www.annmtrader.com.

Thank you for purchasing
this publication of The Wild Rose Press, Inc.

For questions or more information
contact us at
info@thewildrosepress.com.

The Wild Rose Press, Inc.